One Day

I Saw

a Black King

ALSO BY J. D. MASON

And on the Eighth Day She Rested

One Day

I Saw

a Black King

J . D . M A S O N

ST. MARTIN'S GRIFFIN 🐎 NEW YORK

www.stmartins.com

Library of Congress Cataloging-in-Publication Data

Mason, J. D.
    One day I saw a black king / J. D. Mason.—1st ed.
        p.   cm.
    ISBN 0-312-30154-5 (hc)
    ISBN 0-312-30619-9 (pbk)
    EAN 978-0312-30619-9
    1. African Americans—Fiction.   2. Denver (Colo.)—Fiction.
  3. Drifters—Fiction.   4. Alabama—Fiction.   I. Title.

  PS3613.A817O54 2003
  813'.6—dc21

                                                    2003053854

10   9   8   7   6   5   4   3   2

September 11, 2001

This is the day that I cried for strangers and America . . . and humanity.

*To all the victims of the World Trade Center, Pentagon, and
Pennsylvania tragedies,
little birds . . . taking refuge in heaven's arms.*

Peace

IN THE BEGINNING

For unto Us . . .

Sweat poured down her face and burned her eyes. Even the storm raging outside refused to have any mercy. The small room was hot and humid, lit dimly by two lanterns. One behind Roberta and the other at the head of the bed. The girl jerked so Roberta thought she would knock over the light on the table next to her and set the whole place up in flames. The thought almost made her laugh. A vision raced across her mind of the three women running around the room, burning and melting like candles. Roberta wasn't afraid of death. She'd seen too much of it. She'd seen it in midwifing, even in her marriage.

Blood flowed from between the girl's legs in rivers, and Roberta's face remained expressionless as she realized that death would pay them all a visit tonight. She worked feverishly, packing towels and her good bedsheets against the girl's womb to absorb the blood she was losing.

Mattie sobbed, "I can't do this! I can't do this no more . . ."

Shadows danced across the walls, mocking Mattie's torment. Elongated shapes flickered against faded flowers on peeling wallpaper. She'd anticipated Miss Roberta's birthing room, anxious to meet the growing child inside her, but nothing could've prepared fourteen-year-old Mattie King for the pain she'd struggled with for what seemed like days. But it hadn't been days. Or had it? It was like a nightmare that lasted too long. Mattie captured sleep in packets of minutes, only to wake up to her nightmare again and again.

"Momma! Please! Oh . . . please!" She squeezed hard on Agnes's hand until the tips of her mother's fingers turned purple.

Watching her little girl suffer filled Agnes's eyes with tears. "Shhh, li'l girl. It's gon' be over soon, baby." She looked desperately at Roberta, hoping to see some sign of confirmation from the midwife that the promise she'd made Mattie would come true. Roberta remained stone-faced, working hard toward the inevitable.

Foolish heffa, Roberta thought to herself. Agnes always was a foolish woman. Talking about "It's gon' be over soon." Roberta knew better. It wouldn't be over until this child was born and this girl was dead. Only then would it be over. She'd been here before, watching life straddle death. Over the years, Roberta had come to know which side would win out in the end. Mattie King was losing.

The storm outside raged hard and steady like Mattie's pains. There's nothing worse than an angry god. Roberta knew this. Agnes was too foolish to know it. God was pissed off about something, punching his might hard into the black sky, then ripping it open with his will. Roberta wanted to tell Him to hush, but she knew better. No man or woman ever tells God to hush unless they want Him mad at them. *Thy will be done.*

"Pleease, Momma!" Mattie's body jerked against the pain of birthing the big baby. "Please! Make it stop! Momma . . . !" Her eyes pleaded more than her words ever could.

Agnes prayed silently for her daughter. "Mattie," she said, rubbing her hand across the girl's head. "Hold on, baby. Please . . . just hold on for Momma." She stared again at Roberta. "How much longer, Roberta? Ain't it almost here yet?" Roberta ignored Agnes. "Answer me! Please! Say somethin'," Agnes pleaded. "Roberta?"

Roberta watched in horror as the imprints of what looked like small fists pushed against the underside of Mattie's stomach. Fists trying to punch their way through that girl like God punched holes into the dark sky.

He a demon child, Roberta, a voice whispered to her. Chills ran up her spine and she quickly looked around the room to see who'd spoken to her. There was nobody there but the three women. Roberta wiped the sweat from her face with the back of her hand. *He a demon child. Got hell in him, woman!* God continued his attack on the universe, ripping away at the heavens, lighting up the sky like it was daylight in time for Roberta to see a tiny foot emerge from between Mattie's legs. *Kill him!* the voice whispered to Roberta. She looked up again. Agnes stared at her, confused by the expression on the midwife's face.

Agnes had heard Roberta sometimes had spells. She'd heard Roberta wasn't always right in the head. (Lord! Please don't let this woman have a spell. Not now. Not when Mattie needs her so much.)

The voice whispered again, *He demon seed! Break his neck! Break his neck before he lays eyes on you, woman! Don't let him see you!* Roberta's heart pounded fiercely in her chest. Killing him wouldn't be hard, except . . . he wasn't turned. If only he was turned . . . it wouldn't be hard at all, and Agnes would never know.

"Aaagh!" Mattie screamed. "Help me! It's killin' me! Momma!"

"Roberta?" Agnes begged. "Do somethin'!"

Roberta looked at Mattie. "Don't fight him, Mattie girl! Let him do what he got to do!" The harder Mattie fought this boy, the harder he fought back. Roberta had to turn him. Maybe, if she could just turn him . . . She pushed the small foot back inside Mattie and reached inside the girl, hoping to turn the boy. *Kill him, Roberta! He demon seed! Don't let him see you!*

"He ain't lettin' me turn him, Agnes! He ain't lettin' me turn him!" Roberta was getting desperate. He'd be born soon, and by then it might be too late.

Tears slid down Agnes's face as she watched the life slowly leave her daughter's eyes. The girl's small body convulsed uncontrollably and grunts escaped from deep inside her. Agnes knew that Mattie, her precious baby girl, was losing this fight. She started humming quietly, then sang softly into her daughter's ear, "Precious Lord . . . take my hand . . . lead me on . . . let me stand . . . I'm tired . . . I'm weak . . . I'm worn . . ."

Mattie whispered, "I'm tired, Momma. I'm so . . ."

Agnes cried. "When my life . . . is almost gone . . . hear my cry . . . hear my call . . . hold my hand . . . lest I fall . . ."

Suddenly, as Mattie's body went limp, Roberta reached inside her as far as she could and delivered the child. He didn't cry at first, but his small fists punched into the air as if he were mocking God. Roberta quickly cut and tied the cord, hoping to finish before he opened his eyes, but she was too late. He stared at her with coal-black slits, then suddenly started screaming. Fear blanketed

Roberta and she quickly laid the boy on Mattie's swollen stomach.

"Get him! Get him, Agnes!" Roberta demanded.

Agnes stared at a horrified Roberta, who'd backed into the corner of the small room, staring at the screaming child with black eyes. "What's wrong, Roberta? What is it?" Mattie's grip softened on her mother's hand, and Agnes knew her only daughter was gone.

"Get him!" Roberta reached behind her and grabbed an old wooden cane leaning against the wall. "Get him, 'fore I . . ." He'd seen her. The demon had seen her and he knew what she looked like. Roberta's hands trembled.

Agnes didn't understand the fear in the woman's eyes and quickly scooped up the child in her arms. "Roberta!" She screamed. "What the hell is wrong with you?" Roberta's eyes were wild as they darted around the dimly lit room. He'd seen her. Lord have mercy! He'd seen her face.

"Get him outta here, Agnes! I'll take care of Mattie! You just get him and go! Get outta my house!" Roberta gripped the cane in her hands. He'd get no closer to her. She'd never let that monster get any closer to her.

Silent tears flowed down Agnes's cheeks. She turned to where her only daughter lay, giving in to her grieving heart. "My baby's dead, Roberta. My baby girl's dead." Agnes dropped to her knees next to the girl, cradling the naked boy in her arms. Roberta disappeared into the darkness in the corner of the room. Her incoherent ramblings were eventually dismissed by Agnes as nothing more than the mumbling of a crazy woman.

"I don't want him here!" Roberta swung the cane into the air. "I don't want that demon near me!"

"My baby's dead. My baby's . . ." Agnes wailed. The sound of thunder could be heard in the distance. The storm had moved on, taking the spirit of Mattie King with it.

Apparitions

She'd been wrestling with sleep for hours before finally giving up. Agnes sat on the edge of the bed, staring out of the open window into another sweltering Texas night that took no pity on anybody. Crickets sang outside her bedroom window, probably just as disgusted as she was with this heat. She walked over to the fan that was hard at work blowing hot air around in circles and stood there, hoping it would provide some relief from this oven she'd been lying in all night, not the least bit surprised it didn't. Agnes slid into her house shoes, then went into the kitchen. The coolest place in Bueller this time of night was her freezer, and Agnes stood there, savoring the crisp, cold air as it caressed her skin. She filled her glass with ice, then took one of the cubes and rubbed it against her neck and chest until it melted. Several ice cubes later, the tray was empty.

In the living room was a bottle of Wild Turkey she'd kept hidden in the corner of the bookcase. She filled her glass and watched the precious cubes of ice start to dissolve in the warmth of the amber liquid. Agnes capped the bottle, and then stared at it, wondering how long she'd had that whiskey. Abe had bought it, just before he died, as a matter of fact. She remembered how she'd fussed at him about it.

"Abe King? Now I know you ain't bringin' no more of that mess up in my house! Didn't I tell you that I don't want no whiskey round here?"

He looked at the bottles he held in his hands, then back at

her. "Ain't nothin' but a couple of small bottles, baby. Grady gave me a good price on both of 'em. And you know I'm only gon' take a sip every now and then."

Agnes protested, "I don't care how good a price Grady gave you. You ain't got no business bringin' that mess—"

Abe drew back his massive shoulders and looked her square in the eyes. "A man got to be able to take a sip every now and then, Agnes. It don't mean nothin'. Jus' a way to take the edge off, that's all," he reasoned. "I works hard and sometimes I need somethin' to take the edge off." In the end he'd won out, of course. But she watched him like a hawk, daring him to take more than that sip every now and then.

Agnes smiled, then slowly drank from her glass. Abe had been right about most things, and the value of a good drink had been one of them. Since he'd been gone, Agnes had needed to smooth her own edges every once in a while. That bottle of whiskey had come to her rescue on more than one occasion, and tonight would be a night she welcomed the bitter taste burning a trail down the back of her throat. It was bound to take her mind off this heat eventually.

Getting through the nights was still hard. Even after all these years, she still hated sleeping without him. He'd been dead sixteen years, and in all that time, she hadn't had a man in her bed. "That don't make no sense," she said out loud, then chuckled, though she really didn't find it funny. The ice cubes chimed as Agnes swirled her glass and found her favorite place to sit.

She'd always hated that old chair. The first time she saw it, she wondered why anybody would have the nerve to put a price tag on something so hideous. But Abe had sat down in it and insisted on buying it. Agnes smiled, thankful she hadn't gotten rid of it after he'd died. She sank into that old wingback chair, cradled her drink, and then closed her eyes. It had been his chair, and sometimes, she swore, she could feel him in it. She turned her face, then pressed her nose against the fabric and inhaled. The faint scent of Abraham King was held captive in that chair, and she knew that she'd never part with it, no matter how old and ugly it was.

Abraham Theofolus King had blown into Bueller, Texas, like a big old twister. He'd come down from Oklahoma City, talking big, walking big, and looking big. Women came from everywhere just to get an eyeful of that man, half Choctaw Indian and half black. His wavy black hair lay back on his head like ripples in Cranson Creek. He was the kind of brown that looked gold and shone like the sun just before it set down for the night.

She'd overhear women whispering amongst themselves, "Girl, that is one handsome man. Do you hear me?"

"You know you ain't tellin' me nothin' I don't already know. I might wear glasses, honey, but I ain't blind."

"Ain't nobody said nothin' 'bout you. Ooooh! Shhh. Here he come."

"Evenin', Brotha King," the women would sing in unison.

Abe would smile and tip his hat, bowing slightly at the waist. "'Evenin', ladies. How y'all doin'?"

"Fine. Jus' fine."

"I can see that," he'd say coyly, leaving behind two foolish women basking in the glory of the hopes of having him.

Agnes took another sip from her glass. "Abe King wasn't nothin' but an ol' flirt. Up to no good," she mumbled, then laughed to herself.

Plenty of women made fools of themselves over Abraham, but not Agnes. He'd tried on many occasions to put his slick charms to work on her, but Agnes wouldn't hear of it. She'd always been a practical girl, and everybody knew pretty men like Abe King weren't worth two cents when it came to holding down a decent job or keeping their pants buckled up around their waists. Momma had taught her that. "Don't you pay that boy no mind, gal," she scolded when she caught Agnes staring at Abe driving by the house. "He ain't up to no good. Got all y'all actin' ig'nant over him like he God's gift."

"Not me, Momma," Agnes said defensively. "I ain't even interested in that man."

"Well, you make sho' you don't get interested in him. He only after one thang, gal. I know his type. Struttin' round here lookin' like a peacock. You keep yo' legs closed and yo' eyes on God. I don't need that man sniffin' round here like a hound dog," she snapped. "And I don't need no mo' grandbabies to take care of neither. Lord knows Dorothy done gone and got herself in a mess . . ." Momma went on and on about Agnes's sister, Dot, and her two little messes, but Agnes had stopped listening a long time ago. Abe King was a handsome man, and a woman would have had to be dead not to notice. Of course, that hadn't been the first time she'd seen him driving by the house. Seemed like everywhere she went, there he was staring at her and smiling.

"How you doin', Miss Agnes?" he'd say, looking devilish. But Agnes would look the other way and keep right on walking like she hadn't even heard him. Years later, he'd tease that the reason he chased after her was that she'd played hard to get and he'd enjoyed the challenge. The more she resisted, the more he persisted, until finally, at the church social, Abe King got downright foolhardy.

She'd been helping serve the food that afternoon when he came through the line with Pete Jensen. Agnes had seen him watching her all afternoon, but as usual, she'd chosen to ignore him.

"Yeah," she heard him say to Pete, "My momma was dark-skinned too, which is why my daddy chased her down like he did. We King men . . . we like our women dark. Dark and thick, just like molasses."

Despite her best efforts to pay him no attention, Agnes looked up and stared straight into the face of Abe King. He smiled at her, then winked. "Aw, yeah . . . dark and sticky-sweet."

Pete laughed loud enough for everybody to hear, and Agnes was so appalled, she dropped a spoonful of mashed potatoes on the table.

"My plate is over here, Agnes!" Martha Edwards snapped. "What's wrong with you, fool? Can't you see?"

She wasn't sure who had embarrassed her more, Abe or Miss Martha. Agnes planted the serving spoon in the pan of potato salad and ran off. She was mad enough to cuss or spit or something, but ladies didn't do such things. Momma had taught her that too. A few minutes later, Abe found her and apologized.

"I'm sorry, Miss Agnes," he said. "I didn't mean no harm. But you 'bout the prettiest girl I've seen in a long time."

He was patient with her and made love to her with his words. Abe courted her, then six months later asked her to marry him.

Tears rested heavy on the insides of her eyes as the memories retraced steps through her heart. He'd been a world to Agnes, and losing him left a void much too big to be filled by anyone else. The liquor was starting to settle in now, and the weight of her body pulled her further down into that old chair. Agnes prayed time would stop right where it was to leave her lost in her memories of him. She'd been promised that time would make his being gone easier, but it hadn't done that. The more time passed, the more she missed her husband.

"There's been an accident down at the sawmill," the voice on the other end of the phone said. That's all she remembered until the day of his funeral, when she stared down at her husband lying in a casket dressed in his Sunday suit. He didn't look like Abe, just a shell of the man who'd said he'd loved her more than his own life, and from that moment on, Agnes became a shell too.

Mattie had been six years old when her daddy passed, and Agnes gathered up all that she had left and poured it into that little girl. She was the only piece of Abraham that Agnes had, and Agnes adored that child.

I can't do this! I can't do this no more . . .

A lump welled up in her throat when she thought back to that night. "Jesus!" Agnes blurted out, and cried into her hands. She rocked herself back and forth and begged the question again, hoping this time heaven would give her an answer that made sense. "Why? Why both of 'em, Lord?" she sobbed. "Why'd I have to lose 'em both?"

Mattie's death tortured Agnes. Her daughter's pleas for help echoed in her mind to the point she sometimes thought she'd go crazy.

Momma! Please! Oh . . . please!

Nothing could describe the helplessness she'd felt that night. If she could've switched places with that child and taken her burden on herself, she would've. It would've been easier, but instead, she'd been left behind to carry the pain of lost loves and wade through life numb and dead inside.

"You've got yo' grandboy to take care of now, Agnes," Momma said. "You got to go on for his sake. He need you, gal. God's will ain't always our will, but He know best."

In an instant, Agnes's own child was gone and Mattie's son had become Agnes's to raise. He'd never known his real momma, but sometimes he'd ask about Mattie. Agnes could never bring herself to talk about her to the boy. She figured she'd one day be ready to satisfy his curiosities, but that day never seemed to come. Deep inside, she hoped he'd eventually stop asking.

She tended to him and took care of him, but she could never find love inside herself for him. Agnes figured that day would come too, but he was eight years old and it still hadn't come. Most of the time, she couldn't even stand to look at him. Not in his face. Agnes was afraid of seeing too much in his face. Too much Mattie, reminding her of the child she'd loved and lost. She was afraid she'd see some of Abe in him. Surely he was hidden somewhere in the boy too. More than anything, she feared she'd see Fool. The man who'd stolen her baby girl, forced himself inside her and planted a seed her body hadn't been strong enough to bear. To love this boy, most of the time, didn't seem to be an option for Agnes. She took care of him like she was waiting for his real folks to come pick him up and take him home.

John crouched behind the heavy velvet drapes, staring wide-eyed at his grandmother sitting alone in the dark room. The sound of her crying had summoned him from bed. He watched Agnes's laughter transform into tears and pleas to Jesus about what she'd lost. She was probably crying over Mattie. That's what he thought. She missed Mattie a lot. He missed her too, sometimes, but not as much as Momma Agnes did. He never even knew Mattie, so it was kind of hard for him to miss her too much.

John had a picture of her hidden under his mattress. He'd found it in a box hidden beneath Momma Agnes's bed. Sometimes, he'd stare at it before he fell asleep. He'd stare at it long and hard until he could hardly keep his eyes open, hoping he'd dream about her. Then, maybe she'd tell him something in his dream about the kinds of things she used to do and the kind of food she liked to eat. In her picture, she didn't look much older than him. She looked like she was just a girl, and he wondered how a girl could've been his momma. It didn't make sense to him at all.

Momma Agnes slumped down in the chair and tears slid down her cheeks. She looked tired and he wanted to tell her that she needed to go to bed if she was tired. Sometimes, she looked like that after he'd done something to get himself in trouble. She'd have never known about those things if folks weren't so quick to run back and tell on him.

The boy broke Wilson's car window.

The boy been throwin' rocks at Roberta's cats again.

The boy stole ten cents' worth of penny candy and you owe Miss Gwennie a dime.

John wasn't bad when she was around, though. With Momma Agnes, he made sure to behave, hoping that maybe one day she'd notice and smile, then say, "How's Momma Agnes's good boy doin' today?" Then she'd pat him on his head and kiss his face.

He hated to see her cry, and he wished he could do something to make her feel better, but if she knew he was still up, she'd give him a whooping for sure. Her whoopings didn't really hurt, though. Not a lot. But he'd cry anyway and make her think they did.

Agnes slowly got up and started walking toward the bookcase. She stumbled and fell, dropping her glass on the floor. Instinctively, he ran from his hiding place and grabbed her arm to help her up.

Momma Agnes laughed. "Oooowee! Will you look at . . ." When she realized it was John helping her up, she stared at him with red, swollen eyes, then spat in his face. "Boy!" Agnes jerked her arm from his grasp. "Whatchu doin' up?" she slurred.

"You alright, Momma Agnes? You didn't hurt yourself, did you?"

Agnes got up, then staggered back to the chair. "Go back to bed! I said go back to bed!"

"I heard you crying," he said, trying to help her sit down.

She pushed him. "Didn't you hear me, boy? I said get back! Get away from me!" Agnes glared at him. "Don't you make me . . ." She pointed in his face, then pressed her lips together, fighting to keep the tears inside. "Why you gotta . . . look like . . ." Agnes stared at the face that reminded her of how helpless she'd been. She saw shame and hatred, wrapped up in an eight-year-old boy that looked like Fool and the pain he'd caused Mattie.

John didn't know what to do. He stood frozen, wondering if she'd hurt herself. "You alright, Momma Agnes?" John picked up the glass from the floor. "It didn't break. That's good it didn't break or else you could've gotten cut."

Agnes squeezed her eyes shut. Looking at that child hurt her all over again. In his face was hidden everything that had broken her heart, and she wished he'd never been born. "Go away from me, boy!" she said through clenched teeth. "I never wanted . . . I don't want . . . get outta my face, John!" Agnes broke down and her shoulders shook under the weight of her tears. She mumbled again, "How come it couldn't have been you? Mattie. I want my Mattie."

John wanted to say something to make her feel better, but he had no idea what that could be. He turned and walked back to his room. She'd be all right tomorrow, he thought. Momma Agnes was just hot, that's all. It was too hot in that house.

And Revelations

As usual, Agnes had chosen to ignore the obvious, which was no surprise to Dorothy. Agnes had always been guilty of seeing what she wanted to see and turning a blind eye to those things she didn't. Once again, Dorothy's Saturday afternoon visit had found Pete Jensen at her sister's house, fixing something he'd probably broken in the first place. Pete had always been a sneaky man, and Dorothy wouldn't have put it past him to be underhanded enough to sabotage things around Agnes's house, claiming to be repairing them when, in fact, it was all a ploy to get her to call him to come over.

They'd just finished feeding the kids, and Dorothy sat at the kitchen table while Agnes washed the last of the supper dishes.

"Y'all stop runnin' in and out of this house!" Dorothy shouted at the children, who were scurrying around in the living room. The front door slammed shut at least five times before the last of them was finally out of the house, and Dorothy winced every time it did.

"Now, with all them kids you got, I'd think you'd be used to doors slamming all the time," Agnes said to Dot. Between the two sisters, Dorothy had proven to be the more fertile, having given birth to eight children, which included two sets of twins.

"Girl, I can't stand it. Them children know better. They act like they done lost they minds when we come over here. Like I won't whoop they asses in front of you."

Dorothy glanced at Pete, who was supposed to be hard at work fixing the washing machine but instead seemed to spend most of his time getting an eyeful of Agnes's behind. He might've had her sister fooled, and he might've even had his wife fooled, but Dot had figured him out a long time ago. Pete Jensen had been hot on Agnes for years. Of course, Agnes just thought of him as her "friend." Dot shook her head. As old as that woman was, how could she possibly be that naive? For years he'd been buzzing around her like a bee to honey, and everybody seemed to notice but Agnes. If Edna didn't notice, then the woman was either blind or stupid. But Edna had never been one to make a fuss anyway. As long as Pete paid the bills and kept food on the table, she didn't complain about anything he did. All you had to do was ask her on any day of the week and she'd tell you that she had a good man in Pete Jensen. A good man who'd cut off his right arm for ten minutes with the likes of Agnes King.

All in all, though, Pete wasn't a bad-looking man. He was tall and dark, but Dorothy wouldn't admit to him being handsome. His eyes bulged and he was too skinny for her tastes. But he wasn't bad-looking.

"Agnes," Pete said, walking toward her with a black rubber ring in his hand. "Looks like I'm gon' have to replace the belt on this here machine."

"Again?" Agnes asked. "Pete, you just replaced it last month."

"Hmpf," Dot said, then gulped down her iced tea. He'd probably replaced it the month before that too, she thought. Old Pete was smooth. She had to give him that.

He cleared his throat. "Yeah . . . well, that was a different belt, Agnes. This one here is what turn the motor."

"But didn't you say the other one turned the motor?" Agnes asked, looking genuinely confused.

"Naw . . . that one turn the drum. This here belt is smaller . . . see. And it turn the motor to the whole machine. Even the drum won't work if this belt go bad."

Agnes frowned. "So how much is this gon' cost me, Pete?" She'd been putting a lot of money into that machine lately, and she'd been thinking about cutting her losses and buying a new one.

"I'll tell you what. You jus' pay for the belt, and I'll put it in for you no charge." He smiled. "Won't be no more than, oh, three, four dollars."

Agnes protested. "Pete, now you know I can't let you do that."

Dot interjected before Pete had a chance to weasel out of his offer. "Of course you can, Agnes. The man said he'd fix it for free. Let him fix it for free." Pete smiled weakly at Dorothy.

"It ain't really no problem, Agnes. Once I get the part, wouldn't take me but five minutes to put it in anyway."

Finally, after taking twenty minutes to pack up his screwdriver, Pete left and the two women moved their conversation into the living room. After Abe's death, the sisters reserved Saturday afternoons for each other. Agnes and Dot had been best friends, and neither of them would've had it any other way. Both of them knew they'd have been best friends even if they hadn't been sisters, but they'd been blessed to be both.

They were as opposite as two people could get. Agnes, being the older one, had inherited the sense of order and responsibility most firstborn do. Dorothy, on the other hand, had always been wild and spent most of her life in and out of marriages, bars, and church like they'd all come with revolving doors on them. According to Momma, Dot had been the reason behind her arthritic knees, because she'd spent so much time on them praying for her prodigal daughter to come home, settle down, and find Jesus once and for all. Dorothy figured that if Jesus needed the likes of her to find him, then he was the one who needed prayer. In the end, it had taken Agnes to settle Dot's restless soul.

Agnes had been through so much, Dot felt she needed to slow down long enough to offer what little comfort she could. But somehow she'd managed to stop running altogether, and when she did, she remembered she had eight babies she'd dropped off and forgotten about, and she didn't have the strength or desire to start up again.

"The good Lord answers all prayer." Momma beamed. Dot just smiled and nodded. Maybe He does, she thought to herself. Or maybe the Good Lord just didn't know what it was to miss out on a good party.

Summer was winding down, getting ready to let fall have its turn. The late afternoon sun seemed anxious to move on and a slight chill had started settling in. Dot pulled her sweater close around her. "How come kids don't get cold? I must be gettin' old, 'cause all of a sudden, I'm cold all the time."

Agnes smiled. "They too busy runnin' round playin' to worry 'bout bein' cold. Remember when you was runnin' round playin'?" She winked at Dot. "That's why you didn't get cold."

Dot laughed. "Yeah, I was havin' too much fun to be cold. I sho' knew how to have a good time, girl."

"I'll bet."

Agnes had spent years worrying about Dot. Somebody had to worry about her, because Lord knows she didn't worry enough about herself. Dorothy was spontaneous. A big word that made Dot's eyes light up and scared the mess out of Agnes. That girl would pick up at a moment's notice, chasing after some man or dream, or both, only to end up back at home, pregnant and bro-kenhearted. And every time, Momma would drag her into church, get Dot to repent and be born again, hoping this time she'd stay put and get herself together. But Dot's spirit was too wild to let disappointment keep her in one place too long. She'd be off on some other adventure even before she'd left altar call.

All that running had taken its toll on Dot, and so had giving birth to all those children. Strong, spirited children like their momma. Agnes knew Dot had given up the streets for her. Most of the time she was glad she had, but sometimes she saw sadness in her sister's eyes. Not the kind of sadness that came from losing a lover, but it reminded Agnes of the kind of heartbreak that can only come from giving up. Dot had chased after something her whole life and never seemed to be able to catch up with it. Whenever Agnes asked her about it, she'd just shrug her shoulders and say she was tired. Eventually, Agnes guessed that maybe the chase was all Dot had ever been after, anyway.

"Momma Agnes," John called through the screen door. "Can I get some water?"

Dorothy noticed Agnes averting her eyes like she always did when the boy spoke to her. "Come on," she said shortly. John headed for the kitchen. "And wash yo' hands before you go into my refrigerator," Agnes called behind him.

She'd seen Agnes distance herself from the boy since he'd been born. In the beginning, everybody thought it was her grief that had kept her from letting herself get close to him. Agnes seldom held the child, and Dot couldn't remember ever seeing her so much as smile at anything he'd done, like walking or talking for the first time. Then they all thought that maybe she'd chosen to love him from a distance, afraid she'd lose him like she'd lost Abe and Mattie, but eventually Dot recognized the truth, even if nobody else wanted to admit it. Agnes felt no love for this boy. Dorothy had to wonder. If she could see it, could he?

"How he doin' in school?" Dot asked.

Agnes shrugged. "Fine."

"He gettin' big. Tall like Abe."

Agnes sipped on her tea.

John bounced back into the living room, on his way back outside to play. "Hey, li'l boy," Dot called to him. "Come over here and give me some sugar. You didn't even hug my neck when I came in."

He hugged her quickly. Dot held up her cheek to him. "Kiss my jaw."

His lips grazed across her cheek, then he ran out the front door. Agnes never looked at him and he never looked at her. Dot felt sad for both of them. How could two people be so close and so far away from each other at the same time? she wondered. They were like shadows, sharing the same space but never touching. Never connecting to each other. It was as if they were figments of each other's imagination.

It was obvious Agnes didn't want to carry on a conversation about her grandson, so Dot decided to lighten up the mood and change the subject.

"So . . . Pete been over here quite a bit lately. Ain't he?"

Agnes sighed. "Don't start, Dot." She knew nosy questions had been burning the tip of that woman's tongue since he'd left, and it was only a matter of time before she'd decide to try and stir up some dirt.

"All I said was, he been over here a lot. How many times he done fixed on that washin' machine?"

"More times than I care to count. I keep thinkin' it might be best for me to get rid of it and get a new one, but Pete say . . ."

Dorothy grinned. "What do Pete say, Agnes?"

Agnes rolled her eyes, ignoring her sister's obvious chiding. "He say this one is fine."

Finally Dot blurted out, "Oh, girl! Pete Jensen likes you. Can't you see that? Why you think he over here all the time? I'm surprised Edna ain't said nothin'."

"Will you get yo' trashy mind out of the gutter, Dot? Pete and Edna been friends of me and Abe's for years. He jus' helpin' me. That's all. Lord know I need it. I swear, this ol' house seem like it's fallin' down round me sometimes."

"I saw him lookin' at yo' booty," Dot teased. "Smiled, then licked his lips like this." She traced her tongue over her lips, then laughed.

Agnes glared at Dot, then folded her arms defensively across her chest. "Nonsense! That's nonsense and you know it!" she snapped.

Dot folded her arms too. "Don't be sittin' over there actin' surprised. That man been sweet on you since second grade. And you know that!"

"Even if he was sweet on me, Dot—which he ain't—Pete and Edna are good people and they my friends. Now, why don't you mind yo' business and stop tryin' to stir up mess?"

"I ain't tryin' to stir up nothin'. I'm jus' lettin' you know what I think. 'Sides, couldn't nobody but Edna blame you if you got you a li'l bit." Dot winked.

Agnes could hardly believe what she was hearing. "A li'l bit . . . of what?"

"He ain't a bad-lookin' man, Agnes. And I know how long it's been since you—"

"Dorothy Louise! I can't believe what's comin' out of yo' mouth!"

"Now, girl, you know me," Dot said nonchalantly. "I'm gon' say what I think, 'specially with you. All I'm sayin' is, won't nobody know but you and him. Pete ain't gon' tell and I know you ain't gon' say nothin'. Like I said, he ain't a bad-lookin' man. Ain't bad-lookin' at all."

Agnes's eyes narrowed. "Well, then, if you think he ain't all that bad-lookin', then why don't you get you a 'li'l bit,' as you say? 'Cause I ain't interested in no Pete Jensen or no other man either."

Dot smacked her lips. "Child, please. You know I done gave up on men. If one of 'em even so much as breathe on me, I'm pootin' out babies, and I'm gettin' too damn old for any more kids."

Suddenly, laughter burst through Agnes's anger and the two women were beside themselves, clutching at their stomachs, laughing so hard that tears filled their eyes. "Girl! You ain't never lied!" Agnes squealed.

A small, brown face pressed against the screen door, peering at the two women. "Momma!" Dot's son called to her. "Sadie's cryin'."

No sooner had he said it than the wailing child appeared behind him, cradling her elbow. "Mommaaa!" she cried. "Mommaaa!" A band of wide-eyed children trailed behind her.

Dot started to get up and go over to the girl, but before she could, Agnes quickly jumped up out of her seat and scooped Sadie up in her arms. She sat back down on the couch, wrapped her arms around the girl and poured kisses all over her face. "It's all right, baby girl," she said soothingly.

Dorothy stared at Agnes, who was smothering this child with entirely too much concern. "She fine, Agnes. She probably just scraped her elbow a bit. Come here, baby. Let Momma see." She reached out to Sadie, but Agnes pulled her in even closer, then smiled at her sister, pleading with her eyes to let her have this moment.

"Shhh, li'l girl. You gon' be jus' fine." Agnes rocked the girl slowly back and forth on her lap, rubbing her hand across her hair. Memories flooded her thoughts, and Agnes was hurled back in time to a place where Mattie had been small and sweet. A place where Agnes could make it better with hugs and kisses. The child felt good in her arms.

"Y'all go on back outside now," Dot told the other children. Then she looked at John, who stood mesmerized at the sight of Agnes holding Sadie. He looked as if he couldn't believe Agnes was capable of this kind of tenderness. Yes, Dot thought to herself. This boy knew. He knew he'd been unwelcome in his grandmomma's life, and all of a sudden, he seemed to understand this.

Tears threatened to fall from his eyes, but they never did. "C'mon, y'all," he said to his cousins. "Let's go."

The Wages of Sin

Roberta waited quietly, watching the congregation settle into their seats. Crying babies rested on the hips of young women, while older children waddled behind their mommas, reminding her of baby ducks. She hadn't birthed any of these little ones. As a matter of fact, Roberta hadn't birthed a baby in years. Now, the only time she'd visit a womb was to kill babies, not give them life.

Look at 'em all. She glared. *Fast heffas, every last one of them. Got the nerve to be sittin' up in church praisin' God one minute, knowin' good and well they were gon' to be laid up with some man later on this evenin' with they legs all up in the air. Which one of y'all gon' be knockin' on my door next month?* she wondered.

"Let the church say 'Amen'," commanded the preacher.

"Amen!" Roberta's heavy voice carried over the other church members. "Thank you, Jesus!"

What's that fool gal staring at? Roberta wondered to herself. She stared at Mavis, Lula May's whorish daughter, causing the girl to shift uncomfortably in her seat. Roberta had done Mavis two weeks ago. Mavis, like everybody else, thought the midwife was crazy, but she'd come to her like all the others. Crying in the middle of the night, with a knitting needle stuck up her behind. Dumb-ass gal. Of course, crazy old Roberta had to be the one to take care of things, and she did too. The midwife knew her business, whether it be birthing babies or killing them. She knew what to do better than anybody else in the county, which is why Mavis came crying to her when she had no place else to go. Besides, who else is going to do it for forty dollars?

"Thank you, Lawd!" Roberta shouted. Mavis was dumb and she knew it wouldn't be long before the girl came back.

Spreading her legs like butter for them Clark brothers. Both of them, from what Roberta had heard. She was in the store one day when she'd heard them talking. "Yeah! I want me some poo-tang, man. Let's go to Mavis's house. Her momma at work."

Fool gal! If her momma hadn't been sitting right next to her, Roberta would've stood up and slapped her face. Then she would've called her a dummy, right there in church. She'd do it the next time she laid eyes on Mavis, and Roberta knew there would definitely be a next time.

The reverend preached. "We don't always understand where the Lord is comin' from. We don't always understand why things happen the way they do."

"Praise the Lawd!" she shouted.

"Amen!" Agnes's voice shouted from the row next to Roberta's. Reluctantly, Roberta glanced over in Agnes's direction, knowing he'd be there, staring at her like he always did. The little bastard! What was he now? Eleven? Twelve? Roberta held his gaze for only a second before turning her attention back to the preacher. He was still staring at her. She could feel his black eyes burning into the back of her neck, stinging her like a swarm of bees. Roberta closed her eyes. *Lawd, please!* She prayed silently. *Please rid me of that demon, once and for all. He like fire in my blood, Lawd. He tryin' to tear me down. Tryin' to kill me with his hate. Lawd, take that boy's evil eyes off me.*

She took a deep breath, then slowly opened her eyes and glanced again to where he was sitting. Roberta smiled. The boy's head rested against Agnes's shoulder and his mouth hung open as he slept. "Thank you, Jesus!" she shouted. Let that sleeping dog lie.

She stared at him while he slept. He looked harmless enough, like any other boy. He looked like his daddy. Just like him. Suddenly, Roberta was startled by the resemblance. She'd never really looked at the boy before, but he was the spitting image of Fool. The same cocoa-brown skin and heavy dark brows. The same full bottom lip. Agnes pushed against his head gently with her shoulder, then whispered something to him. His eyes fluttered open, and

Roberta quickly turned away. How could he look so much like . . . No. Fool meant nothing to her. He'd never had anything to do with Roberta. "Thank you, Lawd!" she shouted again. Cleta Jewel turned and stared at her and the other church members shifted uncomfortably in their seats. She'd better turn her nosy self back around, Roberta wanted to say. She had every right to shout the Lord's name if she wanted to. When she wanted to. Never mind the pastor or Cleta.

He who begot Fool has fallen. "What?" she asked out loud. Who'd said that? Roberta sat up straight and looked around the church. Who'd said it? The words echoed in her mind as she tried to make sense of what had been said to her. He who begot . . . Fool . . . has fallen? *Fool . . . begot . . . he begot the black-eyed boy. That King boy.* The one who hated her so? The one who wanted her dead? Roberta fought the urge to turn and look at John. Confusion waged war inside her as words and questions demanded her attention. But how can a fool beget a king? she wondered to herself.

"Praise him!" she shouted. A fool can't beget a king. Or can he? *Break his neck!* the voice commanded. Roberta shook her head back and forth, desperate to shake free from the voices and the questions. How can a fool be . . . begotten by a man who ain't a fool? Fool's daddy wasn't a fool. *Oh, yes, he was!* "Yesss, Lawd!" Roberta stood to her feet, raised her arms, and opened her hands to heaven. The fire of God was upon her now. "Thank you!" she shouted. The boy King stared at her. Roberta didn't have to see him to know he watched her. She could feel his eyes trying to burn her flesh. Her soul. A fool beget a king. And a man who wasn't a fool, beget Fool.

John and the rest of the congregation stared at Roberta's massive figure, swaying back and forth like a giant elm tree in the wind. "Thank you, Lawd! Praise be to God!" she said. The spirit of God had consumed her and she dared the black-eyed demon to try to harm her. Fool! He was begotten by a man who was no fool! But by a man who'd done a foolish thing. "Yesss, Lawd!"

"Sistah Roberta," the usher said quietly to her. "Sistah Roberta . . . it's all right now. You wanna come with me?" She tugged on the midwife's arm, but Roberta yanked away from her.

Tears streamed down her wide face because all of a sudden she felt enlightened. "Oh . . . thank you. Thank you, Jesus!" Of course, that man had done a foolish thing. Laying up with that woman like he did. The weight of God's spirit made Roberta weak in the knees, and she struggled to hold herself up. He knew that wasn't his place. She wasn't his woman. Roberta had been his woman. She'd loved him and given herself to him, freely and unconditionally. She'd given him babies and taken care of him. She'd been good to that man. Naw! He wasn't supposed to be laying up with a woman that wasn't his. And that's why Roberta had to cut him. For his foolish act of laying up with that woman and begetting that Fool! Roberta laughed. That's why God had made that boy retarded. Fool . . . was an abomination. His momma and daddy had sinned in the eyes of God and in the eyes of Roberta. *For the wages of sin is death.*

Roberta remembered that night like it was last night. Only, years had passed since she'd last laid eyes on her husband. He stood before her, covered in the stench of that bitch, spitting out lies like fire. Trying to make her doubt her own eyes.

"Roberta! She lyin', Roberta. That boy ain't mine! He ain't mine and I ain't had nothin' to do with that woman!"

Roberta sobbed. "He look jus' like you, Charles! I saw him myself. How can you stand there and lie to me? How can you do this to me? When you know how much I love you?"

"Baby!" He reached out to her, but she slapped his hands away.

"Don't put yo' nasty hands on me after they been all over that woman!"

"I ain't been with that woman, Roberta! How many times I got to tell you that?"

Roberta choked back tears. "I seen you!"

He shook his head in disbelief. "Naw . . ."

"Yes, Charles! I seen you with her!"

"Naw, Baby! You know I wouldn't—"

"I followed you to her house. I seen you kissin' her when she opened up the door, Charles. I seen you with my own eyes."

The man who ain't a fool begot Fool. Charles hadn't been a fool, though he'd done a sinful thing. For the wages of sin . . .

Charles begged her, pleaded with her to forgive him. "Think about them babies we got, Roberta." Babies she'd given him because he wanted them. She never did. Babies she took care of and loved because he wanted them. All Roberta ever wanted was Charles.

He thought she'd forgiven him; after all, they'd made love. Making love to him was as easy as breathing. Then he fell asleep. He awoke to the sensation of the sharp blade slicing open his throat, then stared at Roberta from behind black, dead eyes, pleading to her to help him. His mouth moved, but the words got lost somewhere in the blood.

There's power in the blood.

They sent her away after that night. They sent her straight to a hell they called Richardson's Women's Asylum for the Criminally Insane. From what she could tell, that's where they sent all colored women they thought were crazy. Either there or prison. As far as she was concerned, there was nothing crazy about what she did. He'd been the one who wronged her. Charles had stolen her spirit, then spit it out and stepped all over it to get to Sara Tate, and death was his inheritance. That hell became her home for more years than Roberta could remember, robbing her of her youth, her beauty. She'd been a fine woman before being sent there. The only reason they let her go was because the state stopped giving money to the institution. She'd overheard two nurses talking about it one day.

"This one here ain't crazy. She jus' mean as hell," they'd said, laughing. "They say she killed her husband, but—he probably had it comin'. Niggers always got it comin'. Hell! She'll probably get right out and find another one, just like that," the nurse said, snapping her fingers. "Maybe next time they'll be smart and send her black ass to the chair."

All Roberta had left were her memories of Charles. Memories of his dark eyes and red blood haunted her, tormented her in her dreams and in this boy and the one before him, Fool. Roberta saw Charles in both of them.

It wasn't hard to get back into midwifing when she finally came home. All it took was one poor, desperate woman, calling her up in the middle of the night. "I know you used to deliver babies," she gasped. "My man ain't here, and I'm by myself and—"

"Where you live again?" Roberta had asked.

"Over on West Garrett, near the railroad tracks." The woman grunted. "Number Eight-seventeen! Can you . . . hurry? Please?"

Roberta slipped into her house shoes and grabbed her purse. "I'll be there in a minute." That's how easy it had been to get back into midwifing.

Charles beget Fool. Fool raped Mattie King. He beget the black-eyed demon. Yes! The very same one standing over her, with the rest of the congregation, staring down where her spirit-slain body lay. "C'mon, Sistah Roberta," the usher said, helping her to her feet. "The Lord done bless you again today."

"Yesss . . . he most certainly did." Roberta smiled. *Yo' death is in his hands, Roberta!* the voice whispered. She swallowed hard. *For the wages of sin . . .*

John sat back down next to Agnes. Racine Davis had switched places with her sister and sat next to him. She reached inside her small black purse, pulled out a butterscotch candy, and handed it to him. "She do that almost every Sunday," she whispered to John.

"She just crazy," he said, opening his candy. Racine had a crush on him. That's what Sara Jenkins told him. But she didn't have to bother telling him that. He already knew.

The Mountain

The pale yellow pickup traveled slowly down the dirt road, heading toward Miss Gwennie's store. The ominous figure driving glanced casually at the boy, nodded his head slightly, then turned his attention back to the road.

"Moses," John mouthed, as his eyes grew wide with fascination. He dropped his backpack off his shoulder, gripped it in his hand, then he ran as fast as he could behind the truck, hoping to catch up with it and see in the flesh all six feet five inches and three hundred pounds of the mountain they called Moses.

The sound of heavy footsteps resonated across the wooden porch of Miss Gwennie's store, sounding more like they were carrying thunder than a man.

"Afternoon," said one of the old men sitting outside the store and playing checkers. He didn't bother with the customary small talk or handshake he'd have greeted anybody else with. The old man knew Moses and he knew that Moses wasn't friendly with anybody.

Moses never even glanced in the man's direction. The sound of his voice slowly erupted from deep inside and replied, indifferently, "Afternoon."

He slowly pulled open the screen door to the store, then stood for a moment in the doorway, allowing his eyes to adjust to the dimly lit room. His massive shadow filled the entrance, eclipsing the room from the sun. Moses glanced in Gwennie's direction, then walked slowly toward the back of the store, to the cooler where Gwennie kept the cold pop. She stared at him over the rim of her glasses. Gwennie knew Moses Tate. She'd known him since he was a child, and that boy hadn't been nothing but trouble to his poor momma, Sara, who'd died some years back from cancer. Sara had had to raise those boys all by herself: Moses, who'd been full of hell from the day he was born, and Fool, the retarded boy who'd raped that girl, Mattie King. She shook her head, slowly, remembering how hard it had been on that poor woman, finding out what that boy of hers had done to that girl. Sara cried and wailed like it had been her daughter he'd done that to. "Lord . . . Jesus! Why? Why he have to . . . Why?" The Good Lord work in mysterious ways, she thought to herself. Lord knew Sara Tate needed to rest, which is why he took her the way he did. She wasn't even fifty when she passed.

Moses had moved out of Bueller years ago, fifteen minutes away, in a town called Solo. He despised Bueller, and everybody in it. If his momma hadn't needed him close by, he'd have left Texas altogether, but he had her and Adam to look after. After she passed, he moved Adam to Solo with him and his wife, Sadie. He seldom came into town, except to take care of business. Sadie had been worrying him about getting a phone put in the house since they'd gotten married three years ago, arguing that they needed one for emergencies. Moses knew better. He was more than capable of taking care of all their so-called emergencies like he'd always done. The truth of the matter was, Sadie wanted that phone to run her mouth on all day. But he'd promised her, and had come into town today to pay the deposit so that the phone company could turn it on. Seemed like wasting good money to him, but if it kept her mouth running to somebody else, and not to him, he figured maybe it was worth it.

Gwennie jumped at the sound of the door slamming shut behind the boy, standing in the doorway of her store huffing and puffing like a train. John stood breathless in the doorway of Miss Gwennie's store, in time to see the broad back of Moses Tate moving through the store like he'd imagined a whale moved through the ocean. Moses glanced back over his shoulder, and John quickly grabbed a comic book from the rack near the door, pretending to read it. Gwennie eyed John suspiciously. The little thieving bastard, she wanted to say. That boy was in here being nosy or trying to steal something. Or both.

"If you gon' buy thumpthin', hurry up and buy thumpthin', boy. Thith ain't no library." Gwennie scowled at him over the rim of her reading glasses. She'd forgotten her teeth again today, which were still upstairs soaking in the teacup on the nightstand next to her bed. John ignored her like he always did, fumbling through the pages of comic books and glancing back where Moses stood, hovering over the freezer. He'd grown up hearing stories about Moses Tate all his life, mostly from his best friend Lewis's daddy and uncles. According to them, Moses Tate was stronger than any man in Texas. He was stronger and meaner than Mad Dog the Bruiser, the wrestler he and Lewis watched on television on Saturday nights. Moses Tate's hands were so big, he could palm a whole watermelon, then squeeze his long, thick, black fingers around it and crush the hull as easily as crushing a grape. "Wow," John whispered, staring at Moses.

"Boy!" Gwennie growled. "If you ain't gon' buy nothin' up in here, then get on home, fo' I call yo' grandmomma!"

One time, he'd heard, Pete Jensen was changing the oil filter on his old Chevy when the car collapsed on top of him. His wife watched as the weight of the car slowly crushed the life out of Pete, who was a dead man for sure. But then, Moses pulled up in his truck, lifted that old Chevy and held it up long enough for Pete's wife to pull him out from under the car by his ankles.

"Ain't you th'posed to go right home after thchool boy?" Gwennie asked. "You know Agneth waitin' on you." John looked at the old woman, sighed, then flipped through more comic books. Gwennie rolled her eyes. "Hmpf!"

Moses turned to the rack behind him and glanced at John. Of course that was him, he thought. He'd heard about the boy, but he'd never laid eyes on him until today. He looked just like his daddy. Adam. Or at least the way Adam used to look, years ago. Moses counted the years in his head. The boy had to have been . . . twelve, maybe thirteen years old by now, he figured. Had it really been that long? he wondered. Time had disappeared into a black hole, especially for Adam. Sometimes Moses wondered if everything that happened back then hadn't been somebody's dream or nightmare.

He and Adam never talked about those years anymore, except when they talked about Momma. But it had always been as if nothing else ever happened, until Moses stared at that boy, who looked so much like his brother, pretending to read comic books.

John saw Moses staring at him, then quickly turned his back to the man. His heart beat excitedly in his chest. Had Moses really killed those three men at the old Smith place like he'd heard? He wondered. Lewis's uncle had told them the story about Old Man Davis seeing Moses's yellow truck out late one night, speeding down Smith Road. A few days later, they found three dead men behind the house in the old barn; their skulls had been crushed. "Like watermelons," he whispered, then slowly glanced over his shoulder again at Moses.

"What was you doin' out at that time of night, Mr. Davis?" one of the policemen had asked the old man. Old Man Davis was ninety-seven years old at the time, with dim eyes and a feeble mind. So, most folks didn't take what he said too seriously at all.

"I was on my way to the outhouse," he replied. "I saw that yella truck, and I knowed it was that Tate boy, Moses, so I wave my hand . . . even though that boy mean as hell. I wave my hand anyhow . . . but . . . he don't bother to wave back, but that boy . . . he a mean one. I know he is and I ain't s'prise he ain't wave back. Ain't s'prise at all."

Benita Butler had kept Moses out of prison. She was a white lady who lived just outside town with her two kids. Benita didn't have a husband, but she swore Moses had been with her the night it happened, and nobody could prove otherwise.

John held his breath prisoner inside him, as Moses made his way up to the register, carrying a six-pack of red pop, two bags of fried pork skins, and a bottle of hot sauce. Moses reached down to the candy on the shelf lining the front of the register and grabbed a handful of chocolate bars. John stared in awe of his hands that looked like they could easily crush watermelons and skulls. Moses glanced over at him, then John quickly closed his mouth and pretended to read.

Miss Gwennie quickly rang up his merchandise. "Three twenty-five."

Moses put a five-dollar bill down on the counter, while Gwennie bagged his things, then handed him back his change, but Moses picked up his bag and headed for the door.

"Give the change to the boy," he said, not bothering to look at John.

Moses left the store, letting the sun filter back in like it had done before he'd gotten there. John grabbed his change from Gwennie and quickly followed Moses out of the store, in time to see him drive off.

Lewis walked up behind him. "Man? Was that him? Moses Tate?" he asked over John's shoulder.

"Yeah, that was him." John stared down at the $1.75 he held in his hand. "Check it out, man," he said to Lewis.

"Where'd you get that?"

"From Moses."

Lewis sucked on his teeth. "Yeah, right. Why he gon' give you money?"

John smiled. " 'Cause we kin."

"Stop lyin', man. You and Moses Tate ain't no kin."

"He my uncle," John said defensively.

"If he yo' uncle, then I'm yo' uncle." Lewis slapped the back of John's head and ran. "I'm a monkey's uncle! I'm a monkey's uncle!" he sang. John shoved the money into his pocket, then chased after him, caught him, and put him in a headlock. "Ow! Get off me, boy!"

John laughed. "Punk! You a punk, Lewis!"

"I'm gon' kick yo' ass when I get outta this!"

John leaned back on Dot's front porch, watching his cousins play while she snapped the ends off green beans, then broke them in two, dropping them in a bowl she held in her lap. The sun slowly sank down into its bed hidden somewhere behind the open field across from the house. Dot wasn't like Agnes. He could talk to Dot and she talked back. Most of the time, when she wasn't fussing at kids, she even listened to him, like she cared about what he had to say.

"Guess who I saw today?"

"Sadie! Get up off that ground, girl!" Dot shouted. "Now I know you don't want me to wash and press that head again?" She looked at John. "Who?"

"Moses."

"Moses?"

"Tate. You ever seen him?" he asked.

"Yeah. I seen him. Big as he is, it be hard not to see him. Where you see him at?" She stared at him, seeing questions in his face he didn't know how to ask.

"The store."

"He say anything to you?"

"Naw. He gave me some money, though. Dollar seventy-five."

"I see," she said indifferently.

"I told Lewis, Moses is my uncle. That true?"

Dot stopped snapping beans and looked at John, wondering if what he didn't know was more of a blessing than a curse. Agnes refused to give him answers, and sometimes Dot felt obligated to tell him what she knew, because right or wrong, all the answers to all the questions he asked belonged to him. He'd been born into them.

"Moses is Fool's brother," she said.

He looked at her. "Fool's my daddy. Right?"

Dot nodded. "That's right."

"You know him?"

"I've seen him."

John swallowed hard. "He really . . . you know? Crazy like they say?"

"Fool ain't like other folks. He what they call . . . retarded."

"That mean he crazy?"

Dot sat back and went back to the business of snapping her beans. "Naw, child. He jus' slower in understandin' than most folk and don't know better 'bout most things."

John sat quietly, fingering the change in his pocket that Moses had given him. "Aunt Dot?" he asked thoughtfully. "What did he really do to my momma?"

The expression on the boy's face pleaded for her to shed some light on that dark, uncertain corner of his world. It was at times like this when Dot wanted to march over to Agnes's house and shake that woman silly. She should've been the one telling him what he needed to know. It was Agnes's responsibility to fill in the blanks of this boy's life. Not Dot's.

"Ooooh! I'm tellin'. Momma! Look what William did to my hair!" Sadie pointed to her freshly washed and pressed hair, full of grit and grass.

Dot was livid. It had taken her all morning to wash heads. "William!" she screamed.

"I didn't do it, Momma!" William stared up at Dot with wide eyes pleading innocence.

"Yes, he did, Momma!" Sadie insisted.

Dot glared at both of them. Lord, why didn't she just keep her legs closed? If she'd have kept her legs closed none of these little . . .

"Get in here, Sadie!" Dot pointed at William. "I owe you an ass whoopin'!" she growled.

"But I didn't do it," he whined, throwing his hands up in the air. "Dang!" he mumbled under his breath, then plopped down on the porch next to John.

"I heard that!" Dot shouted from inside the house.

John got up from the porch and headed home feeling like the door had been shut in his face again. Everybody knew something, but no one seemed to want to talk about it. It didn't seem fair to John; after all, Mattie was his momma, and more than anybody else, he figured he had a right to know what happened. Most of the time, he didn't bother asking, but seeing Moses raised his curiosity about Fool and what he did to Mattie King. John had his own ideas of what might've happened, but he never entertained them long. He wished for the truth and he hoped that once he knew it, he could bury it deep in the ground and forget all about it, like you were supposed to do with dead things.

This Day Belongs to Charlie

The bottoms of her feet felt like they were on fire, and anxious to get out of Denver, Colorado, once and for all. Charlotte Rodgers was born here, but deep inside, she'd always hoped she wouldn't be trapped into spending the rest of her life here. Now that she finally had a chance to fulfill at least one of her resolutions of the new year, and she knew she had to take it or risk being buried alive in this Rocky Mountain tomb forever. Choking down a glass of cheap champagne as 1976 chimed into her life, Charlotte promised herself that no matter what, she'd find a way to be happy. She vowed to take hold of the first opportunity that came along and hold on to it with all her strength if it promised even a hint of something, anything that gave her a reason for waking up in the morning. Who knew that opportunity would stroll in looking like Sam?

The brick-red Riviera slowed down and eventually came to a stop in front of the apartment building on the corner of Twenty-seventh and California.

"I'm just going to honk the horn when I swing back by, baby. I ain't getting out and I'll be back about nine."

Charlotte leaned over and kissed him. "I'll be ready, Sammy," she promised, getting out of the car.

She stood on the curb and watched him drive away until his car disappeared around the corner. The sun was just beginning to rise over her shoulder, and she knew she'd have to hurry and pack if she were going to be ready when Sam came back.

Not surprisingly, her daughters were still asleep. Charlotte hurried inside the apartment and quietly closed her bedroom door behind her. She slipped out of her high heels and collapsed on the bed, savoring images of her and Sam coiled together like snakes, making love all night long.

The first time she'd laid eyes on him, she thought he was the blackest man she'd ever seen. Sam was black enough to look sinister, like a child had drawn him and filled him in with a black crayon. But Sam made her knees weak the first time he spoke to her, with a voice that seemed to come from the center of the earth and channel up through him. She melted into his strong, muscular arms while they slow-danced at the club for hours, even through the fast songs.

"Mmmm . . . honey gold . . . honey brown girl." He smiled, gazing deeply into her eyes. "If I dip my finger in you, and put it in my mouth, would you taste as sweet as you look?"

She blushed. "That's for me to know."

"But it's for me to find out, and I'm definitely gonna find out, baby. You best believe that." He squeezed her close to him and cupped her behind in his hands. Sam was thick and hard, and his excitement for her pressed firmly against her thigh, boasting in its size and intentions.

Everything about Sam was smooth like satin; his walk, talk, ways, even the way he laughed, poetically summed him up into one word—charismatic. She'd never met a man like him, and after they made love for the first time, she knew it was a waste of time to bother looking for better. Orgasms with Sam left her trembling, and crying and pleading for him to stop and praying he never would. To put it mildly, she had it bad for this man.

Charlotte stared up at the ceiling, then sighed. Sam had done it again. He'd left the indelible imprint of him all over her, and the thought of washing him off was more than a disappointment. But a shower was in order or this sweet aroma would definitely turn sour before long, she thought, laughing to herself.

After showering, she came back into her room and lightly sprayed a mist of cologne between her breasts; his favorite. Charlotte stared back at the reflection in her dresser mirror. Dark circles beneath her eyes mocked the fact that she'd been up all night, riding Sam until dawn, then begging him not to leave her alone and without him. She was exhausted, but there was no time to sleep. He'd be back soon, and if she wasn't ready, he'd leave without her.

"I'm moving back east, Charlie," he'd told her early this morning. "Ain't shit out here in this sorry-ass city for me."

"You're leaving? When?" she asked, staring down at him.

"Today. My cousin's got a job lined up for me in Memphis, and I got to be there by Monday."

"And when were you planning on telling me this, Sam?" Agitation rose in her voice, but Sam seemed oblivious to it.

"I been telling you," he said casually.

"And what am I supposed to do?"

"What the hell you mean, what are you supposed to do? You do what you've been doing."

"What about us?"

"Us?" Suddenly, Sam noticed the unmistakable glimmer of tears form in Charlotte's eyes. "Awww, hell! What? What is this, Charlie?"

"I thought you cared about me?"

"I do care about you, but I've been talking about leaving ever since you met me. Now you got the nerve to get pissed about it?"

Charlotte took Sam's cigarette from between his fingers, rolled off him, then took a long, slow drag from it. "Fuck it, Sammy," she muttered. "Just . . . fuck it. And fuck you too!"

"Why are you tripping, Charlie? I told you I wasn't planning on staying. I've been telling you that since—"

"Yeah, you been telling me that all along. I just thought—"

"Thought what?"

Charlotte inhaled on the cigarette again. "That you'd take me with you. I thought you wouldn't leave without me."

Sam laughed. "You? Yeah, baby. I'd love to take you with me. But you and two kids? Hell, naw! That ain't happening."

"It ain't like I got an army, Sam. Two kids ain't nothing."

"Two kids is extra mouths to feed and extra bedrooms in an apartment. Two kids is more money than I've got right now, baby. And I damn sure ain't got the patience for them."

"They don't need a lot."

"They're kids, woman. They always need some damn thing, sooner or later."

"But . . . Sam . . ."

"Look, Charlie, I'm going to be staying with my cousin until

I get on my feet," he explained. "And I know good and damn well he don't want nobody's kids living up in his place. You . . . maybe. Kids? Hell, I'm lucky he's letting me stay with him."

"But the girls won't be no trouble, Sam, and I can take care of them. I've been taking care of them."

"That why you laying up here with me at three in the morning? You taking care of them, Charlie?"

Charlotte bit down on her anger and held it inside. "I take good care of my girls, Sam." She'd gotten pregnant with her oldest daughter, Connie, when she was fifteen and left home to be with the father, Dwayne.

"Why don't you just get rid of it?" Dwayne had insisted.

Charlotte smacked her lips, then hit him in the arm with her fist. "Why can't you just be a man and take care of it?"

He shrugged. "Hell! I don't want it."

"Well, I do," Charlotte argued, knowing she was lying. "And I'm going to have this baby, Dwayne. Now, you be the daddy and take care of it. Where can I put my stuff?"

Thinking back, if she'd had that abortion, her life would've been a lot different. She wouldn't be as desperate as she was now, because she'd be free to follow Sam to the ends of the earth if that's what she wanted. And there wouldn't be a damn thing he could say about it.

"It ain't happening, pretty," Sam said quietly, then turned over to Charlotte and gently wrapped his lips around an erect nipple. "Ain't no way I can take you with me. It's a shame, though. Your fine ass . . . I sure hate to let this go."

"Then don't let me go, Sam," she purred. "You can have me for as long as you want. I just . . . I'm tired of not having my own man. I love being with you, and I want us to stay together. I was even hoping we could get married some day."

He smiled. "Is that right?"

"We're good together, don't you think?" She tried smiling. "We don't fight a lot, and the sex is crazy!"

"But do you love me? That's the question, baby."

"Yes," she whispered. "I do love you." Sam rolled over on his back, then laughed again, hurting Charlotte's feelings. "What the hell is so funny?" she asked defensively.

"Your ass is funny, Charlie. Why do you think I'm laughing?"

"Fuck you, Sam!"

"Oh, baby. You been doing that all damn night! But I ain't complaining." Sam lit another cigarette. "Your shit is good. Real good, Charlie."

"But you don't love me?" she asked, trying to hide her disappointment.

"You know I don't. And you don't love me either, so put your lips back in your face, girl."

"I don't want you to leave me." Her voice quivered. "What's wrong with that? Men have been leaving me my whole life, and I'm tired of it."

"It's not you I'm leaving, Charlie. It's Denver."

"Then let me come with you." She pleaded, climbing back on top of him. "Please, baby. Let me come with you to Memphis."

"And what about the kids, Charlie? I can't take you and the kids. I just can't do it. I won't." He just couldn't justify it in his head. Sam had kids of his own. Kids he hadn't seen in years or even spoken to. He hadn't done shit to take care of his own, so why would he take care of some other man's kids?

Charlotte anxiously pressed her lips firmly to his and forced her tongue deep into his mouth, desperate to make him need her the way she needed him. "Then, we ain't got to take them, if you don't want to," she said breathlessly. Charlotte's heart pounded hard between them. The words hastily fell from her lips before she could catch them, but Charlotte didn't dare try to retrieve them now. They'd been set free on Sam's ears and if he didn't know before, he now knew the kind of sacrifice she was willing to make for him. Her children for life in Memphis with him. "If you promise to take me with you . . . we . . . don't have to take them, Sam."

"What the hell you planning on doing with them, then?"

Charlotte shrugged. "I'll figure out something."

"Damn, girl! You don't even give a shit about your own kids!" He laughed. "I know you can't possibly give a shit about my ass."

"That's not true," she said, hurt by his accusation. She gave a shit about her girls, but she'd lost her mind over Sam, the concept and idea of Sam. Or maybe it was the idea of running away with Sam that enticed her so much. "It's time for me to take care of me. I've been taking care of kids since I was fifteen, Sammy. Now it's my turn." She shrugged. "Maybe . . . my mother will take them," she lied. Charlotte hadn't spoken to her mother in years and had no idea how to get in touch with her. "I've got to do this before I get too old." Charlotte raised herself to the tip of Sam's erect penis, then slowly slid down on him. "I ain't old, Sam." She moaned. "I ain't an old woman."

"Naw, pretty. Your fine ass ain't nowhere near being old." He thrust his hips up, meeting hers in the middle.

Charlotte was finishing up packing the last of her toiletries in her overnight bag when she heard the voices of her two daughters rising above the sound of Saturday morning cartoons. She glanced at the clock that told her Sam would be outside in less than twenty minutes.

"What do you want to eat, Reesy?" Charlotte heard Momma Connie ask. Only twelve, Connie was born to mother, Charlotte thought. That's exactly why the two of them didn't get along. Two grown women, even if one of them wasn't grown in age, can't share a household together. It had always been obvious to Charlotte that Connie never thought much of her anyway, and it showed in her light brown eyes, which mirrored Charlotte's, glaring disapprovingly at her every time she took a breath. Connie had a way of spitting out accusations of Charlotte's shortcomings without saying a word. Instead, the girl would roll her eyes, shake her head, and mutter under her breath when she thought Charlotte wasn't paying attention. Like her young ass could do better? But Charlotte knew the truth and she wrestled with it all the time. Connie's pretty little ass would never be the woman she'd been, and sometimes it took a slap across that girl's smart mouth to prove her point.

"I want some cereal," Reesy's small voice answered. Charlotte smiled at the thought of Reesy. That's the one she'd miss, because Reesy was easy on her, and that baby was all about love, and loving her entirely because Charlotte was Momma. Not that any of that mattered, though. Connie always thought she was a better mother to Reesy than Charlotte had ever been, so maybe Reesy would be better off anyway.

"We don't have that much milk, Reesy. Want some toast?"

"No, Connie!"

"Shhh! You're going to wake up Momma."

"But toast makes my tummy hurt."

"Dang, girl! You're worrisome," Connie said in a hushed tone.

"No, I ain't."

Give the girl some damn cereal, Connie, Charlotte wanted to scream. Why did Connie always have to make everything so damn difficult? She'd been that way since she was born. Crying all the damn time, driving her daddy mad and out the door and into somebody else's bed. Leaving Charlotte behind to deal with her hollering ass by herself. Reesy's daddy wasn't much better. He went out and got himself shot trying to rob a house in south Denver when Reesy was two.

"I'll be right back, baby. I got some business to tend to." Meaning he had to go out and do something stupid like take a bullet in the head.

Charlotte slipped into her shoes, then checked herself one last time in the mirror, smoothing her hands down her flat stomach and smooth behind. She still looked good. And why shouldn't she? Hell, she wasn't even thirty yet. Charlotte was still a young woman, with plenty of life left to do the things she'd always wanted to do. She'd go with Sam to Memphis, and if she didn't like Memphis, maybe she'd meet somebody else, leave his ass behind and go someplace like Atlanta. She'd heard a lot about Atlanta, and all the fine black men out there. Maybe she'd even go back to school and get her degree.

She gingerly applied her lipstick, when suddenly she was struck by how simple this was. *It should be harder than this,* she thought. After all, she was leaving her home, her life . . . her children behind, for nothing more than a black hole in front of her and Sam's black ass. Charlotte had been waiting for them all morning, but they hadn't come. Guilty thoughts that should've driven her insane, tormenting her and sounding like her mother.

What kind of woman leaves her own kids for some man she don't even know?

She stared at her reflection. "What kind of woman leaves her kids, Charlotte?" she whispered to herself. "And what kind of woman . . . don't even care?"

But she knew the answer to that question. The kind of woman who wasn't even thirty years old yet but felt like she was fifty. The kind of woman overwhelmed with joy at the concept of having the freedom to come and go as she pleased without one thought to responsibility. A woman who was a slave to the biggest dick she'd ever seen. And a woman tired of hearing other people call her Momma, instead of Charlotte, Charlie, Pretty, or Baby. The choices had been laid at her feet, and as far as she was concerned, it really was no choice at all. Sam? Or the kids? And Sam knew how to make her feel so damn good all the time.

The girls stared at her, no doubt surprised to see her up so early on a Saturday morning.

"Morning, Momma." Reesy smiled. A drop of milk from the bowl of cereal she was eating slid slowly down her chin.

"Morning, Momma," Connie said solemnly from the kitchen.

Charlotte stood in the middle of the room, wearing velvet, leopard-print leggings; her black leather halter top; strappy, gold lamé sandals; and her signature rabbit fur coat, and she held on firmly to the suitcase in her hand. She had no idea what to say. Should she just come right out and tell them that she was tired of being their mother, and that no man had ever fucked her the way Sam had fucked her and that she hoped they'd grow up to be well-adjusted, happy women?

The girls were quiet, probably bracing themselves for the bullets to come shooting out of her mouth over the mess they'd made in her living room. Instead, she stared at them both, took a long, slow drag from her cigarette, squinted through the smoke floating up past her eyes, and casually strolled over to the door, in time to hear Sam honking his horn. Charlotte hesitated, then turned to them one last time. "I got to go," she said. "I just . . . I got to go."

What Little Girls Are Made Of

A week after Charlotte left, social services came rushing in like the cavalry, rescuing Connie and Reesy in the nick of time, promising to take them to a safe place. That's not what they needed, Connie tried to explain. "We just need some peanut butter and jelly and some milk and toilet paper." Her argument fell on deaf ears. As young as she was, Connie knew she could've taken better care of herself and eight-year-old Reesy than could any discontented, underpaid, overworked social worker who didn't know that Reesy was afraid of the dark, or that Connie still hadn't started her period yet.

Social services quickly lived up to Connie's expectations of what she'd come to learn about adults. They'd promised that she and Reesy would never be separated, and of course they lied. Reesy left first. She was cute, eight years old, and desperate to be loved. The Turners took one look at her and it was love at first sight for all of them. Connie was a little too old, they explained. She was a big girl and would be on her own soon. Besides, they really couldn't afford to adopt both children.

Evelyn and Matt Turner waited patiently while the two girls said their good-byes. Reesy was young enough to give in easily to her tears, but not Connie. She'd choke to death on hers before giving these people the satisfaction of seeing her cry. Connie knelt down in front of Reesy and buttoned her younger sister into her coat.

"You'd better be a good girl for these people, Reesy," she

said, nearly whispering. "Don't be talking back or getting an attitude with them when they tell you to do something."

Reesy sniffed. " 'Kay."

"Don't drink more than half a glass of Kool-Aid at dinner and don't forget to pee-pee before you go to bed. All right?"

"All right, Connie."

"I'll come get you soon. When I turn sixteen, I can get a job and get us an apartment."

"Can we go back to our old apartment?" Reesy asked, through tears.

"No, Reesy," Connie said firmly. "I'm going to get us a nice place to live. Nicer than that old rat farm. I'll work two jobs if I have to so that maybe we can even get our own house. Okay?"

Reesy nodded and tried to smile.

"Girls?" The social worker called out to them. "The Turners are waiting."

Reesy flung her arms around Connie and wailed, "Connieeeee!"

Matt Turner came over and gently pulled Reesy from her sister, then lifted her lovingly into his arms. "It's all right, sweetheart," he said soothingly. "You'll see each other again soon. Real soon, just like we promised."

Connie glared at Matt Turner and his wife. Lies laced his promises like they'd laced everyone else's. They might've had Reesy fooled, but they hadn't fooled her.

"You'd better take good care of her," Connie threatened, narrowing her eyes at Evelyn Turner.

"Connie!" the social worker interrupted. "Now you know . . ."

Connie ignored her. "You'd better take good care of her or . . ." Tears quickly flooded her eyes. She stood up, then ran up the stairs into her room and quickly slammed the door shut behind her. The lump in her throat swelled like a balloon, blocking air from getting into or out of her lungs, and she fainted.

Connie sat at the dining room table, listening intently to the case-worker and Earl and Pauline Graves talk about her as if she weren't even in the room, wondering what this strange power was that people seemed to have that gave them the right to decide her fate or future. The house was immaculate, but that's the only thing about it she found extraordinary. Dull-brown furniture filled the living room and unimaginative pictures of trees and flowers decorated the pale beige walls. Pauline Graves was a plain woman with small, round eyes and thin lips. Too thin, Connie thought, for a black woman. Earl too seemed to go out of his way to look average. His white shirt and beige slacks blended in perfectly with the drab decor. Connie wondered if he'd done that on purpose. Pauline was a petite woman, even smaller than she was, while Earl was long and wiry, towering over his wife like a flagpole when they stood next to each other.

The Graveses performed like trained monkeys at a circus, saying all the right things at the right times. They smiled on cue and every now and then glanced affectionately in each other's eyes. "We've never been able to have children of our own." Pauline smiled weakly at the social worker. Sincerity seemed to seep from every pore, every crevice of her being, and Connie shivered slightly at the idea of having to live with this woman. It was obvious to her that Pauline was overacting. "The Lord just hasn't seen fit to bless us with—" In dramatic fashion, she pressed her lips together, then looked desperately to her husband, Earl.

"Adoption costs too much," Earl interjected. "But we're good, hardworking people and we just hope we can provide the kind of home a kid like Connie here can flourish in." He smiled, then held his wife's hand between both of his. She watched this performance for an hour, shocked that the caseworker couldn't see how phony these people were.

As soon as the caseworker left and the door closed behind her, the imposter Graveses peeled out of the costumes they were wearing, and out came the real Earl and Pauline. It didn't take Connie long to realize that Pauline had apparently been lobotomized somewhere between the time they waved good-bye to the case worker and the time the door closed behind her. She was there physically, but emotionally, the woman was completely missing in action. Pauline's hollow eyes stared at nothing and her lips had been permanently curved into what appeared to be a smile.

"Let me show you to your room, dear," she said, staring blankly past Connie.

Pauline cooked and cleaned and talked around Connie, never to her. The girl might as well have been one of those boring pictures hanging on the wall, but even they got more of Pauline's attention than Connie did. At least she dusted them. It was as if the woman went out of her way to make Connie nonexistent, and she appeared totally oblivious to the fact that the man she was married to was salivating over a thirteen-year-old girl right under her roof. She ignored the subtle comments Earl often made about Connie's breasts and behind and closed her eyes to the obvious hunger in his eyes whenever Connie entered the room. She never paid much attention at how he'd conveniently forget to knock on the bathroom door as soon as he heard the water stop running, knowing Connie had just stepped out of the shower. And she shut her ears to the sound of his muffled grunts and groans coming from the girl's bedroom in the middle of the night, when he should've been in bed with her, his wife, grunting and groaning all over her instead. In the beginning, Connie looked desperately to Pauline for a hint of concern, but nothing lived inside those eyes but emptiness. Other things lived in Earl's. In him, she saw the kinds of things that made her flesh crawl whenever he said her name or came close to her. The kinds of things that made her turn away ashamed, even though she'd done nothing wrong.

It started subtly enough. He'd come into Connie's room, claiming to check on her. "You all right?" he'd ask. Connie would nod her head, hoping he'd disappear. In the beginning, head-nodding worked miracles and Earl would smile, then fade away like a pungent odor. Eventually, he stopped disappearing and she'd wake to find him sitting on her bed next to her, staring down at her.

"You sleep?" he'd ask. Earl rubbed his hand against her cheek and smiled. Slowly, he leaned down to her and pressed his lips to hers. Connie cringed and stared back at him with wide, frightened eyes.

" 'Night, baby," he'd whispered, and she'd shut her eyes tight, hoping he'd disappear like he'd always done before. But instead of leaving, he'd slide his hand from her cheek to her neck, then slip it inside her pajama shirt to her breast. She'd never forget his hands. Big, meaty hands, cupping her breasts, kneading them with long, callused fingers. Her body stiffened and a hush fell over something inside her. Earl never had to tell Connie to promise not to tell. She knew she never would because she knew nobody would care. She held her breath, hoping this was all a bad dream and she'd wake up as some other little girl who had no idea what it was to be afraid and alone. She'd be the kind of little girl who'd never seen a man masturbate because of her, and whose breasts had never been touched by hands other than her own.

"You're such a pretty girl, Connie. Any of the boys at school ever tell you how pretty you are?" Connie lay frozen, staring up at the ceiling, her voice held prisoner inside her while Earl kneaded her chest with one hand, and his groin with the other. "Damn!" he breathed.

Gradually, things changed between them. His hands explored more of her, invading everything personal and private about her, until he finally needed more than just to touch her or himself. Her heart tried to force itself from her chest, her soul from her body. Earl pulled back the covers, then stood over Connie and unbuckled his pants. Connie lay stiff and straight, afraid to move, to breathe, to live. He forced down her pajama pants. Then he kissed her mouth, filling it with his full, wet tongue, ignoring the tears sliding down the sides of her face. Connie's eyes fixed on the ceiling, and she wished she could escape and rise up out of the dark room, through the roof, and out the other side. Her heart pounded fiercely between them, but Earl ignored it. Couldn't he see that she didn't want him? Not like that, in a dark room, on top of her, grinding against her until she burned. How come she couldn't just die?

"C'mon, baby," he whispered in her ear. "Open your legs a little bit, baby. Connie?" She tried not to hear him or smell him. She tried not to feel him. But that was impossible. Earl pried open her legs with his knees, then became frustrated when he discovered that she was too dry and he couldn't get in. He spit on the tips of his fingers, then rubbed it on the tip of his penis, providing the lubrication she couldn't. "Shhh . . . ," he whispered. "It's all right. It's all right," he promised, then burned a permanent trail inside her.

"Awww . . . baby," Earl's voice quivered. "It's . . . so . . . tight." He pumped slowly at first, drooling into the pillow beneath her head. "Baby . . . baby . . . baby," he whimpered. Low, rhythmic moans escaped from him, through hot breath seeping into her ears. Connie begged her mind to wander and take her to another place. What was her favorite song, her favorite television show? What was her favorite dessert? The sound of him appalled her.

"Oooooh . . . oooooh . . . ," Earl exhaled. She felt nausea well up inside her, knowing that what he found pleasure in left a disgusting film on her skin.

The pain was excruciating, singeing sensitive flesh, and threatened to split her in two. Connie started to cry out, but he put his hand over her mouth to stop her, then began pumping frantically and sobbing into the pillow. "I love you . . . I love you, baby. I . . ." His voice trembled, then Earl held his breath and released himself inside her, convulsing at the sensation. After he finished, he quickly jumped up, buttoned his pants, and left the room, never even bothering to look at her.

Connie's hands trembled as she buttoned her top and pulled up her pants. She lay still, knowing that she wasn't the same girl she'd been before she'd come here. Everything she'd ever cared about had been taken from her; her home, her sister, and now Earl had taken the one thing she thought it would be impossible for anyone to take. He'd taken her soul.

Like other grown-ups in her life, Earl lied too. It was never all right again. Night after night, she pleaded with him, prayed, she even wished him and herself dead. Nothing worked, and eventually, she realized there was only one thing she could do. One day, Connie just left home. That's all.

Homeless Sweet

She'd been walking all day back to the only place she knew as home. Back to the Five Points, looking for places to curl up in after dark. Everything she owned she carried in her backpack, an extra pair of Levi's, her favorite sweatshirt, clean panties, and peanut butter and jelly sandwiches. Connie tucked a twenty-dollar bill into the pocket of her jeans. She'd left the house that morning, like she always did, pretending to walk to the school bus stop: then she threw all of her books into the Dumpster in an alley behind the house and never looked back. Fear of being on her own threatened to overwhelm her, but Connie wouldn't let it. She couldn't afford to let it. This was serious, and there was no time for being scared. She walked frantically, making mental notes of places where she could hide for the night. Places where she'd be hidden in the shadows, and be safe to sleep, and to think. Safe from strangers. Before she'd been taken away from this neighborhood, she hadn't been afraid of it, or the people in it. She'd grown up here, and had ran and played in these streets without worrying about the dangers. But things were different now. Familiar faces nodded and smiled at her, appearing ominous and capable of doing the kinds of terrible things Earl had done. Connie had been fearless before she left here. Now she fought the urge to be afraid, because she'd learned firsthand what people could do to her. What men could do to her.

Connie stared up at the building she'd grown up in, looming over her. She'd almost forgotten about it. Reesy's favorite hiding place was in that building where they'd spent hours playing hide-and-seek. She made sure no one saw her, going through the door leading to the basement of the building. Connie looked over her shoulder, then hurried down the stairs. She crouched down beneath the space behind the stairs, opened her backpack, and pulled out a sandwich. This was the first time she'd eaten all day, and she had to be careful not to eat too much. Connie ate half her sandwich, then put the rest away, saving it for when she was really hungry. She folded her arms across her chest, then leaned her head back against the wall. Running away was the only choice she'd had. And even though she knew exactly what she'd run away from, Connie had no idea what she'd run to. In some ways, she'd taken care of herself for as long as she could remember, but at least before, she'd had Reesy. Without realizing it, Connie cried quietly to herself. Was Reesy all right? God, she hoped she was. Connie prayed silently that Mr. Turner wasn't doing to Reesy what Earl had done to her. She shivered at the thought, then quickly forced it from her mind. She needed to find her little sister and get her away from those people. That's exactly what she needed to do, she concluded. But Connie had no idea where to look. She dried her eyes with the backs of her hands.

"I'll think of something," she whispered. "Everything's going to be . . ." If only she could make herself believe that everything really would be all right, but it never had been. Fear threatened to fill her thoughts again as Connie scanned her surroundings, knowing that it would be dark soon and there were no lights in the basement. But this was the best she could hope for. Maybe if she was lucky, she could stay here until the weather warmed up outside. It was spring, but April seemed to be hanging on stubbornly to winter. The days were warm enough, but the nights were still cold, and she'd left her coat at home so that she wouldn't raise suspicions. Pauline wouldn't have noticed, but he would've. He noticed everything she did.

"Staying here will be fine for now," Connie said to herself. She raised her knees to her chest and wrapped her arms around them. The cold, damp basement was better than sleeping outside, she thought.

Connie had been up all night contemplating the events of this day, and sleep finally started to set in. She rested her head against the wall again and closed her eyes. She had to learn to sleep when she could, just in case she was caught down here and made to leave. Maybe that's what she should do, she thought. Sleep during the day, then stay up at night. Connie had just dozed off when the sound of voices and footsteps coming down the stairs startled her awake.

"Yo, man. You got papers?" she heard a man ask, coming down the stairs.

"That shit any good, man?"

"What do you care, mothafucka? You getting high for free, ain't you? Here. Roll this."

"A free high ain't no good if it ain't good weed, man. That's all I'm saying."

"Yeah, well, stop saying anything and light this."

"What the . . . ?" One of the men sounded startled, then peered beneath the stairs where Connie was hiding. She shrunk back into the darkness, grabbed her backpack, and clutched it protectively to her chest.

"What?" the other man asked. "What is it? What you lookin' at?"

The first man reached for her, grabbed her by her sleeve, and pulled her out from under the stairs. "What the hell you doin' down there, girl?"

The other man laughed, then stood up and came over to where Connie stood. "Looks like we got ourselves a spy or something." He licked his lips, then ran his fingers through her hair. "She cute, though. You like to party, baby?"

Connie stared at him with wide, frightened eyes and shook her head back and forth. "Don't I know you? You look like somebody I know," the first man said.

"Yeah, I might wanna know your little ass too, baby. What you got here?" one of the men said, grabbing her backpack. He unzipped it, then rummaged through it, letting her clothes fall to the floor. "Aw . . . yeah!" he exclaimed, at seeing her sandwiches. "You hungry, man?" He threw a sandwich to his friend.

"Not yet, but I always get the munchies when I get high." His friend laughed.

"Me too. Hungry and horny." His eyes traveled up and down

the length of Connie, then he moved closer to her and backed her up against the wall.

"You can have it!" she said, crying. "Just let me go. Please?"

"You can go, baby. After we get done, you can go wherever you please."

"Man, let me go first. I'm the one who found her," his friend argued.

"Fuck you!" He spat, fumbling desperately at the buttons on Connie's jeans. Connie slapped his hands away, then cried out at the impact of his palm hitting her cheek. Tears filled her eyes.

"You be cool!" he commanded, pointing his finger in her face. "Be cool . . . and we'll be cool!" He pulled at her jeans again, then stopped when he saw the money sticking out of her pocket. "What's this?" he said, taking her money, then counting it. "You full of surprises. Ain't you, baby?" He laughed.

"What? How much is it? Man! Let me . . . Naw, Man! You tripping!" his friend argued, trying to take the money.

"Get up off me, fool! I found it!"

"And I found her!"

"And I was gettin' you high for nothin'. The least you can do is—"

"How many times I done got you high for free, mothafucka? Huh?"

The two men stood toe to toe, pushing each other back and forth. Connie took advantage of the opportunity and quickly darted past them, ran up the stairs and out the door.

"Hey!" one of them shouted after her. "See what yo' dumb ass did?"

"What I did? If yo' punk ass wasn't tryin' to—"

"Man! Let's light this joint! You done pissed me off!"

"Kiss my black ass!"

Connie ran as fast as she could down to the elementary school two blocks away, then collapsed out of breath in the locked doorway, hoping they hadn't followed her. Now she really did have nothing. No food, no money. Not even clean panties. Connie cried into her hands. She was too tired to run anymore and had no idea where she'd go anyway. So, she stayed there all night, hoping it would be the only night she'd have to sleep outside, but in the back of her mind, she knew better.

She had only been gone a few days when she met Shay, a petite, mocha brown fifteen-year-old with big, sad, brown eyes. Shay had been living on the streets since she was twelve and was a wealth of knowledge when it came to surviving on her own. Her mother had been high for practically Shay's whole life, and she had no idea who her father was. Eventually, she got tired of her mother and left her strung out on a curb near a homeless shelter, mumbling incoherently to herself. Shay had taken care of herself ever since. Connie and Shay sat huddled inside the doorway of an old abandoned building, sharing the last of a cigarette.

Shay shivered. "I keep telling you, girl, you need to get busy. By this weekend, I'm going to have me a room and I don't give a fuck if it has to be with some old pervert. That's better than this shit."

Connie shook her head back and forth. "I don't know how you do that, Shay. Letting them do all that stuff to you. I couldn't do it."

Shay shrugged. "Yes you could and you will too. You ain't no virgin right?"

"No," Connie said quietly. "But I still—" She still cringed at images of Earl hovering over her, grimacing at the sensation of his release. She still felt like throwing up over the stench he'd left on her after he'd finished.

"You could do it. I started doing it when I was eleven and it ain't no big deal."

"It is a big deal. Every time one of them puts their nasty hands on you."

"You know what I do? I just close my eyes and pretend I'm not even me. They're the ones doing it. Not me. I'm just laying there. That's all they want you to do anyway. Young ass. That's all they care about. And the younger the better. I can make some good money sometimes. Especially if I lie and tell them I'm twelve, even thirteen."

Shay's eyes were as frigid as the air. She had old eyes and an old spirit. Connie didn't want to look like that, old and tired before she was grown. "It ain't nothing but a thing, Baby Sister. You do what you got to do out here. One of these days, you're going to get sick of eating out of the garbage and you're going to want some real food. You're going to get tired of sleeping in the alley and you're going to need a bed, even if you have to share it with some old drunk-ass fool."

Connie shook her head, refusing to believe the words coming from her friend's mouth. No matter how hungry or cold she got, no man would ever do that to her again. She'd made that promise to herself and would die before she broke it.

Connie hadn't seen Shay in nearly a week, and she'd been left by herself for the first time since the two had met. Her fingers and toes were numb from the cold, and Connie was tired, scared, and hungrier than she'd ever been in her life. The last time she'd eaten, she and Shay had feasted on hot dogs and fries. Shay had gotten the food from someplace. Connie never asked where. Warm tears rested inside the brim of her eyes as she looked around for someplace safe to sleep.

It was late, and Connie walked slowly down Welton Street, headed toward downtown, when a car slowed down next to her.

"Hey," he said, slowly rolling down the window of the passenger side. Connie glanced at him quickly but kept walking. He was a white man, in his forties, wearing a dark suit with a tie, driving a four-door black sedan. In the backseat was a car seat.

"You need a ride?" She ignored him, then picked up her pace, hoping he'd speed away and leave her alone. She knew what he wanted and the thought made her want to vomit.

"It's pretty cold out here. I can take you where you want to go. It's no trouble." Tears burned trails down her cheeks as she heard Shay's prophecies repeat themselves over again in her head,

One of these days . . . you'll get tired.

"Why don't you get in the car, sweetheart? It's warm in here."

Connie shook her head back and forth and kept walking. She was tired. Sleeping outside alone at night wasn't really sleeping. Every sound, shadow, whisper threatened danger, so the best she could hope for were short naps, light enough to hear trouble approaching.

"I can take you someplace to get something to eat, honey. Are you hungry?"

You're going to get . . . tired, then you'll do it . . .

Yes. I'm very hungry, she wanted to say. Couldn't he just take her to get something to eat and then leave her alone? Couldn't she just say, "Thank you, mister. That was really nice of you," and leave it at that?

Connie came to the corner and stopped. The man pulled his car around in front of her. "I won't hurt you," he said tenderly. "I promise. I won't hurt you."

Of course you will, she thought to herself. A frigid wind blew up the back of her sweater, and before she realized what she was doing, Connie opened the door and quickly crawled inside, welcoming the heat that enveloped her like a warm blanket.

"Are you hungry?" he asked. Connie nodded.

Slowly she followed him up the stairs of the musty motel. He'd stopped at a fast food restaurant and bought her a hamburger. Connie had gulped it down in the car on the way to the room.

"This isn't something I do all the time," he explained nervously. "I just . . . well . . ."

The tips of her toes and fingers ached as the numbness began to wear off. He opened the door to the room and let Connie enter first. She swallowed hard, trying not to think of Earl, trying not to think of this man, standing over her, slowly sliding her sweater down off her shoulders. Just this one time, and that's all, Connie rationalized in her mind. He'd fed her and it was too cold to sleep outside anyway. One time. It wasn't like what Shay did at all. Shay was a prostitute. She'd called herself that, so Connie wouldn't have to. Connie wasn't a prostitute. She'd just been cold and she'd been hungry.

"I'm not going to hurt you. I promise. You've got to believe me." He sat down on the edge of the dresser, then turned her to him and pulled her close. Connie refused to look in his eyes. He rubbed his hand down her hair. "You're such a pretty girl," he whispered. Earl had whispered it too. Was this the kind of thing that happened to the pretty girls? she wondered. She closed her eyes tight, feeling him lean into her. He put his mouth against hers, then kissed her softly on the lips, like he was afraid she'd break if he pressed too hard. "Such a pretty little girl."

"I just close my eyes and pretend I'm not even me," Shay had said. Connie knew how to do that. Earl had taught her.

After he finished, Connie lay in the bed, sobbing quietly to herself, staring at the fifty dollars he'd left on the nightstand.

"I paid two nights on the room," he said over his shoulder before leaving.

"Thank you," she whispered, after he left.

The goal was to make enough money hustling so that they wouldn't have to hustle. When times were good, Connie and Shay shared a room together, slept until noon, and ate like queens. Every night was a slumber party, as the two pranced around in their T-shirts and panties, ordered in pizza, and practiced the latest dance steps. Connie was no longer the big, responsible sister she'd been to Reesy all those years. She was Baby Sister, and Shay looked out for her, teaching her things she needed to know in order to survive and to keep from being picked up by the police.

"All they're going to do is send you back to what's-his-name, or somebody worse. They don't give a shit about people like us." That's what she'd become. A "people like us." Somebody nobody cared about or loved. Someone invisible in the daytime and a filthy secret at night. Different from everyone else. Less than. Dirtier than. And desperate. All the time, desperate.

Shay taught her how to smoke weed and drink gin and juice. Shay told her who she could trust, and who'd stab her in the back first chance they got. And for those times when things weren't so good, she taught her where to find the best food, and the safest places to sleep.

The two girls lay in bed in the dark room, talking late into the night. "Guess who I saw the other day?" Shay whispered.

"Who?"

"My mom, girl. She didn't know who I was, though."

"I'm sorry, Shay."

Shay smacked her lips. "Girl . . . please! Like I give a damn. She's an idiot. Always been an idiot. I ain't thinking about her dumb ass." Shay took a long drag on a joint, then handed it to Connie. "You ever see yours?"

Connie inhaled and held the smoke inside her for as long as she could, then slowly released it through her lips. "No. I don't want to see her either."

"Yeah . . . I know what you mean. My thing is, if they didn't want kids, they shouldn't have had us."

"That's true."

"It ain't like they couldn't take birth control or something. I'd rather not be here at all if this is what I got to end up with."

Connie swallowed hard. "Me either."

Shay turned to Connie and giggled. "Guess what?"

"What?"

"P. D. let me get high with him yesterday."

"So? What's the big deal about that? We get high all the time."

"No . . ." Shay turned over to Connie and raised herself up on her elbows. "He let me try some smack."

Connie gasped. "Girl . . . you didn't?"

Shay laughed again. "Yes, I did. And it was a trip! Girl, I thought I'd died and gone to heaven or something. That stuff was good."

"Shay! You said you wouldn't do that stuff. We both said we wouldn't."

"Stop preaching, Baby Sister," Shay snapped. "It was just one time. One time ain't going to do nothing. It just felt cool, that's all." Shay lay back, smiled, and stared up at the ceiling. "I'm telling you, Baby Sister, it was like leaving this world and the only thing that mattered was feeling good all over. So good that I never wanted it to stop. I didn't care about nothing but flying." She laughed. "I was a goddamned cloud and couldn't nothing or nobody touch my ass."

"How much did it cost, Shay?" Connie whispered.

Shay sighed, then shrugged. "I just had to fuck him. That's all."

But that wasn't all, and gradually, Shay started spending less time with Connie and more time with P. D. Eventually, she even spent more time prostituting. Shay would see Connie but pretend not to. Whenever Connie tried talking to her, all of a sudden Shay didn't have time and had to go, always promising to "get with you later." Shay never did, and soon Connie gave up trying.

One day, Connie saw Shay stumbling down the street, coming toward her. Months had passed since Connie had last spoken to her, and she wasn't the least bit surprised when Shay walked passed her without saying a word.

"Connie?" Shay suddenly called out after her. "Connie . . . is that you?" Connie stopped and stared at Shay, speechless. "Connie?" Shay squealed, then flung her arms around her. "Hey, Baby Sister! That is you?"

"How you doing, Shay?" Connie asked apprehensively.

Shay smacked her lips and rolled her eyes. "Girl, I'm fine. Real fine. Been doing good for myself." She smiled.

Connie stared at her, amazed at how much older Shay looked. The last time Connie saw her had been right after Shay's sixteenth birthday, four months ago. Shay shifted uncomfortably at Connie's expression. "So, how you doing? You been all right?" she asked, trying to smile.

Connie shrugged. "I'm all right. You know. Same old . . . same old."

"Yeah I know." Shay looked off over Connie's shoulder, then pressed her lips together. "Same old."

"Well . . . I guess . . ." Connie started to walk away.

"Me too." Shay smiled again.

Connie had made it to the corner when she heard Shay calling after her again. She turned in time to see her running in her direction. Shay wrapped her arms around Connie, then whispered in her ear. "Don't do this forever, Baby Sister." She sobbed. "You do good, Connie. You do better than me." Shay kissed Connie on her cheek, then hurried off in the other direction.

Connie watched her friend disappear. Neither of them had planned on being out here forever. They were going to get jobs and share an apartment together. They were going to get a dog and some new furniture and fill their refrigerator with all the things they liked: ice cream sandwiches, cold cuts, Dr Pepper. And they were going to get plants. Shay loved plants and flowers.

"African violets are my favorite," Shay told her. "It ain't easy getting them to bloom, but if you treat them right, and if you're patient . . . they'll bloom."

"I ain't doing this forever, Shay. I ain't doing—" Connie wiped away a tear before it had a chance to fall. Seeing Shay had changed her mind about hustling that night. It was August, and this time of year, sleeping outside really wasn't so bad. Besides, she'd gotten used to it.

Edwina . . . Eddie . . . Edwina

"Lord have mercy!" Connie jumped back into the shadows, startled by the woman's outburst. "You 'bout the biggest rat I ever seen." Edwina adjusted her glasses, then squinted, straining to get a better look at the girl rummaging around in her garbage cans in the alley behind her restaurant. No telling how many times the girl's been here, Edwina thought. She was usually long gone by now, but had stayed late tonight because she'd given the cook the night off. Besides, Edwina had been meaning to get that refrigerator cleaned out anyway.

Connie jerked, appearing as though she were going to try and make a run for it. Oh, yes, Edwina thought. She'd seen this one lurking around before. Edwina instantly took on a defensive stance and blocked the only exit to keep the girl penned in.

Connie quickly retreated back into the corner, against the fence. "You'd better leave me alone! I'll kick your ass!"

Curiously, Edwina began to look around the area.

"What? What are you looking for?" Connie asked defensively.

"I'm lookin' for that army you got that's gon' help you kick my ass—*forgive me, Lord*—'cause I know you ain't thinkin' you gon' kick it by yo' self."

Connie eased out of the corner and stood facing Edwina with her fists balled, ready to fight the old woman if she had to. "Get out of my way! I ain't done nothing to you!"

Edwina straightened up and balanced her fists on her broad

hips. "You back here stealin' my food and you got the nerve to stand there and say you ain't done nothin' to me?"

Connie stared at Edwina, confused. "But, you threw it away. It's in the trash!" she argued.

Edwina shook her head. "Don't matter. I still had to pay for it, and you still takin' it without askin'. That's stealin'."

"It's not stealing if it's in the trash!"

"It's my trash. And I didn't say you could have it," she said firmly.

Connie threw the piece of chicken she'd found back into the garbage can. She was painfully hungry, but one drumstick wasn't worth all the grief this old woman was giving her. "Fine! There! You happy? I didn't want your old nasty chicken anyway!" Connie folded her arms across her chest, then rolled her eyes.

"If my chicken's so nasty, why you here stealin' it all the time?"

"Look! I didn't steal it! I gave you back your trashy chicken, so you need to let me go!"

"Where your people, little girl?"

Connie rolled her eyes again.

"Don't act dumb, now, I asked you a question. Where yo' people?" Edwina demanded. "You got a momma? A daddy? A auntie?"

"That's my business, not yours!"

"It's my business if yo' little ass—*forgive me, Jesus*—is out here in the middle of the night diggin' round in my trash."

"I said I don't want your trash! Now get out of my way!"

Edwina looked up to the sky, then sighed. "Lord! I told you I didn't want to be bothered with this mess and now you got me out here in the middle of the night with . . . All I want to do is move to Vegas. Can't I do that? Can't you just let me pack up and move to Vegas? I ain't got time for no street rats."

"I ain't no street rat!"

Edwina looked angrily at Connie. "You a street rat if I say you are, and you a street rat if you out here diggin' around in the garbage for my chicken too!"

"Look! I said—"

"I heard what you said, girl!"

"Then why don't you let me leave?"

"Because He say I can't." Edwina pointed up to the sky.

Connie looked up to the sky where Edwina was pointing, then stared at the woman and frowned. "You're crazy."

Edwina folded her arms across her chest defensively. "At least I ain't the one out here diggin' in the garbage for somethin' to eat."

"You're getting on my nerves with that. I gave you back your chicken."

Edwina sighed, then eyed the girl suspiciously. "Where you stayin'?"

Connie didn't answer.

"I'm tired of standin' out here messin' with yo' fool ass, girl. *Lord, forgive me.* Get inside!" Edwina demanded, pointing toward the back door of the restaurant.

Connie's eyes grew wide. "Why? Are you going to call the police?"

"Get yo' ass—*forgive me, Lord*—inside or else I will. I ain't playin' with you, child."

Reluctantly, Connie did as she was told and slowly opened the screen door leading into the kitchen of the restaurant. Edwina followed closely, then locked the door behind them.

As soon as they were inside, Edwina handed Connie a mop. "Finish up moppin' this floor. And don't take all night. I'm tired and ready to go home."

"I ain't mopping your old nasty floor!" Connie snapped, then threw the mop on the floor at Edwina's feet.

Slowly, Edwina bent to pick it up. She glared over the rim of her glasses at Connie, then said through clenched teeth, "You will mop this damn floor—*forgive me, Lord*—or I'll put a whoopin' on you like you ain't never had a whoopin' befo' in yo' life, heffa! Now . . ." She shoved the mop back into Connie's chest. "Hurry up."

Grudgingly, Connie mopped the floor, hoping Edwina would let her leave without calling the police when she was finished. Connie looked for Edwina to tell her she was done and found the woman dozing off at one of the tables in the dining area.

"Hey! I'm finished!" she yelled, purposely startling the woman awake.

Edwina smacked her lips, then rubbed her eyes. " 'Bout time," she muttered. "Don't take all night to mop no floor." Edwina stood up and motioned for Connie to follow her. Connie sighed. She was too tired and too hungry for this old woman to put her to work all night. It was only a drumstick.

Edwina led her to a room in the back of the house barely big enough for the twin-size bed it held. There was a small bathroom off to the side. "You can sleep here tonight. But don't put yo' nasty ass—*Lord, forgive me*—in my bed without washing it first. There's a shower in the bathroom. No tellin' what the hell you got crawlin' on yo' little stanky behind."

Connie was so shocked by Edwina's offer to let her sleep in the room, she nearly forgot to retaliate. "My behind ain't stanky!" Connie snapped.

"If yo' behind is out there diggin' around in the garbage, and . . . Lord knows what else"—Edwina looked Connie up and down— "then trust me. It's stanky! And you need to put some water to it befo' you crawl in between my clean sheets or you can get the hell out!"

She'd learned how to grab hold when opportunity presented itself, and Connie quickly swallowed her pride, stormed into the bathroom, and slammed the door shut, praying the old woman would disappear and finally let her get some sleep.

Twenty minutes later, Connie came out of the bathroom relieved to find Edwina gone, having been replaced with a plate filled with chicken, macaroni and cheese, peach cobbler, cabbage, corn bread, and a cold glass of lemonade, sitting on a small table near the bed.

Edwina had never had children of her own. The Lord had never blessed her with any despite having been married three times, so she stopped being sad over it a long time ago and figured she must not have needed any. But she knew better than most people that God worked in mysterious ways when He wanted to, and sending this street rat her way for her to take care of had been one of the most mysterious things He'd done to her in a long time. Edwina knew better than to turn the girl away. She'd learned that when God wanted her to do something, she just needed to go ahead and get it done, or else He'd worry her about it until she did. And being that He was God, she knew she'd get tired before He would.

God was the one who told her to let Bobby, her cook, take the night off. And God was the one who told her to stay a few minutes later than she usually did. He told her to go out back and see what that noise was in the alley too.

And when she did, that's when He said, "There she is, Eddie. Now you know better than to let that child raise herself out here in these streets. It ain't safe, and she don't belong there."

Edwina drove all the way home, tired, mad, and mumbling to herself. Of course, she made sure to let the Lord know this arrangement was only temporary. She had plans of her own, and they didn't include taking care of no street rat for the rest of her life. "I'm gon' take care of her 'til she old enough to be out there on her own, Lord. 'Til she can take care of herself and act like a woman's s'posed to act. 'Less she take off first. You know how street rats are, Jesus. Don't appreciate nothin' you do for 'em. Then I'm goin' to Vegas. You got that?" Eddie fussed. "I ain't 'bout to let no other woman's child keep me from followin' my dream. I'm goin' to be retirin' soon, and I'm goin' to retire in Vegas. And that's all there is to that. Hmph! Got me takin' care of some other woman's child. I'm too old . . . I'm fifty-four years old and you know I'm too old to be . . . Hmph! Probably gon' steal everything I got. The little street rat!"

I'll Be Damned

The summer between his freshman and sophomore years of high school, John discovered a fruit like nothing else he'd ever tasted, and he'd discovered it hidden between Racine Watson's thighs. That summer, consuming that fruit was the driving force behind fifteen-year-old John King's existence, and he made it a point to lose himself in it every time her parents left the house.

John and Racine dressed quickly. "Hurry up, John. My momma and daddy gonna be home any minute." Racine slipped into her panties, then expertly reached behind her, buttoning her bra. John stared in appreciation of Racine's full behind. A behind he'd been buried in all afternoon. She'd told him she loved him. At the time, it only seemed right to say it back to her. He wasn't sure if he'd meant it or not, but she seemed to need to hear it, and since she'd been giving him pussy all the time, he figured the least he could do was say it back. Girls liked hearing that kind of thing, like somehow saying "I love you" made things better between you. Had sex been any worse before he'd told her he loved her? he wanted to ask. To John, it really didn't matter one way or another. It felt good even if Racine never told him she loved him.

He was moving entirely too slow for her. Her parents would be turning into the driveway any minute, and this dumb boy was sitting there staring and grinning like an idiot. She threw his other sneaker at him. "Boy! If you don't hurry—"

"Damn, Racine!" he said, ducking. "Why you gotta rush me outta here like this? You know I wasn't finished," he teased.

She jumped into her jeans, then ran downstairs, looking out the window and anticipating her parents' car. "Hurry up!" she shouted back upstairs to him.

John had never said he was her boyfriend, but to Racine, that's exactly what he was. She'd loved John King since they were in third grade, and today he'd said he loved her too. Her heart beat passionately in her chest just thinking about it. He was her man, all right, but if he didn't hurry his slow behind up, this would be the last time they'd be together like this. Her daddy would kill him, and her too, if he ever found out what they'd been doing all day long; eating, having sex, playing Atari, listening to music.

John finally finished dressing and strolled downstairs, when Racine heard her parents' car pull up. "Oh, my goodness!" she screamed, pushing him into the kitchen, then rushing him out the back door. "Go! Hurry, John!"

He turned and kissed her quickly on the lips. "Can I come over tomorrow?"

"If you don't get outta here, boy, you ain't never going to be able to come over ever again! Now, go!" She pushed then shut the door behind him, just in time to hear the keys turning in the front door. That was close, she thought to herself. But wasn't it always with John?

John grinned. Racine was sweet like the candy she was always sucking on. Sweet inside and out. He'd seen magazines where men put their mouths on women's pussies. Lewis swore up and down that he'd never done it because it was nasty, but John knew better. Rumor had it that Lewis was game for just about anything when it came to screwing. Racine wasn't nasty, though. She was clean, which is why he didn't mind. Besides, she'd done it to him first. He laughed. She'd shocked him when she took him in her mouth, but she'd hooked him too. He jumped over the fence and figured he'd head over to Lewis's house to see what he had to eat. Agnes had probably cooked, but he'd rather eat at Lewis's, even if it was just sandwiches, and deal with his grandmother's wrath later on.

"Got to . . . soon as I get this done . . . I'm gon' . . . I . . . need to get me . . . get me some . . . got to . . ." Roberta mumbled breathlessly to herself. She'd been down on her hands and knees all afternoon digging holes in her front yard. The kinds of holes that were too deep for planting and too shallow for burying.

Her nerves had been bad again today. The doctor called it "anxiety." Doctors always made up fancy words for describing things that weren't fancy at all. Bad nerves were just bad nerves. That's all. She didn't need a fancy word for that. "I'll be done . . . in a minute. I'm almost done . . . now. Jus' need to . . ."

Roberta sat up and surveyed her work. Maybe she should run down to the store and pick up a few tomato plants. She'd been thinking about growing her own tomatoes again. Years ago, she'd had a big garden, filled with fresh tomatoes, greens, onions, cucumbers. She frowned. She'd waited too long to plant anything. Roberta should've planted her garden back . . . back . . . She started digging again. Blisters swelled in her palms, but Roberta refused to stop digging. Not until she'd finished what she'd started.

She'd been startled awake this morning before dawn and had slept so hard, she didn't remember dreaming. Her hands shook and her heart raced inside her chest as she hurried out of bed, then picked up that old cane leaning in the corner and searched through the house, looking to see who was hiding inside, waiting to sneak up on her. Except for her, the house was empty. Roberta didn't bother with breakfast and dressed quickly, then went straight to work scrubbing the floors and walls. She even washed the windows, inside and out, before going outside to work in the yard.

The scorching sun bore down on her back, and Roberta knew she had no business being out in the sun like this. She was bound to get sunstroke and end up at the doctor's office for that too. It seemed like lately she was always seeing the doctor about something or other. The last time she went, it was because she'd been convinced her blood pressure medicine wasn't working anymore. "You're fine, Roberta," was all he said. Before that, she'd complained of chest pains she'd been having. "You're fine, Roberta." She wasn't fine, and when she told him this, he fussed at her, claiming she had anxiety. Roberta knew better. Anxiety had nothing to do with how bad she'd been feeling lately, but all he did was write up another prescription, then shoo her out the door.

Roberta glanced at her watch. If she hurried, she'd be done in a few minutes and she could go inside the house, put her feet up, and watch her stories. She never missed her stories. They kept her mind off her nerves. She'd fix herself a bowl of popcorn, watch her stories, and forget all about the feeling that had been tugging at her for days, warning her that something might happen if she wasn't careful or didn't pay attention. The wooden handle stung in her hands, but she held on to it, fighting the desire to let it go and hurry back into her house. Sweat soaked through her blouse, causing it to cling to her like skin. The heat was getting to her and she knew she'd have to hurry . . . before . . . before . . .

Roberta never even heard him walk up, but suddenly she shivered, then stopped working and slowly raised her eyes. John King stood on the other side of her gate, his hands buried in his pockets.

He smiled and stared at her with coal-black eyes. "What are you doing, Roberta?" he asked casually.

Roberta sucked in her breath and held it, feeling as if the world had closed around her, trapping her in it with him. Fear welled up and knotted in her stomach, and she carefully rose to her feet, staggering on the weight of exhaustion and the heat.

"Why are you digging all them holes? You planting something? What are you planting?" John fought back the urge to laugh. Roberta was a trip, he thought. She stared at him with big, wide eyes, afraid he'd lunge at her and say boo. He never understood why she was so afraid of him. As far as he knew, he hadn't done anything to the woman. When he was a kid, he used to mess with her cat, but he'd never done anything to her. Lewis said he'd heard that Roberta believed John was a demon or something. The devil. All he knew was that every time he so much as looked at her, Roberta's eyes rolled up in her head and she'd whisper Jesus' name, praying that the Lord would fly down out of heaven and smite him or something like that. Roberta was one crazy old woman. That's for sure. John figured she was out of her mind, and it didn't have a thing to do with him.

Roberta's mouth hung open, but she didn't bother to answer his questions, so John shrugged his shoulders and started to leave.

"You a trip," he mumbled, walking away.

Panic rose up inside her like vomit, and the sound of her own voice surprised her. "I should . . ." she mumbled.

He stopped. "What? You say something?"

She shook her head meekly back and forth. No. No, she hadn't said anything. She hadn't meant to say anything at all. She cringed, feeling the burn from his black eyes as they bore holes through her. John shook his head, then started to walk away again. What was this? Roberta wondered. Shouldn't he have pulled daggers from the air, then thrown them at her heart? Shouldn't he have spit fire from his mouth and burned her to ashes? Why hadn't he done those things? Why hadn't he killed her like she'd known he would if he'd ever gotten the chance?

All of a sudden, she realized she wasn't shaking anymore. Roberta considered herself for a moment, then looked at this . . . boy. "Of course," Roberta muttered to herself. Of course he hadn't done any of those things. *The truth shall set you free.* He was, after all, only a boy. A child. That's all he'd ever been.

"That's all." Roberta stared at him, astonished at the transformation he slowly made to her eyes. She watched him shrink in size; the fire surrounding him, protecting him, slowly faded. Talons on his hands that she prayed he'd never use on her disappeared. The demon had left him. Yes! The demon had left, finally. No. No, John King couldn't leave. She watched him walking away and started to panic. He couldn't leave. Not now that she knew the truth and recognized him for what he really was. "Boy!"

John stopped, then slowly turned to face her. Roberta laughed. Yes, Lawd! The red fire hidden behind the blacks of his eyes was gone too! Glory! she wanted to shout. She squared her shoulders, finding courage where there had been none before, then she glared at him. "I shoulda killed you that night, boy!" she shouted. "I said, I shoulda killed you the night you was born! I shoulda killed yo' black ass!"

John stared at her like she'd lost her mind. "You crazy, Roberta! Crazy! Ain't nobody got time for your nonsense!"

Look at him, she thought. He's almost a man now. Tall and strong and nearly full-grown. She'd been afraid of this boy his whole life, dodging the sight of him, the sound of him. Even the thought of him, fearing the evil thing inside him was waiting for the opportunity to pounce on her and tear into her flesh. Sadly, she realized she'd spent years running from him to no place in particular. He was always close, waiting, biding his time. And she'd crouched low, hidden in the shadows behind the facade of her proposed insanity, hoping to trick him into leaving her alone. *Fear not. For I am with thee.* Had this been the reason she'd been so nervous lately? This confrontation with this child that had been prophesied and inevitable? Now the time had come for her to face what had been tormenting her all these years and stand fast in her faith. It was time to meet the demon head-on. Her steady hands gripped tightly to the spade hanging down by her side, still burning her blisters. Today she was ready for him, and if he came one step closer to her, she'd take that spade and dig his black heart out of his chest.

Her eyes and lips narrowed. "The night you was born, I wanted to snap yo' neck like a twig, niggah! I shoulda killed you that night. Lawd knows . . ."

He looked so much like Fool. He looked like . . . Charles? Charles's eyes . . . staring up at her through his own blood. Those same eyes stared back at her now, through this boy. Her husband's eyes, full of wonder and confusion.

No one believed she'd been capable of such a thing, but it hadn't been hard at all. It had been as easy as slicing through a hot loaf of homemade bread, blood melting like butter down the sides of his neck, soaking into clean, white pillowcases she'd washed and hung on the line to dry that morning. Roberta closed her eyes, remembering the scent of sun-dried linen, and Charles, like it was yesterday.

"Why'd you do it, Roberta?" someone had asked her. She remembered laughing hard enough to pee on herself, and watching the puddle form on the floor where she stood.

"Why'd I do it?" She repeated the ridiculous question. *Hell! Why wouldn't I do it?* she thought. Charles had lied so much about that woman and that boy of hers, claiming he wasn't the boy's daddy, when the child looked just like him, especially by the eyes. Black eyes. Eyes she'd dreamed of over and over again, and desperately wanted lovingly locked on her until death parted them. Not on that heffa he was fucking. Charles's eyes. Fool's. John King's.

"Bastard!" she growled at him. "Bastard boy!"

John stared at her more confused than ever by her outburst, and he angrily retaliated the only way he knew how. "You outta your mind! Everybody knows you outta your fuckin' mind, Roberta!"

She took a step in his direction, twirling the spade she held down at her side. Roberta smelled opportunity coming. Finally, she might be able to rid herself of this boy once and for all. Right here and now. She could be done with his wicked self, if only she could get close enough. "I want you gone, John Tate! I want you gone, boy!" She'd wanted Charles gone. She'd even wanted his kids gone. *Be careful what you pray for.* None of them were around to be a bother to her anymore. "John Tate!" she growled again, and that's when she noticed it. Roberta blinked in astonishment. He'd winced at the sound of it. Yes. She'd seen him wince . . . no . . . cringe at the mention of his name. His real name. He'd recoiled, like a snake. Like the snake he was. The devil had been caught off guard and he was speechless and paralyzed, momentarily silenced by the mention of his name. His real name. He was John Tate, but no one ever had the nerve to call the devil by his real name. Lucifer. John Tate. She laughed.

"My name ain't no Tate, woman! You know my name! You know who I am!" He seldom gave any thought to that name or had the nerve to associate it with himself. Fool meant nothing to him. He'd been nothing more than a notion, an idea, a glimmer. Until now. Hearing Roberta say his name and Fool's name in the same breath suddenly bonded him with a man he'd never known, or cared to know. She'd given life to what had never been more than a fleeting thought to John. All of a sudden, Fool wasn't a distant character hidden in whispers and gossip. He was real, and Roberta's eyes drilled truth into him like nothing or no one else ever had.

Roberta exploited her advantage. "You a Tate, boy! Yo' daddy's a Tate and that's what you is! You jus' like him. Ever thought about that, John Tate? You jus' like him!" she spat. "Got the same evil in you, I bet. Don't you, boy?"

John's mouth moved but no sound came out.

"Don't bother answerin', child. We know what kind of evil you got in you. Don't we? We always knew. Me and you? We knew what you was . . . are. He raped that girl," she said coldly. "Yo' momma? Mattie? Ain't nobody ever told you to yo' face before. Have they? He caught her up on her way home from school, covered her mouth with his dirty hand, so nobody could hear her screamin'." Roberta closed her eyes, conjuring up images behind them of Fool tearing at Mattie's dress while Mattie struggled beneath him, crying and fighting to get free. John stood motionless, listening to the story he'd been waiting for his whole life. "She kicked and scratched at him. But he was too strong. Too . . . strong. He pinned her down and ripped away her drawers. Mattie cried and cried and tried to scream, but he was strong. He pushed inside her . . ." Roberta curled her hand into a fist. "Pushed—pushed—pushed—harder! Harder, John Tate!" She opened her eyes and stared into his astonished face. "Harder! And harder! Until he pissed you out, boy! That's who made yo' black ass, John Tate! A lunatic! A crazy man! Call me crazy? Hmpf! A fool made you!"

This child. This boy had no idea what to make of the likes of Roberta Brooks, and it dawned on Roberta that she'd been wrong about him from the very beginning. She'd mistaken him for something else entirely. Charles's retribution. A grin spread across her face. *He's a boy, Roberta. Look at him. He can't handle you. You've wounded him. Bruised his heel.*

He never noticed her moving slowly in his direction. John stood transfixed, lost in a story that now had an image, breadth, width, depth. It tasted salty on his tongue. He'd grown up hearing whispers and trying not to hear them. But no one had ever come out and told him the truth. They'd always talked around him, careful not to say too much, but always saying enough for him to know the unthinkable had happened.

"You a Tate, boy. You always been a Tate 'cause Fool is yo' daddy. Fool raped that girl!" Roberta said, inching closer to him. "Fool made you, but . . . you killed her, John Tate," she hissed. "I saw what you did to that girl." Tears streamed down her face. But they weren't tears for Mattie and they definitely weren't tears for John. Insane tears. Tears of relief, knowing she'd gathered up all the faith she had and stood boldly confronting what she'd been afraid of all these years. Charles's wrath, born again in the boy King. "I saw how you tore her up."

Roberta was lying. John knew better than that. How could he have killed Mattie? "You shut up, Roberta! You don't know nothing! You don't know—"

"I know how she scream, John Tate."

"My name ain't no—"

"I know how much blood she lost 'cause of you. She bled to death," she said, approaching him slowly.

"Fuck you, Roberta!"

"You tore her up like he did. Like yo' daddy did. Pushin' . . . and pushin' . . . hard, boy! Too hard for that girl! Hard! You jus' like him." Roberta laughed. "Devil boy. Devil boy kill his own momma, tearin' her up from the inside out, with his bare hands."

"Shut up!"

"And Mattie King screamin' the whole time . . . 'He killin' meeee!' "

"Shut the fuck—"

" 'He killin' meee! I can't do this no more!' " she wailed.

Tears filled his eyes but refused to fall. Roberta was full of nonsense and insane. How could he have killed Mattie? "Fuck you, bitch! You crazy! You crazy, Roberta!"

" 'I can't do this no more! He killin' meee!' "

Now was her chance, she thought to herself. He was off balance and this was the moment she'd been waiting for since the night he was born. *Kill him! He demon seed!* Roberta was a step away from killing him. She was so consumed with thoughts of burying that spade into him, she never saw the hole in front of her. Suddenly, she stumbled and fell toward the ground that raised itself to meet her like an anxious lover who'd been gone too long. Here was her prophecy, come true.

Before John knew what was happening, she'd fallen and was laying facedown on the ground.

"Get up . . . you fat . . . Get up!" he screamed. Served her right. Spewing out all that mess . . . served her right to fall on her fat ass. He waited, expecting her to raise herself up off the ground, but Roberta didn't move. "Roberta! Yo! Roberta!" His chest heaved up and down. She lay still, staring off at something distant. John paced back and forth, uncertain about what he should do, if anything. She'd started this. She'd been the one . . . not him. He hadn't done anything, except . . . except to go over to Lewis's, and . . . That's all he'd wanted to do all along.

Roberta lay still for too long. John slowly opened the gate to her yard and walked over to her. Grudgingly, he knelt down next to her. "Roberta?" She grunted. "What did you do? Crazy ol' . . . Here," he said, reaching for her arm pinned beneath her. "You need to get up. Roberta? You need to . . ." John slowly started to turn her over. Roberta's lifeless eyes stared up at him. "Roberta?" He looked at her hand, still gripping the spade buried deep in her chest, covered in rich, red blood that flowed black into the ground. "Fuck!" he whispered. John released his grip on Roberta and ran.

Patience Is Its Own . . .

Pete Jensen had craved this woman for as long as he could remember. They'd grown up together. Gone to school to-gether. He'd been an usher at her wedding and a pallbearer at Abe's funeral, changing his role in her life like he changed clothes. It hadn't been easy. People gossiped, creating drama where there was none. Gossip that sometimes made its way back to Edna. But he knew the truth and nothing had ever happened between him and Agnes. Nothing until now, that is.

Pete had always made himself available to her, especially after Abe's death. When Agnes needed something fixed, he was there to fix it. When she needed someone to share a cold drink and reminisce with about Abe, he'd been the one she could talk to who never seemed to tire of reliving old memories. He'd been her friend. That's what she called him. His wife, Edna, was one of her best friends. But being her friend had never been enough for Pete. He'd watched her struggle with the deaths of her husband and daughter and seen loneliness smother her into a shell of the woman she'd once been. He'd pursued her since they were in grade school, but she never paid that kind of attention to him. She'd never paid attention to any man until Abe came along. Pete never said anything, but he'd resented the love she seemed so eager to give to Abe. They'd all made such a fuss over his big behind when he moved to town. Abe could've had any woman he wanted, and it pissed Pete off that he chose to go after the one woman he knew Pete wanted. Now Abe was gone. And Agnes? She needed somebody. Pete knew this, even if she didn't.

He'd planned on stopping by just for a minute and pulled up in front of her house, finding Agnes sitting alone on her front porch.

"How you doin', Miss Agnes?" he asked, getting out of the car.

She smiled, looking genuinely glad to see him. "I'm fine, Mr. Pete. How you doin'?"

"Thirsty. Whatchu got to drink?"

Agnes laughed, then got up and went inside. "C'mon in," she called to him.

Obediently, Pete followed.

Pete sat at the kitchen table drinking lemonade while Agnes checked on her supper. He watched her like he always did, but as usual, Agnes was oblivious to his attention. Pete's eyes traced the curve of her breasts, pressed against the front of her dress, and followed the line down to her full hips, finally resting on big, pretty legs that made him shift against the uncomfortable bulge forming in his pants. His mouth watered for the taste of her and his hands itched to touch her. He sipped slowly on his lemonade but drank in Agnes with his eyes.

She went on and on about something she and Edna talked about when they ran into each other at the Piggly Wiggly, and mentioned she'd used up the last of her flour frying chicken and had forgotten to pick up some more while she was shopping. Tomorrow she'd have to send John to Miss Gwennie's for some more, but of course that woman charged entirely too much for flour, and everything else for that matter. She'd have to put John on her insurance after he got his license, which would be in a few months. That way, she could let the boy use the car and drive over to—

Agnes turned, and Pete, who'd been sitting quietly at the kitchen table and now stood over her, was looking down and staring into her eyes the way she hadn't had a man stare into her eyes in years.

"Pete?" she asked, clutching the top of her dress closed. Pete never said a word. Standing this close to her, he couldn't. He leaned into her, backing Agnes against the kitchen counter, pressed his nose to her hair, then inhaled. He reminded himself that he'd only intended on staying for a few minutes. Edna was expecting him home soon, but Agnes smelled so damn good. Pete rested his hands on the counter on either side of Agnes, then leaned down and kissed her softly on her neck. She trembled slightly at the sensation of his breath against her skin.

"Pete!" she said sternly, pushing her hand against his chest. "Whatchu call yo'self—"

Pete gently pushed back, pressing his erect penis against her thigh. "Lord," she whispered, but not in protest. "Pete?"

He prayed he wasn't dreaming. Pete's lips left a warm, moist trail from Agnes's neck to her cheek, ultimately finding her mouth, where he softly brushed his lips against hers and he was surprised when the sweetness of her tongue timidly greeted his. Agnes pressed herself into him, then abruptly pulled away, turning her face from his, ashamed and shocked by what she'd just done. But Pete couldn't let this moment escape him. He'd waited too long for her, so he pulled her into his arms, then kissed her passionately.

"Slow it down, baby," he whispered. "We ain't in no hurry."

Agnes straddled Pete, riding him with the hunger of a woman who'd been without a man for too long. Her eyes were closed, but he didn't dare close his. Twenty-five years of patience had finally been rewarded, and Pete gazed up at Agnes, biting down on her bottom lip, holding his hands in place around her waist with her own.

"Pete," she pleaded. Agnes couldn't bear to look at him, at them, at what they were doing.

"That's it, baby," he whispered, struggling to keep his release inside him for as long as he could. This might be his only opportunity to be with this woman, and Pete wanted it to last as long as possible. He stared into her face, a forty-eight-year-old face, hardly believing she was as old as she was. Agnes's hair hung down around her shoulders, framing her youthful face. Her figure rivaled that of any woman years younger than she was. Agnes was a lady who kept herself looking respectable, but round, full breasts danced above him and soft hips swirled on top of him, leaving a tantalizing aroma of juices saturating the two of them. She was the only woman he'd ever wanted, and at this moment, Pete Jensen would've lived or died for Agnes King.

A lump welled up in Agnes's throat, threatening to choke the life out of her. Tears streamed down her cheeks. *Have mercy!* she mouthed. *Please have mercy, Lord.* Pete Jensen was a married man. He'd been friends with Abe. No! This wasn't right. Agnes knew, being here with this man like this wasn't right. She pushed down hard against him, until it hurt, welcoming the pain as penance for her sin and as relief from what she'd deprived herself of all these years. Pete felt so good inside her, and Agnes felt ashamed. His hands roamed her body, and she loved the sensation of his rough hands gripping her waist. His mouth found her breast and she moaned when his warm, moist tongue flicked against her nipple.

Lord! Why had she let him kiss her? If only she'd backed away, or slapped his face, but the warmth of his lips had drenched something inside her soul, and before she knew what was happening, she had her arms wrapped around his neck, drinking in his tongue like water. Pete filled her with slow, deep thrusts, taking his time, letting her starving body devour his. She wanted it to be over, and she didn't. Once it was over, she'd have to face herself. She'd have to face her transgression, her friend Edna, her guilt, shame, loneliness. Once it was over, there had be hell to pay. *Forgive me, Jesus,* she said over and over again in her mind. *Have mercy!*

John had run home as fast as he could. Images of Roberta falling replayed themselves again in his mind. If only he'd left her alone, he thought. She'd be alive, digging holes in her front yard. If he'd kept walking and gone over to Lewis's like he'd planned, Roberta would be alive now. Alive and crazy, but alive. Panic threatened to overtake him and he stopped. Maybe he could still go to Lewis's. He could act like he didn't know anything about Roberta lying dead in her yard. He could—

He ran into the house, trying to prepare himself how to tell Momma Agnes what had happened. She'd call the police and maybe the ambulance. They'd get there and find out that Roberta wasn't dead after all. She was just unconscious, and they'd take her to the hospital. She'd be all right. He promised himself.

John went from room to room, searching for Agnes. He wanted to call out her name, but the lump in his throat wouldn't let him. Panic in his chest beat too fiercely for him to call out to her without screaming. Maybe she was in her room, he thought, probably taking a nap. John took deep breaths, trying to calm himself. The last thing he needed to do was rush into her room and wake her up from sleeping, as upset as he was. He walked toward the back of the house to Agnes's room and heard sounds coming from behind the door. She must've fallen asleep with the television on again, he thought. The palms of his hands were sweating as guilt consumed him. He should've just kept going. All he had to do was go to Lewis's house like he'd planned.

John slowly turned the doorknob to Agnes's room, praying she wouldn't think he'd done this. He'd explain that he was just walking past her house. No. He hadn't stopped to talk to her. He was on his way to Lewis's and saw her lying there. She was already dead and . . .

He knew better than to open the door to her room without knocking.

Pete could hardly believe it. John swung open the door and stood there with his mouth open. "What the . . ." Pete shouted. "Get the hell outta here, boy!"

Agnes turned quickly and looked right into the face of her grandson. "Oh, Lord!" She scrambled to pull her dress closed and climbed off Pete. "Oh, my Lord!" Her voice trembled. What had she been doing? What in the world had she been doing? She stared at John, who stood frozen in place, then she looked down at Pete. Lord! How could she have been so wrong? How in the world could she have let this happen?

John stood speechless, planted firmly where he stood, his eyes locked on Agnes, trembling shamefully in the corner of the room. His heart beat like a drum inside him. It had all happened so fast, but not fast enough to stop the image of Agnes straddling Mr. Jensen from burning itself into his mind. John's thoughts whirled inside his head like a cyclone. Roberta lay dead in her yard—because of him. Agnes clutched possessively at the front of her dress, her eyes darting wildly between Mr. Jensen and John—because John had forgotten to knock. Nothing, in his mind, had ever been as bad as this.

Uncontrollable sobs escaped from her as Agnes fought to compose herself. She sat on the side of the bed, smoothing out her dress, fumbling with the buttons. Her hands shook so badly, in frustration she gave up. She glared at John, and suddenly she realized she couldn't do this anymore. Bile rose up into her throat as

Agnes stood up between John and Pete, desperate to scream but not knowing why.

"He yo's to raise now, Agnes," Momma had said. "You got to do right by him, jus' like you'd do right by yo' own chil'." Do right. Agnes had always done what was right, to keep from being a burden, to keep people from talking about her behind her back. She'd grown up doing the right thing. She looked at Pete, sitting embarrassed and frustrated on the other side of the bed, then at John, standing there with his mouth hung open, and looking like Fool. Anger welled up inside her and Agnes hated both of them. She hated herself.

"John," she whispered. She looked at him again, and for the first time, Agnes admitted to herself that she didn't want him here. He didn't belong to her. He didn't even belong to Mattie. Mattie was dead! John never belonged to that girl, and he sure as hell wasn't her responsibility to raise. She'd had enough. All his life, Agnes had tried to do what she never wanted to do. What everybody told her it was her job to do. She never wanted him! But he'd been thrown into her arms, reminding her of her own emptiness every time he took a breath.

John couldn't move. Even the sting of her hand across his face didn't uproot him. "Get out!" she screamed in his face. Then Agnes pushed him as hard as she could. "Get the hell outta my house! I don't want you here!" Agnes fought him, clawing at him, kicking him, pounding his chest with her fists. "Get outta here! I want you gone! I hate yo' ass! I always hated—"

Pete Jensen jumped up from the bed and caught Agnes as she collapsed in his arms, exhausted from the weight of depression. "You need to get on, son! You need to go!"

Agnes was empty on the inside and had nothing else to give this boy.

John ran to his room and quickly packed all he could carry. He had no idea where he was going, but it didn't matter. This wasn't home anymore. Maybe it never had been.

Little Bird

Little birds pushed out of the nest before they can fly don't usually live very long. Every time Edwina looked into Connie's eyes, she saw a little bird that was desperately trying to hold on to life but, at the same time, was afraid to. Connie might've had most people fooled, wearing her "hard as nails" attitude like armor, hissing and clawing like a mean old alley cat every time somebody threatened to get too close. Some people fell for it. Edwina never did. She'd seen glimpses of another side of the girl too. As hard as she pretended to be, Connie could be as soft as butter that had been left out all day, when she thought nobody was looking. Sometimes, she just looked as if all she wanted in the world was for somebody to gather her up in their arms and hold her tight enough to squeeze the breath out of her.

She'd seen scared people before, and Edwina knew that if you came at them too hard or too fast, they'd run away as fast as they could to look for a place to hide. Most of the time, she made sure not to let Connie see how much attention she was really giving her, appearing to be indifferent and casual in their conversations.

"So, what did you say yo' momma's name was?" Edwina asked one day while Connie was busy sweeping up the dining area. It was late and Edwina was getting ready to go home for the night. "I just asked 'cause you favor a girl I used to know back when I lived down here," Edwina lied.

"I never told you her name," Connie said, continuing to sweep.

Edwina waited, hoping Connie would mention it, but she never did. "But, you got family, though. Right?"

Connie shrugged, then whispered, "I got a little sister."

Edwina pretended to sort through her purse, stalling for time, hoping to get more information from Connie. Not that she'd know what to do with it. Turning the girl in probably wouldn't do any good. More than likely she'd just end up running away again. Besides, politicians didn't know a thing about taking care of children. They'd put her someplace she didn't belong, which was probably what they'd done in the first place to push the girl out here on her own. "You the oldest?" she asked, sounding surprised.

Connie nodded, then smiled.

"Well, what's her name, Little Bird?"

Connie stopped sweeping, then looked at Edwina, not sure if she wanted to tell her or not. She tried not to think of Reesy, because she missed her so much, and because she didn't want to think that maybe what had happened to her with Earl was happening to Reesy. But Edwina had been nice to her, and she really didn't think telling her would do any harm. "Her name's Reesy. She's eight . . . I mean, she's nine now."

Edwina smiled tenderly. "You ever talk to Reesy?"

Connie shook her head. "She was adopted last year."

"I see," Edwina said quietly. The expression on Connie's face told Edwina she'd asked enough questions for the night. It was late, and they were both tired.

Edwina put on her coat and pulled out her car keys. "Well, you finish up, Little Bird. I'm gon' get on home now."

"Night, Eddie." Connie smiled as Edwina walked out the door.

"Night, baby."

Eddie never had to tell her what their arrangement would be. She'd arrive at the restaurant every morning by five and Connie would already be up and dressed to get to work, hoping that Edwina wouldn't have had a change of heart and decide to make her leave. Connie put in long hours and the work was hard, but she had a warm, safe bed to sleep in and food to eat, and that's all that mattered.

She washed dishes, helped cook, swept and mopped the floors, and kept the bathrooms clean. Sometimes, if Eddie needed help out front, she'd let Connie take phone orders, or help out at the serving counter. After four o'clock, Connie was free to do what she wanted, but Eddie made it clear that the doors to the restaurant were locked promptly at nine, and if Connie wasn't inside by then, she would have to find somewhere else to sleep. Connie made sure she was inside by eight.

"Hey, Eddie." Milo grinned at Edwina as he came through the serving line. "How you doing?" Milo was a regular and flirted shamelessly with any woman who'd let him.

"Boy! Where you been?" Edwina exclaimed, smiling. "You eatin' some other woman's cookin'? You know that's goin' to hurt my feelin's if you are."

"Aw, I just been working, sweets. Ain't nobody feed me like you do." He leaned over the counter, gazed into Edwina's eyes, then winked.

Edwina laughed. "You ain't even a bit of good. What you want, Milo?"

"Give me some of them ham hocks and greens, sweet potatoes, and mac and cheese."

"You want corn bread or a biscuit?"

"Now, what do I look like trying to eat greens with a biscuit?"

Edwina put corn bread on his plate. "Folks come in here asking for all kinds of crazy mess. You want tea or pop?"

"Pop."

Edwina turned to Connie. "Little Bird, go get me a large cola."

Milo stared at Connie and smiled in her direction. "Who's that?" he asked Eddie.

Edwina glared at him. "That is my new help and she is entirely too young for you," she snapped.

"She look familiar."

Connie came back to the counter with a glass of cola and handed it to Milo.

"Haven't I seen you somewhere before?" Milo asked Connie.

Connie glanced at him but didn't answer.

"What's your name?"

Edwina quickly interrupted, "You want cobbler, Milo?"

"Naw, Eddie," he said, staring at Connie. "I know I've seen you somewhere—"

Edwina interrupted again, "That's gon' be five-seventeen."

He handed Eddie a ten-dollar bill and shook his head, frustrated because he knew he'd seen this girl but couldn't remember where. Edwina handed him back his change, and Milo hesitated before leaving. "Man, now you got to move on," Edwina scolded. "I got other customers waitin' behind you."

Milo shrugged, picked up his tray, found an empty table, and sat down to eat, staring at Connie the whole time she worked. Of course he knew this girl. Fine as she was, she'd be impossible to forget, he thought.

He took his time eating and watched as Connie wiped down the tables. The lunch crowd was starting to thin out, and Edwina was busy at the cash register. Now was the time to make his move.

"Now I remember where I've seen you," he whispered over Connie's shoulder. A knot formed in her stomach as Milo inched closer to her. "Didn't you used to hang out with a chick named Shay? She was a little ho over off—"

"I don't know a Shay," Connie lied, then quickly stepped away from him.

Milo followed and stood close behind her again, then reached out and touched her hair. "Damn! You are fine, little momma. How much?"

"Milo!" Edwina spat. "Get yo' hands off that child, and get yo' ass—*forgive me, Lord*—back to work, before I tell yo' woman what you been up to."

Milo slowly backed away from Connie, grinned slyly at Eddie, then left. Connie stood frozen in embarrassment, wondering how much Eddie really knew about her.

"Finish up them tables, Little Bird. I need you on them dishes." Eddie went back to work like nothing had happened, and so did Connie.

Connie finished washing the last of the lunch dishes and decided to take her break on the porch in back of the restaurant. Milo had shaken her more than she'd let on. He knew Shay and he knew Shay was a prostitute. The fact that he'd seen Connie with her meant that he knew she'd hustled too. Sometimes, she couldn't help but wonder how many other people knew and just never said anything. Shay called it "selling pussy," making it sound as nasty as it was. There were days when Connie swore she'd dreamed that time of her life, but Milo reminded her that it hadn't been a dream. And if Eddie ever decided she didn't need Connie's help anymore, it would be a nightmare she'd have to live all over again.

"Child," Edwina sighed, coming out of the restaurant. "This place is wearin' me down." She sat down next to Connie on the steps. "Soon as lunch is over, got to get ready for supper. All this damn cookin'—*forgive me, Lord*—I tell you."

Connie tried to smile. The two sat beside each other not saying anything, until Edwina decided to break the silence. "Don't pay Milo no mind, girl," she said, patting Connie's knee. "He ain't 'bout nothin'." She knew he'd upset Connie, though the girl would never admit it. "He come back up in here with that nonsense again, I'm gon' tell his wife, Shirley, 'bout it. Me and her go to the same church. Milo's behind need to be up in church too, 'stead of runnin' round actin' like a fool."

"It's cool, Eddie." Connie shrugged. "No big deal."

"Disrespect is always a big deal, Little Bird. Don't ever think it ain't."

"Well, I haven't exactly done nothing that deserves much respect."

"You a human bein', ain't you? You God's creature like we all are and for that you deserve respect. Don't ever go thinkin' you don't 'cause of the things you've done. We've all done things, but that don't mean that anybody's got the right to disrespect anybody else." Edwina said things like this to Connie all the time, hoping some of it would sink in and fill the girl with some sense of worth.

Connie sensed a lecture coming on and quickly changed the subject. "How much closer to Vegas?" Every day, Edwina gave a report as to how much more money she'd made that she could put away for her retirement and use to move to Vegas.

Edwina grinned and closed her eyes. "Four hundred and sixty-eight dollars and fifty-three cents so far," she said proudly. "For a grand total of . . ." She pointed at Connie, who imitated a drumroll. "Seventy-seven thousand four hundred and fifty-six dollars and thirty-eight cents! and that ain't includin' the supper rush."

"Sure wish I could go," Connie said coyly.

Edwina shook her head vehemently back and forth. "Naw! Absolutely not. The Lord made me promise to look after yo' little behind until you was old enough to be out on yo' own, in yo' own place, workin' yo' own job."

"But Eddie," Connie whined, "you know I won't be no trouble, and I could help you out."

"Nope. You can't help me doin' nothin', girl. Except makin' me a bill I don't need."

"What kind of bill?"

"A food bill, a phone bill, a 'lectricity bill."

"You'd have those bills anyway."

"I'd have 'em for me. Just me. One. Not two. That's a world of difference, 'specially when it comes to teenagers."

Connie sighed. "So, what am I supposed to do when you leave? Who's going to be my best friend?"

"Don't be silly, Little Bird. I ain't yo' best friend and you know it."

Connie grinned. "Yes, you are, and you know it."

"I take care of you."

"I work for you to take care of me, and I work hard too."

"You too much trouble."

"I ain't hardly any trouble at all."

"You wreck my nerves."

"No more than you wreck mine."

"You ain't goin', and that's final."

Connie looked disappointed. "Then what am I supposed to do when you sell this place and leave?"

"You do what you been doin', Little Bird. You take care of yo'self. Only, you do it the right way. You do what most folks do. Get a job, and find you a place to live that's clean and safe. You pay yo' bills, and buy yo' own groceries. And more important than anything else,"—Edwina put her hand under Connie's chin and raised her face to hers—"you be a lady. Ain't a reason in the world you got to let a man treat you any ol' kinda way." Connie looked away, ashamed. "You such a pretty girl, baby. Too pretty and too smart to let all these men just do whatever they want to you. You got too much goin' for yo'self. I seen them drawin's you got hangin' up on yo' wall. Who taught you how to draw like that?"

Connie shrugged. "Nobody. It ain't nothing. Just designs. They don't really mean anything."

"But they are beautiful, Little Bird. I can't do nothin' like that. Hell, I'm jus' an old Southern woman who know how to do a little cookin', and I got me $77,456.38 saved up. If I could draw like you, I might have me even more than that."

"Yeah . . . right. Ain't nobody going to pay me to make no designs, Eddie, and you know it."

"I know no such thing, and neither do you. You need to get yo' mind right. Get yo' mind off all the mess you been through, and point it towards where you goin', Little Bird."

"Which is where?"

"How am I supposed to know? It's yo' mind and you the only one who knows where to point it. What I look like? One of them psychics?"

"You don't need to bother telling me this stuff if you don't know how to tell me to do it, Eddie. You ain't doing nothing but giving me a headache."

"All I'm sayin' is, you got potential, Little Bird. And you can be whatever you set yo' mind to."

"I ain't even got a diploma, Eddie. Not even a GED."

"So? I look like I got one?"

"No, but . . ."

"But I'm jus' an old Southern woman who can cook, huh? And I'm an old Southern woman who can cook who's got $77,456.38 in the bank too, and that don't even include the supper rush." Edwina grinned. "Ain't no limits, less you make 'em, Little Bird. Trust me, this time. I know what I'm sayin'."

Three years later Eddie sold Edwina's House of Soul Food Cuisine to her nephew, Anthony. She'd been warning Connie that this day would come, and when it finally did, Connie fought back waves of tears and nearly choked on the sadness she felt welling up in her throat. She was seventeen and she'd just started her first real job, working as a receptionist at a dentist's office downtown. Eddie had bought her new clothes to wear to work, and eventually she helped her find and decorate her first apartment.

"What kind of plant is that?" Eddie asked, watching Connie carefully position the potted plant on the windowsill.

"It's an African violet." She smiled, remembering how much Shay loved African violets. "It blooms sometimes. But you've got to be patient with it and you've got to treat it just right. A friend of mine told me about it," she said sadly.

Edwina smiled. "Oh, I guess I know something about that, Little Bird. Yes, I think I do."

In the three years since she'd found the girl in the alley behind her restaurant, Eddie had watched Connie blossom into a lovely young woman, and she was as proud of the girl as she would've been of a child she'd given birth to herself. Connie was better, but Eddie knew she wasn't nearly as good as she could get.

The day Eddie was to fly out, Connie rode with Anthony to take her to the airport. "You sure you got everything, Eddie? You know how forgetful you can be sometimes," Connie said, trying not to cry.

"I am not forgetful, Little Bird," Eddie scolded. "Stop treatin' me like I'm an old woman, and yes, I got everything I need. What I don't have, I don't need."

Connie tried to be happy for Eddie, but once again, someone she cared about was leaving her. She'd tried hard not to let it happen, but she'd failed miserably and had fallen in love with Eddie, who'd been more of a mother to her than Charlotte had ever been. "You'd better write to me, or else!" Connie snapped.

Eddie pressed her hand gently against Connie's cheek and looked warmly in her eyes. "I will, Little Bird. Now, didn't I promise?"

Connie fought desperately to hold back the tears. "You sure I can't come with you?"

Eddie shook her head. "Naw, now I'm through with you."

"God told you to take care of me, didn't he?"

"He did. And I did that."

"Maybe he told you to take me to Vegas with you too, and you just didn't hear him," Connie whined. Sometimes whining worked miracles on Eddie.

"You don't need me to take care of you no more, Little Bird. You grown now, and you got to know what it is to take care of yo'self. You got to know how to live like a woman and not a street rat."

Connie finally laughed. "I ain't no street rat, Eddie! How many times do I have to tell you that?"

"No, baby. You ain't nobody's street rat. You a young lady now, and I'm so proud of you."

A renegade tear escaped and streamed down Connie's cheek. "I'm scared, Eddie. I don't want to be by myself."

"Why not? You think you ain't good company?"

"I know I'm not."

"Little Bird, you one of my best friends, and I know better than that. You need to know how to appreciate yo'self, and the only way you ever goin' to learn how to do that is to be by yo'self. There's so much more to you than you know. Maybe one of these days you'll see that like I do." A voice over the intercom called for passengers to board the plane. "Promise me you goin' to go get that GED?"

"I will," Connie whispered.

"I mean it, Constance. A year from now, I'm goin' to check and see if you got it, and you'd better have it . . . or else!"

Connie wiped away her tears, then rolled her eyes, "Or else what? What are you going to do all the way from Vegas?"

Eddie's bottom lip quivered, and suddenly she did what she'd wanted to do since she'd laid eyes on the girl. Edwina gathered all of Connie up in her arms and squeezed her as hard as she could. "I'm goin' to come back here and give you that ass whoopin'—*forgive me, Lord*—I promised you back when I first laid eyes on you."

Connie melted and rested her head on Eddie's shoulder. "Yes, Eddie." She sobbed.

"I love you, Little Bird," Eddie whispered in her ear. She planted a tender kiss on Connie's forehead, then boarded the plane for Vegas.

She knew well enough not to expect miracles. Eddie had taught her a lot, but Connie still had a lot to learn about life, relationships, and herself. An undercurrent of desperation had propelled her forward for as long as she could remember, and it continued fueling her long after Eddie was gone. Desperately, she worked to maintain employment, a place to live, and to keep food in her refrigerator. All because she'd known firsthand what it was to be without those things, and Connie filed away a promise to herself that she'd never be without them again.

Even in the years to follow, forming lasting alliances with anyone took a backseat to self-preservation for Connie. Friends only got as close as she'd allow them to get, and relationships with men seldom went beyond the physical. Sex on her terms sometimes brought about temporary relief, but it never offered emotional satisfaction. She craved contact, closeness, touching, hoping that maybe sex would surprise her someday and fill her up with any of those things. How else would she get them? Sometimes, she'd manage to convince herself she really didn't need them. Other times, she'd cry herself to sleep, or lash out at some unsuspecting boyfriend, because the truth was, she did need them.

"Damn, girl! You act like you don't even give a shit!"

"I don't."

"Then what the hell am I doing here?"

"You know where the door is."

"Ain't no ties between us, baby. It's about fuckin', for both of us. Ain't that right?"

"Yeah . . . that's right. Now you need to get off me and go home to your wife. I need some sleep."

Falling in love wasn't an option, because as far as she was concerned, there was nothing loveable about men except an occasional orgasm every now and then. Some company and good times. It wasn't personal with men. It never had been.

"You ain't 'bout nothing but breaking hearts, Connie. One of these days, somebody's gonna grab hold of yours, and it ain't gonna be so easy for you to let go," a lover once warned.

Connie doubted seriously that would ever happen. In fact, she knew it wouldn't.

WHAT MEASURE
OF MAN?

Perpetual Motion

Sex wasn't a thing to be rushed. It was good with Terry Matthews, even missionary, because of the way she moved.

"Mmm . . . ," she moaned in his ear. "That's it, John. Right there. Right . . ." He liked the way she wrapped her legs around him. The way she held him and dug her nails into his back.

"Look at me, Terry," he whispered to her. "Look at me, baby."

She opened her eyes and pulled his face to hers to kiss. John knew she was on the verge of coming. Her tongue wrestled with his and he felt himself ready to explode inside her. The whole room smelled like sex. It was a smell that made his mouth water. A smell he sometimes wished he could put on and wear like a shirt.

"Aww . . . baby!" Terry Matthews raised her hips to meet him. Harder. Faster. "John?" she squealed. "John . . . I . . . I'm comin'! I'm comin', baby!"

He came too.

She wasted no time falling asleep after they'd finished. In the morning, he'd tease her about it like he always did, and she'd laugh, then say, "But baby, you've got it goin' on like that." He'd wonder if he really did. Then shrug it off as another insignificant thing in the world. He'd never been the kind of man to beat on his chest and proclaim his dick as the best dick that ever was. It was irrelevant to John, anyway. Good pussy bred good dick in his opinion. Simple as that.

She slept curled up against him, which was cool, sometimes. Other times, he felt crowded and nudged her gently, encouraging her to move over. He wasn't used to having someone sleep up under him like that. At least, not every night. Terry Matthews was the kind of woman who never seemed to get tired of touching. She hugged, kissed, and squeezed on him so much, it got on his nerves, and he'd find himself pulling away from her, or pushing her off him, careful not to hurt her feelings, but enough to let her know he needed his space.

Every day she asked how he was feeling and what was on his mind. Fishing. Prying? Trying to find out how long he was planning on staying, because that's something she'd wanted from the beginning. He'd like to stay, but he knew he couldn't. Terry Matthews was a fine woman, with the prettiest hips he'd ever seen. She was accommodating to a fault, desperate to leave him no excuse for being unsatisfied. She wasn't the reason he was leaving, so how could she be the reason he'd stay? If he told her she was too good for him, she'd argue and think he was full of it, because, he had to admit, that was a lame excuse even if it was true. If he told her he was too good for her, she'd just double up on the good sex and good food and cater even more to his every whim, bending over backwards, or any other way he wanted it, trying to anticipate needs he didn't even know he had.

She needed him and that was the problem. Some men don't need to be needed, and he was one of them. He disappointed her all the time, and she insisted on believing she was the problem. Whenever he told her otherwise, she'd accuse him of lying. So this was the nature of their relationship. He let her need him, while he'd enjoyed the fruits of her good sex, good food, good catering to all his damn needs, continuing to prove himself irresponsible and doing whatever the hell he wanted. Then, like clockwork, he'd stop by her apartment every Friday night to spend the weekends making sweet, slow love to her. That was more responsibility than he knew what to do with. But all in all, it hadn't been a bad trade-off.

She rolled over and laid a warm hand on his chest. "Mmm . . . Can't you sleep, baby?" she purred. Terry Matthews pressed her warm lips against his shoulder and kissed him there.

"Yeah, I'm about to doze off. Night, baby."

He kissed her head and knew he was going to miss her.

Her own slow, heavy breathing echoed in her ears. She'd been running so long. Too long. How far had she come down this road? The exhausted girl turned briefly, looking behind her. The road had disappeared into blackness. She couldn't see them but knew that they weren't far behind. She stumbled but managed to keep from falling. If she fell, she'd be too weak to get back up. The girl struggled to focus on the path ahead of her. It was too dark to see where it led, but she had no choice but to continue running.

The rocks beneath her bare feet were sharp and cut into her soles like pieces of glass, but she kept running. Sweat poured into her eyes and mixed with tears streaming down her face, pooling in the corners of her mouth. She wanted desperately to stop and rest, but the voices behind her were getting closer.

They'd been chasing her for miles. Their voices were closing in on her, laughing and mocking her. "We gon' get you, gal! We comin' after you!" The girl's white dress was torn and dirty. The soft curls that once covered her head and framed her face had become matted and nappy. She was exhausted to the point of collapsing, but she couldn't stop, because if she did, they'd catch her. And if they caught her, they'd tear her apart. That's what they always did. Pulled at her, tore at her flesh like she was meat, until she screamed and died . . . then . . . it started over again. It never ended. They never stopped chasing her and she'd run until she couldn't run anymore.

Rocks dug into her knees when she finally fell to the ground. The voices were even closer now. "We comin' for you! We gon' get you, gal!"

"Noooo!" she cried, clutching her hair. "Noooo! I can't do this! He killin' meee! He killin' . . ."

Her legs felt like lead, too heavy to move even if she could manage to pull herself up. The girl raised her hands to her face and saw that they were covered in blood. Blood so red it looked black. Dark faces of men laughing snarled down on her. It was too late. They'd caught her— again. "We got you now, gal! We got you now!" they laughed.

"Aaagh!" she screamed in agony and terror. Heat tore through her body and she felt the warmth of blood pooling around her. It was finished. The faces that had loomed above her had disappeared, and the girl slowly rose to her feet. She held the child in her hands. He was black, covered in blood, screaming like a man would scream. He fought *to get away from her, squirming in her small hands, until she could no longer hold him. Moonlight broke through the darkness, and she raised her face to where it shone. Slowly, the girl's face began to transform, and Mattie's face became Agnes's as she looked up at the dark sky that opened up into blue and screamed, "I can't do this no more!" Agnes dropped the boy, then raised her arms toward the sky. "I can't do this no more!" The baby fell, crying, kicking, anticipating hitting the ground and feeling the razor-sharp rocks cutting into his back—but just before he did, John woke up.*

He blinked, wondering if his eyes were opened or closed, looking for her, scared to death he'd see her. Who? Mattie or Agnes? Eventually, John's eyes adjusted to the darkness and he stared at the ceiling fan whirring above him. Terry Matthews was sleeping soundly beside him. John sat up on the side of the bed, then rubbed his hand over his head, which felt like somebody had slammed a sledgehammer into it. The room was cool, but he was covered in sweat and had to pee.

"You okay, John?" she called from the bed.

John finished using the bathroom, shook off his penis, flushed the toilet, and then splashed cold water on his face before answering. "I'm fine. Go back to sleep."

He stared at himself in the mirror, wondering how he'd managed to lose track of time. Complacency had managed to set in again. How'd that happen? A decent job, warm home, food on the table, and a body to curl up next to at night; he'd made the mistake of getting comfortable. Comfort fooled him into thinking it was all good when it wasn't. Damn nightmares had a way of reminding him of that. John's nightmares were like alarm clocks that woke him up and told him to move on. Nightmares of a woman he hadn't seen in years pushed him out the door every time he'd made up his mind to settle down. This was the third one he'd had this month, urging him to pack up once and for all and forget all about Terry Matthews and Birmingham, Alabama.

He was thirty-seven years old and couldn't remember what he'd been running from, or to. He'd forgotten why. All he knew was that this place, like all the other places, wasn't his place. Moving was his place. Living on the road was his place. Motels were his place. Fast food and sleeping with nameless, faceless women was his place. As tired as he was of living like that, that kind of life held him captive.

No sense waking her up to say good-bye. He wasn't down for the drama of all that and dressed quickly, packing his things in a duffel bag quietly enough to keep from waking up Terry Matthews. She'd been patient with him. Sweet. Generous. She'd forgiven him for things she had no idea he'd done, all for the pleasure of his temperamental company. Terry Matthews was lonely, and as with other lonely women, he'd taken advantage of her too. He opened his wallet and put two hundred dollars on the nightstand. He knew she needed the money. All that she'd been to him and all that she'd done hadn't been enough to exorcise his demons. He peeled her key off his key chain, then slipped out of the house for the last time.

Women like Terry Matthews were better off without men like John. How come they couldn't see that. Because he was fine? That's what they told him. "John, you a fine man." Silly women. (Fine on a man could open up some women's doors, and legs, just by flashing some attention in their direction.) Being fine was easy. Too easy, and it was one of those insignificant things in the world that in the end didn't mean a damn thing. Fine withered like flowers and faded into old age like everything else.

He tossed his bag into the backseat of his old El Dorado, started it up, and put in his favorite CD: Marvin Gaye, *The Master 1961–1984*, disc three. Leaving before dawn was always the best time to start traveling. Before coffeemakers and televisions came on. Before school buses and rush hour. He never minded driving. That was the only time he felt optimistic about things. Maybe because the road was home. It was where he belonged. Not shacked up with obliging women like Terry Matthews.

He pulled over the shoulder of the on-ramp just before turning onto the highway. "East or west?" he asked out loud, flipping a coin he caught in midair. John looked at the coin in his palm. "West." He pulled back onto the road, then headed toward the Rocky Mountains. He'd never been that far west before, but he'd always planned on making his way out there someday. Today was as good as any. Marvin would be his best friend for the next two thousand or so miles. He turned up the volume, bobbed his head, and sang, "Let's get it on . . . Let's get it on. . . ."

Truncated

He sensed it almost immediately. Denver, Colorado, lacked seasoning, and he'd grown accustomed to places with flavor, like New Orleans. Hot and spicy food, women, and music. Southern to a fault, dripping in molasses and cayenne pepper, burning and sweetening the tip of his tongue, reminding him that he was alive. Or Atlanta, Southern-fried, pecan-pied, funky soul thick enough for him to curl his toes into. Even Texas had a flair for understated, unmentionable drama. The kind of drama people openly wallowed in but turned a blind eye to, feigning indifference. Denver had none of that from what he could see, so he knew he wouldn't be here long. Too bad, he thought. Wholesome places like this, clean and wide open, might do him some good, and might be just what he needed to clear the cobwebs from his memories.

John rolled down the window and inhaled the clean, crisp fall air, savoring the delicate chill that floated just above heat he sensed would seep in later on, filling his lungs, purging the grit from inside him. A man could be born again in a place like this, if that's what he wanted. "Mmm," he moaned, taking in the view of the mountains looming on the horizon like kings, inching toward him as he headed west on I-70. Marvin's voice droned on like it had been since he'd left Birmingham. Funny how he never grew tired of Marvin. That was because Marvin didn't waste time on nonsense. John never had much patience for nonsense. He glanced at his watch, realizing he'd been driving for nearly eight hours, nonstop. His eyes burned to stay open long enough for him to find a room; eventually he turned off the highway, taking the Colorado Boulevard exit, then headed south, looking for a street called Colfax.

"If you goin' to Denver, man, take Seventy west, get off on Colorado Boulevard, go south, and find Colfax. Got plenty of cheap rooms and cheap pussy on Colfax," the old man at the gas station had told him.

He found the cheap rooms easily enough, but as for the cheap pussy, it was nowhere to be found. Of course, at six-thirty in the morning, cheap pussy was probably getting some sleep after working all night. That was fine by him. Hopefully, that meant he could get some sleep without the disruption of moans, groans, and headboards or heads banging against motel room walls. He was too tired for all that.

John took a long, slow drag on his cigarette and lay in bed, watching sunlight slash through the closed faded curtains, daring him to try to sleep this time of morning. He'd hoped that the hot shower he'd taken would've been the sedative he needed to finally let himself fall asleep. It hadn't. He pushed away the urge to call Terry. She didn't deserve that kind of inconsideration, or disrespect, for that matter.

Once again, he'd found himself a stranger in a strange land, wondering what the hell he expected to find here. Too bad he didn't bother asking himself that question back in Birmingham, he thought. "Dumb ass," he muttered, laughing. Somewhere along the line, he'd put aside his search for the promised land he began searching for right after he left home. That perfect place perfectly suited for him, that welcomed him home for the first time every single morning and kissed him good night before he closed his eyes to settle down for the night. He'd heard somewhere that "home is where the heart is," and that was the problem. John's heart wasn't anywhere in particular, except maybe in his car. He'd probably spent more time there than anyplace else.

He doubted seriously that Denver, Colorado, offered anything of substance that would compel him to want to stay. John laughed again. Anything of substance? Had he really been looking for substance all these years? He'd had substance in Terry Matthews and in good paying jobs with retirement plans and benefits. John had been irresponsible with substance his whole life, not knowing how to appreciate a good thing when he held it in the palm of his hand. His eyelids fell lazily, resting closed, until a thump on the wall startled them open; then John put out his cigarette, turned over on his side, and finally drifted off to sleep.

A couple of hours' sleep turned into a couple of weeks, and John found himself leaving his room just long enough to buy something to eat and get cigarettes. Other than that, he wasn't interested in seeing the light of a Colorado day. The motel he'd been staying in turned out to be a halfway house for prostitutes, pimps, and way-ward johns, and it was starting to get to him. On his way back from picking up a sandwich, John casually strolled back to his room, when suddenly, the door next to his flung open. His neighbor, Irene, emerged, adjusting the straps of her short, black slip that clung mercilessly to her plump figure.

"Hey, Daddy," the woman purred, bracing one hand on her hip and toying with the thin gold chain around her neck with the other. Dark circles from wearing too much mascara were smudged beneath her eyes, and a wild mane of auburn hair framed her narrow face. He was used to seeing her in the evenings, with her hair piled high and pinned up, and foundation applied so thick, it looked more like stucco than makeup.

"Where've you been hiding?" she asked, stepping into the hallway, purposely blocking his path to his room.

"Now, you know my ass is too big to be hiding anywhere, Irene."

She smiled and inched closer to him, then ran a long, red, acrylic fingernail up and down his chest. "Your big ass got my mouth watering. That's all I know. When are you going to invite me over for a drink?" She looked up into his eyes and smiled.

The male voice called out from her room, "Irene! Get your black ass back in here, girl! We ain't finished!"

Irene rolled her eyes, ignoring the man calling to her from the room. "What are you doing later on?"

John casually maneuvered his way past her. "You better go see about your man, Irene."

"Irene! Bitch! You hear me? Get your ass off that mothafucka!"

Her man came to the door and glared at John. "Get your own woman, man." He grabbed Irene by the elbow and pulled her back into the room.

"Let go!" she spat, trying to pull away from him.

"What the fuck you think you doing? You got me up in here, and you out there trying to fuck around with—"

"With somebody who's probably got more going on than your sorry ass!"

The door slammed shut behind the couple just as John let himself into his room. Soon, the thin walls gave way to the sounds of Irene's cries and pleas for him to stop, then to the vibrations of the beating he gave her, but John instinctively closed his ears to them. Their routine was as choreographed as a bad dance performance. Irene's man would beat her ass while she begged and pleaded for him to stop, and when he finally did, they'd fuck all night long, and she'd beg him not to stop.

True to form, twenty minutes later, Irene's muffled cries transformed from pain to pleasure. "That's it, Daddy! You know how I like it! You know how I like it!"

John stood staring out the window of his motel room down into the busy street, chewing gingerly on a ham and cheese sandwich. He listened intently for a familiar sound, waited for the urge to overwhelm him, forcing him to pack his bags, get in his car, and move on. No, Denver didn't fit. Or maybe it was him who didn't fit. He wasn't sure, but the road wasn't calling his name this time, and he'd learned not to come if he wasn't being called. Years ago, he'd have hauled tail out of a town like this. That wasn't the case anymore. It hadn't been the case in years. Each time he stopped, he stayed a little longer and rolled out a little slower than the last time. The fire of moving on was a little more than a cinder now. John knew what it was. Moving on was getting old, and so was he. There was no destination in mind, no desire in him to be anywhere right now. Besides, he needed to make some money before he decided to leave. So, finding a job was in order.

"Yes! Yes! Oh . . . that's . . . yes!" Irene screamed.

"Grrrr!" the man growled.

John shook his head. First a job, then an apartment that hopefully came with walls lined with lead.

Who Wants to Live Forever?

He'd been in town a month and had managed to get hired on at a plant making boxes. Corrugated. That's the word they liked to use. Corrugated. Boxes. Same thing. The people at the plant prided themselves on making custom boxes, as opposed to your standard, everyday square boxes. They even had engineers in the place that designed boxes. As much as he would've liked, he just couldn't work up the enthusiasm for boxes that everyone else seemed to have, but it paid good money, and that's all that mattered.

One of the guys he worked with had told him about an apartment building near downtown that was managed by his cousin. The man made a phone call and John moved in shortly after getting hired, welcoming the peace of quiet nights, and a haven from the likes of Irene.

John had been working with two other men, loading up the truck for a shipment that needed to go out. They'd introduced themselves to him, and he'd done the same, but he didn't make it much of a point to remember names of most people. He never saw it as necessary.

The dark-skinned man with cornrows talked incessantly about anything and everything, as if the sound of silence were something he desperately needed to keep at bay. He and the other man, a Hispanic man with a long, wavy ponytail, kept their conversation between them, not bothering to include John, which was fine with him.

"She's about ready to pop, man. Any day now," the black man said, laughing. "I hope like hell this one's a boy."

"You've got too many damn kids, bro."

"No such thing, my brotha. Kids are beautiful and you can never have enough. There were six of us in my family. Four boys and two girls. It was great!"

"Population's at six billion, dude, and you got too many kids. It ain't fair to the rest of the world for you to use up all the earth's natural resources with your family alone," the Hispanic man said jokingly. "I think you're being selfish, but that's just my opinion."

"Allah's got this, man. Let him handle the rest of the world. I got things under control with mine. And in my world, I can make all the kids I want."

"And your wife's cool with this?"

"My wife is cool with us being a family and taking care of our kids together. Raising healthy, happy, well-adjusted human beings is what it's all about, brotha. That's what we're doing."

"She stays home, then?"

"Hell, yeah, she stays home. We can't afford no day care with three kids, man! What . . . I look rich?" The black man laughed.

"Naw, man. But you make babies like you're rich."

"My children are extensions of me. When I leave this planet, when I die, I won't really be dead, because my spirit will continue on through them. It's cosmic, man. You got kids?"

"Got two. One of each."

"Then you know what I'm talking about. When you're dead and gone and buried six feet under, the only proof the world will have that you were ever here will be walking around in your kids, and their kids, and theirs. It's eternal life, my brotha, and you get it through your children. The spirit lives forever if you got kids. That's immortality."

John listened intently, wondering to himself, *Is that how it works?* He fought the urge to laugh out loud. This brotha seemed to have all the answers, John thought. So, why was he out here loading boxes and not president of the company? Most of the time the idea of kids and family never crossed his mind. Then there were the other times, when the thought not only crossed his mind but even lingered there. Threatening that if he didn't hurry up, find the right woman, or even the wrong one, and get down to the business of having kids, he'd miss his chance altogether and die a lonely old man. Then what? According to this cornrowed brotha, John would return from whence he came—*ashes to ashes, dust to dust*—and no one would ever know he had ever been, because he'd have left behind no kids to perpetuate his existence. *Damn. That's fucked up,* he thought to himself.

Even if somewhere along the line he did manage to leave behind a piece of himself, he'd never know it. Every now and then, women had claimed to have been pregnant with his kid, but to his knowledge, none ever materialized. John didn't keep in touch with women from his past, except for his aunt, Dot. And that was only on occasion, letting her know that he was still breathing, and making sure she was too. Other than that, there was no one else. Who knows? Maybe centuries from now, some archaeologist would dig up a few bones and discover that John had fathered an entire nation and never even knew it.

John helped load the last pallet, locked the trailer door, then began walking back toward the warehouse. The man with the cornrows called out to him. "Hey, King, man, am I talking truth or what? A man got kids, he can live forever. Right?"

John turned to him, then shrugged. "Forever's a long time, brotha."

The cornrowed man looked at John, shook his head, then turned back to his friend. "Consider yourself immortal, my man. As long as them kids of yours walk the planet, so will you."

A Rose by Any Other . . .

If indeed there was a home for the perfect kiss, it would be on her lips. John pulled out an old worn notepad he carried in his back pocket and wrote it down. He'd been doing that a lot lately. Thinking profound thoughts and writing them down in his profound-thoughts notepad. He used to never write them down, then get pissed off because he'd forgotten them. These were his proverbs. Every man had to have his own proverbs. Sort of like having his own legacy. Never knew when he might need one. Proverbs had saved his life too many times to count, especially as he'd gotten older and began paying attention to them. Over the years, he'd learned to fight without always feeling the need to use his fists. Young men fought with fists. Old men fought with reason, intellect, and patience. He wrote that down too.

The woman sitting at the table across the room with the pretty mouth inspired him. He watched her wrap those full lips of hers around a barbecue rib, with an uninhibited conviction that turned him on. He laughed. Baby girl wasn't shy about eating, that's for sure. Every now and then, she'd glance over in his direction, staring at him while she licked the sauce from her long fingers, then traced her tongue around her full lips to clean them off too. Using a napkin might've been easier, he thought, but it sure wasn't as seductive. Before long, her attentions would dive back into that plate in front of her, and she'd make him disappear. He couldn't help but admire her for that. First things first. She obviously had her priorities in order.

If indeed there were a home for the perfect kiss, it would be on her lips. He liked that. It was poetic. John believed in poetry because there was a whole lot of truth inside good poetry. He'd been reading a little here and there. Amiri Baraka was his favorite. Baraka had truth down to a science. The kind of truth John could relate to, tangible, with purpose and texture.

"You want some more tea?" the little brown, round waitress asked him. She stood over him, holding a pitcher in her hand, like she knew what his answer would be before she even asked. He nodded his head yes and held up his glass for her to fill. They had some good tea in here. It was sweet the way they made it down South, and he hadn't found another place in town that served tea already sweetened, which is why he'd kept coming back here. A brotha from work had told him about the place. He'd bragged about it being the best soul food restaurant in Denver, but from what John could see, it was the only soul food restaurant in Denver.

He filled his fork with the last bite of greens left on his plate. They'd been some damn good greens. He just hoped they'd been cleaned the way they should've. John hadn't seen anything to make him think otherwise, but some folks didn't clean greens the way they needed to be cleaned. The only greens he'd really ever trusted were Agnes's. That woman could hook them up better than anybody he'd ever known, seasoning them with neck bones and jalapeño peppers. He hadn't had any that good since he'd left home.

The woman with the pretty mouth surprised him and stared back at him again. He could tell she wasn't like most people he'd come across in this town. They were too shy for his tastes. Too shy or too stuck up. Nobody dared to look in his eyes when he spoke to them. John learned years ago the importance of looking into a man's eyes. How are you supposed to know what kind of man you're dealing with if you never look into his eyes? Eyes told his stories and secrets for him. They let you know what was on his mind, even if he didn't have the guts to tell you himself. Looking into his eyes let you know how much or how little a man could be trusted. They'd sometimes even go so far as to reveal his destiny.

Get yo' ass outta my yard, boy! You black-eyed devil! Get outta here, John!

Black-eyed devil. Devil. Never made much sense to him. Had he been a devil because his eyes were black? Or were there devils with eyes a different color than his? Crazy Roberta. Strange how his memories of her sometimes resembled fondness. Crazy or not, Roberta claimed to have had the gift of discerning spirits, and he often wondered how closely she'd come to discerning his.

She wore a skirt with a split up the middle, and boots that came up to her knees. Without giving it much thought, she crossed her legs, then the skirt fell open slightly, revealing soft, creamy thighs that probably tasted even better than that fried chicken he'd just eaten. When she saw him staring, she uncrossed her legs, then pulled her skirt together. John glanced around the room. He hadn't been the only man who'd noticed.

Yes, she was gorgeous. But not the kind of gorgeous that had been pampered or put up on a pedestal. She was tough, maybe because she'd had to be. Something about the desperation she put into eating. More than that, there was something about the way she wasn't afraid to make eye contact with a man, and not be moved by it one way or another. This one had secrets, he concluded. Most people had secrets, but John didn't give a damn about secrets. He never had patience for them. Secrets were games best left for children, because that's who best played the game of secrets anyway. He was too old for them.

"You through?" the little brown, round waitress asked him. "You want your bill?"

John wiped his mouth with his napkin. "Yeah. I'm done."

She gave him good service, so he left her a good tip on the table. She'd poured him sweet tea.

Sweet tea parches a bitter tongue. He slipped into his shades, reminding himself to write that down as soon as he got into the car. Poetic truth. He laughed.

Connie watched him watch her. There had been a time in her life when she'd have turned away, pretending not to be interested, or she might've even been flattered by his attention and smiled at a handsome man like that. Maybe back in the day, she'd have gotten up from her table and written her phone number down on a napkin, or in the palm of his hand. "Call me," she'd say simply. Connie would've initiated a conversation, tried to read between the lines of what he said and what he really meant. Thirty-six years had taught her to stop trying to see into the future or minds. He was good-looking, like a lot of good-looking men. If he'd had anything to say, he'd have said it, and if she'd cared one way or another, she'd have said something too.

"Thanks, Camille," she said to the waitress on her way out the door.

"Oh, Connie," the waitress called out to her. She reached down into the pocket of her apron and pulled out a postcard, then held it out to Connie. "I almost forgot to give you this, girl. She's right on time with it, like clockwork."

Connie quickly read the card, though she knew well enough what it said.

> Ain't no limits less you make them, Little Bird.
>   Love always,
>   Eddie

Connie flipped over the card and glanced at the picture of a Las Vegas hotel with the words MISSING YOU FROM VEGAS spelled out on the marquis.

"Same message?" the waitress asked Connie.

Connie smiled. "Same one, and the only one that matters to Eddie," she said, tucking it into her purse. Connie pulled her wrap tightly around her and headed back to the shop, hoping that maybe today would be the day when those words would finally take root.

Life had been hard on Constance Rodgers. Time had been especially hard on her, forcing her to grow up too fast, and even too much, doing the kinds of things that forced themselves into her thoughts whenever she had too much time on her hands, or too much to drink, or felt sorry for herself. Things that forced her to bury her face and tears into her pillow late at night, because the smell of them woke her up from a sound sleep, threatening to trick her into believing she was still that teenage girl, hustling and cold and hungry. Trying to convince her that she wasn't a grown woman who'd survived and finally moved on with her life, whatever that meant.

Connie had been young and beautiful, living on the streets, doing whatever she needed to survive. Ugly things she'd been taught by men and desperation. Nasty things that left a residue still lingering on her skin and a bitter, gritty taste on her tongue.

Her mother, Charlotte, was her first teacher in the importance of mastering the art of the temporal. Knowing and accepting that nothing lasted forever had been her salvation and her hope, though hope was a word she used sparingly. But this neighborhood, Connie reminded herself while strolling down Welton Street, the Five Points, tugged at her every time she strayed too far away like nothing or no one else ever had. It had raised her and, in its own way, protected her. It taught her how to take care of herself. Like any good parent, the Five Points had seen her hungry and fed her, even if it had been from garbage cans. It had seen her homeless and given her a place to sleep in its dark hallways and alleys. These streets had become her family after Charlotte abandoned Connie and her younger sister as children. Eddie had become her family too, rescuing her from the clutches of homelessness and loving her in a way Charlotte never did.

Constance

Connie was so busy rummaging through her purse looking for her transportation pass that she nearly bumped into John as she came out of her apartment.

"Excuse me." She glanced at him briefly, then hurried down the stairs.

The miss with the pretty lips, he thought to himself, watching her hurry out the front door of the building. So, this is where he could find her? Right down the hall from him.

"Fate and kismet and all that," he muttered to himself. John sat in his car for a moment, admiring the view of Connie from behind as she made her way to the Light Rail. He smiled, then sang, "Bring your sweet lovin' . . . Bring it on home to me . . . Yeah . . ." John laughed, then started up his car and headed for work.

"Next stop, Twenty-third and Welton," the automated voice said over the train intercom. Urban renewal had crept in subtly and the changes that had taken place seemed to Connie to have appeared out of nowhere. This part of Denver seemed to be having an identity crisis going on and was confused as to what its role should be. Was it the hood, or a yuppie, buppie haven? Good or evil? Light or dark? Right or wrong?

A television and radio station now occupied the building that once housed the old community health center, and the Tea Emporium had sprouted up from a vacant lot. The Ensino Cabaret that hosted world-class musicians and singers, and boasted valet parking, sat directly across the street from Justine's Hair and Weave shop, and Edwina's House of Soul Food Cuisine, where she'd lived all those years with Eddie. There was a soulful class erected here now, with the soulful part hanging on for dear life. It reminded Connie of herself, because she wasn't sure where she fit in anymore either. Living and dying a thousand times before turning forty definitely had that kind of effect on a woman. Uncertainty. Confusion. A Peter Pan complex?

Connie rode the commuter train on her way to work and gazed out into the city. She'd been born here. Abandoned here. She'd run away from foster homes back to here. Connie had been homeless here and had little doubt she'd probably grow old here. It was only natural; after all, the Five Points had been the only constant in her life, the only thing she'd ever felt connected to.

Yolanda was the closest thing Connie had had to a best friend since Eddie. More than anything, Connie admired Yolanda because she'd had a dream and made it come true, bringing the Ivory Coast, a boutique specializing in African and African-American art and artifacts, to life. Twice a year, Yolanda had traveled to Africa herself, trading and buying Kinte cloths, batiks, shea butter, and sculptures. She was an agent to one of the local artists, as well as a broker for more established African-American artists throughout the country. Because of Yolanda, the Ivory Coast was fast developing a reputation as one of the more exclusive shops in the country. But what Connie admired most about Yo was that she never let any of that go to her head. Her store might have developed national recognition, but Yo managed to keep the atmosphere intimate and personal. "Bougie is as bougie does," she'd said to Connie. "And I ain't got no kind of patience for bougie, girl. I'm all for keeping it real."

They'd met a year ago at the grocery store of all places. Connie had just started a new job at the electric company working for twelve dollars an hour and benefits, no doubt. As far as she was concerned, she'd finally made it. She was still answering phones, but now she was answering phones for a conglomerate, and that was the difference. Connie was at the checkout counter paying for deodorant and tampons when Yolanda walked up to her, dressed in full African garb, complete with head tie and gold bangle bracelets from wrist to elbow. "Ooooh, girl!" she exclaimed to a shocked

Connie. "That is bad!" Yolanda said, referring to Connie's bracelet. "Girl, where'd you get that?"

Connie reluctantly held out her wrist and let Yolanda admire it more freely. "I, uh . . ."

"This is beautiful. I've never seen anything like it, and girl, let me tell you," she said, smiling, "I have seen some jewelry in my day. But, nothing like this. Where'd you say you got it?"

Connie heard sarcasm where there was none and immediately became offended. She swallowed hard before answering. "I made it," she said, expecting the woman to say something smart, like, "Oh . . .I thought so. It looks homemade."

But Yolanda surprised her. She stepped back, put her hand dramatically over her heart, pressed her lips together, and stared at Connie. "You're an artist? Oh, I should've known. Of course you are." What the hell did she mean by that? Connie glared at the woman. The word "artist" or the phrase "I make my own jewelry because I'm too cheap to buy that shit they sell in the malls" was not tattooed on her forehead the last time she checked.

"Do you have other pieces? I'm sure you do."

"That'll be six ninety-five, please," the cashier said impatiently to Connie. Connie hurried and paid the cashier, anxious to get away from this lunatic, looking like Mother Africa.

"Maybe you could get me one of your catalogs? Or do you have a Web site?"

Connie grabbed her bag and headed for the door. This woman was getting on her nerves, and if girlfriend wasn't careful, she was coming dangerously close to getting cussed out.

"Forgive me," Yolanda said, following her. "I neglected to introduce myself."

"That's not necessary," Connie said shortly.

"My name is Yolanda. Yolanda Edwards."

"That's nice," Connie said shortly, continuing in the direction of her car.

"I own a shop over on Twelfth and Broadway, and . . ." Finally, it wasn't Connie who lost it but Yolanda. "Sistah! Will you please stop and let me talk to you?"

Connie stopped, turned abruptly, and glared at Yolanda. "Did it ever occur to you that I don't want you talking to me . . . sistah?"

Yolanda sighed. "Look," she said, trying to calm what could easily turn into a volatile situation. "I'm just admiring your work. It's an extraordinary piece."

"It's not a big deal."

"Of course it is," Yolanda said, surprised by Connie's obvious frustration. "It's a beautiful piece of art, and I'd like to know if you have more? Do you ever sell on consignment?"

"I don't sell . . . period. I made it because . . . well . . . it's personal. I make it for me."

Yolanda smiled. "I see. So, you don't have a catalog?"

"No."

"No Web site either, I suppose?"

"I just make the stuff because I—"

"You're an artist."

"I ought to knock you in the mouth for that!"

"For heaven's sake, why?" Yolanda asked, astonished.

"Because I work at the electric company!" Connie snapped, feeling stupid as soon as she'd said it. Yolanda laughed, offending Connie even more. "What the hell are you laughing at?"

"You. Who else is standing here looking dumb?"

Connie took a step toward Yolanda and balled up her fist. "Oooh! If we weren't out here . . ."

"Girl, you couldn't give me a proper beat-down even if your life depended on it, so back it up . . . sistah."

"I wouldn't waste time with a beat-down," Connie said matter-of-factly. "I'd just cut you." With that, she turned quickly and headed toward her car. She was in no mood for this idiot.

Yolanda hurried to catch up with her. "You could make a lot of money," she said breathlessly.

"Leave me alone."

"Your work is incredible, girl. Why do you have to be so negative?"

Connie stopped. "Negative? Your crazy ass is stalking me, and I'm negative?"

Yolanda laughed. "You wish I was stalking you, but sistergirl, you are not my type. I like my women tall, dark, and handsome . . . with big dicks!" Connie stared at Yolanda, astonished; then, without meaning to, she laughed. "I'm telling you, sistah, if this one piece is any example . . . Look." Yolanda reached into her purse and pulled out a business card. "The name of my shop is the Ivory Coast. Come in and see it. Bring some of your jewelry, and I guarantee it'll sell."

Connie had kept Yolanda's business card on her coffee table, looking at it for weeks before finally taking her up on her offer. She dropped off a bracelet and threatened to set the store on fire should Yolanda try to steal it. A week later, Yolanda called and told Connie to come pick up her money. From then on, the two were business partners. Connie worked at the electricity company all of six months before making up her mind that she hated it. During that time, her jewelry had been selling like crazy at the Coast, and Connie even found herself getting orders for pieces. Working a full-time job, and trying to keep up with demand, proved to be more trouble than Connie cared to deal with. So she quit the electric company and went to work full-time with Yolanda, who had a workshop in back of her store, so Connie could make her jewelry there instead of messing up her kitchen doing it. It was a match made in heaven.

"Hey, girl," Yolanda sang out to Connie, who was just coming into the store.

"Hey. Sorry I'm late. I missed my train and had to wait forever for the next one."

"No problem. Guess what? Ethel Simpson called. She's writing an article for the *Spectrum* and wants to know if she can interview us." Yolanda beamed.

"You serious?"

"Dead. Look at my face. Don't I look serious? And elated? And tickled pink?" Connie curled up her lip. "Okay, so I'm too dark to be pink, but you know what I'm saying?"

"I know, Yo. Sounds wonderful. I'm happy for you, girl."

"For us, Connie. She wants to talk to both of us."

"Why? The Ivory Coast is your baby. Not mine. I'm just the hired help. Remember?"

"The hired help who's got people breaking down the door to get some of that jewelry of yours."

"Yeah, I don't understand it either."

"Well, as long as it sells, I don't have to understand it. Anyway, she'll be here at four, with a photographer."

"A photographer?" Connie frowned.

"Yes. A photographer. Gonna get a photo of that pretty face of yours," Yolanda said, pinching Connie's cheek.

"I don't want my picture in the paper."

"Camera shyness is not cute, Connie."

"I'm serious, Yo. I really don't want my picture in the paper."

"Why on earth not?"

"Let them take yours. I'd rather not do the photo shoot. Okay?"

Yolanda stared at Connie, wondering how she could be so guarded about the most inconsequential things. It was all Yolanda could do to keep from jumping over the counter and screaming into Connie's ear, "Lighten up, girl!" But Connie wore her defensiveness like armor, and Yolanda doubted seriously she'd have gotten through to the woman anyway.

"Oh. I almost forgot. Reesy called. She said to call her when you got in."

Connie grimaced. "Did she say what she wanted?"

"Nope. Just said for you to call her," Yolanda lied.

Connie dialed the number, and Reesy answered quickly and entirely too perky for Connie's taste. "Hey, sis! How are you?"

"Fine, Reese. What's up?"

"What. No small talk this morning?" Reesy asked sarcastically.

"Nope."

"Not even a little bit of chitchat? How are you this fine day, Reesy? How are Justin and the kids, Reesy? You feeling all right, Reesy?"

"Reesy. I just got in and I need to get to work," Connie said impatiently. "What's up?"

"Jade's got a dance recital Saturday at one. Can you come? I'll pick you up."

"I've got to work."

"I'm sure Yolanda will give you a few hours off, Connie. C'mon. Don't do this. She really wants you to come. Girlfriend's going to tap a solo." Reesy laughed.

"Really? How exciting," Connie said teasingly.

"You know you want to come, so stop playing."

"No, really, girl, it sounds really nice, but I've got to work Saturday."

"Connie, she specifically asked me to call Aunt Connie and beg her to come. So I'm begging, sis. Please?"

Connie sighed. "You know begging on behalf of that girl is my downfall every time."

Reesy laughed. "I know. That's why I threw that little ditty in there."

"Well . . . what time is it going to be?"

"One o'clock to three. I can have you back at work no later than three-twenty. Yolanda will hardly know you're gone."

"I'll have to ask Yo if it's all right."

"I already did, and she said yes."

"Reesy!" Connie glared at Yolanda, standing at the end of the counter and pretending not to be eavesdropping.

"I'll pick you up from the shop at twelve forty-five. Cool?"

"I guess it's going to have to be."

"Love you! Smooches!"

Connie knew getting pissed off at Reesy was a moot point. The woman had nerves of steel and was oblivious to snide comments, lip smacking, eye rolling, cuss words, or anything else Connie had in her arsenal to let her sister know she'd crossed the line by going behind her back to finagle time off from her boss. But the bottom line was, Saturday afternoon she'd be sitting in the front row of her niece's tap dance performance, when she'd planned on getting a pedicure on her lunch break—spending money she didn't have—and daydreaming about that trip to Jamaica she'd promised herself. Well, so much for planning ahead. Besides, she hadn't seen a good tap dance performance by an outta-sight six-year-old in ages.

Sistah, Sistah

Seven years ago, Reesy had suddenly reappeared before Connie's eyes as if by magic. The romance of their reunion had tattooed itself onto her heart as one of the sweetest episodes of her life. Seventeen long years apart hadn't been enough to dull the memories they held of each other. From time to time Connie found herself replaying that day over again in her mind, nearly drowning in waves of emotions welling up inside her, much like they had then.

Connie stood frozen in the doorway of her apartment, holding her breath, afraid that the sight of Reesy's honey-gold, heart-shaped face would disappear if she so much as blinked. Reesy had grown up into a delicious woman, but that little eight-year-old girl was still there, hidden behind familiar almond-shaped eyes that filled with tears the moment she saw Connie.

"It is you. Isn't it?"

Connie smiled broadly behind tears of her own. "It's me . . . if it's you." She shuddered.

Reesy slowly reached out and touched Connie's cheek, remembering how pretty she'd always thought her sister was, and relishing how pretty she still was, even after all this time. They kissed gently, careful to avoid any sudden movement that might shake them awake, then stared into each other's eyes, saying absolutely nothing, because words were unnecessary. The two women embraced, holding on tight to each other, trying to recover the years they'd lost, heartbroken in the knowledge that they probably never would.

"How'd you find me?" Connie asked, her voice cracking.

Reesy sniffed, then laughed. "In the phone book."

All Connie cared about was that Reesy was okay, and that she'd been taken care of and loved and untaught all the things Charlotte had spent so much energy teaching them when they were children. Reesy's life growing up was as different from Connie's as it could've been. The people who'd adopted her, the Turners, had tried for years to have children of their own before finally choosing to adopt. They'd intended to adopt an infant, but decided to consider an older child when they were told how many older African-American children needed homes. And so they agreed to meet some of these children, and they fell instantly in love with Reesy.

"I've been so blessed, Connie," Reesy said, smiling. "Mom and Dad have been incredible to me, and from day one, I belonged to them, and them to me."

"That's wonderful, Reese." Connie beamed. Maybe God was good for something after all, she thought. Maybe he did pay attention to her prayers begging him to make sure Reesy was okay.

Reesy had grown up with birthday parties and family vacations. She'd gone to high school, proms, graduations, and even college, before dropping out in her sophomore year to become a full-time wife and mother.

"Justin and I met in the eleventh grade. After graduation he went to Arizona State, and I stayed here and eventually went to CU. My parents were furious when we told them we were getting married." She laughed. "And they absolutely lost their damn minds when we told them we had to get married because I was pregnant."

"You've got kids?" Connie gasped.

"I've got two." Reesy beamed. "Two beautiful, incredible boys."

"I've got nephews?"

"Yep," Reesy smiled. "Very handsome nephews. Alex, the oldest, is four, and J. J. is three."

"I'm so happy for you, Reese. I can still call you Reesy, can't I, Miss Married Lady? Or should I address you more formally now?" Connie teased.

"If you call me Clarice, I'll cuss you out!" Reesy warned.

"So what does everybody else call you?"

"I'm Momma to my boys, and Reesy to absolutely everybody who loves and cares for me. I'm only Clarice to people who don't know any better. Clarice." She frowned. "That's an old woman's name. I've always hated it."

"I remember . . . Clarice." Connie laughed.

Reesy glared at her sister. "All right . . . Constance. Don't start!"

"Brat! Some things never change." she said, pinching Reesy on the arm.

Reesy's eyes grew wide in astonishment. She gasped. "I don't believe you did that."

"Oh . . . I'm sorry, Reesy. I just—" Connie didn't know what to say. She'd been catapulted back in time, forgetting all about the fact that her little sister was a grown woman now with kids of her own, and much too sophisticated for pinches.

Then Reesy surprised Connie, giving the all-too-familiar response. "Big butt!"

The two stared at each other, then fell over laughing hysterically.

Reesy listened intently as Connie painted a very broad picture of her past.

"Most of the time, I just remember being scared. But I couldn't let on that I was. Out on the streets you had to be tough, or at least look tough, and act tough. Eventually, you might even convince yourself that you really were . . . tough."

"Oh . . . Connie," Reesy whispered. "I'm so . . . oh, sweetie." She reached out and held Connie in her arms. "I'm so sorry." She sobbed.

Connie kissed Reesy's cheek. "It's cool, Reese. Now it's cool, because I don't have to live like that anymore."

"You shouldn't have had to live like that at all."

"Girl if I'd had my way, I wouldn't have."

"You were a kid, Connie, and I just hate thinking about you being out there, all alone."

"Yeah, but I had help. My friend, Eddie—she's the one who got me off the streets. She's wonderful, and kind of adopted me in her own way."

"I'd like to meet her."

"I'd love for you to meet her too, but Eddie retired and moved to Vegas. I haven't seen her in years, but she writes. She always writes."

"I'm glad you had somebody."

"Me too. And now I'm glad I have you."

Reesy's cell phone rang. "Hello?" she asked into the receiver. "Hi, baby. Yeah . . . I'm at Connie's. Yes! It is her." She smiled at her sister. "Not yet, but I will. Okay. Love you too." Reesy hung up.

"You will what?" Connie asked suspiciously.

"Justin and the kids really want to meet you. Please come over Saturday? Justin's going to barbecue and I'll make a cake and—"

"Reesy—"

"I want you to meet my family, Connie. I want them to meet my sister. And don't tell me you're busy, sis. That's totally unacceptable."

"Your family sounds great."

"They are great, and I want my great family to meet my great sister," Reesy said proudly. "You're my dream come true, Connie. Do you have any idea how long I've prayed to find you?"

"Seventeen years?"

"Seventeen freaking years! And I'm so elated that I want the whole world to know who my sister is."

"A lot's happened."

"Yeah . . . so? We've got the rest of our lives to catch up. I say we start with a barbecue."

Years ago, they'd both had Charlotte in common, but after she left, Connie and Reesy had both been shaped by histories completely opposite to the other's, and eventually, it shone through in their personalities. Reesy had been raised to have ideals, and Connie had always found that she could never afford such luxuries. Reesy had expectations, and Connie knew better than to expect much of anything. The Turners had even taught their daughter that she deserved nothing but the best life had to offer. Connie had always found it best to take what she could get and make the most of it.

Despite her best efforts, Connie's familiar shield of defensiveness rose up between her and her sister, putting a wedge between them. Reesy seemed determined to make it her mission in life to tear it down. It wasn't intentional, but it was instinctive. Connie was conditioned to keep her distance from people. It had been a skill that saved her life on more than one occasion. She listened to what people said with their mouths, saw what they really meant in their eyes, and heard what they tried not to say in the tones of their voices.

Reesy talked a lot, and she talked fast, saying exactly what was on her mind. A dangerous trait as far as Connie was concerned. People who talked too much often neglected to listen to themselves and, without meaning to, sometimes said things they shouldn't have. So, Reesy talked, Connie listened without responding on cue, and Reesy usually took it personally.

Reesy's phone calls caught up with Connie eventually. She'd left numerous messages, but as usual, her sister hadn't deemed any of them important enough to return.

"You've been avoiding me, Connie. And don't bother trying to deny it. I know."

Connie sighed. "I haven't been avoiding you. I've just been busy."

"Doing what?"

"Working," Connie said, trying not to sound sarcastic.

"And what else?"

"There you go again. Being nosy."

"And there you go again, trying to keep me out of your life."

Connie sighed. "Why are you doing this?"

"What?"

"If I had something to talk about, Reesy, I'd talk about it."

"No, you wouldn't."

"Yes, I would."

"No, you wouldn't, because you'd rather keep everything locked up inside you instead of talking to me or anyone else about it."

"That's my prerogative."

"You know, you really take the cake, Connie. Why can't you let me in? Why can't you trust me?"

Because you're a nosy, self-righteous know-it-all, that's why. Connie thought it, but she didn't say it. "I'm just not like that, Reese. I know that might be what you're used to, but . . ."

"We used to be close, Connie," Reesy whispered. "Closer than close."

"We were kids."

"We were sisters, and we still are."

"I'm doing the best I can, Reesy. I really am."

"So am I."

"I just need some time, sis."

"To get used to having somebody who cares about you?"

"I'm fine, Reese. Really. I've got to go, sis. I'll call you later," Connie said, anxious to hang up the phone.

"I'll call you first, Connie. I always do."

Of course she'd lied and Reesy, no doubt, saw right through it. Connie hadn't been all right since she'd peed on the stick and stared down at the plus sign beaming back at her. She was pregnant— again. But this time was different. This time, she was thirty years old, and the thought of having a child lingered on her longer than it had any of the other times. This time, she was actually considering having it.

Shame. Embarrassment. Confusion. Second thoughts. Every emotion known to desperate, single pregnant women rose up inside her and emanated from Connie's flesh like a vapor she was sure Reesy could smell. "You're what?" Reesy screeched. Connie had stopped by Reesy's, at a time she knew Justin wouldn't be home. The last thing she needed was a double team.

"Pregnant, Reesy. What part of that word are you having a problem with?" Connie said, through clenched teeth.

Judgment shot out of Reesy's eyes like darts, and Connie could've cut out her own tongue for telling the woman this. "I see. So," Reesy said, clearing her throat, "what are you planning on doing about this?"

"What do you mean, what am I planning on doing about this?"

Reesy rolled her eyes. "Are you going to keep it?"

Connie sat across from her sister, toying with the strap of her purse. "I'm not sure."

"Who's the father, Connie?" Reesy blurted out. Reesy had lost track of the men in her sister's life. Connie spewed out a different name every time she and Reesy talked, so she wouldn't be the least bit surprised if the woman didn't know.

"The father?" Connie asked, staring at her sister. "What's that got to do with anything?"

"Does that mean you don't know?"

"I know who the damn father is, Reesy."

"Then who?"

Connie was speechless. She suspected she knew, but no, she wasn't certain at all.

"You don't have a clue. Do you?" Reesy said arrogantly.

"The father isn't the issue here," Connie said coldly. "I'm the one having this baby. Not the damn father."

"Is that what you're planning on doing? Having this baby?"

Connie stared at her sister, offended at the contempt she saw behind her eyes. "You act like you don't think I should. Is that what you're trying not to imply?"

"I didn't say that," Reesy said defensively.

"Then what are you saying? Come on out with it, Reesy."

"I just don't think you've been very responsible, that's all," Reesy said smugly.

Connie took a deep breath, hoping it would counteract the anger welling up inside her. "It was an accident, Clarice. Accidents happen."

Reesy leaned forward, rested her elbows on her knees, and stared Connie in the eyes. "And how many 'accidents' have you had over the years, Constance? From the expression on your face, I'm sure this isn't the first one."

Connie quickly grabbed her purse, then stormed out the room to the front door. "Obviously, coming here was an accident too. I can do without that judgmental attitude of yours right now, sis."

Reesy followed behind her. No, she didn't need to say it, but . . . yes. She needed to finally get it off her chest and just say it, because without even trying, Connie had it coming. "I might be judgmental, but at least I'm not out sleeping with everybody who so much as breathes on me. And you're surprised this happened? What the hell do you expect, Connie? How irresponsible can you be? Ever heard of birth control or how about condoms? Ever heard of keeping, and this is just a concept, your damn legs closed?"

"Fuck you!"

"Kiss my ass!"

Connie slammed the door shut behind her.

———

She'd wanted to stop making excuses, and blaming everybody else, and using abortions as alternative forms of birth control. For probably the first time in her life, she'd made the decision to finally be a woman and take responsibility for her actions. Connie decided against an abortion, which had been too convenient for her in the past. Having that child was something she could do. It was something she had to do. She'd watched Reesy with her children and envied her for more reasons than she'd ever be comfortable admitting. Connie had never let herself entertain the idea of her own children, but it didn't mean she never wanted any. She just never figured she'd have them. Maybe the child she was carrying would put her a step closer to that kind of reality, and maybe it was time for her to make someone else the center of her universe for a change, instead of letting the cosmos revolve around just her. Eventually, Connie somehow managed to convince herself that motherhood was something she looked forward to, even savored. Then there were the other times, when the idea of raising a child scared the hell out of her.

Of course, Reesy came rushing in once she accepted the fact that Connie was planning on keeping the baby, carrying armloads of reassurance Connie embraced reluctantly. She bought books on pregnancy and how to raise children, encouraged Connie to spend more time with her nephews, and even went so far as to buy clothes and diapers.

"Isn't this adorable?" Reesy beamed, holding up a small yellow sleeping gown.

"Is the baby really going to need all this stuff, Reese?" Connie asked, sorting through the bags Reesy had strewn on Connie's bed.

"Not really." She smiled. "But it's your first baby, Connie. Everybody always buys too much for the first one and it's perfectly acceptable. As a matter of fact, it's tradition."

Reesy went with her on visits to the doctor and even signed Connie up for Lamaze classes, which she promised to take with her. But ultimately Connie's apprehensions broke through the barriers of all her feigned securities and good intentions and stampeded all over them like a herd of wild horses. This was a child, not a hamster. And she couldn't just put it away when she was tired of playing with it. She couldn't forget to feed it, and she couldn't leave it alone in the cage while she was out at the club until the wee hours of the morning partying and shaking her groove thing all over some fool who hardly deserved it. She knew absolutely nothing about raising a child, and Connie hated to admit it, especially to herself; she wasn't sure she wanted to know.

The baby moving around inside her would need things from her she couldn't find in a book or in a mall. Connie had always been Connie's first priority, out of necessity, not conceit. She'd been taught to do whatever it took to take care of herself no matter the sacrifices or risks. That's what she knew. It's all she knew, and to think she could do the same for a child was unfathomable. As much as she wanted to believe she could be the kind of mother Reesy was, or even the kind of mother Edwina had been to her, Connie knew better. The truth was, she was probably more like Charlotte than she wanted to be, and a baby deserved so much better than that.

When Jade was born, Connie held her in her arms, anticipating the sensation of that innate mother instinct, rising up inside her like lava. The small, brown package she held in her arms slept quietly, completely unaware of the danger she was in, trusting that her mother wouldn't let her fall, or go hungry, or get cold. Unfortunately for Connie, Jade didn't come with instructions or a warranty. Maybe if she had, Connie would've kept her. But it wasn't as if she could get a new one if she happened to accidentally break the one she had. Babies, little girls, were fragile, and at that time in her life, Connie feared she was capable of hurting the most precious thing she'd ever seen. Jade had been like something too exquisite and too expensive for her to be trusted with. The tiny child sleeping in her arms scared her more than anything or anybody Connie had ever faced, and she knew in a moment that she had no business trying to be anybody's momma.

It hadn't been an easy decision, but she had nothing to offer her child, and every time she looked in the mirror she saw her own sorry-ass excuse for a mother, living in a one-room apartment, making next to no money, and completely screwed up in the head. The three of them discussed it shortly before Jade was born, and Reesy and Justin agreed to take the baby, just until Connie got herself together. But right before their eyes, the baby had grown into her lovely, little brown self, and into a family Connie could never give her. How could she deny Jade of that? So, she never did, choosing instead to step back into the role of aunt. Just close enough, but never close enough again.

Despite their differences, Connie had to admit, Reesy made a beautiful mother. Reesy was responsible and sensible. She was grounded and her family meant the world to her. She was the epitome of the stuff mommas and wives were made of. Reesy cornrowed hair, baked, actively participated in the PTA. Reesy knew how to listen intently when her man complained about the injustices of his job, without rolling even one of her eyes, or huffing impatiently from boredom. She knew that whoopings weren't always necessary and that sometimes a thing called "time out" sufficed just fine. Reesy smelled like homemade cookies and lilacs and expensive perfection.

Connie, on the other hand, smelled like Earl, garbage, and Zovirax. She could roll a joint with the best of them, had mastered the art of freak dancing, could down half a forty-ounce before coming up for air, and fuck a marathon if she had to. No. Definitely not the kind of stuff mommas were made of.

Thinking back, Connie honestly believed she'd done the right thing. Jade was a happy, well-adjusted six-year-old and Connie was her favorite aunt in the whole wide world. Jade told her that each and every time the two saw each other.

The commuter train slowly made its way to Fifteenth and Broadway. Connie had promised to have a necklace finished today for a customer and needed to get in early to get it ready. Reesy would be picking her up for Jade's recital later that day. Jade had been prancing around in tights and tap shoes for the last three months. Before that it had been ballet shoes and a tutu.

Connie got off at the next stop, a block away from the store. Yolanda wouldn't be in until at least ten, which was fine for Connie. She welcomed the quiet sometimes, especially when she was working. Creativity flowed like a waterfall in quiet.

How Do You Do?

John huffed and puffed as he slowly walked up the three flights of stairs that led to his apartment. *These people must be part fish,* he thought. How else could they survive in a place with no air? He'd been in Denver three months and still hadn't gotten used to this altitude. His shoulders and back ached from lifting all that cardboard, and all John had been able to think about driving home was jumping into a hot shower, drinking a cold beer, catching the last half of the double header on television, and maybe ordering a pizza. As tired as he was, though, he didn't mind it. Over the years, he'd become addicted to this kind of tired. Hard work had a way of keeping everything he didn't want to think about at bay, pumped his heart hard in his chest, and squeezed out toxins through his pores. Some people called that sweat. He preferred to call it purging.

John slid his key into the lock on his door, then turned just in time to see a woman run up the stairs, stop in front of her apartment, and begin rummaging through her purse. He smiled when he saw her; the woman with the pretty mouth and creamy thighs.

"Where are my damn . . . shiii . . . ," she mumbled, oblivious to him. "C'mon, c'mon! Why now? Why the hell—" She tilted her large bag from side to side, dancing like she was stepping on a pit of hot coals.

John watched her work up to one of those dances he'd seen women do in church when the Holy Ghost felt a little too good to them. Her hips swayed from side to side as she paced back and forth, hesitating momentarily and pressing her knees together. She stopped, then braced herself against the door, closed her eyes and shook her head back and forth.

"Okay, okay," she whispered. Gradually, she took her hand off the door and slowly began sifting through her purse again, obviously frustrated that she couldn't find whatever it was she was looking for. "Did I leave them . . . no. I didn't even take them . . . oh, oh," she said, bracing herself against the wall. "This is not . . . good, Connie. Not . . ."

All of a sudden, it dawned on him what was going on, and John posed the question, "You got to pee?"

The woman glared at him, then pressed her lips together and reluctantly whispered, "Yes."

He grinned, then swung open the door to his apartment. "C'mon," he said, leaning his head in the direction of his apartment.

She stared at him as if he were out of his mind. What made this fool think she'd trust him enough to just walk into his apartment and use his bathroom? But she quickly composed herself, rushed inside John's place, grabbed the keys from his hands, then slammed and locked his front door behind her.

"I'll wait here," he shouted through the locked door. He'd hardly known what hit him.

On her way out, Connie surveyed his apartment. She'd seen him before, a couple of times, as a matter of fact. She peeked into the bedroom, not at all surprised that there was no bed in it. A pile of dirty clothes lay in one corner, and an open duffel bag with more clothes in it was in the other. His bed, or, rather, two mattresses stacked on top of each other, lay in the middle of the living room, where this man obviously spent the majority of his time. Everything was within an arm's reach of everything else; the television, the stereo, a stack of CDs, an ashtray, and an empty beer bottle. Boyfriend definitely preferred to keep things simple, she concluded. Connie looked up at a seductive Pam Grier snarling at her from a poster he'd taped to the wall. Pam, Pam's breasts, and Pam's 1970s Afro seemed to threaten Connie to get out of Pam's man's apartment or suffer her mighty *Sheba, Baby* wrath. Amen.

Connie opened the door and handed John's keys back to him. "Thanks."

"Anytime."

She walked down the hall to her apartment, casually reached into her coat pocket, and found the keys to her apartment she'd been looking for. Connie shook her head, then looked down the hall in time to see John staring at her before disappearing into his apartment.

Cassandra Wilson's rich, sultry voice filled Connie's apartment, inspiring designs she sketched of new pieces she'd been toying around with. Funny how the two went together, she thought, music and inspiration. Cassandra inspired rich and sultry, while Lil' Kim, for instance, inspired something else altogether. Connie laughed.

Images of Mr. Good-looking down the hall kept invading her thoughts in increments of split seconds. That's all she'd allow them at any one time, but they were persistent and insisted on coming back again and again. That man knew full well how fine he was, she concluded. The epitome of tall, dark, and handsome, he could've easily been the poster child for the Drop-Dead-Gorgeous Brothas Club of America if there were such a thing. Milk-chocolate brown, with rich, dark eyes and lips made for sucking on. A tall man, he had to be at least six two, maybe six three. Probably one of those country-fed boys from down South, who grew up on grits and greens and pig feet and had no idea what a bowl of cereal even looked like. The South bred thick men. Men with some bulk to them that never looked anything like fat. But instead looked like muscles, bulging and banging all over the place, screaming for women to stand up and take notice, or else. Damn, she loved muscles and tight behinds, teasing from behind baggy denim. If she remembered correctly, his shoulders were so broad, he had to turn sideways to get through the doorway of his apartment. Connie smiled, then took a sip of her Merlot. He had what were commonly referred to as "penetrating eyes." The kind of eyes that convinced a woman to say yes when the word "no" dangled on the tip of her tongue.

When's the last time a man had this kind of effect on her? she wondered. Not in ages, she concluded. Not that that was a bad thing, because the last man who'd gotten her all worked up like this, Jamil Henderson, nearly got his face slashed to pieces with a chisel. So yes. Brotha had better keep his distance . . . or else.

But the last date she'd been on had been with Yolanda's brother's golf buddy, Carl. Connie rolled her eyes in disgust. That had been months ago, but the memory was still fresh enough to make her stomach turn.

"Girl, he's fine," Yolanda insisted. "He's got his master's degree and a good job, and he makes damn good money."

Carl stood an inch taller than Connie. If she'd worn stockings that night, she'd have probably towered over the man. She could've handled the fact that he was short, but what got on her nerves was the incessant talking he did about himself and all the complaining he did about "these Denver women who didn't know what the hell they wanted from a black man." Yeah. She'd slept with him, that same night, as a matter of fact. She'd been just that horny and desperate. Before Carl came along, Connie had gone cold turkey on the sex thing after she'd broken up with Jamil, her intended chisel victim. Eight months without some sex was entirely too long, and that night, Carl transformed into a short walking complaining-too-much penis she'd hoped would provide her some relief to take the edge off. But just as she'd suspected, he'd been too wrapped up in himself to even think about accommodating a little foreplay, and too preoccupied to care one way or another about her orgasm, or lack thereof.

"I'll call you," he had the nerve to say on his way out the door. Much to her relief, he never did.

Now, Mr. Good-looking down the hall had been the first man to pique her interest in a long time. But she had him all figured out, just by looking at him. He knew he had it going on and no doubt wallowed in it. She'd known men like him her whole life. Pretty men, committed to the game—playa's, dogging, using, and abusing the hearts, minds, and bodies of unsuspecting women. Good thing she'd never been like any of those women. She knew better than to put all her faith into men like him. She also knew better than to waste all of her energy trying to change him into something else. Connie made jewelry, not men. Besides, the memory of Carl had reminded her that she'd grown tired of one-night stands and convenient sex. She'd tasted the flavor of making love with Jamil. Not enough to take it for granted, but enough for her to know that intimacy was so vastly different from fucking, and so much sweeter.

Ultimately, Jamil had ended up being a worthless piece of trash and waste of good oxygen, but before she saw him for what he really was, she'd loved him and she'd made love to him. Connie hadn't been a virgin in years, but Jamil was her first lover, and yes, she relished the idea of making love again. Someday.

Over the years, memories of men melted into one another. Faces blurred, circumstances became questionable, and sex . . . Sex for Connie had nothing to do with passion or love. An act as routine as breathing and, inasmuch, taken for granted. It had always been a means to an end. A tool, sometimes a weapon, from which none of the things she craved most would ever derive. Love. Acceptance. Reassurance. All of the above. Or none of them. Instead, what she ended up with more times than not was rejection, pain, and eventually an incurable STD from men who had all been toxic one way or another. Leaving remnants of their own issues inside her every time they had an orgasm, and she'd soaked it all up like a thirsty sponge until she'd become saturated in the insecurities, lies, desperation, unplanned pregnancies . . . herpes.

One day a knight surprised her and came riding in on the white horse like knights tend to do, sweeping her off her feet into his strong arms, holding her close to him, keeping all the dragons at bay. Connie truly believed it would be Jamil who'd change her life forever. And, in retrospect, she figured he'd done that. Just not in the way she'd hoped.

Beautiful Jamil, whose name meant "handsome" in Swahili. He'd sworn he'd been born with that name, but Connie had heard his real name was Byron. Not that it mattered. He could've called himself Geronimo and she'd have embraced it, like she'd worked up the courage to embrace him and the concept of him. He'd definitely been handsome. Tall and ebony-skinned, with locks dancing on the tops of his shoulders, and full, soft lips that had mastered the art of transforming lies into poetic justice. Jamil the artist, the painter, the sculptor, the activist, speaking out on the unity of the brotherhood and the beauty of everything black, who'd forgiven her transgressions and transgressors and taught her the beauty of who she was in creation and as the creator.

"Baby," he spoke softly into her ear, his warm breath lighting on her shoulder like butterflies. "You've got a natural eye and talent for creating," he said about her jewelry. Connie would have never pursued her interest in jewelry making if it hadn't been for him. He showed her how to solder and polish and shape and bend and transform the ugly into something to be cherished. "Don't stifle it, Connie. Let it come through, and see if you don't discover your true, beautiful self in the process, sweetheart." He'd encouraged her and eventually even had the nerve to whisper "I love you" in her ear, convincing her he'd actually meant it.

Without even realizing it, Connie had been waiting for him her whole life, and when he opened his arms to welcome her, reluctantly she dropped her defenses, put away her shield, and allowed him closer than any man had ever been, giving him carte blanche access to her soul. Gradually, she allowed herself to trust him, and she stepped out from behind the shadows of who she'd been her whole life into who she'd dreamed of being, because he'd encouraged her to.

"It's time, to be set free, love," he whispered. "You can't be free if you don't come out of hiding. I'm here for you, Connie. Trust me."

Jamil opened her eyes to see that all that filth she'd been raised in didn't have to belong to her. She had the power to discard it, throw it away, and start all over from scratch and transform herself into something beautiful too; she could be born again and be clean and even happy. "It's all right to believe in something, baby. To have faith . . . even hope for the future." He'd given her the confidence she'd never had, daring her to be more than what she was. He'd given her herpes, then rode off into the sunset, hoping to never be heard from again.

A year later, she did see him again, sitting with a group of people at a coffee shop. "You dirty bastard!" she shouted. "Do you know what you did to me?"

He looked around nervously to his friends, then back at her. "I'm sorry, Connie. I never meant to hurt you."

Sorry. Connie shook her head in disbelief. Sorry had always been the most pitiful word in the English language, as far as she was concerned. Too many people hid behind it, buried their sins under it, and used it as an excuse for all the ridiculous notions that popped into their heads to justify their lack of consideration. Sorry was the magic word, like "abracadabra," that was supposed to make all the right things appear out of thin air. But sorry didn't cure herpes or cancer or child abuse or even broken hearts.

She'd loved Jamil, but at that moment she glared at him, hoping to singe his flesh with the loathing she shot from her eyes. Connie pulled out the chisel she carried in her purse for protection and waved it in his direction. She'd wanted to do this for a long time. Slash him to pieces, knowing it would make her feel better. Connie had wished for this day so hard, the universe had had no choice but to bring it to life, and here she stood, salivating at the thought of scarring him, the way he'd scarred her.

"Connie!" Jamil jumped back, startled.

Connie walked slowly toward him. Jamil had made the mistake of leaving her with too much time, wallowing in the same kind of irony that erupted and festered on her genitals. How many men had she fucked; strangers, unclean and unsavory? Men who'd never given a damn about her. Men she'd let pass through her like she'd been nothing more than air. Those were the kinds of men who left women with things like shame, regrets . . . herpes. Not men like Jamil. He was hope and love and promises. He sang her love songs and made love to her, patiently waiting for her to come, even if it took all night. So, yeah . . . she had to cut him.

"You owe me, Jamil," she growled. "You owe me this." Connie waived the chisel in his direction, daring him to try and get past her.

"I . . . I understand, Connie," he said nervously. "I understand how you must feel. I felt the same way when I found out."

He had no idea, she thought. How could he? Jamil had been a whole new world for her. He'd been a fresh beginning and the core of the family she'd have one day. She'd seen him with Jade, and how good he'd been with her, and Connie knew that he'd be a wonderful father and husband. And he'd baptize her and make her clean and new all over again. Jamil washed away every face that grunted unsympathetically above her, only to leave her filthier than all of them put together.

Connie backed him into the corner, then, just as she lashed out at him, one of his friends grabbed her from behind and took the chisel out of her hands. "Damn, man," he said, staring at Jamil, who stood trembling against the wall. "What the hell did you do to her?"

Connie snatched her arm away from the man, cursed Jamil, spit in his face, then left his filthy, lying ass standing there knowing good and well he'd been a terrible figment of her imagination. For his sake, she thought, he'd better hope she doesn't see him again.

She filled her glass again, then admired her latest design. Jamil used to tell her that the lines of her drawings flowed like rhythms. "There's freedom in your work, love. If you'd stop being afraid, you could enjoy some of that in your life." In retrospect sometimes, she concluded, he hadn't been all bad, and he hadn't been all good. That's how most people were, not necessarily good or bad. Just people being people, and all of them had demons in some form or other. Connie wondered what demons Mr. Good-looking down the hall might be harboring. Men like him had plenty. She gulped down the last of her wine, closed her drawing pad, turned off the light, then stretched out on the couch and fell asleep to the sound of Cassandra's singing.

Come on, Dance, Pretty Baby

Connie sat at the table, nursing a vodka Collins. Yolanda bounced up and down in the seat next to her, snapping her fingers, talking about everybody that passed by them.

"No, she didn't come in here with that on. Somebody should've loved that girl enough to tell her, she's too fat to be wearing spandex. Girl, did you get a look at that brotha? Damn! I thought I saw a ring on his finger. Did you see a ring on his finger?"

Connie spent most of the evening shrugging her indifference and drinking too much. She'd only come to the club because Yolanda nearly cried at the thought of coming by herself. The woman pleaded to Connie to come with her just this one time, and she swore she'd never ask her again. Of course, she'd said that the last time.

Connie stared out onto the dance floor, at the swaying bodies huddled together beneath the large silver disco ball spinning overhead. Time stood still in places like this. Connie had practically been raised in nightclubs. Shay had taught her how to get into the twenty-one-and-older clubs when she was fourteen. Back then it had been easy. Innocent eyes and cleavage was all it took to get past bouncers in those days. Connie had taken advantage of her looks back then. Or had they taken advantage of her? She'd come to places like this, sat on laps, sucked down drinks, compliments, and promises of what some old fool could do for her, then danced herself into a frenzy, nearly passing out from exhaustion. Even that had been a way to survive, she concluded. Back in those days, she had no place to really go home to. So all the drinking and dancing had been her way of numbing herself for what she knew would come later in the evening. "Last call for alcohol," the DJ's voice would call out when the lights came on. That was her cue to find someone, anyone, to take her home with him for the night. If he was nice enough, maybe for the weekend.

Connie glanced at her watch. Eleven-thirty. Too early for last call. She hadn't been all that different from these people. Desperation would creep in for most of them when the lights came on. Maybe not her kind of desperation, but some kind. And then the rush would be on, and matches would be made, couples united, even if it was only for one night. Men hoped for a pair of warm thighs to curl up between and lose themselves in, and women would hope for a long-lasting, once-in-a-lifetime, something-kind-of-special relationship. In the end, everybody would end up sober, disappointed, and back here again next week to play the game all over again. She sighed at her own pessimism.

John wondered what expression that was Connie wore on her face. Boredom? Indifference? Hell. Weren't they one and the same? He'd been watching her from across the room since he'd come in and saw her sitting there. Connie wore a knit knee-length black skirt, split up one thigh. She crossed one leg over the other, prob-ably oblivious to the fact that she'd just turned him on—and the other brotha standing next to him at the bar. Connie's red sweater was scooped low in the front, revealing plenty of cleavage to pique a man's imagination, but hugged on tight to the rest of her. She twirled a strand of her naturally light-brown hair, avoiding stares from men who were more interested than she'd give them credit for.

He'd been on his way home from work when he decided to stop in for a beer. John hadn't even showered yet and made the effort to do everybody a favor and stand as far into the corner as possible. He'd outgrown clubbing years ago, but every once in a while, the lure of them beckoned his curiosity and he'd stop in, have a few drinks, maybe get a little dancing done, then go home, relieved he hadn't been missing out on much of anything after all. He gulped down the last of his beer and was just about to leave when the DJ decided to slow it down for the first time since he'd been there, and Jodeci begged him to find some sexy sistah, lure her out onto the dance floor, and make some magic, regardless of how bad he might've smelled. John quickly made his way over to Connie. She'd been turning down men all night, but she didn't turn him down.

He pulled her close to him, wrapped one arm low around her waist, and gently took her hand in his, bracing it close to his heart. "You enjoying yourself?"

She shrugged. "Sure, I am."

"Liar," he teased, relieved that she didn't seem to notice how much he needed a shower. And if she did, she didn't seem to mind.

Connie laughed. "Is it that obvious?"

"Obvious? Woman, I thought you were about to doze off there for a minute."

"I probably was. Places like this just don't excite me very much."

"So why bother to come?"

"My friend got down on her hands and knees, promised me her firstborn son, money. The woman begged me to come. I thought she'd slit her wrists if I didn't."

"Well, then you did the right thing."

"That's me. I'm a sucker for doing the right thing," she said sarcastically, staring up at him. "And what are you doing in a place like this? I wouldn't really figure you for the clubbing type."

"I'm not. Anymore."

"A handsome brotha like you? Lots of pretty women in this city and you can find the bulk of them in the clubs. Or church. Or both. You go to church?"

"Not lately."

"Me either. How about we get up one Sunday morning and go sometime? Me and you," she teased.

"Why would we want to go and do something like that?"

Connie chuckled. "Hell, I don't know. I heard somewhere that salvation worked miracles on people."

John threw his head back and laughed. "For some people, maybe, but I think people like us learned the truth about salvation a long time ago."

"Which is?"

"Other people wear it better than we ever could."

Connie frowned. "I'm not sure I appreciate that 'people like us' comment."

"What's wrong with it?"

"It implies that something just ain't right about us. If I were you, I wouldn't be so willing to embrace it, but if you insist, then you need to leave me out of that loop."

"You're offended?"

"I'm offended," she said playfully. "I used your bathroom once. I don't think that makes us—"

"Kindred spirits?" He looked deep into her eyes. "I think we got each other pretty much figured out. Like minds and such."

"You let me use your toilet. I wouldn't exactly call that grounds for being soul mates. You know nothing about me."

He smiled. "Denial. It's cute on you."

"Denial nothing. You don't know me, and I don't know a thing about you. Nothing that isn't obvious."

John smiled. "Obvious? If you see obvious in me, why can't I see it in you?" Connie stared at him. "I don't know." He shrugged. "Something tells me we might be more alike than we know."

Of course he was teasing her. Wasn't he? she wondered. He was practically a stranger to her, but something about him was familiar, and he claimed to recognize that familiar in her too. Connie found it odd that she wasn't uncomfortable with the notion of being transparent to him. In fact, she felt strangely calmed by it. They danced two more songs, slow and close. Connie's head rested against his broad chest, and the deep, rhythmic beating of his heart soothed her, nearly lulling her into a trance. The DJ abruptly interrupted her solace with booty-shaking, earth-quaking music that startled Connie back to reality.

John led her off the dance floor back to her seat, then leaned down and whispered in her ear. "Thank you."

"You leaving?" she asked.

"Yeah. I'm on my way out."

"Can I come?"

"You wanna go home?"

She shook her head. "No. Not right now."

"Where you wanna go?"

"Anyplace. Just outta here."

He shrugged. "Then let's go."

Connie told Yolanda she wasn't feeling well, then left with John. Neither of them said much during the drive. After giving him directions, Connie rolled down the window and let the cool breeze whip through her hair. Fall was her favorite time of the year. It was a cooling down time. A time to prepare for the hibernation and seclusion of winter.

John parked the car across the street from the old Stapleton airport. He turned off the radio and popped in an Earl Klugh CD.

"Nice spot," he said.

"Yeah. It's quiet now. When I was younger, I used to come out here and watch the planes take off. The old runway is over there," she said, pointing toward a dark open field. "I used to imagine I was on one of those planes."

John lit up a cigarette. "Going where?"

"Shoot. Anywhere was fine with me. Didn't matter. Maybe someplace secluded, surrounded by ocean with just me and a servant boy who kept my glass filled with something blue that had fresh orange wedges on the rim. At night, he'd hand-feed me lobster." She laughed. "You ever been on a plane?"

He shook his head. "No. I'm a road man. I like the highway."

"That's almost like flying. Isn't it?" She smiled.

"Sometimes."

"Where are you from?"

John took a drag from his cigarette. "Born in Texas, but I'm from all over. Been on my own since I was about fifteen."

"I knew you were from the South."

"How? Can you hear my accent?"

"Accent?" She laughed. Connie reached over and squeezed his upper arm. "Big collard green, corn bread, red beans and rice brotha. They only grow those down South. Not up here in Colorado."

"That's because everybody here is jogging and eating salads and shit. Trying to lose weight and live forever. I like to eat and I ain't running unless some mothafucka bigger and badder than me is after my ass."

She laughed. He liked the way she laughed.

"You've been on your own since you were fifteen?" Connie asked. "Why so young?"

John shrugged. "That's just how it worked out."

"Yeah . . . I can understand that. I left when I was fourteen."

John leaned back and inhaled again on his cigarette, then let the smoke escape from his lips and watched it rise up and out of the window. There it is, he thought. Beautiful, teenage girl living on her own, probably in the streets, doing whatever with whoever. He glanced at Connie, who lay with her head against the seat, staring serenely across the field to that old runway. That explained what he'd seen in her the first time he laid eyes on her in the restaurant. Street people recognized street people, no matter how good they cleaned up. Despair rested beneath their eyes, like dark circles from never being able to sleep completely, soundly, and having to watch their own backs because no one was going to do it for them.

"So, where are you going when you leave here?"

"What makes you think I'm leaving?" he asked.

"Please. This place is not you. That's obvious. Besides, didn't you tell me you have this love affair going on with highways or something like that? People in love with highways don't stay put for too long. They go through withdrawals, like any addict."

He laughed. "Damn! Is that one of those *obvious* traits you see in me?"

"Actually you're not that complicated."

"Is that right?"

"It is. So, where you going when you leave here?"

John sighed. "To be honest with you, baby, I don't have a clue."

"California's supposed to be nice. Ever been there?"

"Not yet. Maybe I will make it out that way."

Connie wrapped her arms around herself. The chill was getting to her, but she dismissed the idea of rolling up the window. John noticed her shivering and took off his jacket, then placed it over her shoulders. "That better?"

"Much." She smiled. "See . . . there you go again. Throwing me off guard, being chivalrous and coming to my rescue." Connie laughed.

"Well, somebody's got to do it. Otherwise, you'd be pissy and cold."

"Our introduction was memorable, to say the least. How many other times have you met women because they were about ready to pee on themselves?"

"None."

"And because of that, you'll never forget me. I've left what you call a 'lasting impression.' "

John stared into her eyes. "Yes. You certainly have, baby girl."

"What's your name?" she asked, smiling.

"John. John King."

"John King." Connie smiled and extended her hand for him to shake. "I'm Connie Rodgers."

He gently took her hand in his. "The pleasure's mine," he whispered.

Looking into his eyes, she saw it. It had been something she'd sensed about him, hidden behind those dark eyes of his and cool exterior. He'd never admit to it, of course. Men like him never did, but Connie recognized it. Vulnerability.

He shifted uncomfortably, then let go her hand and started the car. "I'd better get you home."

Connie lay back and pulled his jacket close around her.

Slowly, they walked up the stairs, then stopped in front of her apartment. Connie unlocked her door, then slid John's jacket from around her shoulders and handed it to him. "Thanks for the ride home," she said. "And for the conversation. It was cool. Much better than sitting up in that tired club all night."

He leaned against the wall and quietly asked, "You ain't going to invite me in?"

Instinctively, she'd known they'd end up here, at a moment like this, where he'd hope to come inside and she'd hope he wouldn't ask. Connie had rehearsed in her bathroom mirror a way to tell a man she had herpes, and it never seemed to come out right. No matter how she said it, the statement fumbled and fell awkwardly from her lips, and she'd stand there, staring at herself, embarrassed by how absurd she appeared. She hadn't told what's-his-name? Carl. And guilt plagued her the whole time he was there. Telling him would've been the right thing to do for him, but the humiliation would've been all hers. Her only consolation had been insisting that he wear a condom.

"C'mon," he coaxed. "We could . . . talk some more?"

"Right. Talk." She smirked.

"I'm serious. I got a few beers in the fridge. I could get them, come back over here and—"

"And?" She owed him the truth, if for no other reason than for the fact that it hadn't been given to her. At least if Jamil had told her, she'd have had some options, like running for the hills as fast as she could, leaving him in a cloud of dust. Connie wanted John

King to come inside as much as he wanted to. Keeping something like this from him really wasn't her decision to make. Jamil had made it for her. "I should tell you something, John."

"Baby, you can tell me anything you want." John smiled.

"You might not be so anxious to come in when I tell you."

"Why don't you let me be the judge of that?"

Connie looked down at her feet, down the hall, then to the wall behind him. Anywhere but in his eyes. "I've . . . um . . ." She leaned in close to him.

John grinned, expecting a kiss. "You smell good," he whispered.

Connie ignored his flattery, then got down to the business of blurting out her confession. "I've got herpes, John." She pressed her lips together in embarrassment, quickly stepped inside her apartment, and breathed a sigh of relief. There. She'd done the right thing. She'd told him the truth and cursed Jamil under her breath for being too much of a punk to tell it to her. "I'll see you around," she said, trying to smile as she closed the door behind her, refusing to give him the opportunity to make even one unintentionally crude comment.

John stood speechless outside her front door, which had just slammed in his face. What the hell? he wondered. Herpes? He scratched his head, then walked slowly down the hall to his own apartment. Damn! Miss Rodgers definitely had a way of dampening a brotha's spirit, he thought, adjusting his hard-on.

Connie peeled off her clothes, took a quick shower, then crawled into bed. Confessions sometimes left behind grime, and she'd found it was best to wash them off right away, before they had a chance to set in and leave behind unsightly stains, ruining a potentially decent outlook on life in general. He'd been a nice man, she thought. Connie turned off the lamp next to her bed, pulled the covers up around her chin, and closed her eyes. Behind them were images of John King, hovering over her, filling her mouth with his tongue, then trailing kisses down her neck to her breasts. "Man!" she muttered, wishing she could have just fallen asleep and forgotten all about him. Connie sat up and fluffed her pillows, then turned over on her stomach, squeezing her eyes shut, tight enough to block out any visions of him, and of the things he might be doing to her now if only she'd kept her mouth shut. Her imaginary John balanced himself above her. Connie's knees were raised as high as they could go as he thrust himself back and forth slowly inside her. "Mmm . . ." she moaned, then turned over on her back. This was too good a fantasy to let go to waste, despite her frustration. Connie slid out from underneath the covers and slowly traced one hand down the front of her body, grazing her nipples with the tips of her fingers. Her other hand slid down her stomach, finding the warm, welcoming spot between her thighs.

"Mmmmm . . ."

She smiled.

Can I—We?

John sat inside his car, started it up, and turned the heat on full blast. "Damn!" he muttered, folding his arms across his chest. "It's too damn cold." The slate-colored sky seemed ready to drop a blizzard on his head at any moment, but he'd been assured by the weatherman to expect "some possible flurries in the morning, but plenty of sunshine in the afternoon." Yeah, right. John looked up in time to see Connie coming out of their apartment building, on her way over to catch the light rail. He honked to get her attention. "You want a ride?"

Connie hesitated before answering. After her confession the other night, she hadn't expected he'd have much to say to her. Most men would never have spoken to her again. But this man? He was just a trip, and Connie began to realize and accept the fact that he wasn't most men. "I don't know." She shrugged. "It might be out of your way."

"Which way is that?"

"Broadway and Twelfth?"

"It's on my way," John said, leaning over and opening the door. "C'mon."

As hard as it was, he fought the urge to stare at her. Just the other day, the woman had admitted to him that she had herpes, leaving him hard and speechless. Sitting next to her now, he was just . . . speechless.

"I really appreciate this," Connie said, breaking the silence.

"Not a problem," he said casually. "Like I said, it's on my way."

"Oh yeah? Where do you work?"

"Broadway and Alameda."

"What do you do?"

John glanced at her, then grinned. "Make boxes."

"Well, I guess somebody's got to do it," Connie said indifferently. John drove down Welton, turning left onto Broadway. "You like what you do?"

"It's a job."

"That's too bad." She smiled.

"Why is that?"

Connie shrugged. "You spend most of your life there. Just seems like work should be more than just a job."

"Yeah, well . . ." John hadn't spent most of his life anywhere in particular, but he didn't see a reason to have to explain that to her.

Relief. That was the first word to come to Connie's mind. He knew the truth. She'd blurted it out to him because blurting was the only way of admitting that she had an incurable STD. She'd practiced tactful, but tactful confessions always seemed to come out sounding dumb, so she opted for blurting. The next word she thought of was disappointment. The man was definitely the object of a few fantasies, so yes, she was terribly disappointed that she'd been forced to stop at fantasies of him instead of experiencing all of him. Connie stared out the window, twirling a strand of hair, glancing at John every now and then out of the corner of her eye. Fine was the third word to come to mind. (See disappointment.) Whatever. That was the fourth, followed by the usual slew of clichés . . . such is life. That's the way the cookie crumbles. No use crying over spilled . . . et cetera. She sighed.

John pulled over in front of the Ivory Coast. "Thanks again," Connie said, getting out of the car.

"Anytime."

Connie turned to him one last time and smiled. "You should come into the store sometime. If you see something you like, I'll give you a discount."

"I might just take you up on that," he replied, suddenly caught up in those light brown eyes of hers. John waited until she was inside, then drove away.

Carpooling in the mornings quickly became a routine. Eventually he stopped asking if she wanted a ride, and she'd climb into the car, taking a seat next to him as if that's the way it had always been.

Connie offered to pay him for gas, but John refused. "I'd have to come by here anyway, baby girl. Keep your money."

She laughed, getting out of the car. "You're too good to me."

"You're welcome."

"Why don't you come inside? Just for a minute." John sighed. "Please? I think you'll be impressed."

"That what you're trying to do, baby. Impress me?" he teased.

Connie rolled her eyes. "Somebody, and I ain't mentioning no names, has a tendency to be a little full of himself sometimes." John laughed, knowing she was right. "But, like I said . . . I ain't mentioning no names."

"I think we both know, all that sarcasm flowing past those pretty lips of yours really ain't necessary," he said, opening his door. "C'mon. Let's do this. Impress my ass so I can get to work."

Walking into the Ivory Coast, John felt like he'd been catapulted from Denver, Colorado, straight into some Ashanti village, and as if answering the call from ghosts of African warriors, John immediately migrated to Zulu spears hanging on the wall. Men were so predictable, Connie thought to herself, admiring the width of those shoulders when he wasn't looking. John admired Zulu spears.

"These the real thing?" he asked, carefully removing one of the spears from the wall.

"Yep. Genuine articles from the Zulu Nation," Connie said proudly. "Yolanda picked those up on her last trip over a few months ago."

John carefully placed the spear back where he'd gotten it, then gazed at one of the batiks hanging next to it. "This is cool."

"Yeah . . . that's one of my favorites. I think it's from Ghana."

Women like her were irresistible without even trying, and it had taken a great deal of effort on his part to keep his hands to himself. The sandy brown mane framing her face begged to be touched, but he fought the temptation by shoving his hands into his pockets, thinking he should've paid more attention in health class when he was in school. They'd shown films of people with diseases such as syphilis, gonorrhea, herpes, and not one of them looked like her. Brown, beautiful, and soft.

"So, you said you make jewelry?"

"I make some of it," she said, leading him over to the display case. Connie unlocked the cabinet and pulled out a ring she'd recently made, then handed it to John. "This is new. What do you think?"

"Aww. That's nice. You make this?"

"Yeah." She smiled. "I think it turned out pretty good."

"Pretty good? Naw, baby girl. This is nice." John's eyes grew wide when he happened to glance at the price tag on the inside of the ring. "Eight hundred dollars? Damn!"

"What? That's white gold and real opal."

"You got something working-class folk can afford up in this place?"

Connie laughed. "It's custom-made, John. A one-of-a-kind piece."

"And I can appreciate that. I just can't afford it, that's all." He handed it back to her.

Connie carefully put the ring back into the case, then pulled out a silver bracelet and slipped it onto his wrist. "How about this?"

Instinctively, he leaned close to her and inhaled the scent of Connie's hair. Jasmine, he thought to himself. He loved the smell of jasmine.

John admired the bracelet. "I like it."

"It looks good on you, and it's sterling silver. I think you should get it."

He eyed her suspiciously. "This custom too?"

"Very," she said, laughing.

"How much?"

"I told you I'd give you a discount."

"How much?"

"Twenty-five."

"With the discount?"

"Are you really that cheap?" she asked, teasing.

"Baby, I'm broke. There's a difference."

"It goes for fifty."

"Then it's a good enough deal," he said, pulling out his wallet. "And yes, I'll take it."

John lay in his apartment, trying not to think about Connie. She wasn't making this easy on him. Smiling, touching his arm, smelling like jasmine, and looking so damn good all the time. She wasn't making it easy at all. Sex was the sweetest part of a woman, and he knew it had to taste sweet on her. John stared at the television, but he wasn't watching it. Connie wasn't far enough away, just down the hall, plaguing his mind with ideas of what he could be doing to her right now. Falling in love. Contrary to popular opinion, he was capable of love. Each and every time he thrust himself inside a woman, he loved her. But it was a love that seldom lasted longer than an hour, maybe two, depending on his stamina.

There was an art to lovemaking. Fucking required no particular set of skills. But making love was good sex, and good sex required love and sacrifice. Inhibitions weren't allowed. Naked bodies slapping up against each other, slurping and grinding, didn't leave space for inhibitions. Defenses had to be left outside the door and a man had to be willing to pour out everything that was inside him through his semen.

Loving wasn't hard when he was having sex. Being loved wasn't hard. It was before sex and after sex when love retreated. When it was over, it was over. That's how it had always been for him. But lately, something inside him had been nagging at him. Tugging at him, whispering in the back of his mind that maybe he needed more. But more of what? The problem was, and had always been, he really didn't know. John figured it had probably always been there, but he'd just been better at ignoring it before. In the past, emotional ties to women proved detrimental to his ego. Physical ties lasted long enough to get to the orgasm, then he'd put on his pants and move on, taking that empty feeling he'd carried with him his whole life. Ultimately, for John, only moments mattered, because that's how he lived his life, wrapped up in moments. Never reaching too far behind or too far ahead. Only ghosts lived behind him, and as far as he knew, there wasn't anything in front of him until he got close enough to touch it. Contemplating a future with someone in his life just never made much sense to him, and he'd tried making sense of it, every time he'd had sex and fallen in love. But then he'd come, and it would make even less sense.

Connie was definitely tugging at him. The thing was, he knew she wasn't even trying. Hell, if she'd been trying, she'd have thrown some good sex up in his face, then told him about her issues. But she'd come at him through the front door, arms wide open, bearing truths at her own expense. He figured that was admirable.

Bottom line was, he was lonesome. No, he never had a problem admitting that when it happened. He'd been in Denver a few months now and missed the intimacy of a woman. Maybe that's all it was, he concluded. Maybe he just needed to snuggle up between warm thighs and lose himself in tongue kisses. He missed that. But he hadn't put forth much effort in finding it either. Believing he was on his way out at any moment, he just hadn't taken the time to make that kind of connection. She was down the hall and he knew he wouldn't be leaving Denver anytime soon. John flicked off the television, then got up to take a shower. Right now, he definitely needed more . . . of her.

Connie glanced over at the clock on the nightstand and it reaffirmed what she already knew. Eleven forty-seven at night was entirely too late for anybody to be knocking on her door. She crawled out of bed, slipped into her robe, and cautiously tiptoed to the door. "Who is it?" she asked, eyeing the baseball bat balanced in the corner, ready to do battle with somebody's head.

"It's John."

She cracked open the door and stared right at his handsome face, feeling heat rising up in hers.

He looked freshly showered, dressed in a clean white T-shirt, sweatpants, and slippers. "Hey," he said casually.

"Hey."

"You sleeping?"

Connie stared at him with a perturbed look on her face. "No. I'm standing here in the middle of the night, talking to you."

"I know it's kinda late," he said, ignoring her obvious sarcasm.

"Yeah, John, it's pretty late." Connie yawned.

"I was just wondering if you were in the mood for company?"

"Actually, for me, it's too late for company."

"I see."

"Really?"

"It's just that . . . well, I was . . . thinking about you, and I was just wondering . . ."

"Wondering what?" Obviously he had something on his mind. Connie suspected she knew what that was, but she decided to wait and see if he'd actually have the gall to come out and say it.

John held up a small box in his hand. "We cool with condoms?" He smiled.

Connie stared at the box, then glared at him. "You bastard." The icy tone in her voice sent a chill up his back, but John quickly shrugged if off. "I know you did not come over here at this time of night, expecting me—"

"Hoping." He grinned. "I came over here hoping."

"Whatever!" she snapped, trying to keep from raising her voice. "Don't you think we're a little old for booty calls, King?"

"Not really," he said, staring blankly at her.

Connie's eyes narrowed. "How dare you think that you can come over here in the middle of the night and . . . You know what? Don't worry about giving me a damn ride to work in the morning!" she said, pointing in his face. John stood speechless, patiently accepting the verbal lashing she gave him. "You ain't about shit, and this little late-night visit of yours proves it! Give her a ride, be nice, act like a gentleman, then dive right into the panties! Was that the plan, John? You would've been better off taking the damn gas money!"

John stood silent for a moment, then asked, "That mean no?"

That's what it was supposed to mean, but Connie had done a poor job of convincing herself that she truly meant everything she'd said in all her ranting and raving. *No more sex for convenience, Connie,* she'd vowed to herself.

Connie rubbed her tired eyes, sighed, and then muttered more to herself than to him. "I promised myself I wouldn't do this anymore."

"Do what?"

Annoyance spread over her face. "One-night stands, John. They've gotten a little lame over the years. Know what I mean?"

"Who said it had to be for one night? What are you doing to-morrow night?"

"You just don't get it, do you?" Connie stared at the man, in awe of how casually he stood in her doorway, in the middle of the night, believing he was all the reason in the world she should let him in.

"Naw, but I'm trying." He grinned. "I'm really trying, baby."

"I thought we were friends, John."

"We are."

"And do you make it a habit of banging all of your friends?"

"Friends that look like you."

"I don't believe this," she muttered. Connie stared back at John, fighting to hide the silent war waging inside her. No, she didn't want to do this. And yes she really wanted to do this, and she wanted to do it with him.

"You deserve better, sis." Reesy's words resurfaced in her mind. "Hold out until someone special comes along. I guarantee you, it'll be worth it and you'll feel so much better about yourself." According to Reesy, Mr. Someone Special could materialize at any second, and the last thing she needed was the scent of meaningless sex all over her when he did. Of course, the last and only time in her life Mr. Someone Special did show up, he left herpes behind to remind her of just how special he'd been and how special she hadn't been to him. Connie learned from that experience exactly what she'd suspected was true all along. That sex wasn't significant enough to be reserved for someone special.

She stared at John's broad chest, then all of a sudden, out of the corner of her eye, she spotted her pathetic, little convictions quietly slump down the hall in defeat and hurl themselves out the window. Of course she wanted this like he wanted this, and after all, he did have condoms. The man never batted an eye, and as hard as she tried, Connie couldn't keep the smile from spreading across her lips, and she stepped aside to let him in.

Candles soothed her, and she hoped they'd soothe him too. Butterflies fluttered relentlessly inside her stomach. Tonight, she'd flip the switch and turn this encounter into something else besides sex, because that's not what she needed. It was the tenderness she craved. Someone who felt nice on the tips of her fingers. Who kissed her slowly and nibbled on her, savoring her like she was a gourmet dinner instead of gulping her down like fast food. Tonight, she'd be the one to use him. He'd be the instrument, not her. She'd take from him what she needed, and when she was finished, she'd politely dismiss him. No harm done. No hurt feelings, false senses of commitment, or feigned devotion. Things like that weren't necessary between two consenting adults like them. They knew better.

She turned off the lights. John watched her slowly slip out of her robe. Connie stood naked before him, stepping back slightly when he instinctively reached out to pull her closer to him. "You've got to let me do this," she said softly.

He leaned back on the bed, smiled, then nodded his head in approval. "Yes, ma'am."

Baby girl is glorious, he thought to himself. Candlelight flickered against her skin, teasing him with nipples that appeared to dance against the darkness. Connie's voluptuous figure was too enticing for words. Her full hips begged him to grab onto them and pull her down to where he needed her most. On his lap. Slowly she walked over to him, then took his hands in hers. She straddled him, and he leaned in to kiss her.

"No kissing," she whispered, leaning back.

He nearly protested. Of course there'd be kissing. He'd wanted to kiss her from the moment he'd laid eyes on her, but he kept his protests to himself, confident that she'd change her mind later.

She ran her hands over his broad chest, flattening her palms over his heart, then gently pushed him down on his back. Connie grazed her lips across his chest, finding one of his nipples with her tongue, then traced warm, wet circles around it until it peaked in her mouth.

"Mmm . . . ," he moaned. The tips of his fingers lightly trailed over her shoulders and down her back.

He's being good, she thought. If he continued being good, she'd let him stay. John's penis throbbed hard between their bellies. He wrapped his arms around her, then turned her over on her back. Hovering over her, he stared, admiring the curves of her beautiful body, and gathered up her breasts in his hands, smothering them with kisses. He savored the taste of nursing from her, while Connie moaned and wiggled beneath him. Gradually, his kisses traveled downward, lured by the aroma of her juices. His tongue craved her, almost as much as she craved it. Connie slowly spread her legs, anticipating the warmth of his mouth between her legs. She stared up at the ceiling, her eyes glazed over from the sensation of him, the idea of him, the strength of him. His tongue teased her navel, then, as he traveled further down her body, she suddenly remembered.

"No!" she said, squeezing her legs together, before he'd made a mistake. "Damn!" she muttered, in frustration.

John raised up and hovered over her. "It's cool," he said. "No problem, baby."

She sighed. "The condoms are on the nightstand."

He sat up and pulled a condom from the box, then handed it to her. "Put it on me?"

John lay back, resting one hand beneath his head, running his fingers through Connie's hair with the other, while he watched her expertly slide the latex over his penis. "Come here," he whispered when she'd finished, then pulled her on top of him. He started to kiss her lips, but again, she pulled away from him.

"I said no kissing, John."

He stared into her eyes. "Nonsense," he said. John raised his mouth to hers and filled it with his tongue.

Sex to Connie was one thing. As personal as it was, she'd learned how to make it impersonal. She'd mastered the art of going through the motions, faking satisfaction and orgasms, and leaving it in the bed, or on the floor, or on the couch, or in the backseat of a car, where it belonged. But kissing—kissing meant something else altogether. It meant affection, admiration, sometimes even love. Kissing was sacred, reserved for those she deemed worthy. But somehow, she'd managed to allow herself to get lost in his kissing, realizing just how much she'd missed it.

She wondered if he knew he was still holding her in his arms. Connie didn't think he did and started to pull away. John pulled her back to him, then mumbled, "What?" in his sleep. Maybe he did know. She decided not to wake him, because then he might want to leave, and she wasn't ready for him to leave. Not yet. He'd been willing to give her what she'd needed, and what she'd been missing most. Patience. Compassion. She kissed him lightly on the chin, then stared over his shoulder out the bedroom window and watched azure begin to creep across the sky in the dawn. That was the last thing she remembered before finally falling asleep, satisfied, for the first time in ages.

Mortal Man

Neither of them had any idea where they were going, but they followed the signs on the sides of the road that read LOOKOUT MOUNTAIN.

"Damn," he muttered. "It's beautiful up here."

"Sure is. I'm surprised there's no snow yet." It was the bottom half of October and fall had been playing peekaboo, showing up on chilly mornings, hiding behind springlike temperatures at midday, then coming out of hiding again at sunset, bringing nippy evenings with it. Connie leaned back, absorbing the view of Colorado from the heights of the mountain road they traveled. "If I'd known about this place when I was younger, I'd have escaped to here and lived off nuts and berries," she joked.

"Not a bad idea, sugar. Not bad at all."

John and Connie found a clearing on the side of the road and spread out a blanket, overlooking a valley, still lush and filled with evergreens. She couldn't remember the last time she'd cooked, but Connie had gotten up early that morning and prepared a virtual feast fit for African-American Kings: fried chicken, homemade biscuits, potato salad, corn on the cob, baked beans, and cole slaw.

John ate so much, he thought he'd bust wide open. " 'Scuse me." He belched, then smacked his lips and licked his fingers. "This was good, baby," he said, kissing her cheek. "You really put your foot into this."

She smiled, uncharacteristically proud of herself. "You want some more chicken?"

"No. I'm cool." He gazed down into the valley beneath them, untouched by anything to do with humans, and drank in the view. "Man! It doesn't get any better than this." John closed his eyes and inhaled the cool, crisp air, filled his lungs to capacity, then held his breath. "I'll bet the air here is light enough for a man to grow wings and fly if he wanted to."

"I thought you said you were a highway man?"

"I was . . . until now."

"Where would you go if you could fly?"

"Aw, baby. I'd head straight for the clouds." He stared into the sky, then pointed. "That fat one right over there. I'd fly up there, lay my happy ass down, and just, hell . . . be."

Connie laughed. "Be? Be what?"

"Be nothing. Be everything, I guess. Just chillin' for all eternity." Too bad real life couldn't be that simple. He'd declare his wish at the top of his lungs and fate would have no choice but to give it to him, because he'd be a god and the universe would have to obey his god wishes. But in real life, wishing was a moot point and he was nowhere close to being godlike. Realizing that doused him with disappointment, which shone on his face.

"What happened to you, John?" Connie asked, her voice filled with sincerity.

"What do you mean?"

"I mean, what happened to send you out into the streets at fifteen? What happened once you got out there? What happened to make you who you are now?"

"Damn! What do you want? A history lesson?" He laughed.

Connie rolled her eyes, feeling insulted by his sarcasm. "Forget it. I was just trying to get to know you a little better, but if you don't want to talk about it, that's fine with me. It really is no big deal."

John grinned, then asked sarcastically, "Oh, so now you're pissed off?"

"You give yourself way more credit than I do. No, I'm not pissed off," Connie snapped.

"I'm sorry," he said humbly.

"Why? Because you think you pissed me off? Or because you think you're all that?"

"Hell!" he said, laughing. "Right now, I'd say it was a little of both." John took her hand in his and kissed her palm. "This day's been too perfect, Connie. We've got a great view, shared a great meal, and I, for one, am in a great mood."

"So, what are you trying to say?"

"Don't blow this, and . . . I'm sorry?"

"I told you. It's no big deal."

"Then accepting my apology ought to be easy."

"Fine." Connie pulled her hand from his. "You're forgiven."

"Thank you, baby girl."

Connie eventually lost her diligent battle to keep from laughing. "You're welcome."

John rested his head comfortably in Connie's lap, closed his eyes, and listened intently to the tranquility of peace and quiet. "You sleep?" she asked him.

"Almost. I feel good, baby."

"Mmm . . . me too. I wish we didn't have to go back."

"We don't. I got a blanket in the trunk. We can stay up here and live off them berries if you want."

"What about the nuts?" She giggled.

He grinned, then grabbed the crotch of his pants. "Girl, we've got plenty of good, wholesome nuts right here. Don't worry about the nuts."

"That's terribly offensive."

"You like it, though."

"No . . . I like you. Not your offensive behavior. There's a difference."

"Then that's all I care about."

"So, you going to tell me why you ran away from home?"

"You still on that?"

"Yes."

"What happened to 'it's no big deal'?"

"It isn't. But tell me anyway. I'm curious."

"Nosy is more like it."

"Please?"

John stared up at the vivid blue sky, wondering if he could resurrect a past that was just as clear. So many years had passed, details had become blurred, particulars faded, but the emptiness he'd always felt was crystal clear and right where it had always been, tucked safely inside him. "I just remember being hungry when I was a kid. Not for food or anything like that. Hell, we used to eat damn good. Agnes was always hooking up the eats." He grinned.

"Agnes?"

"My grandmother. She's the one who raised me until I left," he said thoughtfully.

"Well, what were you hungry for, then?"

"I don't know exactly, but I needed something, and I could never figure out what that was. Still don't know. I thought that when I hit the road, eventually I'd find it, but—"

"You never have?"

He shook his head. "No. I think if I'd found it, maybe I wouldn't still be out here like this."

"You ran away hoping to find something, and I ran away to get away from something," she muttered, more to herself than to him.

"What?"

"Nothing. Finish what you were saying. Why'd you leave?"

"She told me to get the hell out." He shrugged. "So, I did."

"The two of you didn't get along?"

"The two of us didn't get anything, period."

"What about your mother?"

"What about her?"

"Where is she?"

"Dead. She died having me."

"Oh. . . ." Connie sat thoughtfully, toying with the watch on his arm. "Do you think your grandmother might've resented you for that?"

"She probably did."

"Do you ever talk to her?"

"Naw."

"But you miss her?"

It was hard for him to miss Agnes. Memories of her had all converged into that one, and it was only that one that remained timeless in his mind. Anges, straddling Mr. Jensen, riding him as if he were a horse. Her smooth, brown thighs cocooned him, and Agnes's face was raised toward the ceiling as though she were straining to see heaven. That's what he remembered about Agnes. She looked like she'd been set free. All his life, she'd been perfect and proper, pinned up and in, but not that day. Her hair had fallen from the bun she'd kept it in and fell down to her shoulders. Her dress was open, revealing breasts he knew were warm to touch, like hot biscuits fresh from the oven. But it was the look on her face he remembered most. She stared at him like she'd seen a monster. She stared at him like Roberta had before she died.

You black-eyed demon!

All of a sudden, John had become the enemy, and Agnes fought for her life to get him away from her. It was as if, finally, all the warnings Roberta had given her had become real. The crazy woman's spirit had hurried before him and gotten to Agnes before he'd had a chance, warning her to get away from him, once and for all, before he killed her too. Like he'd killed Mattie. Like he'd killed Roberta, without even trying.

The fresh air seemed to baptize him from the inside out and John inhaled buckets of it, holding his breath for as long as he could, disappointed that he couldn't hold it forever. With baptisms came confessions and truths that rolled off tongues like water. John lay in the comfort and warmth of Connie's lap, feeling an overwhelming desire to express what he felt.

"I imagine most men meet up with their mortality eventually."

Connie smiled. "What's that supposed to mean?"

"It means, he comes to a crossroads. A place where he realizes he's not going to live forever after all, and he's got to make a choice to keep on living like he's been living—for himself—or do the right thing."

"What's the right thing?"

"You know? Settle down into his own woman, his own house . . . kids."

"Have you met up with your mortality, John?"

He smiled. "That's not even the right question to ask, Connie. The question is, would I recognize it if I did?"

"You'd better hope so."

"I do hope so. Forty is inching up on my ass pretty fast. Kind of makes me wonder if somewhere along the line, I didn't pass right by it and never even noticed."

Gazing into her eyes, he wondered if mortality might look something like her, light brown hair and eyes, pretty full lips. *Don't get attached, John,* he'd taught himself. He'd learned that lesson well, and staying in one place because of a woman had never been an option. But if Connie Rodgers was that elusive mortality he'd believed was lurking in the shadows, maybe he ought not to be so quick to leave. Maybe he needed to slow down for a minute, just to get a closer look.

"So you miss having those things? A wife? Kids?"

He shrugged. "Sometimes I think I do. Most other times I try not to give it much thought at all. I mean, this is just me. I try not to read more into it than I need to. I live the way I do because it's the only way I know."

"It had to have been hard, though. Especially when you were younger. And don't try to gloss it over, King. I've been there. I remember how hard it was teaching yourself your own lessons, raising yourself. And I also know how lonely it can get sometimes too."

"It does get lonely, and yeah, growing up on my own was hard. I figured I was a pretty tough kid when I left home, but no matter how tough a boy thinks he is, until he's out on the streets with nowhere to go and a hundred and sixty seven dollars in his pocket . . ." He swallowed hard. "It was hard."

Hard had been getting off the bus in Shreveport, not knowing where he'd sleep at night. He stayed at the bus terminal as long as he could before the shift manager finally told him he had to leave.

Hard had been begging for odd jobs, doing anything and everything on both sides of decent because he'd been unable to get a real job. Hard was having his ass kicked by heroin addicts who knew when he had a little bit of money in his pockets, then having to beg for food, sleep in alleys, prison and more prison. Missing home had been hard. Missing Momma Agnes and Aunt Dot, a pot of hot greens and a pan of corn bread, clean clothes, when he was fifteen, yeah . . . it had all been hard.

John was nineteen when he was arrested and sent to prison for four and a half years for assault. He'd confronted a liquor store owner who'd accused him of stealing. John never denied he'd hit the man. He'd hit him a couple of times because there'd been a lot of anger in him when he was young. Anger that he'd learned from other desolate, angry men his age, and pounding on somebody's ass seemed like pretty cheap therapy back then. Who knows? If he'd gotten away with it, maybe he'd still be beating people down. Fighting wasn't the answer then, like it wasn't always the answer now. In retrospect, none of it had been worth four and a half years in prison, and stupidity draws life's hardest lessons. He'd have to remember to write that down.

"Aw! Yo' black ass is bad out there in them streets, ain't you, pretty boy?" Cellmate Ace had growled at him. "This ain't no streets, boy," he said, cornering John. He had stared into Ace's cold eyes, trying to hide the fear in his own. "This here the pen, and you—" He pointed his finger in John's face. "You my bitch now, niggah!" John was taller than Ace, but Ace was thick and powerful from years of lifting weights. The men fought, but Ace won, hitting John hard enough to send him face first into the sink, knocking him unconscious.

"That's my ass, pretty," Ace said, breathless and zipping his pants when it was over. "Don't you be givin' my ass away to nobody, or I kill you, boy."

John sat up all night in that cell, staring at Ace's perverted ass sleeping in the cot on the other side of the room. The next morning, at dawn, Ace awoke in time to see John's fist racing to meet his face. "Mothafucka!" John screamed over and over again, pounding into Ace's mouth. "Mothafucka! Die you . . . Die! Fuck you!" Guards raced to the cell and pulled John off Ace, who lay bleeding on his cot, choking on his own blood. Fortunately for John, he didn't kill the man, or he'd have ended up with a lifetime membership to the federal prison system. What he did get was solitary confinement and two years added onto his sentence. Ace left him alone after that. They all did.

Connie saw memories flooding his eyes. Like her, he was full of things he'd just as soon forget. Talking about them only spread them like manure, and she knew better than to press him for details about his past. "Maybe it's love you've been looking for, John. Somebody to love you for who you are."

Where the hell did that come from? he wondered, gazing into her lovely face. John couldn't help but smile. "That's not my dream, sweetheart. It's gotta be one of yours."

"Sometimes it is. I ain't gonna lie." She smiled. "You think I'm crazy for wanting something like that?"

"Even if somebody were to come along and love us, would we know how to let them?"

Connie's eyes watered, and she swallowed hard. "I'd like to think so."

"I think it's a funny thing about people like us."

"There you go again, with that 'people like us' thing."

"People who grew up hard, on the streets. We've seen the ugliest side of living, Connie. Shit like that fucks with your mind for the rest of your life."

"Only if you let it," she said, trying to propel herself into optimism. "My sister, Reesy, tells me I need to bury the past, and finally move forward with my life."

"She ought to bottle advice like that and sell it," he said sarcastically.

"I think it's good advice. Not easy, but good."

"It's damn good advice. Is that what she's done? Put her past behind her?"

"She shouldn't want to. After Charlotte left us . . ."

"Charlotte?"

"Our mother. If you can call her that. Reesy and I were separated. We were just kids, but Reesy had a different kind of life than I did. But she's right. I wear my past like a second skin. It's not so easy to forget when it's so much of who you are."

"No, it's not. So why don't you make like a snake and shed it?"

"Look who's talking. Why don't you?"

"I'm not the one living in the past, baby. I'm right where I am at any given time. Right here. Right now."

"You keep telling yourself that. Maybe one of these days you'll really believe it."

"So this sister of yours," John said, changing the subject. "She cool?"

Connie shrugged. "She's my sister. The only one I have and I love the mess out of that girl. But I don't know. Before we were separated, we had a small piece of the universe in common." Connie smiled. "We called her Momma."

"And now?"

"Now I think the only reason we put up with each other is

because we're sisters. Reesy doesn't get where I'm coming from. Not that I blame her. I mean, how can she if she's never been there? I don't much understand her either. She has her own ideas about how our relationship should be and ends up disappointed when I fall short of those ideas. I'm not exactly the kind of big sister she can show off to all the girls at the country club." Connie laughed.

"Sounds like she wants things on her terms."

"She does, but she'd never admit it."

"And you?"

"I'm detached and attached." She laughed. "She's all I have, King. I might not like her as much as I did when she was eight"—Connie grinned—"but she's the only connection there for me. For some reason, I need that. I always have, which is why I guess I've never really left the only place I've ever known as home. It might not be perfect, or even good for me, but it's a connection too, like Reesy."

"Better than nothing," John whispered. Connection. That was a word that never seemed to be able to sink into his soul. As a kid, he imagined that maybe that's what he'd wanted from Agnes. Maybe that's the thing he'd been hungry for. But as a man, he'd learned to live without it.

"Feeling a part of something or someone . . . anchored, I guess . . ." Jade's smile quickly came to mind. That was the only other connection she had in her life. One that Jade would probably never fully realize, but Connie would always cherish it from a distance.

He sat up and gazed into her eyes. John softly traced the outline of her lips with his fingertip, wishing he could be the one to give her what she needed. He wanted to be the man who loved her the way she needed to be loved, but John knew better. He was eternally nomadic, just passing through, on his way out. The last thing he needed to do was take Connie's heart with him. He pulled her face to his and kissed her tenderly. "Let's put this stuff up and walk off some of this food. You starting to get fat," he teased.

Connie glared at him. "Don't make me kick your ass, John King."

"Don't make me promises you don't plan on keeping, girl." He grinned. "You know, I'm liable to enjoy the hell outta that."

Extensions

Connie had never been big on birthdays or holidays, but Reesy had taken advantage of a perfectly good Thanksgiving, using it as an excuse to get "the family" together. A concept Connie still wasn't all that comfortable with. She'd never fit in with Reesy's adopted family, who always seemed a little too apologetic as far as Connie was concerned. *No hard feelings, dammit!* she found herself wanting to scream at the top of her lungs when Ma and Pa Turner bought her expensive gifts, or asked once too often, "How have you been, Connie? You doing all right, sweetheart?"

"I've been good and yes, I'm fine," she'd say, squeezing out smiles and warmth she really didn't feel.

"They care about you, Connie. They're just trying to show you that," Reesy argued in their defense.

"Those people don't know me."

"Only because you won't let 'those people' know you."

"I don't need them on my side, Reese. That's why they have you. So that they can be on your side." Connie grinned.

"It's not about you needing them. It's about them wanting to mend a few fences. Why can't you let them do that?"

"I don't blame them for anything. Sometimes, shit just happens."

"Not shit. Your life happened and maybe if they'd—"

"They'd what? Adopted me too? Sweetie, who's to say I would've turned out any differently if they had?"

"At least you wouldn't have had to deal with that pervert . . ."

"Earl wasn't the only pervert in my life. He was just the first, and if I don't blame them, Reesy, why should you?"

Reesy rolled her eyes, then turned her attention back to mashing potatoes. Connie was taking her usual stance again, conceding the battle, refusing to speak up for herself. Choosing to hide behind a wall of indifference rather than confront the things or people that even remotely hurt her. Maybe blaming Reesy's parents was a mis-directed waste of energy, but Connie's anger, directed at somebody, anybody, made more sense to Reesy than it did for the woman to pretend every terrible thing in her life hadn't happened. Reesy wasn't like that. Unlike Connie, expressing her feelings out loud was a crucial key to survival for Reesy. Despite what Connie be-lieved, Reesy's life hadn't been all peaches and cream either after they'd split up. She'd been teased ruthlessly by other children after they found out she was adopted. Suddenly, her eight-year-old world had been turned upside down, everything she'd ever loved was gone, and strangers were raising her. She cringed at the memories of the horrible things that shot out of the mouths of babes.

"Your momma didn't even want you! She just ran away from home, 'cause you ugly!"

Reesy remembered praying to God not to let them see her cry, but she always did cry, wondering how close to being right they probably were. After the tears fell, the taunting would get worse, other children would circle around her and take turns pushing her toward one another. Of course she had to fight back. What choice did she have? Fight back, stand her ground, or suffer through that kind of torment for the rest of her life all because she was afraid.

When they were children, it had always been Connie who'd talked back and stood toe to toe with Charlotte, even at the expense of a backhand across the face, or a fist in the chest. Now that they were grown, Reesy often found herself staring into her sister's eyes, looking for that rebellious spirit that lived in her back then, but there was nothing in Connie's eyes now but defeat. Their roles had changed and Reesy now felt compelled to defend her sister like she'd done a few weeks ago while they were waiting at the checkout counter in the department store. Some woman casually stepped in front of Connie, pretending to be looking at scarves, then decided she was comfortable where she was and claimed her place in line like she'd been born into it.

Reesy watched in dismay as her sister pretended not to notice. "Uh . . . sis? That woman just crowded in front of you," she'd said, loud enough for the woman to hear.

Connie glanced at the woman, then shrugged. "It's not a big deal, Reese. I don't care."

For Reesy it had nothing to do with the deal or how big or small it was. It was the principle of the thing. "Excuse me. Miss," Reesy said over Connie's shoulder. "But the line is back here."

"Reesy," Connie tried to interject.

"We're not standing here for our health, Connie."

"You're making a big deal out of—"

"Out of the fact that she needs to get to the back of the line like everybody else, and if you're not going to say something, Connie . . ." The woman muttered to herself, stuck her nose in the air, then coolly made her way to the back of the line.

Connie went on to explain that things like that didn't bother her, and that it wasn't Reesy's place to say anything to the woman because she was plenty woman enough to say something her damn self. Whatever! was all Reesy remembered saying.

Sometimes for Reesy, trying to understand Connie was like trying to put together a five-thousand-piece puzzle in the dark. As soon as Reesy thought she had the woman figured out, she'd look closer and realize that the pieces just didn't quite fit after all. She could be hard as a rock one minute, then softer than a marshmallow the next, and there seldom seemed to be a medium. Reesy was more comfortable with mediums.

"It's my life, Reesy," Connie would preach. "And I've lived it long enough without you telling me how to do it."

"I'm not trying to tell you how to live your life. I'm just trying to get you to stop wasting it," Reesy argued.

"To you I'm wasting it because I don't live the way you think I should. But you know what, Reesy? I'm not you."

"I never said you had to be anything like me."

"No, but you don't mind implying it. You don't like the way I dress, live, wear my hair."

"Now you're exaggerating." Reesy folded her arms defensively across her chest.

"Girl" Connie mimicked, sounding like her sister, then flipping her hand in Reesy's hair. "You need to do something about this head. You look like a throwback from Woodstock."

Reesy laughed. "Well . . . you do."

"Because I like looking like a throwback from Woodstock and you need to leave it alone, because I'm not going to your *stylist* and sitting up in a beauty salon for four hours just so I can come out looking like a black Farrah Fawcett."

"I don't look like . . ." Reesy started to argue, but she knew from the look in Connie's eyes that it was a lost cause. "Fine. I'll stop talking about your little hair."

"Good."

"But I can't promise I'll stop talking about anything else."

"What's that supposed to mean?"

"It means"—Reesy explained, counting on her fingers—"I still think you need to get a real job, with a real 401K, IRA, something."

"Clarice?"

"I still think you need to start dating nice men for a change and not brothas who show up on Sunday nights on *America's Most Wanted.*"

Connie laughed. "You're wrong for that."

"I'm wrong for wanting my sister to do more than settle for whatever she can get? That makes me a bad person?"

"That's not what you're doing, and you know it. You want to make me over into you."

"No, I'm just trying to make you into a better you."

As usual, Connie rolled her eyes, signaling that this conversation was over and any contribution she might make to it was hereby withdrawn.

Loving Connie, as far as Reesy was concerned, meant straddling a fence. On one side was utter adoration for her older sister, inflated by memories of Connie taking care of the both of them when they were girls. On the other, Reesy struggled to accept the woman her sister had become, a doormat for people to wipe their feet on, while Connie shrugged it off as the norm. Being the martyr seemed to be her calling in life. Making due, and settling for the scraps life had left over, then wondering why she ended up hurt and disappointed all the time. Sometimes, Reesy wondered if finding Connie and having her in her life was worse than never seeing her again. She hated it when she felt that way, but Connie had given up. As a kid, she'd had the nerve to stand up to Charlotte, so why not Earl? Instead of letting him do those disgusting things to her, why didn't she scream, or hit him, or, hell, something? Anything besides lying there and letting him put his filthy hands all over her. Connie had let Earl use her like she still let men use her. Most of the time, Reesy tried to keep her opinions to herself, but that was usually pretty impossible to do.

Connie managed to make it through dinner, sitting between her niece, Jade, and J. J. her nephew, at dinner. Alex, her other nephew, sat across from them. She adored the children, though most of the time they managed to wear out their welcome on her nerves within a matter of minutes, doing kid things that only reminded Connie that patience was a virtue she sorely lacked. Six-year-old Jade was the youngest, J. J. was nine, and Alex ten.

"Aunt Connie?" Jade whispered to Connie at the dinner table. "What's a nonconformist?"

Connie frowned, wondering how such a big word could come from such a small mouth. "A what?"

"A nonconformist?"

"Where'd you hear that word from?"

"Daddy. He said that's what you are. Is that a bad word?" Jade asked, looking concerned.

Connie smiled. "Some people probably think so."

"What's it mean?"

"It means I do my own thing and I don't care what other people think."

"Oh," Jade said matter-of-factly, stuffing a forkful of dressing in her mouth. "Then . . . that's what I want to be when I grow up." Connie laughed.

"What's so funny down there?" Reesy's husband, Justin, asked.

"Nothing, brother-in-law," Connie responded. "Just enjoying this good food. That's all." Connie would have to remember to talk to him later about putting words like that in that child's mouth.

After dinner, Connie helped Reesy and her mother with the last of the dinner dishes. She listened quietly while the two women talked incessantly about intimate things like family vacations, relatives, and Reesy's father's high blood pressure. These things were a part of who Reesy was now, Connie concluded, and so far removed from who'd she'd been when they were growing up. Reesy spoke as if these things, these people and events, had always been part of her life, and Connie wondered if she'd ever given much thought to her BTTDs, Before the Turner Days. But Connie knew better. For Reesy, there really hadn't been life before the Turners.

Ma Turner dried her hands. "Well," she sighed. "I think me and your father need to get on home. You know how he is."

"He's probably asleep, Momma."

"I'll get Justin to carry him out to the car again." She laughed. "And don't forget, we're having dinner on Christmas Eve at the church."

"I know. I know." Reesy hugged her mother and kissed her cheek like she'd done every time Connie had seen the two of them together.

Ma Turner turned to Connie. "Connie," she said entirely too sincerely. "I hope you're planning on coming too. We'd love to have you."

"I'll try." Connie smiled, knowing that if Reesy didn't mention it, which was absolutely wishful thinking, then she wouldn't mention it either, and Connie could have her Christmas Eve all to herself.

"Please do, dear. Families really should be together during the holidays." Ma Turner smiled, then gathered up Pa Turner and left.

Families. The word might as well have been spoken in Greek as far as Connie was concerned. Reesy's clan thrived on the concept, which was obvious in absolutely everything they did; family dinners, churches, even vacations, all confirmed the significance of the family bond in a way completely foreign to Connie. She was more like John. Intrigued by the notion of it, even curious about the flavor of it, but ultimately, neither one of them would have any idea what to do with a family if they ever had one. Connie had even entertained the idea of someday having another child, but after Jamil and the disease he left behind, even that thought never stayed for long. Families were best left to people who knew how to handle such delicate things. She'd probably just end up dropping and breaking one.

"I guess I'd better get out of here too," Connie said, finishing the last of her glass of wine.

"How come your friend didn't come with you?"

"My friend?"

Reesy smiled. "Don't act like you don't know who I'm talking about."

"John?" Connie had casually mentioned she and John had been seeing each other, over the phone, then regretted it as soon as she had. Reesy had been prying about him ever since, and Connie had been avoiding dishing out any more information about the man, knowing her sister would find something about him to disapprove of. In Reesy's world, suburbia was Camelot, marriages were ordained by God and parents came in pairs. Every piece of the puzzle had to fit perfectly, or else it belonged in the trash, and Connie knew instinctively that John would never fit her sister's idea of "right."

"I was hoping you'd bring him tonight. Didn't you ask him to come?"

"Now, why in the world would I do something like that?"

Reesy propped her hands on her hips, then stared at Connie, wondering how she could have the audacity to ask such a stupid question. "So he can meet your family. Dag!"

Connie laughed. "I'll tell you what, Reesy. The next time you come over to the hood, I'll introduce you to him."

"Promise?"

"No. But if it'll get you off my back . . ."

"You're so wrong, Connie."

"I'm full, girl. And I need to go home before I do some really rude business in your bathroom."

"Well, make sure you say good-bye to the kids before you go."

"They're asleep, Reesy."

"Wake them up. Jade will be so hurt if you don't say bye to her. You know how that child is."

"No. How is she?"

"She's just like you."

"Well, then . . . fix her!" Connie laughed. "Get that child some counseling or something, now, before it's too late!"

"She adores you. Everything is Auntie Connie this and Auntie Connie that."

"Reesy, stop it."

"What? I'm just talking about your niece."

"That's not what you're doing and you know it."

"She loves you, Connie."

"And I love her too."

"I never said you didn't."

"So, what is it you are trying to say, exactly?"

"I just think you need to spend a little more time with her, Connie. That's all."

"Reesy—"

"Connie, she's your daughter."

"She's *your* daughter. Yours and Justin's. Remember? March thirteenth, 1999? Adoption? Sign on the dotted line?"

"I remember vividly. Sometimes, I'm just surprised you do."

Reesy's statement begged for an argument, but Connie was too tired and full to accommodate. "Don't start this, Reesy."

"You hardly ever come around anymore. I practically have to kidnap you just to get you to come see her and I can't help but wonder—"

"That's enough, Clarice." The sternness of Connie's voice silenced her sister like it had when they were children. "Don't you dare accuse me of not caring for that child. It's never been easy for me and you know it."

"I know," Reesy whispered. "I know you love her, and I'm sorry, but she's close to you for a reason. It's deeper than blood, Connie. There's a bond there that—"

"There you go again, with this bonding thing. I do the best I can, Reese."

"I know, but—"

"I'm grateful to you and Justin for taking my baby." Connie felt her eyes pool with tears she hoped wouldn't fall. "If she'd have ended up where I did . . ."

"We love you and we love Jade. She's never going to ever want for anything with so many people caring about her."

"I can't be here all the time. You're her mom."

"I'm just saying that you need to take advantage of this time, Connie. Before you know it, she'll be all grown up, and I just don't want either of you to miss out on knowing each other. You and I lost so many years. I don't want you to have to suffer that with your daughter. She's too young to understand now, but someday she'll wonder."

Someday, Jade would be all grown up, and maybe even married with her own kids. And someday, Connie would sit alone gazing out of the window of her small apartment, wondering where the time went, hoping that Jade might find the time to call and say something terribly sweet about how much she missed and loved her aunt Connie. Then she'd promise to come by later and take her to the movies or out to dinner. The image of being a lonely old woman, desperate for company, lingered entirely too long for Connie's tastes, so she figured she'd better stop being stubborn and take her sister's advice. After all, sometimes Reesy knew what she was talking about.

"Can she come stay with me this weekend?"

Reesy smiled. "This weekend would be perfect."

Connie ran inside her apartment and answered the ringing phone, just before it rolled over into her answering machine. "Hello?" she asked breathlessly, putting down her purse and pulling off her coat.

"Little Bird?"

Connie smiled. "Hey, Eddie. Happy Thanksgiving."

"Happy Thanksgivin' right back atcha, baby. You sound like you jus' got in."

"I did. I just got in from spending all evening at Reesy's." Connie sighed, then plopped down on the sofa and slipped out of her shoes.

"That sounds nice."

"It was all right," she said indifferently.

"Jus' all right?"

"I've never been big on stuff like that, Eddie. You know that. How was your holiday?"

"Chil', please. Mine was jus' fine."

"Did you cook?"

"Now, you know better than to ask me a question like that. 'Course I didn't cook. I cooked all them years at that restaurant, and after I sold it, I made myself a promise not to cook all that food."

"What did you make, Eddie?"

"I didn't make much. Jus' a small ham, and a turkey breast, a small pot of greens, some sweet potatoes, cole slaw, macaroni and cheese, peach cobbler, and two sweet potato pies. That's all. You know, I refused to cook like I used to."

"No chitlins?" Connie asked, knowing the answer.

"Ten pounds. But that's it!"

Connie laughed. "And who ate all that food?"

"I had a few of my bingo friends over, and a few folks showed up from church. Why you laughin'?"

"Because some things never change," Connie said reflectively. At least, Eddie never did. Eddie was warm and comfortable like flannel pajamas, hot chocolate, a cozy bed. Connie clung to her memories of Eddie, careful to keep them safely tucked away, close to her heart. Eddie belonged to her, whether she knew it or not. Whether she wanted to or not. And Connie wouldn't have it any other way.

"You doin' anything special for Christmas?"

"I hope not," Connie said teasingly.

"Now, you ought to not be like that, Little Bird."

"I'm too full for a lecture, Eddie."

"I know yo' sister done invited you over."

"Actually, her mother invited me to dinner at their church."

"That sounds nice."

"It sounds dreadful."

"There you go."

"I'm not going."

"What did I tell you 'bout actin' like a brat, Constance."

"Just because I don't want to sit up under those people and pretend I'm having a good time does not make me a brat, Edwina. Do you have any idea how much energy it takes to laugh at things that aren't funny, and act like you give a shit when you don't?"

"'Course I know, girl. I wasn't born yesterday. But that's yo'—"

"Don't even say it, Eddie. Reesy's my family. Jade's my family and even the boys are my family. But Ma and Pa Turner are not my family."

Eddie knew better than to argue. Once Little Bird had her mind made up, there was no changing it. Too bad she couldn't be so decisive about other matters in her life. Like setting her sights on settling down and having children of her own. Connie had never gone into much detail with Eddie about how Jade had become her sister's daughter. Eddie just remembered her calling late one night, crying into the phone about how she wanted to do the right thing for once in her life. And about how Jade needed things she couldn't give her.

"Reesy's a good mom, Eddie. You ought to see her with her own kids. And she's got a nice home, and a husband."

"You ain't givin' yo'self a chance, Little Bird. You more than capable of bein' a good momma too, baby. You jus' need to stop bein' so hard on yo'self."

Connie sniffed. "No. I'm not being hard on myself, Eddie. I'm just being realistic. I'm almost thirty years old, and I'm still screwed up. A baby deserves better than to have a mother too fucked up to take care of herself, let alone a child."

"Connie," Eddie pleaded. "Don't do nothin' rash, now. Jus' think about—"

"I have thought about it," Connie cried. "And I think that if I really love this child, I need to do what's best for it. And I'm not the best, Eddie. I wish I was, but . . . I'm not."

Eddie had hoped things would change, and that Connie would call her up one day and say Jade was home with her. But that never happened. The thing is, even though Connie never said it, Eddie knew that Connie wished Jade was home with her too.

"Well, you and that new man of yours got plans for the holidays?" Connie hadn't told her much about him, so Eddie wasn't sure what to think of him. Little Bird hadn't seemed interested in any man since she broke up with that pretty black one she sent Eddie a picture of. He didn't look like much of nothing to Eddie. Good-looking, though. Good-looking and good for nothing, with hair hanging down his shoulders that was longer than a woman's. All Connie would say about him was that he wasn't who she thought he was. Most men weren't, until you married them. It had taken Eddie three marriages to finally learn that lesson.

"We haven't really talked about it. John's like me. He's really not into this whole holiday thing, Eddie. It's just not a big deal to some of us."

"You don't talk much about him. Is he a good man?" Eddie asked cautiously, careful not to push Connie into her usual defensive stance.

"There's not much to say, Eddie. We haven't known each other that long, and besides, we're just kicking it. That's all."

"Kickin' it? What's kickin' it, baby?"

Connie smiled. "We're just hanging out. Nothing serious."

"Well, you want it to be serious?"

Connie sighed. "No, Eddie. I don't."

"Why not?"

"Because I just don't."

"He ain't the serious type?"

"You're probing."

"Little Bird, I ain't probing. I'm gettin' in yo' business. Call it what it is, girl."

"I think you just did." Connie laughed. "I don't think he's the settling-down type, Eddie."

"And that's fine with you?"

"It is what it is. I just keep it all in perspective." Perspective made all the difference, as far as Connie was concerned. Keeping it real. Keeping it at arm's length. Keeping her defenses up. That pretty much summed up her life in a nutshell. "You jus' need somebody nice, Little Bird," Eddie said sadly. "I think that's what you need."

"Well, if you ever run across Mr. Somebody Nice," feel free to give him my number. But let him know, I've got issues, Connie joked.

"Everybody got issues, Little Bird. Some folks jus' know what theirs are better than others."

Ladies Knight

K-Ci and JoJo crooned in the background, and sandalwood incense perfumed her small apartment. Connie and Jade had just finished soaking their feet in a sea salt and tea tree oil bath, then exfoliated with an apricot peel. They'd wrapped their hair up in towels and snuggled into matching white terry cloth bathrobes Connie had splurged on earlier that afternoon.

"Hold still, girl. I don't want to get any of this in your eye," Connie gently scolded.

"What's this for again?" Connie smoothed a thick layer of the green concoction over Jade's small face.

"It's an avocado mask."

"Looks like guacamole to me." She frowned.

"That's exactly what it is."

"So why don't you call it a guacamole mask?"

"Because it doesn't sound as good as an avocado mask."

"What's it supposed to do?"

"Make your skin soft and supple and minimize wrinkles."

"I got wrinkles?"

"Not after we wash this off." Connie wiped her hands on a towel. "Don't touch your face. I don't want that mess all over my furniture."

Jade giggled, staring at her aunt Connie's face covered in the green goop. "You look funny."

"Look who's talking. But you know what?"

"What?"

"We're going to look absolutely beautiful before this weekend is over."

"You already look beautiful, Aunt Connie. Am I going to look as beautiful as you?"

Connie smiled. "Child, you're going to look ten times better than your old aunt Connie. Trust me."

"How come you didn't let J. J. and Alex come? They wanted to."

"Do you think those two knuckleheads would've let us put guacamole on their faces and apricots on their feet?"

"No." She giggled.

"They can come next time and we'll watch movies and order pizza or something."

"I'm glad they didn't come. They get on my nerves."

"They're your brothers, Jade. They're not supposed to get on your nerves."

"Well, they do. They always play video games and never let me play. Then they always want to call me names and stuff."

"What kinds of names?"

"Names like Big Head Girl and Snaggety Tooth Girl."

"Well, you just need to bop 'em! Right upside their hard heads."

"I can't. Momma says we shouldn't hit."

"I guess she's right. Maybe you could do it when she's not looking?"

Jade laughed again. "You're funny, Aunt Connie."

Connie fumbled around in a silver cosmetic case, picking through bottles of nail polish. "What color do you want on your toes?"

"Um . . . red."

"Red? Figures. What about a nice coral?"

"Nope. Red," Jade insisted.

An unexpected knock at the door interrupted them. "Damn!" Connie mumbled.

"Aunt Connie!"

"Sorry, baby." Connie had forgotten all about the guacamole on her face until she opened the door and saw John standing there. He'd started to say something, but the creature standing in Connie's doorway left him momentarily speechless. "Connie?"

Connie's mouth hung open. "Uh . . . she's not here."

"Aunt Connie." Jade laughed in the background.

"She's . . . she had to go to the store. I'm her sister. Reesy."

"No, she's not." Jade screamed, laughing so hard she nearly fell over. "That's Aunt Connie."

"Is this a bad time?" John asked.

"Kind of."

"Want me to come back later?"

"No."

"You ever want me to come back?"

Connie folded her arms defensively across her chest. "Not really."

"You embarrassed?"

"About?" Connie asked defensively.

"All right. Hey, I just thought I'd stop by and say hello. Hadn't seen you in a few days."

"Hello and good-bye, John," she said, pushing him out the door, but John casually strolled right past her.

"Can I come in?" He was getting a kick out of this, and she knew it.

A tiny clone, wearing a green mask and white robe like Connie's, jumped off the sofa and greeted him. "Hi."

"Hello."

"I'm Jade." The little girl laughed, then pointed at Connie. "And that's my aunt Connie. Not my mom."

John pretended to look shocked. "That's Connie? You sure about that?"

"Yeah. That's her, all right."

"Jade. Time for bed," Connie snapped.

Jade laughed harder. "But you said I could stay up as long as I wanted."

Connie glared at John. "Can I help you with something?"

He walked over to her, peered down at her lips outlined in guacamole, and gave her a quick peck. John smiled. "That is you."

"What do you want?"

"I just wanted to see you, that's all. If I'd have known you were having a masquerade party, I'd have dressed up in something scary too." Jade grabbed her stomach and doubled over, hysterical in laughter.

Connie hit him playfully on the arm. "Yeah, well, you should've kept going. Didn't nobody ask you to come by here."

"But I missed you, baby. Where have you been?" John tried slipping his arms seductively around her waist, but Connie maneuvered her way out of his grasp.

"I've been busy," she said, trying to keep from laughing. "Very, very busy."

He ran his finger down her cheek and licked the guacamole from it. "I can see that."

Jade frowned. "Ewww!" She laughed. "That's gross."

John did the same thing to her. "Actually, shorty, it's not bad." He turned to Connie. "You got some chips?"

It wasn't exactly the kind of evening he'd planned on spending with Connie, but surprisingly, John was enjoying himself. He lay on the sofa with his head resting on Connie's lap. Jade sat contentedly on his stomach, bouncing bare feet with red painted toenails, eating a bowl full of cheese puffs. She'd watched every kid movie ever made and had just about laughed herself silly.

She's cute, he thought to himself. Looking at Jade made him wonder again if he might have remnants of himself left behind somewhere. John had gotten so good at cutting his ties and washing his hands of situations, he'd never looked back, never called. So if there were John Jr.'s running around in the world, he'd never know it. He quickly pushed the thought but of his mind. If he weren't careful, thinking like that might break his heart.

Sometimes, Connie couldn't take her eyes off her daughter. She twirled one of Jade's braids between her fingers, wondering how it had even been possible for something so perfect to come from the likes of her. Reesy often mentioned how much Jade resembled Connie, but she could never see it. They both had the same amber-colored eyes, but Jade's sparkled like crystal against her darker, sienna brown complexion. Connie stared at the girl, looking for hints of someone else in her. She had no idea who Jade's father had been. She'd been conceived during a time in Connie's life when love had absolutely nothing to do with it, and she'd played Russian roulette with sex, sometimes counting her blessings that herpes and a baby she hadn't planned for had been all she'd ended up with. Whoever her father was, he, like Connie, never deserved this baby.

"You comfortable?" she asked John, gently running her fingertips across his forehead. He seemed as mesmerized by these movies as Jade did.

"Aw, baby, I'm cool. What about you? You all right?"

She smiled. "I'm cool too."

Jade's stamina eventually wore thin, and Connie tucked her in on the sofa. Then she and John went to bed and made slow, languid love. Afterward, she lay contentedly in his arms, tracing figure eights on his chest. "How come you never wanted kids?"

"I never said I didn't want kids. I just said I hadn't given it much thought."

"If you did think about it, would you want any?"

John sighed. "I don't know. It's not that easy. You know? Having kids changes everything . . . your whole life. Your whole outlook on life."

"Jade's mine," Connie whispered. She had no idea why she'd said it, but at that moment the words seemed to need to roll off her lips. Another confession? Sure. Brought about by the comfort of the evening. The comfort of him. Maybe even by the three of them spending an evening together like a lot of families did.

"Nine?" he asked, confused. "I thought you said she was six?"

"No. I mean, she is six. But she's mine. Not nine. I had her. Reesy and Justin have been raising her since she was born, and adopted her two years ago."

"She know?"

"Are you kidding? No. Reesy's Momma. She does everything for her. Always has."

"Damn," he muttered. "That's a trip."

"It's . . . Most of the time, I'm fine with it, but, I mean, I don't regret what I did, but sometimes I wished I'd have kept her. In those days, I was really fucked up, John. Raising a kid just didn't seem like something I should've been doing. At least Reesy's got her and not some stranger or system. I know she's taken care of, and I can still see her whenever I want."

"That's cool."

"I didn't grow up like my sister. She had it good, you know? Good people, who took good care of her. Sometimes, I think about how differently things could've turned out if Momma hadn't left, or how'd they'd have been if I hadn't gotten stuck in foster care. I ended up with people who didn't give a damn about me. I definitely didn't want that for Jade. That's why I left. I just got tired of all the bullshit. Foster Momma Pauline was a damn zombie, and Foster Daddy Earl . . . it wasn't cool. I'm just glad Jade doesn't have to go through that."

"Earl wasn't cool, Connie?" he asked quietly.

Connie swallowed hard, then sighed. "No, he wasn't cool, John."

"How old were you?"

"Thirteen," she whispered.

He turned over on his side, then pulled Connie close to him and wrapped her securely in his arms. John kissed her head. "It's all right now, baby," he whispered. "All that's over now."

Most of the time, yes, she thought. It was all right. But then, there were times like this, when she was faced with trying not to remember how awful her nights had been with Earl, wondering if it were even possible for it to ever be over. Connie kissed John's broad chest, then closed her eyes. She was glad he was there.

Do You See What I See?

The word "shopaholic" was synonymous with Reesy. As were the words "charge it," "designer," and "who the hell buys shoes from Wal-Mart?" Connie and Reesy had spent the afternoon shopping at the new mall, built in the middle of nowhere between Denver and Boulder. Actually, Reesy was the one doing all the shopping. Connie couldn't justify paying those exuberant prices on the exact same things everybody else was wearing. Thrift stores had always been and continued to be her mainstay as far as wardrobe went. But Reesy had the easy lure of plastic feeding her motivation. The woman had every credit card known to woman and would whip one out faster than a gunfighter at the OK Corral.

"Connie?" Reesy modeled a dress against herself in a three-sided mirror. "You think this will make me look fat?"

Connie was busy sorting through blouses but glanced quickly in her sister's direction. "No."

"I knew you were going to say that."

"Then why'd you ask?"

"Girl, I don't even know. I swear, you're as bad as Justin is when it comes to shopping. He lies to me too, hoping I'll hurry up and make up my mind so we can leave."

"Smart man," Connie mumbled.

"Did you say something?"

"I have never lied to you, Reese."

"You just did. You know this thing would make me look like a whale."

"If I thought that, I'd have said it."

Reesy rolled her eyes at Connie's size-ten frame. She hadn't worn a ten since she was ten, and somewhere along the line, her sixteens had become a little too comfortable. "I hate you. How come I had to end up being the fat one?"

"You're not fat," Connie said indifferently.

"You always say that. I am fat, and you know it."

"Reesy, why do we always have to have this conversation? You are not fat. Look at me when I'm talking to you. Read my lips." Connie emphasized every syllable. "You . . . are . . . not . . . fat."

"Yes, I am."

"This is why I hate shopping with you. I can't stand listening to this."

"You have to listen to this, Connie."

"No, I don't." Connie rummaged haphazardly through another rack of blouses.

Reesy walked over to her and put her arm over Connie's shoulder. "Yes, you do."

"Why? Why do I have to listen to this every time we go shopping together? Hmm? Why?"

"Because I'm fat and you're not and you're my sister and nobody else will listen to me talk about how fat I am, so you have to. It's your birthright." Reesy smiled, then patted Connie's shoulder.

Connie kissed Reesy's cheek. "You're not fat. Now let's change the subject."

"Okay. But skinny people always tell fat folks they love that they aren't fat, when in fact they really are."

"I'm not listening to you. I stopped listening to you a long time ago."

"Look at this." Reesy pulled on excess flab around her midsection. "Look. If this isn't fat, what is it?"

"Love."

"Love?" Reesy laughed. "Girl, love ain't got nothing to do with this."

"Sweet baby girl," Connie said, holding Reesy's face between her hands. "You pushed two beautiful kids out of that body of yours. Kids given to you by a man who still thinks you are da bomb and is trying to hit it every chance he gets. There's love in those layers. So stop complaining."

Reesy shook her head. "You're so full of shit."

"You ain't buying it?"

"No."

Connie shrugged. "I tried."

"So, you in love yet?"

"What makes you ask me something like that?"

"You and what's his name have been seeing each other for a few months now."

"So?"

"So, if you were in love, would you tell me?"

"If I were in love, Clarice, believe me, you'd be the third person to know."

"You never talk about him. What's up with that?"

"There's not much to say about him."

"I don't believe that."

"Believe what you want."

"You haven't even told me what he looks like, Connie. Is he fine? Tall? Short? Fat? Skinny? What?"

"He's good-looking. You like this skirt?"

Reesy snatched the skirt from Connie's hands, then hung it back up on the rack. "Why won't you tell me about him? I spill my guts to you about everything and you hardly tell me anything."

"If Justin only knew."

"He suspects."

"That you tell all his business?"

"That I confide in my sister."

"If I had something to share with you, Reese, I would."

"Share everything, Connie. We're sisters, girl, and that's what sisters do. I want to know everything about you."

"You already know more than enough, Reesy. Some of the shit you know about me makes me downright uncomfortable."

"Tell me about this man in your life. Is he funny? Intelligent? Is he . . ." Reesy rambled on excitedly.

"He's cool. All right?"

"Cool? What the hell is cool? Come on, sis. You can do this." Reesy egged Connie on. "He's cool and what?"

"Anybody ever tell you that you are one nosy woman?"

"No."

"You've just been told."

"What's the big secret? What is he? An ex-convict or something?"

Reesy had no idea how close to the truth she was, and Connie had no intention of confessing this to her, or she'd never hear the end of it. "He's handsome, Reesy. But not the kind of pretty-boy handsome you're into."

"Pretty boy? Since when do I like pretty boys?" Reesy asked defensively.

"Since you married Justin."

"Justin is not a pretty boy."

"In any case, you probably wouldn't find John attractive at all."

"I don't appreciate that pretty-boy comment, you do know this? But we're making progress here and I'm not going to dwell on it. What's he do for a living?"

"Well, let's see. He eats, sleeps—"

"Connie."

"Right now he's working for a box manufacturer in Lakewood."

"Right now? What's he do all the other times?"

"Whatever he wants, I suppose."

Reesy frowned. "He can't keep a job?"

"I guess he can keep one when he needs one."

"I'm not sure I like the sound of this, Connie. This brotha doesn't sound too stable if you ask me."

"Let me think. Do I remember asking you?" Connie put her finger to her chin. "Hmmm, . . . nope. Don't remember asking you one way or another."

Another scrub, Reesy concluded to herself. She could tell that much from the brief description she'd managed to peel from her sister. Connie was definitely holding true to form, digging out her men from the bottom of the barrel instead of picking a fresh one from the top.

Reesy probed further. "I'm serious. Where's he from?"

"All over," Connie said indifferently.

"No. Where was he born?"

"Texas."

"How old is he?"

"He's grown, Clarice."

"You don't know a thing about this man, do you?" Reesy said, folding her arms defensively across her chest.

"I know he's not all up in my business like some folks around here." Connie spotted the exit and headed straight for it. She could feel an argument coming on, and the last thing these good mall people needed were two black women body-slamming each other in this nice department store, then brutally cussing each other out.

Reesy hurried behind her. "Does he have children? A family? Is he married, Connie? Please, tell me he's not married."

Outside in the parking lot, Connie stopped abruptly and turned to her sister. "I don't know. I don't want to know. And you don't need to know."

"You're sleeping with him, Connie. You'd better know."

Connie threw her hands up in the air in frustration. "Why don't you just tell everybody in the parking lot my business, Reese!"

"Why do you insist on getting involved with losers? I don't understand you. Don't you think you deserve better than some box boy, who can't keep a job and probably has kids strolled from here to the Mississippi?"

"And you wonder why I never tell you anything?"

"Honey, you're my sister, and I care about you."

"Thank you for that, baby. But I really can take care of myself. How many times do I have to tell you that."

"Did I say you couldn't?"

"Pretty much. You're saying I'm thinking with my ass and not with my head and that I'll probably end up regretting laying eyes on this man."

"I didn't say that. You just did."

Connie sighed. "He's cool, Reesy."

"He doesn't sound like the kind of man you need to settle down with, Connie."

"Who says I want to settle down with anybody? That's not what I'm looking for, Reese. That's your life. I'm not you. I like his company. That's what he is to me. Company. That's all I need."

"You need more than that. Face it. You need more than somebody else's leftovers or rejects."

"What do you think I am, Reesy?"

"Don't be silly."

"Don't get it twisted, sis. He and I have a lot in common. More than you'll ever know. I like him. We kick it, and have a good time kicking it. Neither of us is looking for more than that."

"What are you so afraid of?"

"What?"

"It's almost like you set yourself up for heartache and rejection. Like you go out of your way to find somebody who's going to disrespect you and treat you like trash, lulled into a false sense of true love by good looks."

"He doesn't treat me like trash," Connie said defensively. Reesy was desperately trying to push some buttons now, and Connie sensed an argument would be the final word in this conversation.

"Not yet. But honestly, Connie, do you think he doesn't have it in him?"

Connie clenched her teeth. She and Reesy would never see eye to eye on this. What surprised her most was how much Reesy's assessment of John infuriated Connie, and how compelled she felt to come to his defense. "He's just a friend," she said calmly.

"A friend that'll break your heart."

"And that's my business."

"I don't want to see you hurt again. Remember Jamil?"

"Every time I take my medication," Connie snapped.

"So, I'm wrong for not wanting to see you go through something like that again?"

"Then look the other way, Reesy. Everybody gets hurt, and sometimes, there's nothing anybody can do about it. I'm a grown woman, and I was handling my business long before you got here, and I'm handling it now."

"And look at what it's gotten you." Reesy stared at Connie, knowing she'd gone far enough, wishing her legs were long enough to kick her own self in the behind for that snide little remark. "I'm just saying—"

"Oh, I know what you're saying, Reese. We need to go," Connie said, through clenched teeth.

"Yeah. We do." Reesy pulled out her keys, then headed in the direction of her car.

Connie and Reesy drove home in silence. Connie thought about the things her sister had said. "And look at what it's gotten you." No. She didn't want to look at what it had gotten her. Connie was pretty good at reminding herself of her own mistakes, she didn't need Reesy or anybody else to do that for her.

Why are you doing this to yourself again, Connie? she asked herself. The truth was, John had a restlessness to him that threatened to uproot him at a moment's notice. The man lived to pack up and leave. John was a magician whose best trick was the disappearing act to keep his ghosts from finding him. He'd made it clear that staying in one place wasn't something he did well. John insisted on calling it a way of life, but it sounded more like running to her. Something besides that little old lady he called his grandmother pushed him out that door and on his own at fifteen. She suspected that secret would stay buried inside him forever, unless John decided to unveil it, especially to himself. His pride would probably never allow it, though. Men like him would rather run than show vulnerability. One thing was certain. John was even better at denial than she was. Most of the time, she tried adopting his live-for-the-moment attitude and go-with-the-flow philosophy. For Connie, it was all a matter of keeping things in perspective. He'd break her heart if she let him, and therein lied the challenge. She wouldn't let him.

I Come Apart

John lay alone in the darkness, staring up at the ceiling. Sleep wouldn't come, but thoughts swirled around in his head like the cigarette smoke swirled into the air. Connie always seemed to be on the tip of his tongue, the scent of her saturated his nostrils, and images of her danced behind his eyelids whenever he so much as blinked.

"What the hell are you doing, John?" he asked himself out loud.

Women had always played an intricate role in his life. Women like Mattie, who insisted on mothering him from the grave, pushing him up and out and through life whether he wanted her to or not. Her role had always been to ward off contentment whenever it got too close. She knew better than anyone, it just didn't suit him. Momma Agnes preferred the role of straight-arming him despite the fact that it had been her acceptance he'd hungered after more than oxygen. She'd taught him the value of keeping things in perspective. A man can never be objective enough if he's too close to the situation. Roberta had prophesied over him, tagged him, and labeled him before he ever had a chance to figure himself out. Convinced he was fathered by Satan, he carried her words with him everywhere he went, whether he intended to or not, laughing at the ridiculous notion of what she believed, and embracing it at the same time. Women he'd slept with, who claimed to love him, without the benefit of even knowing who the hell he was, had all played roles in his world, and he'd played his in theirs. Keeping them just within reach for when he needed one of them, but never so close that he couldn't breathe without inhaling them. John had made the mistake of inhaling Connie and allowing her to get closer to him than he'd planned, slipping into a place inside him he'd forgotten existed, and that had been the problem. He'd forgotten it, let down his guard, and given up his vigil of watching over it. She'd gotten close enough for him to care for her. He cared to be near her and missed her when he wasn't.

From time to time, he'd entertain the concept of love, falling into it like most people did, but never for long. Careless men *fell* in love. Conscious men waded into it. John picked up his pad lying on the floor next to the bed and wrote that down. Besides, he'd realized years ago that love had little to do with it. More times than not, it had all boiled down to timing. That's what made unions. Not love. With Connie, he figured, maybe the timing had been too right. Or all wrong, depending on your perspective. Timing left him vulnerable to suffer things most people suffer through at one time or another. Things like loneliness, hope, and what-ifs. What if he chose to stay here? What if he committed to the possibility of settling down? What if he asked her, no, told her that she was his woman, and that's all there was to it? His life had never entertained foolish notions of what-ifs because there'd never been room for them.

Connie probably relished thoughts of what-ifs more times than she'd admit to. She was careful not to mention them, though, but he could hear them in the questions she didn't ask and see them hidden behind those pretty eyes of hers. He'd always been selfish, and John rested in the knowledge that he hadn't changed. It was his selfishness that kept him with her. Everything about her felt good to him, satisfied and fulfilled him, and he stayed because he'd miss those things if he left. He knew what he was doing. The longer he stayed, the longer he was leading her on. The longer he allowed her time to build castles on what-ifs. John knew it wasn't fair to Connie, but what surprised him was that he even gave a damn.

If things had been different, he thought, maybe he could promise himself to her and everything good that was supposed to come with him. But things weren't different. Connie was wounded and so was he. What the hell could two wounded people ever do for each other, except lick each other's wounds? He inhaled deeply on his cigarette. If either of them had been different, what's to say they'd have anything to do with each other? To John, the irony was that the circumstances of their lives had been what united them and held them in place together. Like spirits attract like spirits. He'd have to write that down.

He knew the truth, even if she didn't. They desperately needed each other. And they desperately needed someone better than either of them. They needed someone strong enough to pull them up and give them the determination to stay up. But those superheroes would never understand people like John and Connie. So it came full circle. They needed each other.

"That's fucked up," he whispered.

Something about the way she felt lingered on him long after they'd made love. How could a woman who went out of her way to be as hard as Connie did be so soft? Her skin was like silk, daring him not to touch it. John closed his eyes, smiling at the images of her forming in his mind. Connie lay on her back, her nipples rising up to greet his mouth, begging him to swallow them whole. Her thick thighs cocooned him into her, and the deeper he thrust, the deeper she wanted him to. He slowly slid his hand down into his boxers, imagining it was Connie's tongue leaving a wet trail up and down the length of his dick. She wrapped those pretty lips around it, moaning even more than he did at the sensation of her tongue flicking across the head. Remembering the two of them, envisioning them, and craving her one more time, helped him achieve one last orgasm before he finally turned over and fell asleep.

Sometimes, he felt like he was the road. The long, black strip before him narrowed in the distance but opened up for him as he drove, welcoming him, embracing him like he was its long-lost son. This was his element. Endless and empty is how he preferred it because it made him feel as if he owned it. No one else existed on this stretch of des-

tiny and John laughed out loud, savoring his freedom. He'd rolled down all four of his car windows, letting the wind share his ride with him.

It didn't get any better than this, and John muttered, "Make this last forever. Please! Don't let this road ever end."

It didn't matter where it led as long as it kept going. That's all he cared about. The wind whipped at his unbuttoned shirt, and the sun burned like fire. He gazed out in front of him and watched haze settle over the end of his black rainbow, knowing he'd melt if he ever reached his destination. But John didn't care. Music. A man on the road needed traveling music. Sweet soul music. The kind that made his heart bleed and his eyes water, reminding him of his own humanity.

John reached down to turn on the radio, only to discover that it didn't work. "Damn!" he said out loud. How could he keep driving if his music didn't work? It all went together. Music, highway, him.

He was pissed, but only for a moment. John leaned back and smiled. The warm wind hugged him and he knew what it was to feel good. "No need to hurry, man," he told himself, easing up off the accelerator. "Take your time and enjoy the ride. Make it last a lifetime." John laughed, then casually glanced into his rearview mirror. Terror gripped him as John slammed on the brakes and skidded to a stop, then turned abruptly, looking in the backseat. It was empty. Of course it was empty. John chuckled and rubbed his eyes. "Been driving too long," he muttered. "Starting to see shit."

John turned back around, took a deep breath, and slowly pressed his foot on the gas.

"Whatchu doin' way out here?"

"What the . . ." Startled by the sound of her voice, instinctively he looked up into the rearview mirror again. She was there, but when he turned around, she was gone.

John eased slowly down the road, wondering what this new trick was his mind decided to play on him.

"You know you ain't s'posed to be way out here."

John slowed down, then came to a complete stop, staring at the mirror. The pretty, dark-skinned girl sat in the backseat of his car, wearing a dress so white, it nearly blinded him. She stared straight ahead, gazing out at the black ribbon of road they traveled on as if she were talking to someone in the distance.

"Who are . . ." John turned around again, but the girl was gone. The

heat was getting to him, and beads of sweat rolled down his face. His shirt now clung to him like a second skin, and suddenly, the air seemed too thick to inhale.

"Whatchu doin' way out here, boy?" John stared at her through the mirror. He recognized this girl. He knew her, but from where? She never looked at him, but he knew he was the one she was speaking to. He was the one she scolded. "You know you ain't s'posed to be—"

"I'm trying to . . . I know . . . I know . . ." John's head started to throb. It had to have been the heat. The heat was getting to him. It was too hot out here. All of a sudden, it was too hot.

"I done told you! You ain't s'posed to be way out here!" she said, angrily pointing her finger. "I done told you that!"

John turned to the backseat and began swinging his arm wildly back and forth in the air, anxious to rid himself of this—ghost! "Get the hell . . . Get outta my car!"

The voice came again. "You know you too far, boy. You ain't s'posed to be—"

"Shut up!" he screamed, into the mirror. "Shut the fuck up!" The girl kept talking, telling him he wasn't supposed to be here. Reminding him that he wasn't supposed to be here. Convincing him he wasn't supposed to be here. John covered his ears with his hands. "Shut up! Shut up!" Suddenly, the sun started to fall from the sky, hurling angrily toward his car sitting on that abandoned highway, and John screamed at the blinding light and scorching fireball coming toward him. He felt himself burning.

The sound of the alarm clock startled him awake, and John sat up, abruptly rubbing the sleep from his eyes, realizing he had only been dreaming. He glanced at the clock, then at the sun rays bursting through the window. John lit a cigarette, then lay back down and stared up at the ceiling.

Was it time to move already? he wondered. Seemed like he'd just gotten here. Hell, he had just gotten here. The thing was, this time he wasn't ready to go. Most of the time, when Mattie told him to leave, he was ready to leave, but not this time. John was tired. He was tired of moving and tired of being by himself all the damn time. Sometimes, he could admit that to himself. Most other times, he didn't bother.

He inhaled deeply on his cigarette, then closed his eyes to the smoke swirling up around his head. "I ain't ready to go yet, Mattie," he muttered. "You ain't making my ass do shit. Not this time."

Now, he concluded, maybe it was finally time to stand his ground.

In the Recesses

Her relationship with Jamil had haunted Connie since he'd left, turning her emotions inside out, then back again. She'd wrestled with her regrets, rage, and even the revelation that she still had feelings for him. Loving Jamil had always been as easy as taking a breath. Unlike most men she'd known, his intentions with her had always been more ambitious than sex. He'd expected more from her, encouraging her to open herself up to him and lay everything about herself on the table for everybody in the world to see, like him. Jamil wore his emotions on his sleeve and expected her to do the same. "It's not good to keep it inside you, sweets. You've got to come clean with me. Tell me what's on your mind. How else am I going to know?"

"Hypocrite," she muttered.

Days like this reminded her of what putting yourself on the line could do. Loving him had left her exposed, vulnerable. Raw. Open. Connie sipped on a cup of hot peppermint tea, fighting a constant silent battle to keep her emotions intact. Outbreaks were getting easier to deal with as time went on. In the beginning, she'd cry nonstop for a week, curse God and Jamil and anybody else she could think of, contemplate suicide, then watch Jerry Springer and forget about feeling sorry for herself for an hour. Nowadays, Connie found that quiet was better therapy than talk shows, and being alone, and peppermint tea, and patience.

John hadn't seen or heard from Connie in nearly a week, and that didn't set well with him at all. He missed her. He tapped lightly on the door to her apartment, several times, before she finally answered.

"Hey. What's up?" she asked quietly, peeping out at him.

"What you been up to?"

"Not much." She shrugged.

"You gonna let me in?"

"I'm really not up for company right now, King. I'll give you a call later on." Connie attempted to close the door, but John blocked it with his foot.

She sighed in frustration. "What the hell is your problem?"

He leaned down, nearly touching his nose to hers. "What the hell is your problem, Connie?"

Connie rolled her eyes, turned abruptly, and left John standing in the doorway. He followed her inside and closed the door behind him. "You sick?"

"I'm . . . yeah," she said, curling up in the chair, then started twirling a strand of her hair. "I'm sick."

John sat down on the sofa across from her. "You been to the doctor?"

"No."

"Maybe you should."

"I don't need to see a doctor, all right?"

"Hey, I'm just worried about you, that's all."

"Worried about me?" Connie's eyes narrowed. "Since when do men like you give a shit about anybody?"

"Since men like me got a thing for anybody like you," he teased.

"John, you know, I'm really not feeling well and I'm not in the best of moods right now. Why don't you just do us both a favor, take my attitude personally and leave?"

"If it were personal, I would. But we both know I haven't done shit to you. So, why don't you tell me what's up?"

"It's none of your business, King."

"Is it Reesy?"

"No."

"Some blast from the past come back to haunt you?"

"Something like that," she mumbled.

"Well. I'm listening."

"To absolutely nothing. I told you, I don't want to talk about it."

"But I want to talk about it. Now, I'm here for *you,* trying to be sensitive and sympathetic to *you,* and you're giving me the blues. What's up with that?"

"You know what, John? This is my personal business. I never asked for your sensitivity," Connie said coldly.

"And what if I just want you to have it, Connie? Why you gotta have a problem with that?"

Why in the world was she even having this argument? Connie wondered. She didn't know whether to laugh at him or to cuss him out, but she did know this wasn't something she wanted to talk about . . . especially now, and especially with him. John sat defiantly on her sofa, with his arms crossed over his chest, glaring at her, waiting for her answer, and Connie knew that if she wanted him gone, then she needed to tell him what was going on, then laugh at him, then cuss him out, then throw him out.

"I've got . . ." She hesitated.

"What? What is it, baby?"

Connie hated saying it. She hated feeling it and knowing it. She hated . . . it, and the fact that it was a part of who she was now. Most of the time, she was cool and the issue practically didn't even seem to exist. But eventually, it always reared its ugly head, reminding her of the consequence of trusting too much.

"Herpes, King. I've got an outbreak."

To his knowledge, he'd never known anybody with herpes and had no idea what an "outbreak" was supposed to look like. He'd always figured something like that might look like leprosy. He'd never seen lepers, but she looked fine to him. She always looked fine to him, even now, sitting in that chair, covered from head to toe in a baggy gray sweat suit, trying to cover up those delicious curves of hers.

"That's what's got you all bent out of shape?" he asked indifferently.

Connie laughed, then stared back at John in disbelief at the ignorant question he'd just let fly out of his mouth. This man was really a piece of work, she thought. An ignorant, inconsiderate, idiotic piece of work that really needed to get out of her sight.

"Yeah. That's what's got my ass all bent out of shape. And you know what? I think it's time for you to get the hell up out of my house."

"You've got some serious issues, baby," he said, shaking his head.

"I've got issues? I've got herpes, *baby,* and I think that gives me the right to have some damn issues!"

John sat silent for a moment. He stared at her, then calmly posed the question, "You think the whole goddamned world is wrapped up in your shit?"

"What?" Connie could hardly believe the things this man was saying to her.

"Mothafuckas lied to you, and you believed it?" he said angrily. "I thought you were brighter than that, baby girl."

"What the hell are you talking about?"

"I'm talking about you and this fallacy you got going on in your mind that the sun rises and sets around your pussy."

"John . . ." Connie choked back tears. "You need to go." She got up and walked over to the door.

"No, not until I say what it is I got to say."

"I don't want to hear what you got to say." Connie held open the door and said sternly, "Get out."

John casually leaned back on the couch. "You've been lied to, Connie. All the Earls and Johns and whoever the hell else told you that everything you are is between your legs lied to you."

Connie quickly closed the door. The last thing she needed was all of her business to become the business of the entire third floor of her apartment complex. "This isn't about—"

"Don't tell me what this isn't about," he interrupted. "You come hot and hard, leading with your ass like a man is supposed to sacrifice small animals to it. Bringing it like it's the shit. Then as soon as something happens to your 'shit,' you want to curl up in the dark and disappear. When are you going to face the fact that there's more to you than just pussy, Connie?"

The knot in Connie's stomach swelled inside her with every word that came from his mouth. She wondered if he really knew how close to the truth he'd been, or if there were other motives hidden behind his insults. Motives too obscure for her to fathom. "But this isn't about . . . The doctors told me—"

"That you have herpes. Well, hell, woman. You ain't the only one, and I'd be willing to bet the sun's going to come up tomorrow like it always does in this bullshit city, despite the fact that your ass is up in here tripping because you got herpes." John was pissed. Pissed that Connie would wallow in a dark room over circumstances she had no control over. Pissed that she'd been denying him, her, and leaving him to try and convince himself that she wasn't the only woman in the world, and that he didn't need her ass anyway.

"Hell! As much as I've had my ass down there, I wouldn't be surprised if I didn't have it."

The two glared at each other in silence, daring the other to say something, until, out of nowhere, Connie laughed. She grabbed her stomach with one hand, covered her mouth with the other, then stumbled over to the sofa and fell down next to him.

"What the hell is so fuckin' funny?" he asked, obviously offended. "Did I miss the joke?"

She shook her head. "I'm sorry. Really." She swallowed. "I'm sorry."

He started to get up. "Naw, I'm outta here."

"No!" Connie protested, then straddled his lap to keep him from leaving. "Please, don't go. I always trip when I'm like this and I'm sorry, King."

"Yeah, well . . . your ass needs to be sorry." He looked wounded. "Got a brotha all worried over some bullshit."

"It's not bullshit, King. This isn't an easy thing to deal with, man. Every time I have an outbreak, it resurrects all that mess from my past that I'd just assumed never happened and dangles it in my face. That's not cool."

"Maybe if you didn't sit up in the dark thinking about it, you wouldn't have to worry about it dangling in your face, Connie. You ever think about that?"

"No. Not really."

"There are some things in our lives we just don't have no control over, baby girl. You've got herpes. It's yours now, and ain't nothing you can do about it. But damn! Don't sit up tripping over it. That ain't going to make it go away."

She smiled. "How'd you get to be so wise?"

"It's got nothing to do with being wise. It's about surviving and letting it go."

"Letting it go? It's not that simple."

"Who the hell said simple had anything to do with it? I know it can't be simple, Connie, but it is necessary."

"Maybe you're right." She shrugged.

"Hell yeah, I'm right. That ain't even a question."

"I guess somebody like you has learned that lesson well. Huh? About letting stuff go?"

He grinned. "Baby, I had no choice but to learn it. Circumstances in life can kick your ass if you let them. I say let life beat the hell out of somebody else. I ain't got time."

Connie wrapped her arms around him and squeezed. "Thanks for coming over, and for all that sensitivity," she whispered into the crook of his neck.

John held her close, relishing the warmth of her against him. "This mean I can't get me none for a while?"

Connie stared at him. "Excuse me, but weren't you the one who just said my pussy wasn't all that?"

"No, now, I never said that."

"I distinctly remember you saying that, King."

"Your pussy is bomb, baby girl. I just said that the world didn't revolve around it. I never said I didn't."

John's chest rose and fell slowly beneath her hand as he slept. He'd insisted that if he spent the night, they'd have to sleep fully clothed on the couch, because he wouldn't be able to handle the pressure of feeling a warm, soft thigh brush up against him in the middle of the night and not being able to "do that thang."

Sometimes, John King could be just what she needed, Connie thought, closing her eyes. She was pinned comfortably beneath him, but she wouldn't dare complain. It felt good. Being without someone had become too easy. After Jamil, Connie made the decision to never allow herself to get that close to a man again, no matter how wonderful he seemed. Betrayal had come dressed up in the perfect package and walked away laughing at the fool it had made of her, and Connie had wasted the last two years feeling like an idiot. Maybe King was right. Maybe she'd wasted enough time feeling dumb and hadn't spent enough time getting over it. But that was easier said than done. Or was it?

"You've got herpes. It's yours now, and ain't nothing you can do about it. But damn! Don't sit up tripping over it. That ain't going to make it go away," he'd said.

He'd been right about that. It always came back, and she always sat around blanketed in self-pity when it did. Connie had been running in circles, and for what? Jamil? Jamil was gone, and Jamil never warranted the kind of attention she'd given him. But Connie resurrected him every time she had an outbreak, and every time she rolled around feeling sorry for herself. She doubted seriously he was giving her memory that same consideration.

John mumbled something, smacked his lips, nuzzled his chin in the crook of her neck, then snored lightly. Connie willed herself even closer to him than she already was. Maybe she'd make a promise to herself, she thought. Maybe, when the sun came up, she'd make it a point to finally wash her hands of Jamil, admit that herpes was something that was a part of her life now and nothing would change that short of some miraculous cure, and deal with it. Yeah. Connie smiled. Just deal with it, get over it, and get on. Connie slowly opened her eyes. Okay, so maybe tomorrow was too soon to expect everything to be peachy keen all of a sudden.

"This might take a while," she whispered. Connie closed her eyes again, then wrapped her arms tightly around John's midsection. Well, tomorrow would be a practice day, she concluded. The first of many, no doubt.

Lest We Forget

"Hello?" Connie asked into the receiver.

Reesy hesitated before responding, straining to read her sister's mind on whether or not she was still mad at her. "Hi, girl. It's me."

"Oh. Hi, Reesy," Connie said dryly. It had been weeks since they'd last spoken to each other, or, rather, screamed at each other in the mall parking lot. Yeah, she'd gotten over it, but she wasn't about to let Reesy off the hook that easily.

"How are you? I called you, a couple of times, as a matter of fact. Did you get my messages?"

"Sure. Yeah, Reesy. I got them. I've just been busy lately and haven't had a chance to call you back," Connie lied. "So, how've you been?"

"Fine. You know, same old, same old. Nothing new ever happens around here. What about you? You been okay?"

"I've been great. Thinking about taking a trip to Vegas this spring," she lied again.

"Vegas? You and your friend—what's his name?"

"John. Yes. Girl, I need a vacation. I don't think I've ever had one. Not a real one, anyway. And besides, Eddie's been begging me to come out there for a visit anyway."

"Really? Oh, girl, you'll love Vegas. Justin and I have been quite a few times."

Connie sighed. "Yeah, well . . ."

"Anyway, I'm sorry, Connie. About . . . you know. The other day at the mall. I didn't mean to come off so disrespectful."

"And judgmental?" she asked casually.

"Overprotective," Reesy corrected. "I just want you to have the best life has to offer."

"But that is judgmental, Reesy. Who are you to determine what that is?"

"Will you stop? I'm trying to say I'm sorry."

"Well, you should be sorry. I know you care about me, sis. Believe me, anybody who'd look for my ass as long and hard as you did has got to care about me."

"I do," Reesy whined. "You mean the world to me."

"And that's fine, baby." Connie laughed. "You're so—"

"Sweet?"

"Little-sisterish."

Reesy grinned. "Is that good?"

"Hmmm . . . I don't know. I guess."

"Well, I don't want you to get hurt."

"You want me to come live in your garage, so you can look out for me?"

"Girl, please. You can share Jade's room."

"You are too funny."

Reesy hesitated, wanting to ask more about John. Connie was so sensitive when it came to that man, but Reesy suspected that there was more going on than her sister was telling. "So, you really do like this guy, huh?"

"I really do like him, Reesy. And don't tell me how wrong I am for liking him. Do you know how long it's been since I've been interested in any man?"

"Kind of."

"He's not like you might think."

"But Connie, how much do you really know about him?"

"I know all I need to know right now, Reese. I know what's important to know."

"Well, why don't you bring him to the church for dinner Christmas Eve? We'd all love to meet him."

"I'm not even coming to the church on Christmas Eve, so why would I bring him?"

"Don't tell me that."

"What?"

"You promised you'd come."

"I did not."

"When Momma asked you at Thanksgiving, you said you'd love to come."

Connie laughed. "I said I'd try to make it, Clarice."

"It's because it's at the church, isn't it? I swear, you act like you're allergic to the house of God."

"God don't live there and you know it. Stop being dramatic."

"That's blasphemous, Constance," Reesy scolded.

"Now you're starting to sound like your mother."

"Connie," Reesy whined again. "Please come. You know how bored I get at things like that when you're not there."

"How would I know something like that if I'm not there to see it?"

"I'll pay you."

"Nope."

"I'll be nice to your man."

"First of all, I never said he was my man. And second of all, I don't need you to be nice to anybody on my behalf."

"You're so selfish," Reesy snapped.

"And you're a brat."

"I'm telling Mom," she whined again, then suddenly became quiet.

"Just like old times," Connie murmured. "I guess you think about her sometimes too, huh?"

"Not often. But, yeah. I think about her. Wonder where she is?"

"Don't bother wondering, Reesy. She's not worth it."

Between the two of them, Reesy had been the one to give their mother the benefit of the doubt. She'd been the one to love Charlotte unconditionally, forgiving her lack of mothering for something as simple as a hug from the woman every now and then, because more times than not, she was the one on the receiving end of those hugs.

"How's my baby doing?" Charlotte would croon to Reesy, curled up on her lap. "You Momma's lovebug, Reesy?" Reesy would nod and the two would giggle away all Charlotte's crap like it never existed.

Connie, on the other hand, had been the less forgiving daughter, and the one who absorbed the brunt of Charlotte's temper and frustration, because "she was too damn old to be acting like that" and "who the fuck did she think she was, with that smart-ass mouth of hers?" Being the oldest, it had been Connie's responsibility to pick up the slack left behind by their mother, taking care of herself and Reesy when Charlotte wasn't in the mood, or wasn't home, or wasn't interested. Connie watched suspiciously, painfully aware that it was Charlotte's guilt that usually fueled hugs and kisses planted all over Reesy. Other times her affection had been fueled by being high or drunk or both. Anger and contempt for the girls fueled everything else in the woman's life. Connie knew this. Reesy didn't. And when she left them, Reesy cried because she missed their mother. Connie had cried because, suddenly, she'd become the mother, and it scared her more than her younger sister ever knew.

Connie heard Reesy sniff on the other end of the phone. "You crying?"

"Crying? Girl, no. I'm just . . . I've got allergies." Connie wasn't fooled one bit. "So, you're not coming to dinner Christmas Eve?"

"No."

"Well, what are you going to do, then? You and John got plans?"

"I haven't given it much thought."

"Then at least send him. He can come to the church, and you can stay at home. Girl, we are not sweating you. It's him we want anyway."

Connie laughed. "Better him than me."

Their phone call didn't last long. Connie had a way of cutting it short whenever the discussion changed to the new man in her life. Reesy sat back in her chair, sipping gingerly on a cup of chamomile tea. Justin was away on business, and the children were all asleep. Quiet nights like this were like gifts for Reesy. She adored her family, but she adored rare moments of peace and quiet just as much, savoring the taste of them like she savored her cup of tea.

Thoughts of her sister drifted back to her. Connie was getting too old for this, Reesy concluded. Migrating to sorry excuses for men like birds migrated south for the winter. How come she couldn't see that she deserved so much better? How come she never even made the effort toward someone better? She'd tried fixing Connie up with some of Justin's friends, nice men, with aspirations much more admirable than which fast-food restaurant had the best value meal, or what kind of rims they wanted on their car. Connie made it clear that she wasn't interested in Reesy's matchmaking efforts, crying the same old tired song about being perfectly capable of finding her own man.

"More like her own lowlife," Reesy muttered. From what she could see, Connie wouldn't know a real man if one bit her on the leg.

She'd become so good at letting her past be her excuse for every bad thing that happened in her life, and Reesy had grown tired of hearing it. They'd both been abandoned and abused by Charlotte.

After Reesy had found Connie again, she struggled constantly to keep from letting her own guilt consume her. She'd been blessed with everything wonderful in her adoptive parents, and Connie had suffered the consequences of Charlotte's abandonment in the worst way. She'd been a child, hurt and alone and afraid on the streets, with no one but herself to take care of her. And yes. The thought of her sister out there alone threatened to torment Reesy into insanity sometimes. But her mother had been right. Nothing that happened to Connie had been Reesy's fault, and it was wrong for her to feel guilt over something she had no control over.

"I don't mean no harm, Reesy," her mother had reasoned, "but did it ever occur to you that maybe she wants you to feel guilty?"

At the time, Reesy was shocked that her mother would even suggest such a thing. "Momma, no. Now, why would she want something like that? Connie is just . . . she can't help it that things turned out the way they did."

"She wallows in her past, baby. Yes, it was horrible, and no child should ever have to live such a terrible life, but sometimes, it's as if she's not even trying to get past it. If she really wanted to, don't you think that she could?"

"It's not that easy, Momma. I'm sure she's tried, but—"

"Well, how come she refused to go to counseling with you? How come she doesn't get away from that place? The worst years of her life have been down there in that part of town. Why does she stay there?"

Reesy shrugged. "I don't know, Momma. I guess for some people, it's just not easy to move on."

"Then if she insists on living in the past, let her. But you have no reason for feeling responsible, Clarice. Connie's a grown woman, and if she insists on wallowing in that filth, then that's her business. You can't let that eat you up, baby. You've got yourself and your own family to look after. Connie's too old for mothering now."

"You're right, Momma. You're absolutely right. I guess I can't help her if she doesn't want to be helped."

Connie mistook her help for criticism. Maybe she was too hard on her sometimes, but only because that seemed to be the only thing Connie understood. Hard. Unyielding. No doubt this new man in her life was the same way, and no doubt he wasn't a bit of good either. None of them ever were. Even Jamil, who'd had them all fooled, ended up leaving Connie behind to deal with that disease he gave her and probably passed on to other foolish women too. If she was hard on her sister, it was because she loved her enough to be hard on her. Watching her settle for less than that was hard for Reesy, and if admitting that came across as criticism to Connie, then so be it. She'd criticize until Connie came out of that fog she was in and realize that what Reesy had been trying to tell her all these years was right. She just hoped Connie wouldn't get stuck wandering in that fog before this John King finished with her.

If Only

Connie strolled through the gallery, sipping apprehensively on an expensive, bitter-tasting white wine, fighting to keep the grimace from showing on her face. Ultimately, the grimace won.

"That bad, huh?" the distinguished baritone voice asked over her shoulder.

She forced herself to swallow the expensive concoction and prayed the expression on her face wasn't as terrible as she suspected it was. "No, I like it. I like it a lot," she said, referring to the painting.

"Then it must be the wine you find so distasteful." The warmth from his breath lightly brushed across her neck, the scent of his cologne wafted slowly up to her nose, and without realizing it, she closed her eyes and inhaled deeply.

Connie gazed up into the most precious brown eyes she'd ever seen, swallowed, then absentmindedly held out her hand for him to shake. "I'm Connie."

The handsome man slowly raised her hand to his mouth and kissed it. "It's a pleasure to meet you, Connie. I'm Sean."

Of course you are, she thought to herself. What else would he be but a Sean?

She and Sean floated from painting to painting like butterflies in mating season, admiring the artist's work and enjoying each other's company. Sean was the perfect gentleman. He was intelligent and couldn't have been more irresistible if he'd tried. He and Yolanda's artist clients had grown up together.

"I'm proud of him. He's worked hard to bring his dream to life, and it's paid off."

Insecurity had never been a badge she'd worn openly, but this man was too incredible not to be intimidating. Everything about him was impeccable, from the way he dressed to the fluid way in which he moved. "Are you an artist too?"

Sean shook his head, then laughed. "I wish. I do own a small gallery, though, not too far from here. He'll be showing there next fall," he said, gazing into her eyes.

Suddenly he ran his fingers lightly over her forearm. "What are you doing after the show?" His eyes traveled up over the swell of her breasts, then rested on her full lips.

"I'm uh . . ." *Going home, but first, I'd planned on stopping by John's crib to see if he was still awake so that we could get our freak on until the sun came up.* John. John King. The man she was currently involved with. The man she sometimes even found herself falling in love with. Before she even had a chance to respond, he gazed seductively into her eyes and smiled.

"Some friends and I are partying at a hotel downtown," he said. "I'd love for you to come."

Connie smiled. "Well, I'd love to come."

"Perfect." He grinned, showing off flawless white teeth. "Can you excuse me? I've got to make a quick phone call." Sean excused himself.

Before Connie had a chance to relish in the moment, Yolanda had grabbed her by the arm and dragged her into the ladies room and pinned Connie into a corner. "Do you know who that is?" Yolanda asked, in a low growl.

"What? Who?"

"That man you were talking to. Do you know who that is?"

"Yes." Connie put her hand defiantly on her hip, then glared at Yolanda. "His name is Sean."

"I know what his name is!" she exclaimed, trying to keep her voice down. A woman passed by them on the way out of the ladies' room, staring quizzically at the two women huddled in the corner. "Hi. How you doing?" Yolanda asked sarcastically. "His name is Sean Davis." Yolanda waited, hoping the name would register to Connie, but Connie stared back at her blankly. Yolanda leaned in close and whispered. "Sean Davis is one of the biggest freaks this side of the Mississippi."

Connie smacked her lips and laughed. "So? Last I heard, being a freak wasn't against the law."

"Correct me if I'm wrong, but didn't you tell me you were looking for the real deal? A true-to-God, cross-your-heart kinda relationship with a man? Didn't you tell me, late one night when we were both drunk and spilling our guts, that you wondered what it was like to be in love?"

Connie shrugged. "Well, yeah."

"Then don't waste your time, girlfriend. Mr. Davis ain't even trying to hear the word commitment. He ain't listening for the words love, togetherness, or devotion for more than the few hours it's going to take him to *get his*. After that, you're history, believe that."

Connie looked at Yolanda in disbelief. "And just how do you know so much about this man, Yo? Don't tell me you and Sean have gotten it on."

"Now you know better than that, sistah. Don't nobody partake of these treasures"—Yolanda pointed to her groin—"unless it's on my terms, and I don't do one-night stands."

"Excuse me?" Connie asked, knowing full well Yolanda had gotten caught up in a few hit-and-runs herself.

"Well, I don't do them unless it's my idea."

"So, how do you know? Let me guess. Somebody who knows somebody who knows him told you he was a dog."

"Yeah, and . . . ?"

"And people make up stuff all the time, Yo. Did it ever occur to you that maybe what you've heard was nothing more than a rumor from some pissed-off sistah who got diss'd by the man?"

"My friend was not diss'd by Mr. Davis. She turned him down."

"Uh-huh." Connie rolled her eyes.

"Fine. I'm only trying to save a sistah some heartache, but if you insist on going there—go."

"I just might, Yolanda," Connie said, as she brushed past her to leave the ladies' room.

"Don't say I didn't warn you."

It wasn't until later that evening when Yolanda saw Sean leaving with another woman that she realized Connie had heeded her warning after all. The two met at the door together and headed for their cars.

"So, I see you do listen to me," Yolanda said, smiling coyly.

As fine and tempting as he was, the lure of Sean Davis dissipated in comparison to what she knew she was drawn to in King. Connie shook her head and chuckled. "Am I sprung, or what?" She muttered the question. The man wasn't even here and yet he was here, in her mind, in her heart. Sean Davis, art gallery owner, handsome, with rich brown eyes, and more class than she'd ever seen in any man, paled in comparison to John, box maker, nomadic, rough calloused hands, who could kiss a woman's good sense into oatmeal. Sean was standing at the starting line, and Connie was in no mood to go back to the beginning. She had managed to keep up with John all the way to the halfway point, and curiosity was getting the best of her. Would they finish this race together? Who knew? But she'd come too far to quit now that it was just getting good.

"I was hoping you were still up." Connie smiled as she sashayed into John's apartment, wearing a long black knit dress that clung to every curve and a pair of black sling-back stiletto pumps.

John's eyes traveled the length of her. "Damn, Momma! That dress is wearing the hell out of you. Where you been this time of night?" He glanced at the clock on the floor near his bed. "I thought you told me you turned into a pumpkin after midnight?"

Connie twirled around in a circle. "Don't I look like a pumpkin to you?"

He grinned, took her hands in his, then pulled her close to him and kissed her softly on the lips. "Not any damn pumpkin I've ever seen."

"When you going to get some furniture in here, John?" Connie sat down on the mattress in the middle of the room and seductively slid out of her shoes.

"I got furniture," he said, stretching out across the bed in front of her, trying to remember if he'd ever been this excited to see someone. No, he concluded. He hadn't. "This is as real as it's going to get up in here, baby."

"That's too bad. How about we go to the flea market? I could help you hook this place up for cheap," she joked.

"So where you been?"

"Like you care."

"You know I do."

"I've been out. As opposed to in?" she said sarcastically.

He grinned. "Why you trying to give me attitude? What did I do to you?"

"I never said you did anything to me."

"Then tell me where you've been."

"Sounds like somebody is calling himself, checking a sistah. Now, I could be wrong, but that's what it sounds like to me."

"Naw, you ain't wrong. Where you been?"

"Well, if you must know . . ."

"I wouldn't keep asking if I didn't want to know, sweetheart."

"I had a date," she said smugly. "Sort of."

John shivered slightly at the unfamiliar twinge of jealousy surging through his veins. "A date? Who the hell with?"

Connie stared into John's lazy expression, then smiled. "One of Yolanda's artists had a showing at a gallery down on Broadway, and while I was admiring one of his sketches, this real attractive brotha introduced himself to me, and spent the better part of the evening gazing into my eyes. You don't know him, though."

"I'd better not know him," John said sternly, feeling another unfamiliar twinge of possessiveness.

"Well, you don't. So there."

"How was it?"

"The exhibit? It was nice. Extremely abstract and he did something with barbed wire I just couldn't quite comprehend. I mean, I wasn't feeling it, but . . ." She shrugged. "Anyway, it was catered. Cajun." She smiled.

"Cajun? In Colorado?"

Connie laughed. "Yes. In Colorado."

John shook his head. "Can't be real Cajun, then."

"No, it was. I met the caterer and the sistah is from Louisiana, born and raised. I had the best chicken creole I've ever had in my life. Actually, it was the only chicken creole I've had, but it was incredible. Have you ever had that?"

"What the hell kind of question is that?"

Connie laughed. "Oh, I forgot, Mr. 'I spent plenty of time in New Orleans and I've had everything from genuine blackened catfish to chicken creole to voodoo gumbo and everything in between.' "

"So," he said, eyeing her suspiciously, "you really digging this dude?"

She shrugged. "Yeah, I dug him. He was a perfect gentleman, well mannered, catered to my every whim, and did I mention how fine he was?"

"Yeah . . . you did."

"He was tall. Almost as tall as you, dark-skinned with the most beautiful brown eyes I've ever seen, and had a goatee, which I find very sexy. Oh! Owns a gallery over on Sixteenth Avenue, drives a beautiful silver Audi." Connie looked down into John's eyes. "You jealous?"

"Nope," he said, suddenly indifferent. He raised up the hem of her skirt, then kissed her thigh.

"Nope? Why not? Brotha was all that."

"If brotha was really all that, then why are you sitting here with me and aren't curled up somewhere with him at two o'clock in the morning?"

Connie laughed. The man at the gallery had been tempting and so had his invitation for drinks at some remote little bar he knew down in LoDo, but she'd insisted on him bringing her home.

"He wasn't my type," she joked.

"Oh, and I guess that must mean I am?" John sat up, then planted a trail of kisses from her neck to her chest, pushed her gently down on the bed, and hovered over her.

"Sometimes you are. Mmm . . . like now."

"So, you diss'd him? For me?" He smiled. "I think I'm flattered."

"Well, you ought to be. He's got an Audi and damn good manners."

John laughed. "But I've got you, baby girl."

"Aren't you the lucky one?" She smiled.

They made love, and then John drifted contentedly off to sleep while Connie lay next to him, reflecting on her life and all the changes lurking around it. When they'd first met, he'd talked about men coming face to face with their mortality and eventually wanting to settle down. There were moments in her own life when she found herself looking eye to eye with her own mortality, wondering if the day would come when she'd finally stop living like a teenager and settle down into the reality of marriage, even a family. She turned over and curled up against his back. John reached behind him, tenderly took her hand in his, then draped it over him, pulling her closer. This was one of those mortality moments. Sleeping next to him was something she'd grown fond of. Having a man around as a permanent fixture wasn't necessarily a bad thing. Or maybe the notion of having John around as a permanent fixture wasn't such a bad thing. He was comfortable, unpretentious, and unassuming. John didn't hold her up to any kind of expectations, and she suspected he probably appreciated that in her too. Neither of them demanded anything from each other, but they craved each other, despite their best efforts not to. If he'd stay, she'd stay with him. She knew this. If he did decide to leave and asked her to go with him, she'd definitely give it some serious thought.

John turned to her and kissed her tenderly on her head. "Hey? What's wrong?" he asked groggily.

"What makes you think something's wrong?"

"You're still awake. So, what's wrong?"

"I'm thinking."

"Oh, shit," he mumbled.

"What did you say?"

"I asked what were you thinking about, baby?"

Connie sighed. "Life. My life."

"What about it?"

Connie sighed. "King, do you think it's too late?"

"Too late. For what? Thinking about life? Yeah, baby. You need to think about that in the morning." He kissed her cheek. "After you've had a good night's sleep."

"No, I mean, for wanting things like marriage and kids? Hell, John, I'm thirty-seven years old. Who in their right mind is going to want my old ass?"

"I want your old ass."

"I'm serious."

"So am I."

"You're not serious. All you know is now, and for now you want me, but what about tomorrow, or the day after that? What about next month? Or next year?"

Sleep threatened to reclaim him at any moment. John answered groggily, "Tomorrow ain't even here, Connie. What's the big deal about tomorrow? Ain't shit you can do about tomorrow."

"You can hope."

He kissed her softly on her forehead. "If you got now, Connie, and if it's all good, why waste the energy hoping for something that doesn't exist?"

"You're hurting my feelings, John King."

"I'm not trying to."

"I know. I just wish you could understand."

"Understand what, Connie?"

"That there's a bigger picture, baby. A much bigger picture than just living from day to day."

"Then I haven't seen that picture."

"You're not looking for it. I am. I want something more than just living for the moment. How come you don't?"

Connie was probing too hard and too late at night. She wanted answers to the meaning of life, and all he wanted was a good night's sleep. John fought the urge to show his annoyance and then sighed. "Because I've learned that the moment is the only thing that's real. It's the only thing I can put my hands on. I can smell, taste, and see what's going on right now, and that's all I've got."

She sighed. Everything he'd said was true, but knowing that wasn't enough. There had to be more than just the now. Otherwise, what was the value in the next breath she took, or the heartbeat that was certain to follow this one? Connie turned to face him, then curled up in his arms. John felt so good sometimes, so right and right for her. But he also felt so temporary. "If I could draw a picture of you and me, I'd draw us just like this. And then I'd frame it and we'd be this way forever."

"That's a nice thought, Connie, and I can understand wanting to keep special moments in your life, but—"

"No, I don't think you do, King. This"—she pressed her lips into his chest and snuggled as close as she could to him—"this is all I've ever really needed and wanted. I love this spot, John, and if I could stay here for the rest of my life, that would be fine with me."

"Well, you can have it, girl. Anytime you want it. You know where I live." He laughed.

"Until you leave."

"Connie . . ."

"We know it's going to happen. You can't stay here, and it's only a matter of time before you're gone. We both know this."

"I ain't good at this, Connie. I ain't good at—"

"Commitment? Falling in love? Me either. The whole notion scares the mess out of me."

"So what is it you want?"

"I don't know. I guess I want what we have, only I want it permanently. I want it to last."

"What we have? What do we have, sugar? Me and you, we get together, we fuck, have a good time."

The carelessness of his words cut deep, and Connie suddenly snatched away from him, then stared down at him with tears in her eyes. "Why am I surprised?" She crawled out of bed and quickly slipped back into her dress.

"What? Connie . . . baby, come back to bed. What did I say? Connie?"

"Fuck you, John!" she snapped, before slamming the door behind her.

John sat up in bed, confused by what had just happened. What the hell did she expect? What did any of them expect? Sometimes, women made his head spin. They all insisted that they wanted honesty from a man, but the moment he gave them that, they started tripping. Connie was like the rest of them. She didn't want honesty. She wanted him to tell her what she wanted to hear. He thought they understood where each other was coming from, but somewhere along the line, Connie had made the mistake of taking this thing to some other level, insisting on dragging him along.

She showered as soon as she got back to her apartment, scrubbing as hard as she could, in water as hot as she could stand. It's all about sex, she thought to herself. She and John had understood that from the beginning. He needed sex, and so did she. They'd both gotten what they set out to get in the first place. So, when did she decide she wanted more than that?

"All of them can kiss my ass," she growled to herself.

She dried off and slipped into an oversized T-shirt. Connie crawled into bed. Tears slid quietly down the sides of her face. Despite her best efforts, she felt sorry for herself, pathetically replaying memories over and over again in her mind of all the dumb decisions she'd made in her life that led back to where she was now. Still wanting. Waiting. Concluding that King had been right. A person's life is summed up in the moment at which they are in time, and nothing else really mattered.

Connie heard a light knock at her door and reluctantly got up to answer it, knowing he'd be standing on the other side of it.

Her shoes dangled off the tips of his fingers. "I'm doing the best I can, Connie."

She took her shoes from him. "Are you?"

John came inside and closed the door behind him. "I'm not sure what it is you want from me."

"Exactly what I get, King. The truth. I know that everything you said was the truth and sometimes it hurts, but that doesn't make it wrong. Look, I can't blame you for any of this."

"Any of what?"

"I'm the one who let myself get all caught up in the idea of something more between you and me. I did that and I can't blame you."

"Maybe there is something more between you and me."

"I don't think so, John."

"Yes, you do think so. Otherwise, you wouldn't have stormed outta my place, pissed off."

"I'm not pissed." Connie started to cry.

"Baby," he whispered. John gathered her up in his arms. "Look, just one day at a time, Connie. That's all I'm asking. One day, and then tomorrow, we'll do what we've got to do. But right now is all I've got to give you. It's the only promise I know how to make. The only one I know how to keep." He lifted her chin and raised her lips to meet his, then kissed her passionately. "We've got right now, baby girl. That's all we need." Then John picked her up in his arms and carried her to bed.

For him, it probably was just that simple. And for now, she'd concede his moment to him, but Connie knew she wanted more. She'd reached the point in her life where an occasional promise would've been nice. Someone who knew how to keep them would be even nicer.

In a Perfect World

"Hello," Reesy sang, opening the door, feigning enthusiasm for the man standing in the doorway with her sister.

"Hi," Connie said, smiling broadly. From the look on Reesy's face, she knew right away that bringing John hadn't been a good idea.

"How you doing?" John asked nonchalantly. A toothpick dangled menacingly from his mouth, and Reesy had to resist the urge to snatch it from between his lips, hurl it to the ground, and stomp on it, smashing it like an insect.

He looked ominous to Reesy. Tall, dark, and too brooding to be handsome. John King stared back at her beneath hooded eyes, filled with a roguish indifference she found unsettling. Reesy wondered why women ever found men like him attractive. Reesy could tell just by looking at John, she'd had him pegged right from the start. He wasn't capable of caring about anybody but himself. Of course, Connie wasn't interested in hearing anything Reesy had to say about him, and she would no doubt end up having to learn this the hard way.

Reesy had insisted on Connie bringing him. "If he's going to be around my baby—"

"Your baby?"

"—then I need to meet this man," she'd told Connie over the phone.

"Or else what?"

"Or else you can visit her at the house. I don't just let my children around anybody."

"Jade isn't just your child, Reesy," Connie said defensively. "I'm the one who gave birth to her. Remember?"

"Of course I remember, and I'm the one raising her. Remember?"

"What makes you think I'd put her in harm's way, Reesy? Do you really think I'd be that irresponsible with my daughter?" *My daughter.* The words echoed inside her as if she were hearing them for the first time, and Connie took a deep breath, straining to make them real. Jade was her daughter, as much as she was Reesy's, and nothing would ever change that.

"It's not about you. It's him I'm not sure of. People are capable of anything these days, Connie. You know that."

"Yes. I do know that, and you know I'm not going to let anything happen to Jade." Connie had worked hard to avoid an argument during that conversation, but the expression her sister wore on her face the moment she laid eyes on John clearly indicated that a confrontation between them was inevitable.

The three of them went into the living room. John and Connie sat close to each other on the caramel-colored leather sofa, while Reesy sat across from them on the loveseat. "Justin's out golfing. He should've been here by now," she said, nervously glancing at her watch. "He gets so caught up in that silly game sometimes."

Where was this coming from? Connie wondered, staring at her sister, who'd transformed into superdiva somewhere between inviting them inside and sitting down.

"John? Do you golf?" Reesy asked smugly.

"Naw," he said simply.

"I don't golf either, Reesy. In case I forgot to mention it." Sarcasm laced Connie's voice.

Reesy ignored Connie altogether, choosing instead to focus on John. "Connie's told me so much about you."

Connie started to protest, knowing good and damn well she had hardly said two words to the woman about the man. But John stepped up to the plate, sparing Reesy a very embarrassing moment that Connie was dying to release all over her smug behind.

"And she didn't bother telling you that I don't golf?" John looked at Connie and kissed the tip of her nose. "Shame on you."

"It slipped my mind completely, baby," she said seductively. Connie and John gazed passionately into each other's eyes, creating an intimate circle just big enough for the two of them, while Reesy shifted uncomfortably in her seat, under the pressure of being the outcast. Eventually, Connie cleared her throat and turned her attention back to Reesy. "So . . . where are the kids? Are they ready to go?"

Reesy's cold stare cut into Connie like a steel blade. Her pretentious smile quivered in the corners, fighting diligently to stay in place. "Jade's upstairs in her room, and the boys are downstairs watching a movie."

Connie inhaled deeply against the frustration welling up inside her over her sister's holier-than-thou attitude. She'd seen this side of Reesy before, but never in this concentrated a dosage. But then, the woman had gotten it honest. After all, she'd been the Turners only child, and Reesy had been unfairly raised a Black American Princess (BAP) through no real fault of her own. Reesy sat regally on her leather throne, looking down her nose at John, while he sucked indifferently on his toothpick, seemingly unimpressed by her vain attempt at superiority.

Little sister didn't approve, John concluded to himself. Not that it mattered one way or another. No, he didn't golf, wear Dockers, or read the *Wall Street Journal*, and obviously, yes, she had a problem with that. He'd met people like Reesy before. John imagined himself an annoying ripple in the otherwise peaceful lake of Reesy's expectations and the thought made him smile. He felt sorry for her, though. Riding high up on her invisible horse, he knew for a fact that it was going to hurt like hell the day she fell off. The Reesys of the world played dangerous games of forming opinions of people they didn't know based on assumptions and speculations. From the look in her eyes, she'd formed an opinion of him long before he set foot in her home. He couldn't help but wonder how much, if any, of what she assumed about him was true. He made a mental note to ask her what those assumptions might be the next time he saw her. He knew something she'd never admit to, though. The two of them had more in common than little sister could ever be comfortable with. She'd fall over backwards at the thought of being like him. Just like she'd made assumptions about him, he made them about her, and the bottom line was, fate would never allow the two of them to see eye to eye about anything. John felt relieved by that thought.

Connie shifted uncomfortably against him, seemingly torn between trying to rise above her sister's obvious disapproval and trying to be real with him. It was bad enough she'd had to pacify Reesy in the first place to get an audience with her daughter. Connie's daughter. Reesy had been the one to encourage Connie to include Jade in her life, but sometimes Connie sensed that Reesy never wanted her to get too close. She'd always made sure to push thoughts like that from her mind whenever they threatened to become too real, excusing them to insecurity and even envy she knew she harbored deep inside. Reesy sat on a throne in Jade's eyes. Connie would never have that luxury. Despite her sister's reasoning behind the importance of Connie being an intricate part of Jade's life, Reesy certainly never had a problem injecting stipulations, consequences, and ultimatums, though. Not cool, Connie thought. Not cool at all, and she knew that she and Reesy would have to talk about this eventually.

"Connie also tells me you're from Texas? What part?"

"Northeast."

"Dallas?" Reesy probed.

"No."

Reesy waited for him to elaborate. He never did.

"Are you going to tell the kids we're here, Reese?" Connie asked impatiently.

Just then, Jade burst into the room. "Aunt Connie!" she squealed, then jumped into Connie's arms.

"Hey, baby." Connie beamed. "How are you?"

"Fine. Hi, John." Jade smiled.

"What's up, shorty?"

"Look!" Jade held out her hand to John, showing him a small tooth. "It came out yesterday. See?" She pointed to the empty space in her mouth.

"You pull that out yourself?" he asked, sounding concerned.

Jade shook her head. "It fell out."

Connie asked, "Did it hurt?"

"Nope," Jade said proudly. "And I wasn't scared neither."

"You weren't scared *either*," Reesy corrected her.

"And I wasn't scared either."

"Go downstairs and tell your brothers it's time to go, Jade." Jade jumped out of Connie's lap and ran to get her brothers. "Stop running," Reesy called after her. "It's really nice of the two of you to take the kids to the park." Reesy smiled. "It's pretty cold outside, though. You sure you want to do this? They're forecasting snow."

Connie attempted to smile. "We really don't mind, Reesy. The snow, or the kids either, for that matter."

"Do you have kids, John?"

"Not to my knowledge," he said casually.

Reesy's smile disappeared, and Connie quickly jumped in to salvage what was left of a volatile situation. "Jade's crazy about him, if you can't already tell."

"It appears so. Well, then . . . I guess, in the end, that's all that matters. Isn't it?" said Reesy, trying to sound sincere.

Connie sat bundled up on a park bench, sipping on hot chocolate and watching while John played with the children on the playground. She wondered who was having more fun. Him or the kids? All of them called his name relentlessly, and he made the effort to give each of them the attention they demanded. She saw a new facet of him emerge, fascinated by how natural some things seemed to come to him. The children adored him. Especially Jade, who insisted on him pushing her high enough into the air for her to kick a hole in the sky. He laughed and tried to accommodate as best he could. Lately, Connie and John had been spending much more time together, and what had surprised them both was that neither of them seemed to mind.

Watching John with Jade, sipping hot chocolate on a cold day, Connie felt sentiment begin to wash over her. "Must be the cocoa," she muttered to herself. She took another sip from her cup, then stared at the two of them together. Warm tears pooled in her eyes, threatening to wash away the beauty of the image held in them. There was the perfect picture of a dream. Jade laughed, then ran and jumped into his arms. John swung her high in the air, laughing too. Connie wanted to fold them up nicely and tuck them away in her pocket. How simply perfect, she thought, and how basic it all seemed. This was something most people took for granted, shrugged away as being no big deal, but for Connie, it was absolutely precious. How could anything that natural ever be a burden? How could it have been so elusive to her all these years?

She'd never let herself entertain the notion of raising Jade for more than a few minutes here and there. Notions brought about by sentimental moments, melancholy moods that begged fantasies of what it would be like to be a mother. Connie watched her little girl laughing and playing, and she saw Jade being happy, and being happy with *her*. Would it really be such a mistake to turn back the clock? she asked herself. Or maybe, to stop it dead in its tracks and write a whole new story where the roles changed and new characters were introduced. With everything going on in her life lately, maybe fate was telling her that it was time for her to finally reinvent herself instead of settling for the hand she'd been dealt. Connie had denied everything she felt passionate about for so long. Hiding beneath the guise of independence and indifference, knowing all too well she'd been lying to herself.

She had tried to recall what had been so wrong in her life, in her, that she'd convinced herself she shouldn't keep her baby. The only clear reason that she could come up with was fear. Her fear had chased her from owning up to that responsibility. Fear told her she wasn't worthy of being Jade's mother, and she didn't deserve to be happy. Tears filled Connie's eyes as she suddenly realized she wasn't afraid anymore. In fact, she hadn't been afraid in a long time.

John sat down breathless next to Connie. "I'm tired, y'all! I'm an old man! I need to rest!" He laughed. "They're a trip."

Connie handed him her cup, and he gulped down the last of her cocoa.

"Damn!" He grimaced. "Baby, you got a beer in that bag?"

"Now, you know I didn't bring beer."

"Well, next time we come out here remind me to stop and get a six-pack."

She laughed. "Next time? I'm surprised to hear you say there'll be a next time."

"Why? Ain't you having a good time? You need to get over there and let me give you a push in that swing."

"No, thank you. I've seen how high you push."

He shrugged. "That's the way they like it."

"Well, I'm cool on that. Besides, you might hurt me," she said, teasing.

"Never. Never in a million—no, make that two million years."

Connie smiled. He was such a beautiful man. Warm and rich like the hot chocolate she drank. Connie leaned over and softly kissed him on the cheek. He smiled gloriously. Then, Connie gathered up all her courage, inhibitions, and doubts and whispered, "Sometimes . . . I think . . . I'm falling in love you, John King."

John stared at the children on the playground. Words like that had never come easy for him. Sometimes, they were even harder to hear than to say. But today, they fell easy on his ears, and on his heart. He took her hand in his, slid off her glove, then kissed her hand. He stared deeply into her eyes and kissed her.

"John?" Jade called to him. "Can you push me again or are you still resting?"

He smiled at Connie, then yelled back to Jade, "I'll be right there, shorty!"

He hadn't said he loved her. But Connie hadn't even expected him to. She was learning that with John, it wasn't necessarily what he said or did that mattered so much as what he didn't say. If she listened carefully with her eyes, her heart, and the tingle she felt in her lips after he'd planted kisses on them, she heard every word.

Shoofly

"Yo! King!" the foreman called into the cafeteria. John had just finished his lunch break and was on his way back out into the plant. "Yeah?"

"You got a phone call in the office. Long distance."

"This is John," he spoke into the receiver.

"John?" the elderly female voice asked.

"Dot?"

"Hey, baby." She laughed. "How you doin'?"

He smiled. "I'm fine, baby. How you doin'?" He and Dot didn't speak often, but hearing from her was always something he appreciated. He'd always managed to keep a link to her, no matter where he was. More than relatives, he and Dot had always been friends. Even when he was a kid, other than Lewis, she'd been his best friend. Easy to talk to, and listen to. She'd never treated him like one of her kids, but as if he were as old as she was.

"I'm sorry for callin' you at work, John. I called the house and a woman answered. She gave me yo' number at yo' job. That's all right, ain't it?"

"Yeah . . . that's fine."

"She yo' wife?" Dot asked, trying not to sound nosy.

"Naw, Dot. She's not my wife."

"Yo' girlfriend?"

"You know, you're getting all off into grown folks' business," he teased.

"Chil', please. I don't care who that woman is."

"Good."

"So, how long y'all been together?"

He laughed. "You're a trip. Anybody ever tell you that?"

"Them kids do. All the time." She laughed. "I don't pay them no attention."

"So, what's up, Dot? I've got to get back to work here in a minute."

"I know, baby, and I ain't goin' to keep you. I'm callin' 'bout Agnes."

He and Dot rarely ever talked about Agnes. He'd ask how she was doing every now and then, if Dot didn't mention it first, but she'd never called him to talk specifically about his grandmother. "What's going on with Agnes?"

Dot sighed. "She ain't doin' too good, John. Agnes been sick. She been sick for a while now, like I told you. I knew she hadn't been feelin' well, but . . ."

"What's wrong with her, Dot?" he asked impatiently.

"You know she got sugar?"

"I know."

"Agnes had surgery about a month ago, John. They had to remove one of her kidneys."

"She all right?" he asked, surprised at how unfazed he was by what Dot had just said.

"They want to put her on dialysis. The other one is failin' too, and the doctor don't think she gon' be able to go much longer with it. So, they want to start her on dialysis soon."

"I see," he said. "I'm sorry to hear that, Dot. I really am." John had no idea how to feel hearing news like that. He thought he should feel something, but nothing welled up inside him. He wasn't surprised.

"Well, you know how stubborn she is. She don't want to do nothin' she don't want to do."

"Yeah, I remember."

"I don't know what I'm goin' to do 'bout that woman. She ain't even listenin' to me. I told her she need to do what the doctor say do, but Agnes jus' bein' hardheaded, like she always is."

"Well, look, Dot. I've got to get back in here and—"

"I know you got to go, John, but could you jus' call her?"

"Dot—" he started to argue.

"I know y'all don't talk much."

"We don't talk at all."

"Jus' call her and check on her. Let her know you doin' all right, John. She'd be glad to hear from you. Jus' call and say hello."

"Yeah. I'll give her a call."

"You say it, but you won't do it. I swear you 'bout as stubborn as she is." John chose to ignore Dot's comparison between him and Agnes. As far as he was concerned, he and Agnes had never shared anything between each other. Except for Mattie, there'd been no connection. He'd known that his whole life. He'd accepted it years ago.

"I'll give her a call, Dot."

"Please do, John. She'd like to hear from you. Agnes ask about you all the time, baby. Let her know you doin' all right for yo'self."

"No problem."

"When you comin' to visit? She'd like to see you. We all would."

"We got to go, man," John's coworker said, tapping him on the shoulder.

"Dot, I've got to get back to work."

"I understand. And John? Please think about comin' home for a visit soon. We miss you, baby."

"All right, I'll let you know. Take it easy, Dot."

"Bye, baby," he heard her say as he hung up.

He seldom even thought of Agnes. She'd faded into the back of his mind over the years, and sometimes he had to wonder if he hadn't really just dreamed her. After he left Bueller, he'd never bothered looking back, because there hadn't been anything there for him anyway. Ghosts of a dead girl and rumors of a retarded man he'd grown up knowing was his father lurked in Bueller. Roberta's pissed-off spirit probably still haunted the place too. No doubt looking for him.

He'd grown up calling her Momma Agnes. Those words together felt awkward on his lips now. And why shouldn't they? He was a grown man, and he hadn't needed a momma in years, if ever. Long ago, he'd faced the fact that Agnes was pitiful. She'd been more pitiful than all of them; John, Mattie, even Fool. Agnes had been a woman who'd insisted on being lonely and miserable, then took it out on him, making him feel like a visitor in what should've been his home. She'd made it clear to him his whole life that she had no use for him. As a kid, knowing that hurt him. As a man, he realized she'd done him a favor. Agnes had taught him lessons on what it was to be in a room with someone, in a relationship with someone, and to be disconnected. Knowing that lesson had saved his life on more than one occasion. It made it easy for him to pick up and pack up and go where he wanted to go, with no thought of anyone else but himself.

Dot had no right asking him to see about Agnes. For what? he wondered. She'd never given a damn about him.

In the Seat of Wisdom

"I really 'preciate the ride home, son." The old man sitting next to John worked with him at the plant, but John had never seen him before. "That ol' truck of mine 'bout on its last leg. I 'call myself rebuildin' that transmission last summer, but you know how transmissions is. Truck ain't never been the same."

Rush-hour traffic crept along Colorado Boulevard. The snow falling steadily wasn't helping matters either. John wondered why people living in a place like Colorado didn't seem to know how to handle snow when it came to driving.

"Damnit!" John growled when the car in the next lane nearly swerved into him.

"Fool ass!" the old man shouted. "Dumb ass! How the hell you gon' live in Denver and don't know nothin' 'bout drivin' in the snow? Hell! The shit ain't even stickin' good."

"I don't know, man," John said, shaking his head. "I just don't know."

"So, where you from, son? 'Cause I know you ain't from here. Seem like you got too much sense to be from here."

"I'm from all over," John said nonchalantly.

The old man laughed. "Aw, I see. You one of them."

"One of what?"

"One of them brothas who think it's cool not bein' from anywhere in particular."

John shrugged. "It's true whether it's cool or not."

" 'Course it is. I s'pose you ain't got no people neither? Man like you, probably ain't got no use for kinfolk." John didn't say anything. "Me? I'm from Macon, Georgia." He volunteered, as if John had asked the question. "Ever been to Macon?"

"I been there."

He laughed. "Well . . . even if you hadn't you wasn't missin' much. Left outta Macon goin' on thirty-six, maybe thirty-seven years ago. I go back every now and then. Got a brother still living there and I go back to see him. I miss him. Don't miss Macon, though. Ain't shit in Macon." He looked at John. "You got anybody to miss?"

"Naw, man. Can't say that I do."

The old man grinned. "Not even a woman? C'mon now. I know you got to have a woman you done left behind that you miss from time to time. I know I got me a few. Don't miss the bullshit they brung, but I sho' miss 'em from time to time. You ain't got no woman you missin'?"

John shook his head. "No. Don't miss any of them." And he didn't, not enough to have stayed or to have gone back to see any of them. Not even enough to call. Except that, every now and then, the smell of something familiar awakened brief memories of a particular smile, laugh, or touch. He missed aspects of women, holding the value of those aspects in the back of his mind, frozen in time, like photographs. "Not much anyway."

"What's wrong with you, boy? Ain't you never had you no good pussy?"

John couldn't help but laugh. "I've had plenty of good pussy."

"But none good 'nuff to miss?"

"You asked me if I missed a woman, man. Now, if you want to know if there's some pussy I miss—"

"Boy!" he laughed. "I was startin' to think you was dead or gay. You know you remind me of my boy. Bobby. He ought to be 'bout yo' age now, I guess." The look on the old man's face told John that he and Bobby weren't as close as he'd have liked.

"Bobby live here in Denver?" John asked.

The old man sadly shook his head, then stared off into the distance. "Naw. I ain't seen him in . . . Damn!" he muttered. "Got to be goin' on ten, eleven, years now."

"Sorry to hear that." John was careful not to pry. Some things were just personal, and should be left that way.

"Things happen sometimes. I'd heard he joined the service some years back. Army . . . or . . . no. The marines. His grandmomma told me he was in Germany, but that was a few years back." His voice trailed off. "Me and his momma . . . we split up when he was a little boy. She got married again to a good man, from what I hear. Where yo' daddy?"

John drove in silence, not bothering to answer that question. Some things were just personal, and should be.

"I s'pose you ain't got no use for one of those neither?" John glanced at the old man, then turned his attention back to driving. "He dead?"

"No."

"You know who he is, though?"

"Yeah . . . I know who he is."

The old man nodded. "He musta done somethin' pretty bad fo' you not to want to talk 'bout him. Hard as hell for a boy to forgive his daddy." A forlorn look glazed over the man's eyes. "He forgive his momma anything, but boys don't ever forgive they daddies." He turned to John. "You got kids? You got boys?"

"No. No kids."

"Well . . . when you get some and if you get some boys, make sho' you don't ever fuck up, 'cause boys will hold it against you. Girls won't, but boys will. I always wondered why that was. I figure boys expect more from they daddies then girls do. Boys know what a man's made of 'cause he made of the same thing, don't matter how old he is. Girls don't know nothin' 'bout what it is to be a man, so they ain't got no problem forgivin' them. Boys never do."

John sighed, trying to hide his impatience. "That's too bad, man. Sorry to hear about you and your son."

"Don't be sorry for me. I'll hear from him again, eventually. Always do. He'll catch up with me. What 'bout you? You ever catch up with yo' daddy? Ever call him?"

John flicked on his left turn signal, turning down Martin Luther King Boulevard. The old man said he lived on Thirtieth and Elm, and John was in a hurry to get him home. He talked too much. "No, I don't call him. My daddy don't know who the hell I am."

"Bet he do. Bet he'd know you if he saw you."

"Well, that's not something I'll ever have to worry about, because he ain't never seeing my ass."

The old man grinned. "It ain't yo' ass he wanna look at anyway, son. It's yo' eyes."

"My eyes? Why my eyes?"

"So he can see some of him in you. He look into yo' eyes and see hisself. That's all he want. To see hisself in you, so he know that when he die, there'll be a part of him left behind, and then he know that he gon' live on in his son." John turned down Elm Street. "This here's my place."

He pulled over to the curb in front of the old man's house. "Ain't shit about him in me."

"You tellin' me, or you tellin' yo'self?"

John was too tired for the man's philosophy lesson and he had little patience for conversations that resurrected thoughts of Fool, who'd never been of any consequence to John anyway. He sighed. "Well . . . here you go, man. I've got to be going now."

The old man opened the door to get out, and then turned to John before leaving. "You know why they call it seed?"

"What?" John asked.

"Cum, boy! Sperm! Know why they call it seed?" John stared at him. " 'Cause once you plant it in a warm, moist pussy, it grows into what it came from." The old man laughed, then got out of the car. John slowly pulled away from the curb, hearing the old man calling to him in the distance. "You got him in you, son! He there, all right! You might not like it, but he can't help but be there!"

You jus' like him. Ever think 'bout that, John Tate? He raped that girl. But you killed her.

John just shook his head and turned his car in the direction of home. Seed or no seed, he and Fool didn't have a thing in common as far as he was concerned. It didn't matter to John if the man were dead or alive. He was nothing. And that's all there was to it.

Always Be a Part of Me

Reesy casually strolled into Connie's apartment, greeting her with an icy stare. "You summoned me?" she asked coldly.

"Thank you for coming, Reesy. How have you been?" Connie couldn't believe how nervous she was. The palms of her hands were sweating, and her heart raced anxiously inside her chest. She'd been anticipating and dreading this conversation they were about to have for weeks. Rehearsing what she might say, mulling over her thoughts, making sure she'd given this all the attention it deserved. The last time she'd given this much thought to anything was when Reesy and Justin asked her if they could officially adopt Jade.

Reesy sat down and crossed her legs. "Oh . . . so, now you want to know how I've been?"

"You losing weight?" Connie asked, smiling.

Reesy rolled her eyes. "No."

"Justin and the kids okay?"

"Justin and the kids are fine, Connie. Now, why don't we cut the crap and get down to why you really asked me over here," Reesy hissed.

Her abruptness caught Connie off guard. She'd never seen this side of her sister, and Connie resisted the temptation to greet Reesy's defensiveness with some of her own. Now was not the time, she'd concluded. "I thought we needed to talk."

Reesy looked around the apartment. "Where's what's his name? Is he living here now?"

"I didn't ask you over here to talk about him, Reesy," Connie replied shortly.

"Well, maybe I want to talk about him, Connie."

"John's none of your business."

"John's my business if he's going to be around my kids. You're a grown woman, Connie. You can do what you want, and if that happens to be surrounding yourself with assholes, that's your business, but I'm not going to let my kids—"

"I want to talk about Jade."

"Jade?" Reesy's demeanor softened slightly. "What about Jade?"

Connie hoped like hell that Reesy would see the reason behind what she was about to say, hoping they could have a rational conversation about the future of the child they both adored. Connie took a deep breath. "Well . . . you know how you've been saying that I need to spend more time with her?"

"Yes. And you've been doing that."

"And I've loved it, Reesy. I think Jade's loved it too."

"Jade loves you, Connie. What's your point?" Reesy eyed her suspiciously.

"My point is, I'd like to have a more consistent role in her life."

"Consistent? What do you mean? Consistent?"

"Weekends? I'd like weekend visitation, Reesy."

Reesy shrugged. "You can see her any weekend you want. What's the big deal?"

"I'm talking about every weekend, Reesy. I'd like to have Jade come live with me every weekend." Connie swallowed hard as Reesy's eyes narrowed, staring back at her.

"Live with you?"

"Yes."

"What's this about, Connie? What's going on? Did he put you up to this?"

"Up to what?"

"That's what I'd like to know. What's going on?"

Connie's impatience was starting to show, and she hated having to explain herself to Reesy where Jade was concerned. "I just want to spend more time with my daughter. What's wrong with that?"

"Your daughter? Now, see, that's what I'm talking about. She's six years old, and lately, all of a sudden, she's your daughter."

"No. Not all of a sudden."

"Why are you tripping, Connie?"

"I'm not the one tripping. I'm trying to step up and do what I should've done a long time ago. Why are you tripping, Reesy?"

"Because I'm the one who's raised that child. I'm the one who's taken care of her ever since she was born. Where were you?" Reesy tallied all the times in her head when she'd practically had to get down on her hands and knees and beg Connie to spend more time with Jade. Now, all of a sudden, since John King had come into the picture, Connie seemed to want to cut and paste together her own version of a family. As far as she was concerned, he wasn't good enough for Connie and he sure as hell didn't deserve a place in Jade's life.

Reesy's insensitive words cut through Connie like daggers, and she fought the urge to set free her own anger, burning the back of her throat. "That's not fair, Reesy."

"No, it isn't fair. Neither is this conversation. That man put you up to this, didn't he? I'm not surprised. That asshole walks around like he's God's gift, gives you some good dick and you lose you damn mind!"

To hell with you! she wanted to scream. Connie swallowed those words, trying to maintain a cool head despite Reesy's best efforts to make her lose her temper. "I'm her mother, Reesy."

"You gave birth to her, Connie, but I'm her mother. Years ago, you begged me to be her mother, and that's what I've been doing for the last six years."

"Years ago, I needed to get myself together."

"And you think you've done that? You run around here with men from Mars and you think you've gotten yourself together?"

"It's not about him!" Connie snapped. "How many times do I have to say that? This has nothing to do with him!"

"Doesn't it, Connie? This man waltzes into your life, and suddenly you're playing house and want to be Mommy? And you expect me to believe he has nothing to do with this?"

A tear escaped and streamed down Connie's cheek. She stared back at Reesy, then quietly said, "And what if he does? For the first time in my life, I might have something to look forward to, Reesy. Is that wrong? I'm putting the pieces of my life where they belong, and maybe having him in my life has allowed me to do that. Tell me . . . is that a mistake, Reesy?"

"If you think he's the one, Connie, then you do what you've got to do. Maybe I'm wrong. And maybe I've got the wrong impression of the brotha. But you're talking about my baby, Connie."

"My baby, Reesy. We agreed a long time ago that when I was ready, when I'd gotten myself together—"

"Are you saying you want custody of Jade? Is that what you're telling me?"

"I'm not saying—I wouldn't do something like that. Not right away, Reesy."

"Not ever, Connie! This is ridiculous. Listen to what you're saying. You want to take this child from the only home, the only family she's ever known because you've suddenly gotten yourself together?" Reesy snapped her fingers.

Connie looked stunned, then murmured more to herself than to her sister, "When you're ready, Connie. She's your daughter, whenever you're ready." She stared glassy-eyed at Reesy. "How many years have you been telling me that, Reesy?" All of a sudden, Connie realized it was time to come to terms with what she'd suspected was true all along. Reesy's song and dance about Connie's relationship with Jade was just that. A song and a dance designed to reinforce the fact that Reesy was perfect in all her good intentions, and Connie was perfect in making a fool of herself. Reesy had spent years drilling motherhood into Connie's head, making sure she never let amnesia set in like Connie had sometimes prayed it would. For the first time Connie understood, the woman was no different than most people, and she had only been talking out of the side of her head, saying what she thought Connie wanted to hear, knowing all along that she never meant any of it.

"When she was two—three, hell, Connie, even four years old, then I could see it. But you want to step in now and just snatch her up from her home? Does that make sense to you?"

"It's all starting to make sense now, Reesy."

"That's my baby, Connie. I'm Mommy. Justin's Daddy."

"Reesy, just listen to me."

Reesy picked up her purse and walked over to the front door. "No, you listen. Whatever fantasy trip this man's got you on, whatever you want to do with your life, fine. You live like Cinderella up in here with Prince Charming if you want to. You're a grown woman, Connie, and I can't stop you. But Jade's not playing."

"It's not like I just came up with this idea yesterday. I've always wanted her, Reesy. Why do you think it's been so hard for me to spend time with her? You have no idea what it's been like. Wanting my child and not believing I could have her. Falling in love with her each and every time she so much as smiled at me, then having to turn her over to you again, like I'm returning a cup of sugar I've borrowed. I've never felt I deserved Jade. I never felt I was good enough."

Reesy's eyes narrowed. "And you're good enough now, Connie? You deserve her now?"

"I do." Connie swallowed hard. "I take it you don't think so?"

"I just can't help but wonder how much of this has to do with Jade and how much of it has to do with John?"

"I love my daughter."

"I love my daughter too. I love her enough to fight like hell to keep her." Tears rested inside Reesy's eyes. She loved Connie more than anything, but not enough to let her tear her little girl apart. "You might be happy now, Connie. Lord knows I hope you are. But when he breaks your heart, when he leaves, and I think we both know he will, then all you'll have left is Jade. She hasn't been enough for you all these years. What makes you think she'll be enough for you without the whole package?"

"You haven't been listening to me. I loved that little girl enough to give her away, Reesy. Because I knew I couldn't be the kind of mother she needed back then. Could you have done it, Reesy? Could you have given any of your children away?"

"I'd die for my children, Connie. Jade included. Can you say that?"

Connie sobbed. "I die for her every time I have to give her back to you."

"Have you given any thought of what something like this could do to her? Suddenly, Auntie Connie's Mommy, and Mommy is Auntie Reesy? Have you thought about her at all?"

"So I should settle for the fact that you get to have it all, Reese? You get to have your family and mine too? And what does that leave me with?"

"We are all your family. You haven't lost Jade, but you're the one who chose to play a different role in her life. You could've stopped the adoption, Connie. But you didn't."

"I didn't know. I didn't expect—"

"To change your mind? Like it's that simple. You can just change your mind, and we just hand her over to you like it's no big deal? And what happens when you change your mind the other way, Connie? Jade's not a volleyball."

"I'm sick of my time with my daughter being on your goddamned terms! I'm tired of asking for permission to see her, and having to bring her home when you say! I did what I did because I thought I was doing the right thing."

"You did do the right thing."

"And I'm the one suffering from that."

"Connie—"

"You have everything, Reesy. They took you and left me behind. You grew up with people who loved you. Who cared for you. All I've ever had is me."

"You've got us, Connie. We love you. We've always loved you."

"I need my own, Reesy. How come you can't understand that?"

Desperation swelled in Reesy's voice. "Don't do this to her. Please, Connie. Don't do this to Jade."

Connie held open her apartment door. "I think you need to leave, Reesy."

Reesy walked out into the hallway, then turned to Connie one last time. "I'll fight you for her. I'll fight you with everything I've got."

Connie bit down on her bottom lip. "Yeah. You've made your point, sis," she said, closing the door behind her sister.

Fruit of My . . . ?

Reesy sat at the foot of her daughter's bed, watching her sleep. Jade looked so much like Connie sometimes, she thought. But looking like her wasn't enough for Connie to threaten to take Jade away from the only home she'd ever known. Reesy remembered the first time she held that tiny baby in her arms and swore a silent allegiance to be the kind of mother to Jade that Charlotte never was to them. She'd never intended on keeping Jade permanently, and Reesy tried as best she could to keep the reality of their special situation in perspective. In time, she'd truly hoped that Connie and Jade could be together, but the years droned on and Connie drifted in and out of questionable and unsavory situations that left her too preoccupied to be bothered with Jade. Reesy knew how much attention children demanded, and despite her best efforts to believe otherwise, Reesy knew that Connie's attention was usually focused on herself, or some man . . . in this case, John. She took a deep breath and tears filled her eyes. Finally she could admit it, even if it was only to herself. No. Connie wasn't good enough for Jade. She never deserved that little girl, and it was this revelation that broke Reesy's heart. It was this revelation she knew she'd never utter to another soul.

Justin woke up next to an empty space that should've been filled by his wife. He crawled out of bed, knowing exactly where to find her. "Baby?" he whispered, peeking into Jade's bedroom. "It's late, Reese. Come back to bed."

"Why can't she see what she's doing, Justin?" she asked quietly. "Why can't she see how utterly selfish she's being about this whole thing?"

He came into the room, then knelt down in front of her. "I don't think she sees it that way at all, baby."

"But it's so obvious."

"To you and me . . . yeah. But to Connie . . . I think she just wants something special for a change, Reese. She's had a lot of crap dumped on her her whole life."

"And now she wants to dump that crap on this baby?"

"Now, you know better than that. She'd never intentionally hurt Jade, just like you wouldn't."

"Something like this would hurt her and confuse her, Justin. But Connie's too shortsighted and wrapped up in that man to see that."

"Well, then, we need to give her some time. I'm sure eventually she'll see that what she wants to do isn't right."

"Not as long as he's around. She got this mess from him, only she won't admit it."

"You don't know that for sure, baby."

"Of course it's about him. Or the two of them. I don't know. I guess she's got this notion that building families is as easy as building skyscrapers with blocks."

"You can't fault her for wanting a family of her own, Reese. Maybe she really loves this guy, and maybe he loves her too."

"I've met him, Justin, and believe me, he's not capable of loving anybody but himself."

"That's your opinion, Reesy. But it's not necessarily fair. You don't know what goes on between them when the door is closed."

"And I don't want to know."

"Then how can you jump to that conclusion?"

"I'm not trying to jump to conclusions. But I know how she is. When it comes to men, Connie thinks with everything but her head, and then she ends up getting hurt every single time."

"She's been hurt since you've known her. I, for one, can't fault her for hoping for better than what she has."

"She doesn't have a damn thing in him."

"And what did she have before him?"

"She had—"

"Nothing, Reesy. Connie's been more out of love than in. It's just that when she's in love, she's usually hooked up with the wrong kind of guy, but I don't know. I just don't think she's wrong to hope for someone to come along to share her life with."

"She's not wrong for that. I don't blame her for wanting someone. But I don't think she needs to drag Jade along on the search either. That child needs stability. Connie never had that growing up and look at how she turned out."

"Reesy."

"I'm not going to let her take her from me, Justin. Not now. She's too late for all this now."

Justin sighed. "Fine, then we won't let her take her from us." He stood up, took her hands in his, and pulled her to her feet. "It's late, and I've got to go to work in the morning."

"I'm not going to be able to sleep."

Justin led her to the door. "Then you can watch me sleep."

On the way out of the room, Reesy stopped and kissed Jade softly on the cheek. "This is my baby, Justin," she whispered to him. "Mine."

"I know, Reesy. We all do."

Shhhh . . .

John opened his eyes, slowly, sat up on the side of the bed, and lit a cigarette. Connie slept soundly next to him. He didn't remember his dream, only the essence of it, still lingering on his pillow. It was a dream filled with breaths of discontentment, restlessness. Filled with faces of people he didn't recognize but who all sounded like someone he knew, and even had names he remembered. Moving. All of them moving, in circles and straight lines, and up and down. Each of them saying things that made no sense but all alluding to something similar, something familiar. John closed his eyes, trying to recall the words he'd heard in his dream. Words that danced just outside his memory, threatening to come into view but never materializing into anything logical.

want
long
so . . . long
wanting
finding . . . my . . . my . . . self
wanting

It was happening again. It. That was the only name he'd ever given it, because he'd had no idea what else to call it. It . . . was the thing that compelled him to be the kind of man he was, and the kind of man he wished he wasn't. He needed to be here with her. He needed to stop running up and down the road to nowhere and finally accept that he was at a point in his life where he could admit there was never anything out there for him, and that he'd been running all this time for absolutely nothing. But "It" wouldn't let him settle down. John sighed deeply. All he wanted to do was settle down, with his own woman, home, maybe even kids. Suddenly, he squeezed his eyes shut. The bright light seemed to fill the room, and it blinded him. He knew exactly what was happening without even thinking about it. There was no way he could miss it. His mortality, pulling at him in the opposite direction of It. It—the drive, the force, the invisible hand that propelled him into the galaxy. John felt himself being torn in half.

Despite his best effort, John couldn't keep his mind off Agnes. According to Dot, she wasn't doing well at all. John thought he didn't care, but he was wrong. Agnes was supposed to live forever, wasn't she? When he was a kid, she'd seemed immortal. John figured maybe all kids felt that way about the people who raised them. They didn't grow old, or get sick. They certainly didn't die. Agnes's frown was supposed to be a permanent fixture in the universe as far as he was concerned, like the sun and the moon.

He laughed at himself, then started up his forklift. She'd never been any more or less than any other woman, he concluded. Pete Jensen could attest to that, John thought, remembering the two of them together. Dot had been begging him to come home for years, and he'd never been compelled to accommodate. Did he now? Now that Agnes was ill? What the hell did that have to do with him? After all, she'd broken his heart and never batted an eye.

In Light End Me

Connie had been toying with the food on her plate since they'd sat down to have dinner. She'd wanted to discuss this with him for days, but John had seemed distant and moody lately, preoccupied by recent phone calls from his aunt in Texas, though he'd never admitted it. Connie knew there was something serious going on for him back home, but whenever she asked about it, John never seemed to want to talk about it.

"Reesy and I had an argument the other day."

"Oh yeah?" he asked indifferently, shoving food into his mouth.

"She's under the impression that I want custody of Jade."

"Where'd she get that idea?" John asked dryly.

"From me, I guess," Connie said casually. "I mentioned that I wanted to spend more time with Jade. That I'd like to . . . I mean, eventually, I think she needs to be prepared for the truth. Don't you?"

He shrugged. "Eventually. Maybe," John answered carefully.

"Reesy seems to think I'm going to rush into her house with the police and demand that she give me back my daughter," she said, trying to make light of the concept. "Which is ridiculous."

John sighed. "Yeah, it is."

"I just tried talking to her, but she was being so unreasonable, and she went off."

"Like you'd just threatened to take her kid away from her?" he said coldly.

"She's my kid too, King," Connie said defensively. "I gave birth to her, but people seem to forget that."

Frustration showed on his face. "Nobody's forgotten it, Connie. Least of all Reesy, I'm sure. But just because you had her doesn't make her yours."

"I love that little girl and nobody seems to want to give me credit for that," Connie said, on the verge of tears.

"I don't know who nobody is, but everybody knows you love her. Again, that doesn't make her yours."

Connie stared at him through her tears. "I want her to be mine."

"That doesn't make her yours either," he said, starting to raise his voice. "Reesy's Momma, Connie. That's it."

"That's not it!" she snapped. "I wanted her to have better than I could give her. Reesy agreed to help."

"To raise her, and that's what she's been doing, and that's what she's been doing Jade's whole life."

"She's been wonderful to her."

"So, then, what's the damn issue?"

"The *damn* issue is that it's time for me to stop running from my responsibilities. I ran away from home, and I've been running ever since. I ran away from my own daughter, and it's time to stop and face her with the truth."

"She's six years old!"

"I know that. It's not like I'm going to all of a sudden announce that I'm her real mother."

John pushed his plate away, angry that he'd even been dragged into this conversation. This was Connie's business, Reesy's business, and it had nothing to do with him. "But you're not her 'real' mother, Connie. Reesy's her real mother."

"I had her!"

"Period! You had her, and you think that gives you the right to go in and fuck up her world?"

"I'm not fucking up her world!"

"You tell her this, you try and get custody, that's exactly what you'd be doing."

"I'm not saying I want custody."

"What the hell do you want?" he asked heatedly.

Connie cried. "I want my family, King. My own family."

It was clear to him now. He'd wondered where this had come

from, now all of a sudden he knew. "And does this family include me too, Connie?"

Connie turned away and sobbed.

"You can't wrap it up like a present, Connie," he said grimly. "Jade and I have nothing to do with each other, and we never will. It just won't work."

Connie slowly got up from the table and put on her coat. Space. She needed to put space between herself and John, between herself and even the idea of Jade. Life always seemed to come full circle for Connie. The reality that nothing was permanent had been what kept her alive back when all she wanted to do was vanish. Connie peeled his key off her keychain, then placed it on the table. "Leave mine on your way out," she said quietly.

Christmas wreaths and lights decorated downtown Denver, but Connie's mood was anything but festive. She sat on a bench, in the middle of the Sixteenth Street Mall, gazing beyond the swarms of holiday shoppers and horse-drawn carriages. She'd been desperate—again, trying to hold a future captive and design it to her specifications. One moment, the future had been crystal clear, but now it was what it had always been for her: faded and tattered. John made it clear that he definitely didn't belong to her. He would pass through her world, take a piece of her with him, and keep right on going. Her throat ached from holding in the sadness welled up inside it.

She'd been clinging to John like a girdle, because she'd believed herself to be falling in love. "No," she whispered. Love wasn't worth the anxiety. Regrets hadn't been formed in the future yet, but they were plentiful in the past, especially hers. Connie inhaled the frigid air and held it in her lungs. She needed a new breath of air to strengthen her, for wherever it was she was going. And she knew one thing for certain. Wherever she went, she'd go it alone. Unfortunately, that was the way it had always been.

The apartment was dark when she got home, and Connie assumed John had finally done what she feared he'd do: leave. Strangely, a sense of relief fell over her. The fear of his leaving had hovered over her like a dark cloud since they'd met, and now that it had happened, she could once again pick up the pieces and get on with the rest of her life. Whatever that meant.

She pulled off her coat, then turned on the lamp on the end table. His figure slowly materialized in the doorway of the bedroom, as if by magic. "I'm trying to do the right thing," he whispered. "Why don't you?"

"What are you still doing here?" she asked, staring at him.

He shrugged, then chose his words carefully before answering. "I'm your man, baby. I'm supposed to be here." Connie was tired. She sat down, leaned back, and rested her head on the back of the sofa. Her emotions moved like waves inside her, and she couldn't decide if she was happy that he'd stayed or not. "Where have you been?" he asked.

"Walking. Thinking." John sat down next to her. "I thought leaving was what you did best?"

He sighed. "It used to be, but I'm tired, and I can't think of anyplace in particular I want to go."

She sighed. "You can do like I do and run around in circles."

"And get dizzy?" he teased.

Connie surprised herself and almost laughed. "You get used to it."

John took her hand in his. "We need to slow it down, baby girl. Folks like us tend to be skittish enough already without running full speed ahead on things like this."

Connie sighed. "Maybe we shouldn't do things like this at all. Maybe we should put everything back in place, forget we ever met and leave well enough alone."

"Naw . . ." He put his hand beneath her chin, turned her face to his, and gently kissed her on the lips. "That's not something I'm ready to do."

"It might be the best thing to do in the long run."

"There you go again." He smiled. "You know, for someone who's always accusing a brotha of walking out on a situation, you're pretty quick to turn tail and run your damn self."

"I can't help it if I can't handle the stress of having you in my life. I never know from one day to the next if you're staying or leaving."

"Damn, baby." John sighed. "How many couples you know got it all figured out?"

"One. Reesy and Justin."

"Reesy and Justin are cartoon characters. Real people ain't that damn perfect."

Connie laughed. "The black Ken and Barbie."

"Made out of plastic."

She sighed. "I don't know what to expect with us, King."

"Why you got to expect something?"

"You want me to be like you and live for the moment. I can't do that. Life for me has always come in big packets of time, bigger than moments. They're either all good or all bad. Seldom anything in between. For me to live for the moment would mean breaking up those chunks into pieces, and I just don't have the energy."

John laced her fingers between his. "Know what I think?"

"What?"

"I think me and you got enough to deal with in each other right now. We want to be together and make this work, but neither one of us knows how to do that."

Connie laughed. "The two of us makes absolutely no sense. Is that what you're saying?"

"That's exactly what I'm saying."

She stared deeply into his eyes, hoping to see everything hidden inside them. "Why are you still here, King? Why haven't you left me behind, brokenhearted like all those other women in your past?"

"What makes you think I've broken any hearts?"

"Don't even try to deny it. I'm not naive. I know what's up. I might not know who, but I know what. Broken hearts from here to Florida, or Virginia, or wherever the hell you left from, coming here."

"I don't know about broken." He shrugged.

"Why haven't you broken mine?" she whispered. "I keep expecting you to, but you prove me wrong, every time."

He'd asked himself that a dozen times since he'd met her, but John never sat still long enough to let the answer sink in. "Staying ain't easy for me, Connie."

"I know."

"Leaving ain't as easy as it used to be either. I don't know." He sighed. "Maybe it's just . . . I'll be thirty-nine in a few months. Seems like yesterday, I was seventeen."

"So you're still here because you feel like you're getting old?" she teased.

"No. I know for a fact that I'm getting old. I also know that I've made my mistakes, then packed up and moved on, never bothering to look back at any of them."

"Why not?"

"What the hell would I do about them? I couldn't fix them. I just made them and left them behind, because there was nothing else for me to do."

"You say that like it's a bad thing. I wish I knew how to do that."

"Sometimes, it was necessary, and probably even saved my ass on occasion. Other times, it was an excuse not to give a damn about anyone or anything. That's not necessarily good."

"No. I guess not."

"I've known some beautiful women . . . generous, and all they said they wanted was me. But I never appreciated any of them, and whether they'll ever realize it or not, I'm the one who lost. Not them. I don't want to make that mistake this time."

Connie stared back at him. "Do you know how jacked up I am? I mean, I really could use some serious counseling, King. You could do so much better than me."

He laughed. "Baby girl, jacked up or not, it's all good with you."

"I've got herpes," her voice quivered. "I've done some terrible things in my life."

"Who hasn't?"

"Reesy."

"No, I'm talking about real people. Not Reesys."

Connie laughed. "It's just—"

"I know, Connie. You did whatever you felt you had to do to survive. We both did and here we are. We survived, baby. The problem is, that's all either of us knows how to do. We know how to survive better than most people ever could, but if we're going to be together, then we need to know how to do more than that. We need to learn how to live. Now how are we going to take care of a kid if we can't do that? Especially with each other?"

Suddenly, it became clear what he was saying, that the two of them were too screwed up to be responsible parents. And that Jade deserved absolutely every opportunity to grow up into the wonderful, beautiful woman Connie knew she'd be. That she was in a place that would allow her to do just that. Connie sobbed. "It wouldn't be easy. Would it?"

"Not for any of us. Not now. Later on—maybe." He shrugged. He had no idea what would happen, but for the first time, he wanted to hang around long enough to find out.

"So . . ." She dried her cheeks with the back of her hand. "Is this your way of asking me to be your girlfriend?"

John smiled. "Yeah, will you be my girl?"

"This means you plan on hanging around for a while?" Connie sniffed. "You're not going to cut out on me anytime soon, are you?"

"That's what it means. That's exactly what it's supposed to mean."

REVELATIONS

Windows

Agnes had been looking underneath the bed for her other shoe when she came across that box filled with old photographs. She'd put it there years ago, but this was the first time since then that Agnes felt compelled to open it. She sat on the bed and put on her reading glasses, carefully pulling each photo from the box, one by one. Agnes chuckled at black-and-white snapshots of her and Dot, with their hands on their hips, posing when they were girls. She even came across an old picture of Momma, blurred and faded. As usual, Momma was frowning. That woman frowned even through smiles. "Look at her, with her old mean self," Agnes said affectionately. When she'd hidden that box away, it had been because those pictures had made her cry. Now they reminded her of the sweetest things she'd been blessed with in her life, and she wondered why she'd waited so long to look at them.

Handsome Abe King smiled at her, looking like the dream he'd stepped out of, then back into. He was still in her heart, only not as heavy as he'd once been. Abe had been like a fine meal. Everything about him had tasted, smelled, and looked so good. But as with most fine meals, eventually all that was left behind was the memory of it, and an empty plate. Agnes had nearly let herself starve from the emptiness he'd left behind.

She gazed into the faded eyes of her daughter, from infancy to young womanhood. Agnes laughed. "Lord have mercy," she said, looking at a picture of seven-year-old Mattie wearing a bow that was even bigger than her head. Mattie smiled a toothless grin at Agnes. "What in the world was I thinkin'?" She shook her head. Agnes counted the years in her memories. If Mattie were alive today, she'd have been fifty or so years old, Agnes thought. She'd have gone off to college like Agnes and Abe had planned, gotten married, and had kids of her own. By now, she'd even have had grandchildren of her own. "My goodness," Agnes whispered. "I guess . . . ain't nothin' promised."

Mattie had been thirteen in the picture Agnes held in her hand. Agnes remembered that picture vividly. School had just started, and Mattie had begged Agnes to let her wear her hair down for that picture. "Momma?" Mattie had whined. "Please? Can't I wear my hair down jus' for school pictures? All the other girls are goin' to be wearin' their hair down." Reluctantly, Agnes agreed and she rolled Mattie's thick hair up the night before, then tied it up with a head scarf. The next day, that child walked out the door on her way to school, thinking she looked entirely too cute. Agnes stood in the doorway, watching Mattie's little behind bounce down that street like she was some kind of movie star.

Nothing in that picture predicted the future. Nothing in Mattie's bright eyes predicted the hardships or her death, which would come later that year. Mattie's life had changed without warning, and over the years, Agnes had beat herself up a thousand times, counting all the ways she'd let her child down, only to conclude that ultimately, Momma had been right. God's will wasn't always our will.

Memories crept into Agnes's mind of her peering through the screen door and seeing Mattie standing in the front of the house. Agnes was furious at that child, who didn't seem to remember what it was to come straight home from school anymore.

"Mattie!" Agnes called out. "Get yo' behind in this house, gal!"

Mattie didn't move, which infuriated Agnes even more. "Chil'! I know you heard me!" Agnes swung open the door, then stopped at the top of the porch steps.

Mattie stood planted in the front yard, with her legs trembling beneath her. She walked hesitantly toward Agnes, clutching at the front of her torn dress, tears falling down her cheeks, pooling in the corners of her quivering mouth. Agnes's panic propelled her down those steps and across the yard to her daughter. "Mattie? What happened? Tell Momma what happened, Mattie."

Agnes felt herself drowning in dread as Mattie's glazed expression looked beyond Agnes, even through her. She wrapped her daughter up in her arms, squeezing her hard enough for the truth to come out and convince Agnes that something silly had happened. Mattie had fallen down and skinned her knees, or she was so afraid of getting in trouble for not coming home from school that she thought tears would sway her mother's anger. Tears and a torn dress that Mattie held together with her fist.

"Tell me . . . what . . . happened. You tell me . . ." Agnes spoke slowly, sternly.

"He . . . hurt me, Momma," Mattie whispered, through her sobbing. "He . . . hurt . . ."

Mattie never said his name, but she didn't have to.

"All I can think about is how he was always lookin' at her sometimes, followin' behind her. I'd hear the girl tellin' him he needed to go home," Roberta Brooks had told Willie Pool. He drove over to Agnes's house as soon as he'd heard it.

"Roberta say he stared at Mattie all the time, and one time, he walked up to her and reached out his hand to try and touch her. They was walkin' past the sto', which is how Roberta saw 'em. And sho' 'nuff, I asked Gwennie. She saw 'em too. Mattie backed off, of course, but he kept comin', and she had to jus' tell the boy to leave her alone befo' he finally run off."

"Mattie . . . did Fool do this?" she whispered quietly to her daughter, who lay in bed staring out the bedroom window. "Is he the one, baby?"

Mattie never said a word. She buried her head in her pillow and cried herself to sleep. She might as well have said, "Yes, Momma. It was Fool."

Agnes's heart sank into her stomach as she curled up behind Mattie and cried tears of her own.

When had her ache dulled? she wondered. There hadn't been a particular time or place when that had happened. It was just that days blended together, strung along in time, and managed to turn into years. She supposed it was the little things that dulled the pain. Cleaning the house, going to the grocery store, cooking, eating, and sleeping. Life's routines often taken for granted that meant so much more than folks gave them credit for. She dug deeper into her box and pulled out a picture of John. It was a school picture, and he looked to be about ten or eleven in it. He smiled handsomely at her. Had he always been so handsome? she wondered.

"Agnes!" she heard Dot call out, coming into the house. Agnes had been so immersed in her memories, she hadn't even heard her sister's car pull up.

"I'm in here, Dorothy!"

Dot followed the sound of Agnes's voice to her bedroom, then sat down on the bed next to her. "Chil'," Dot said breathlessly. I'm sorry I'm late, but Sadie took off with my car and just now got back. You ready to go?" Dot had come to take Agnes to her doctor's appointment.

Agnes smiled, then handed John's picture to Dot. "Look at this."

Dot looked at it and laughed. "Oooohweee! Check him out. That boy sho' had some big ol' teeth."

"He was handsome, though, wasn't he?" Agnes asked proudly. Dot looked thoughtfully at Agnes. Something had slowly come over her sister in recent years. She didn't known what to make of it at first, but Agnes seemed to soften as she grew older, and a calm had washed over her. Maybe the fact that she hadn't been feeling well had something to do with it, Dot concluded. Agnes's sugar had been bothering her more and more as time went on, and it seemed like every time Agnes went to the doctor, they'd find something else wrong to compound all the problems she'd already had. Agnes was still recovering from the recent surgery she'd had, where they removed one of her kidneys. Now it appeared the other one was failing too, and dialysis seemed to be the only solution.

"Look at this one." Agnes laughed, handing Dot a picture of John when he was five. "He got Mattie's smile. Don't you think?"

Dot nodded. "I spoke to him the other day." She wasn't going to tell Agnes about it at first, but looking at her sister, Dot didn't think it was fair of her not to let Agnes know her grandson was fine.

Agnes casually continued flipping through the pictures in her box. "Really? How he doin'?" she asked, trying not to show her enthusiasm.

Dot knew better. She knew Agnes was full of questions about where he'd been and how he was really doing. When was he coming home? Was he ever coming home? "He say he doin' fine. He in Colorado, Denver."

"He say anything else?"

"Just to tell everybody hey."

"Well, I hope he takin' care of hisself. From what you tell me, he don't never seem to stay no place too long." Dot had asked her what happened the day John left, but Agnes wouldn't talk about it. She could be as stubborn as a mule when she wanted to be, and she had outstubborned Dot that day for sure.

"Well, we got to get goin' to the doctor's office, Agnes. We gon' be late enough as it is."

"I ain't goin', Dot," Agnes said quietly.

"What? Agnes, how you gon' sit here and tell me you ain't goin' when I done rushed my big ass all the way over here to get you? How you goin' tell me that?"

"I'm sorry. I meant to call, but—" Agnes lied. She hadn't meant to call Dot, because she hadn't decided she wasn't going until that moment.

"Agnes, now you got to go this time. You missed the last appointment. You know they got to run them tests."

"I'll call and tell 'em I'll come in another day. I'm jus' . . . I jus' get tired of lettin' them folks poke all over me," she complained.

"How else they goin' find out what's goin' on?"

"I'll call 'em and make another appointment for next week."

"Agnes—"

"Dorothy." Agnes smiled weakly. "I jus' need to rest. That's all."

Dot knew there was no arguing with Agnes when she got like this. She'd made up her mind, and Dorothy had no choice but to leave Agnes right where she was, caught up in memories kept hidden in an old shoebox.

Agnes stared out her bedroom window, wondering if he was looking at the same sky in Colorado that she was looking at in Texas. She felt sorry for the way she'd treated him when he was a child. Purposely keeping him at arm's length, especially in her heart, blaming him for things he never had anything to do with. Agnes hoped there'd come a day when she could apologize to him. Only now she wouldn't be apologizing to a boy but a grown man. She closed her eyes and tried to imagine that small face all grown up, full and handsome. She missed him, almost from the moment he left home. But it never really mattered. Agnes had learned, just because you miss somebody doesn't mean that it's enough to bring them home.

No Heart Feelings

Connie and Jade lay in bed talking late into the night. After their last conversation, Reesy was apprehensive about letting Jade spend the night at Connie's, but Justin convinced her that keeping the two apart was the wrong thing to do, and Jade needn't suffer because the adults in her life couldn't work through their differences.

A candle flickered on the nightstand, casting shadows on the walls and ceilings.

"Hey, Short Stuff, I've got an idea. Tell me what you think, okay?" Connie said softly.

"Okay," Jade whispered back.

"What would you think about me and you taking off this summer on a vacation? We could catch a plane or maybe a train over to California, and hang out at—"

"Disneyland?" Jade asked excitedly.

Connie laughed. "How'd you know I was going to say that?"

Jade gasped, clasped her hands together, then squealed, "Oooh! I wanna go! I really wanna go!"

"Now, how'd I know you were going to say that?" Connie stared affectionately at her daughter. New ideas invaded her thoughts daily about all the things she missed out on with Jade. Some things were more elaborate than others, like trips to Disneyland, and others were as routine as making her lunch every day for school, or taking her the dentist. She longed for a whole future with Jade, not just a pretend one.

Jade lay staring past Connie at the candle next to her. "I can't wait to go to Disneyland, Aunt Connie."

"Me either, baby."

"And is Mommy coming too?"

Connie felt her heart rise up and get caught in her throat. "What, sweetie?"

"Mommy? Is she coming with us? She'd like Disneyland."

But I'm Mommy, Connie wanted to say. *I'm going to Disneyland with you, Jade.* Connie pressed her lips together, holding those words captive inside her. "You want Mommy to come? I thought it could be just you and me, Short Stuff. Wouldn't you like that? Wouldn't you like it if we went by ourselves?"

Jade stared at Connie with big, sad eyes. "But if she doesn't come, she'll miss me too much. Then I'll miss her too much too. Don't you want Mommy to come, Aunt Connie?"

Connie pulled Jade into her arms and kissed the top of her head. "Of course Mommy can come," she promised. "We can all go together."

Let Sleepin' Dogs

Change. He sensed it coming. Not the kind you could see immediately with your eyes, but the kind that sounded like a train, whirring down the tracks in the distance. Lately, John had been feeling uneasy. He hadn't been able to place it at first, because it hadn't been obvious. His relationship with Connie had been surprisingly comfortable. Being with her had become as natural as breathing, and John didn't feel the pressure of the usual tension he'd felt in other relationships. There was an easiness between them. One that flowed and fell into place naturally. They fit, like pieces of a puzzle. And for John, whose natural tendency was to gear up and be prepared for the next move, that eagerness had disappeared, and he was in no hurry to go anywhere.

But there was a pressure mounting in his life. It had nothing to do with Connie, but it had everything to do with him.

"You need to come see 'bout her, John," Dot said over the phone. "Agnes ain't doing well. She ain't doin' well at all."

"I'm sorry she's sick, Dot. But I ain't sure when I'm going to be able to get down there. I got this new job," he lied.

"She family, John. I know things ain't been good between y'all, but you know I wouldn't ask you to come if I didn't think it was important. She jus' . . . she been askin' 'bout you fo' a while, now, and I think she really do want to see you, baby."

"I'll see what I can do," he said before hanging up. Their conversations had become scripted lately. Dot would call, tell him how sick Agnes was, and then beg him to come home. In the beginning, he'd tried shrugging off her pleas, but lately he'd found that was getting harder to do. He remembered how when he was a boy, he'd always try to come to Agnes's rescue when he felt she needed him. "Here, Momma Agnes," he'd say when he saw her trying to lift something heavy. "Let me get that for you. Let me help you up, Momma Agnes. I'll run to the store for you, Momma Agnes. You don't have to." He'd wanted her to need him around, but Agnes never seemed to think much about him or his attempts to please her. Eventually, he stopped trying, and now Dot was asking him to come see about her, like his presence was as significant as Jesus' had been to Lazarus. As if his coming to see about her would mean Agnes would get up and walk again, her blind eyes would fill with light, and everything wrong would be right again. Dot put entirely too much emphasis on John, and so did Agnes, if in fact she really was all that eager to see him.

Connie set his plate down in front of him, then sat down next to John at the table. He'd been so quiet lately. Not necessarily depressed, but perhaps melancholy was the word that best described his demeanor. She knew it had something to do with his grandmother, but whenever she asked about her, he never seemed to want to talk about it, except to say she was sick. Connie knew that there was more to it than that. John had been raised by his grandmother, and even though he'd never come right out and said it, his grandmother had been the reason he'd left home so young. Connie knew that still waters ran deeper in John when it came to that woman than maybe even he knew, and that she'd probably been the woman that had ruined him for all other women. She'd been the first woman to break his heart.

"Guess what?" Connie asked enthusiastically. John ate without answering. "Yolanda sold that new piece I made the other day. Can you believe it?"

"That's good, baby," he said, trying to match her enthusiasm with some of his own, but he knew that he'd failed miserably.

"We got fifteen hundred dollars for it." She laughed. "Never in a million years would I have ever expected that I'd have anything worth fifteen hundred dollars. Apparently, the lady wants me to make a matching bracelet for it. Isn't that wonderful?" John smiled. "So, how was your day, baby?" Connie asked, concerned.

"It was all right."

"You look tired. You feeling all right?" Connie pressed her hand against his cheek. John closed his eyes, turned his face into her palm, and then kissed it.

"I'm fine," he said assuredly. Connie wasn't convinced.

After dinner, John took a shower and went straight to bed. Connie sat alone in the living room, sipping on a glass of wine. The past several months, things had been wonderful between them. She'd learned so much more about him as he gradually opened up to her, sharing his feelings, his fears, even his aspirations. He seemed more surprised than she did that he'd even had aspirations. Aspirations required hope for the future, and of course, John had always prided himself on being a man who "lived for the moment."

John wanted to open up his own construction company. He loved working with his hands, and over the years he had learned carpentry work, electrical wiring, and construction through odd jobs he'd held here and there. He nearly blushed when he told her that. Connie smiled at the memory of this big, strong man blushing like a little boy. Yeah, she thought. His mortality had definitely reared its ugly head with that little piece of information. But they both knew better than to think happily ever after was a guarantee. Leaving was what he'd done best. It was as natural for him as blinking, taking little to no effort at all. For a man like him, the hardest part of life would be to stop running from it. Connie knew this and she accepted it because she really had no choice.

The sound of her humming woke him up. John opened his eyes and looked at Connie, who slept soundly next to him. He shrugged it off and figured maybe he'd just been dreaming. No, he distinctly heard it this time. He sat up quickly, then flicked on the lamp on his side of the bed. The brightness from the light blinded him, and it took a moment for his eyes to adjust. Gradually, they finally did, and that's when he saw her. A dark-skinned girl, sitting cross-legged on the floor across the room, wearing a white gown almost too bright to look at. She hummed a melody he found familiar but couldn't place. John knew this girl. She looked like the girl in the picture he'd hidden underneath his mattress when he was a kid. *Mattie?* he wanted to say, but the words wouldn't come. It was Mattie. He rubbed his eyes in disbelief of what he was seeing. She wore two curly pigtails on either side of her head, and wisps of bangs framed eyes that looked past him but stared right at him. John looked over at Connie, who was still sleeping. *Wake up, Connie!* he tried to say, but his voice failed him again. He reached over to shake her, but she was too far away from him. *Connie! I ain't crazy! It's her! It's* . . . John stared at the girl, sitting on the floor, still humming to herself. He'd dreamed her before, but not like this. This was Mattie. The Mattie everybody loved and cried over. Not the desperate Mattie in his nightmares. *My God! Mattie!* He reached out his hand to her, longing to press it against her face and kiss the lips he'd imagined tasted like butterscotch candy. *Momma!* he mouthed. She rocked back and forth, humming the familiar song that seemed to give her comfort. Tears burned his eyes and clouded his vision. He quickly wiped them away, afraid he'd lose sight of this girl whose skin was as dark as mahogany, and whose full lips pursed together sweetly while she hummed. This girl whose rich brown eyes were bright and alive. *Momma!* He tried calling to her again. His momma. No matter what anyone else said. Yes! She was his and belonged to him. The girl was more beautiful than he'd ever imagined. If only he could make her hear him, feel him. If he could make her know him. Then he'd be right. He'd be the right kind of man he'd wanted to be his whole life. He'd be full and finally—satisfied.

Suddenly, the girl stopped rocking, and soon her humming stopped too. Mattie King was no longer looking past him anymore. She stared into his eyes. Into him and he smiled. *It's me, Momma,* he wanted to cry out. *It's me. Your son.* She'd seen him, finally, she'd seen him. And tears of relief fell freely from his eyes. His mother had laid eyes on him for the first time, and John knew everything would be fine. From now on, everything in his life, in him, was going to be fine.

Then, without warning, she started screaming. Mattie's body rolled over onto the floor, shaking, screaming. Convulsing. Screaming. Bleeding. Screaming. She pulled violently at her hair and gown, screaming and kicking her legs wildly against nothing. Screaming. John cried. *Momma!* he tried to shout. *I'm sorry, Momma!* The words wouldn't come. He struggled to get out of the bed, but it held him prisoner and he couldn't get to her—he couldn't help her. Connie still slept. How could she sleep through all that terrible screaming? Blood seeped through Mattie's white gown. *Mattie!* Her screaming was unbearable and he wished he could make her stop. He wished she'd never seen him. Blood soaked into the beige carpet and splattered across the walls. It covered him. *Stop it, Mattie!* His voice burned, pushing hard against the inside of his chest. *Wake up, Connie!* How come she won't wake up? *Dammit! Wake up!*

"Wake up!" The sound of his own voice penetrated his nightmare, and John suddenly opened his eyes. The room was still dark.

"John?" Connie asked, startled, then she sat up next to him. John fought to catch his breath. "Baby? Are you all right?" She turned on the lamp, then cradled his head against her breast and held him like he was a child. "Shhh . . . it's okay, baby. It was just a bad dream."

It was more than that. So much more. "I got to go," was all he could say. It's all he could think about, and the only thing that made any sense. "I got to go . . . now."

Connie held on tight to him. "It's over now. John, you're fine. It was only a nightmare."

His demons had gotten too close. He'd never let that happen before. "You don't understand. I got to go, Connie," he said breathlessly.

Connie kissed him. "Not if you don't want to, John. You can stay."

"No, I can't stay. I can't stay here, baby. I got to go," he whispered. She'd hoped that together they could work through whatever had been bothering him. But looking at him now, Connie realized he'd have to do this on his own.

"Fine," she said. "That's fine, baby. Just not tonight. You go do whatever it is you have to do. But you go in the morning, okay?" She kissed him again, then held him in her arms. Eventually, Connie managed to fall back asleep, but not John. Morning couldn't come soon enough for him.

Take Me to the River

The weight of Dot's heavy hips propelled her forward and down the wooden steps of her front porch. "Lord have mercy!" She laughed. "Boy! Is that you?"

John grinned. Dot had always had the kind of curves that made a man's knees weak, only now there were just more of them. "Hey, Dot."

She stood on the bottom step and waited for him to step into her arms. "C'mon over here and give yo' ol' auntie a hug, boy!" Dot wrapped her heavy arms around him as he bent and kissed her cheek. "I said to myself, who in the world is that fine piece of man comin' up in my yard? Now, I know I ain't got me no boyfriend, and done forgot I had him." She stared into his face, looking for some semblance of the boy she'd last seen. "Look at you." She beamed. "Damn! You one good-lookin' man." Dot laughed again. "If you wasn't my nephew boy, and if I was ten years younger, I'd be all over yo' fine behind like ticks on a hound dog!"

"My ass would be in some serious trouble, then." He laughed.

"Damn right you would be." Dot grabbed him by the arm. "C'mon in the house. Sadie? Sadie, gal! Come see who here!"

A pregnant Sadie came into the living room, smiling from ear to ear when she saw him. "John? Aw, dang! Check you out!" she said, hugging him.

"Check me out? Check you out, little momma. How you

doing? Besides looking like you ready to drop that baby any second?"

Sadie rolled her eyes and smacked her lips. "I'm fine." She patted her swollen stomach.

"Andre, didn't Grammy tell you to take yo' li'l ass outside?" Dot snapped at a little boy who looked to be about six or seven.

"But I wanna watch Power Rangers, Grammy," he whined.

"You betta power yo' ranger on outta my house, boy!" Dot snapped. "You know betta than to talk back to me."

"You heard Grammy, boy!"

"But Momma . . . ," he whined, clinging to Sadie's hip.

She gently pushed him away. "You wanna whoopin'?"

The boy dragged his feet on his way out the door. *It figured Sadie's whiny ass would give birth to whiny kids,* John thought to himself.

Dot went into the kitchen, then came back with a tall glass of sweet tea. She and John sat in the living room, talking about old times and catching up on new ones. "You move around so fast, I can hardly keep up with you. And whatchu doin' up in Denver, Colorado?"

"Just passing through, Auntie," he said, wondering if he really would just keep on passing through like he'd intended, or if he'd stay put this time and try to get himself together. John was more uncertain about his life now than he'd ever been. Too many monkey wrenches had been thrown into the scheme of things. Connie was one of them.

"Get cold up there, don't it?"

He nodded. "Yeah, it does."

"I keep all yo' postcards. Every last one of them." Dot's eyes still sparkled when she talked about traveling. Sometimes she missed it, but most times she didn't. Road running was for young people filled with eager spirits and tireless bodies. Dot could barely remember being that young.

"When you and that woman gon' get married?"

Her question caught him off guard, but he didn't show it. John shrugged. "What makes you think we're getting married?"

"You been stayin' with the woman, John. Don't you think you ought to marry her?"

"Why would I want to mess up a good thing? We cool just like we are."

"Hmpf! I bet she ain't cool."

"I didn't come all the way down here to listen to you stir up some trouble, woman," he teased.

"I speak my mind, John King. And right now, my mind is tellin' me to tell you that it's better for you to marry that girl than to keep on shackin' up with her. You ain't gettin' no younger, boy," she fussed.

"How's everybody else doing?" he asked, trying to change the subject. But Dot could be as relentless as a pit bull sometimes and refused to let him.

"You love this woman? Or is it all 'bout gettin' you some easy cootchie?"

He nearly choked on his tea. "Uh—"

"And don't bother lyin' to me, son. I know you gettin' some. Gettin' plenty and I can tell jus' by lookin' at you."

"That's personal, Dot."

"To hell with personal, boy. Who you think you talkin' to? I tell you one thing—if you gettin' as much cootchie as I think you gettin', then you need to marry that girl. Don't make no sense for you to be wallowin' all up in her cootchie and not be willin' to marry her. That's jus' selfish, John. Plain selfish."

He smiled. "You sound bitter, Auntie. Is that what happened to you? Somebody get all your cootchie and refuse to marry you?"

Dot's eyes narrowed as she stared back at him. "I got eight kids, John. And I been in love at least fo' times. Out of all fo' of them men, do you know only one of them ask me to marry him? Now, that's some sorry shit, and I gave up all my cootchie! Not 'cause I was dumb, but 'cause I was in love. That's jus' somethin' a woman do when she in love. Her man want some . . . she give him some."

John grinned. "Some what, Dot?"

Dot stared at him, bewildered. "Cootchie, boy! Pay attention."

"So why didn't you marry the one who asked?"

" 'Cause he got killed. Some fool woman in Tyler shot him, claimin' he was her man, 'cause he told her 'bout me." Dot put her hand to her chest. "Broke my heart too. But what I'm tellin' you is don't wait 'til it's too late, boy. The older you get, the harder love is to come by, and if you care anything for this woman, you need to go ahead and do right by her, and yo'self."

John stared at Dot, surprised at her mention of the word "love."

"I never said I loved her."

"You don't have to. You wearin' it like a shirt."

How come everybody insisted on summing up a relationship between a man and a woman with the word love? he wondered. Like love was the end-all and the answer people needed to explain what really shouldn't have to be explained. He and Connie accepted each other, and that seemed to be what both of them needed most. Acceptance. Instead of a man telling his woman he loved her, he should have to tell her, "I accept you, baby, and everything about you from the bottoms of your stinky feet to the top of your nappy head and everything in between." As far as John was concerned, society's perspective needed to be changed on that love thing, starting with wedding vows. "Do you promise to cherish, accept, and love your woman when the concept of love suits the mood? And when it doesn't, then do you promise to get yourself a six-pack, watch the game, and stay with her, even when the two of you can't stand each other?" He'd never told Connie he loved her. She'd never asked him if he did. All he knew was that lately, without her in his life, breathing wasn't as easy as it had been before he'd met her.

They talked about her children, her grandchildren, and Dot caught him up on the latest gossip about everybody in town that he remembered from his childhood. Finally, they got around to the matter at hand and the real reason he'd come back to Bueller. "You been to the house yet?" Dot asked the question knowing the answer already.

"Not yet. How's she doing?"

She shrugged. "Bein' hardheaded. The doctor say she need to go on dialysis. She say she ain't doin' it."

"She say why?"

"Everybody know why, John. Agnes jus' don't want to live no more," Dot said sadly. "I think she been sad so long, too long, and she tired."

"What is she? Seventy?"

"Jus' turned. She ask me 'bout you all the time."

"What do you tell her?"

"I tell her you doin' all right for yo'self. That's all I know to tell her. Why? Is there somethin' else I should be tellin' her?"

"Ain't nothin' else to tell, Dot. That's plenty."

"How long you plannin' on stayin'?"

"Not long," he said too quickly.

"You got to get back to Denver?"

John hesitated before answering. "Not necessarily."

"Where you headed, then?"

"I don't know where I'm going, Dot. I guess I'll find out when I get there."

"Ain't you tired yet, boy? Ain't you tired of runnin'? You nearly forty years old, John. And you got yo'self a real nice woman up there in Denver. Why don't you stay put this time, baby?"

"What makes you think I'm running to anything, Auntie?"

"It ain't what you runnin' to and you know it. It's what you runnin' from."

"I ain't running from anything, Dot. I got nothing to run from. I just like to be on the move. What's wrong with that?"

"You ain't got to lie to me, boy. I know better and so do you. I want to ask you somethin', John, and you think long and hard before you answer me."

"I'm listening."

"What you plan on doin' when you get too old to run anymore?"

John finished up his tea, never bothering to answer Dot's question, because he had no idea how to answer it.

He kissed Dot's cheek, then headed for his car. She stood on the steps of her front porch, then called out to him, "Agnes ain't the only ghost you need to deal with, John King."

He laughed. "I don't think your sister would appreciate you calling her a ghost, Dot."

"That's what she is to you, ain't she?"

"That's what we've always been to each other," he said indifferently.

Texas was still full of drama. Drama he didn't need and had learned to live without years ago. Coming to see Agnes had been hard enough, and he still wasn't sure why he did come back. It wasn't like she'd asked him to. He'd spent his childhood bending over backwards, kissing her ass, hoping she'd treat him like he was part of the family and not the furniture. Agnes hadn't given a shit about him. So why was he back? It was simple, really. He'd missed her.

Momma Agnes

Bueller had been filled with castles when he was a boy. Now, petite homes lined the roadways, and John couldn't believe how different the world is viewed from a child's eyes. Apprehensively, he approached the door of the house he'd grown up in, astonished at how much smaller it looked to him now. He almost expected to see Agnes, standing in the doorway, calling him to come inside to eat. What surprised him most was that he didn't feel anything. Not happiness, or sadness. No remorse, no regret, no hard feelings. Nothing. It was like walking up the steps of a stranger's house. Even as he tapped lightly on her door, John anticipated nothing. He hadn't even bothered to brace himself for seeing Agnes again after all these years. A lifetime had passed since he'd last seen her. That boy who'd run out of the house died ten times, and like with Mattie, all that was left of him had been hidden inside memories.

He knocked several times, but Agnes didn't answer. John slowly turned the doorknob and walked inside. An old woman might be able to get away with an unlocked door in Bueller, but Agnes couldn't have pulled that mess in say, Atlanta, he thought to himself. The sound of the television could be heard coming from the living room. Agnes had replaced the heavy, velvet drapes she'd had when he was a kid with vertical blinds, and the floral, Victorian couch and loveseat with a conservative, olive green sofa covered with beige patterned pillows. The only thing that hadn't changed was the burnt orange wingback chair he found her sleeping in. Agnes was thinner than he'd remembered. A baby blue knit shawl draped over her shoulders, and glasses balanced delicately on the tip of her nose. Her dark, brown face, framed by sprinkles of gray, had somehow been held captive in a time warp. She was beautiful to him. She'd always been beautiful.

Agnes's eyes fluttered. At first, she thought she'd gone ahead and died. Lord knows she'd been praying hard enough for it. Then she thought maybe she was dreaming. *Goodness gracious! What a handsome man,* she thought to herself.

"Hello, Agnes," John said.

Agnes sat up slowly and adjusted her glasses. "John? John . . . is that really you?" She slowly reached out her hand to him, then pulled it back, disappointed when he didn't take it and press it between his own. But she couldn't blame him.

John sat down on the couch, then cleared his throat. He hadn't expected her to have this effect on him. Even now, years later, John was surprised to discover butterflies still fluttered inside him whenever he was close to her. "How you doing, Miss Agnes?"

"Miss . . . ?" Agnes started to correct him but thought better of it. After all, he wasn't a little boy anymore. And how silly would it have sounded for a grown man as big as him to go around calling her "Momma Agnes"?

"I'm doin' fine, John. Jus' fine." Agnes smiled warmly.

John's heart beat like an anxious lover's, seeing her smile at him, but he quickly blanketed it with indifference. "That's not what I hear. I hear you haven't been feeling well."

Agnes frowned, but even then she looked lovely to him. John fought the urge to stare. "Dot tell you that?"

"She did."

"She jus' worry too much, that's all. I'm doin' all right. How you been?"

"I've been pretty good."

"You married? Got any kids?" Agnes struggled to hold in her enthusiasm. She was so glad to see him, but it was obvious he wasn't as happy to see her. Time had been what had healed her wounds. Loneliness helped too. Over the years, she'd worried about him, even when she didn't seem to be worrying. She'd prayed over him, beseeching God to look after him, because she'd been too

selfish to do it. This grown man wasn't the image she held inside
her memories. But it was the boy John that bound Agnes to her
regrets. For as long as she could remember, sadness filled his eyes,
and looking at him now, she could still see a hint of it buried
beneath the darkness. Sadness she'd planted in him. He was always
so eager to help, but Agnes only pushed him away. Now, here he
was, reluctantly offering his help again. *Not this time, Lawd. I'm not
going to push my boy away this time,* she thought to herself. So much
had happened between them before he left—of course, he had his
healing to do, and Agnes suspected she might have to wait a while
longer.

John shook his head. "No, ma'am. I'm not married, and no kids."

"I'm surprised." She smiled. "A good-looking man like you? I'd
think all the women would be fallin' all over themselves tryin' to
get to you." She'd been right. Abe King had been born again in
John. John's broad shoulders reminded her of her husband's. He
was strong like Abe too. She could see it all over him. How lovely
it would've been if he'd have gathered her up in his arms and
hugged her close, Agnes thought. "Dot say you stayin' in Colorado
now?"

"Yes. I just left there."

"You like it up there? I hear it's nice."

"It is nice."

"You know yo' friend Lewis got married? Got three kids too."

He was surprised she'd remembered his friend Lewis. "Oh yeah?
Who'd he marry?"

"Barbara Ann's daughter, Racine."

John smiled. "Good for him."

"I hear he got a good job over at the soup factory, supervising.
And Racine teaches over at the school. I saw them the other day at
church and they asked about you."

They sat in awkward silence before Agnes spoke up again. "You
know Roberta passed?" John showed no emotion, but yes, he knew
Roberta had died. "She had a terrible fall in her yard. Fell on a
spade she was using to dig holes. It happened right around the time
you—" She caught herself. It was so nice to see him, the last thing
she wanted to do was to use this opportunity to stir up ugly memories.

"Why won't you let them put you on dialysis, Miss Agnes?"

Agnes sighed, then rolled her eyes. "I ain't 'bout to let them do no mess like that to me. I'd be up at that hospital three times a week for that dialysis and I ain't got time."

"What else do you have to do?"

John's smart-aleck tone caught Agnes off guard. He'd never had the nerve to speak to her like that before, and she didn't appreciate him thinking he could get away with speaking to her like that now. "I beg yo' pardon?"

He leaned forward, rested his elbows on his knees, then looked Agnes straight in the eyes. Something he'd never had the courage to do when he was a boy. "What's going on in your life that you can't spare three days a week? Especially if dialysis can keep you alive?"

Agnes shifted in her chair. "What kind of living is that? Lettin' folks hook me up to a machine three times a week, then bein' sick in between? I don't think that's how I want to spend the rest of my days. No, thank you."

"What kind of living are you doing now, Miss Agnes?"

Agnes stared at him, annoyed by his impertinence. "Don't you talk to me like that, boy. I know how I want to live out my life, and it ain't bein' hooked up to no machine, havin' doctors piece me back together so they can keep me here one minute longer than the good Lord intends."

"So, you want to die? Then, why don't you just tell everybody that, so they'll leave you alone?" John's tone bordered on anger. Maybe her dying would be best, he thought. Maybe her death would finally bring him the peace he craved. He now realized that it had been Agnes's spirit that haunted him all these years. A spirit dressed up to look like Mattie. But it was never Mattie, because he'd never known her. He'd known Agnes. He'd needed her, and as long as she lived, John knew he'd always need this feeble old woman.

His indifference hurt her feelings and it showed. "If you came all the way down here to tell me how I ought to be handlin' my business, you shouldn't have wasted yo' time, John."

"I didn't come back here to tell you how to handle your business, Miss Agnes."

"Then why you here? 'Cause Dot asked you to come?"

"Dot's been asking me to come back for years, and I never did. Not until now, that is."

"So, why you back now? Jus' for the satisfaction of seein' me die, I s'pose?" Agnes was fishing, hoping something sweet would fall from his lips, reassuring her that he did care for her, more than he was letting on.

"You know better than that," he muttered. Volcanoes erupted inside him. Emotional volcanoes shifting violently between joy and sorrow at seeing his grandmother again.

"I know you didn't come to see me. Don't even bother denyin' it, 'cause I know better. I can't say that I blame you. I didn't do right by you, and I know it."

"No, you didn't," he said sharply. Agnes shifted uncomfortably in her chair at the sensation of John's gaze fixed on her. "But that was too long ago to matter to me anymore."

"I'd like to think that was true," she muttered.

Looking at her, he knew it wasn't true. He'd lied to himself all these years, erasing her like a stray mark on a piece of paper, or at least he thought he had. "Even if it isn't, what difference would it make?" John asked. "My life started over when I walked out that door and I put you and everything about this place behind me. I went on with my life, Miss Agnes. Don't you think it's time for you to get on with yours before it's too late?"

"Been too late, boy." Agnes laughed. "Whatchu think? Dialysis is gon' give me back the last twenty-five years of my life? Doctor say if I'm lucky, I might get another year or two out of it. What am I gon' do with two years? I done lost everything that ever mattered to me. Abe, Mattie—you. What I need to live longer for? I died years ago, John King. I died long before you left."

"We both did," John said reflectively, "but hell! At least you'd have a chance at some kind of happiness."

Agnes stared into his eyes. Dark, handsome eyes that made a woman wish she could drown in them and lose herself altogether. She'd done everything in the world to keep from looking into those eyes when he was a child. Lord! How many more blessings had she let get away from her? "Right now, I'm happier now than I been in years. Seein' you. I been prayin' for the last twenty years for you to come home, and when I open my eyes and seen it was you standin' there . . ." Tears filled Agnes's eyes. "I have missed you, John King. More than you ever gon' know or even believe."

"Agnes . . ." John shifted uncomfortably in his seat. Why now? Why was she bothering with all this now? "Twenty years ago, I needed to hear this. Now, it really doesn't make much difference."

"It make all the difference, boy." Agnes pressed her lips together to keep from crying. "It make a difference 'cause you still need to hear it, and Lawd know I need to say it. After Mattie died, you became my baby, and I know I didn't do right by you, but in my heart, that's what you is, John. My baby."

John swallowed hard. She was too late with all this now, he thought. Thirty-nine years too late, and Agnes didn't need to bother telling him any of this. "You need to do what the doctors are recommending, Miss—"

"I wasted so much time, cryin' and missin' what I lost in Abe and Mattie, that I forgot all about you. You was my blessin', right under my nose, only I didn't pay no attention. When you don't pay attention to God's blessin's, he always take 'em away from you. Then you end up missin' 'em when they gone, and all of a sudden, you realize that you had a gift right in the palm of yo' hand. Somethin' precious and priceless. Then, before you know it, it ain't there no more. The hardest thing is admittin' it was all yo' own fault. 'Cause nobody snatched it from you. You was jus' foolish and threw it away and you can't never get it back. I'm more sorry for me than for you," she said sadly. "You still a young man and you got plenty of time to find somebody nice, settle down, and have yo' own kids. But I'm jus' an old woman, and I done used up all my time." Agnes pulled a handkerchief from a pocket on the front of her dress and blew her nose. "I never thought I'd ever see you sittin' here, son. But I done learned my lesson," she said proudly. "And while I got you here, I'm gon' do right by you. Even if it's only for a few days or a few minutes. I got this gift in my hand." Agnes held up her hand, with her palm facing heaven, "and I ain't gon' throw it away this time."

John pretended to rub his eyes, wiping away tears before they slid down his face. He'd spent his life wondering why she couldn't love him, wondering if she'd blamed him the way he'd blamed himself over the death of Mattie. John had craved Agnes, like a thirsty man craved water, hoping that someday he'd know she loved him. He looked over at her. Agnes's eyes were filled with sincerity, her smile filled with apologies.

He cleared his throat. "I ain't a child anymore, Miss Agnes. A lot's happened. I'm a grown man now, and if you're looking for miracles—"

"Oh, but I got my miracle, John. I got my boy, my grown man, sitting here in my living room after I ain't seen hide nor hair of him for over twenty years."

John felt the warm trail of a tear stream down his cheek. He couldn't remember the last time he'd cried. "It's too late to fix this, Miss Agnes!"

"Don't you dare tell me that!" Agnes cried. "We are goin' to fix this, son, 'cause we both here! We here now, and I ain't lettin' you leave till we do!"

"But none of it matters, Momma."

"It does matter, boy! 'Cause you and me love each other! And love always mean something!"

Of course he loved her. He'd loved her his whole life, and suddenly John's world came to a point in Agnes's face. He wiped the tears from his eyes and held out his hand to her, hoping like he'd never hoped before that she'd reach out and take it. Agnes smiled, then placed her small hand in his, and John slowly raised it to his cheek and held it there. Lost in the warmth of it, in the scent of her.

Agnes stood up slowly and walked over to where John sat. He started to get up too, but Agnes leaned down and placed a frail hand on his chest, holding him in place, then kissed him softly on his forehead.

John's body stiffened. How long had he wished for that kiss? He'd waited a lifetime for it, knowing it was all he needed to heal, to right all his wrongs, to purge him of his sins.

"I do love you, baby," she whispered, staring into his eyes. "Jus' took me some time to remember how much, that's all." She stepped back, allowing him room to stand, then Agnes straightened her shawl. "Now . . . I got to finish gettin' my nap. Yo' ol' grandmomma is tired. You can go on and put yo' bags in yo' room, if you like." She smiled up at him.

"No, I uh, I got a room over at the inn off the highway."

Disappointment showed on her face. "Oh. Well, that's fine. You be back tomorrow? Dot brought me over some mustard greens when she found out you was comin'. I need to get 'em cooked 'fo they go bad." She smiled up at him. "I know how much you always love my greens."

John gazed into her ageless eyes and smiled back into them. "I'll be back, Miss . . . Momma Agnes," he whispered.

Agnes blushed. "Good. And don't make me have to come out there lookin' for you neither. I know you know what time supper is. It ain't changed. I'll see you then?"

He grinned. "Yes, ma'am."

Stretching out on her bed, Agnes smiled broadly, knowing she'd rest better tonight than she had in a long time. Her boy was back. He might not be here long, but he was back for now, and that's all that mattered. When he'd run away all those years ago, Agnes stood nightly vigils on the front porch, hoping he'd come home. He never did, but she never stopped wishing he would. He was such a pretty man, and Agnes was no fool. There was more of his grandfather in him than he realized. Women flocked to that boy, like they'd flocked to Abe so many years ago. He just needed to get himself together, she thought. Find him a nice woman and have some kids. She'd have to remember to talk to him about it tomorrow after supper. Maybe dialysis wasn't such a bad idea. It might only buy her a few extra years, but now that John was back, maybe those extra years would be worthwhile, and maybe she'd even get to see her great grandchild, if that boy hurried up and made her some. She laughed.

Agnes pulled the sheets up close around her neck. He was her boy. Always had been her boy, because that's how God had planned it. God knew what was best. He always knew, and over time, Agnes had come to trust that. That boy loved himself some greens, she thought. She'd make a big old pot of them tomorrow, just for him. And a pan of corn bread too. Big as he was, he'd probably eat the whole thing in one sitting. It sure was nice to have him home, she thought. Agnes smiled as she felt herself drift off to sleep for the last time.

———

John left before the funeral service ended. He stood outside the church, loosened his tie, and closed his tired eyes, swollen from the tears he'd finally allowed himself to shed. No, life had never been fair. He and Agnes together were to embark on the journey they'd missed out on so long ago. But they'd be denied it once again. John inhaled deeply, wondering what course his life should take now. Armed with a different kind of ammunition, where were his excuses? Her death had put him face to face with what had driven him his whole life, and John cringed at how much time he had wasted. Thirty-nine years had swirled down the drain like dirty water, and all that was left was a fragile old woman lying dead in a coffin, and him, more lost than he could ever remember being in his life.

Connie's presence loomed in the distance. He missed her, but even that wasn't enough to send him back to her. He promised her before he left that he'd call. But he hadn't done that. John couldn't bring himself to call Connie, even to set her mind at ease that he was all right. Because, truthfully, John wasn't sure he was all right. His life had become gray matter. For years, he'd lived in perfect contrasts, black and white, big and small, tall and short. There hadn't been room for uncertainties. Now, that's all he seemed to have left.

Moses had heard about Agnes, and he'd heard the boy had come home. The minute he saw him standing out in front of that church, he knew who he was. Funny how he always knew. John was almost as big as Moses, though his middle wasn't as thick. Moses climbed out of his truck and walked toward John, who was walking toward his own car. Out of the corner of his eye, John caught glimpse of Moses coming toward him. The Mountain was an old man now. But that didn't make his stature any less intimidating.

Moses and John stood toe to toe. "I heard 'bout Miss Agnes," Moses said to John. "I'm sorry fo' yo' loss." John stood frozen in place, shocked that Moses had spoken to him, and that he even seemed to know who he was. "You don't know who I am, do you?" Moses's deep voice bellowed from deep inside him.

"I know you," John answered.

"She was a good woman. I never knew her personally, but folks say she was good people."

"Can I help you with something?"

"How long you stayin'?"

"Why you wanna know?" John asked defensively.

"I think you need to come see him."

"See . . . Fool?" John asked, surprised.

"Adam. Adam Tate. Yo' daddy."

John was tired and was in no mood for what this old man was asking. All he wanted to do was get the hell out of Bueller, Texas, as soon as possible. He needed to put space between him and this place, and even between him and Connie. John needed space to sort out all the things he was feeling, and to try to get his life back to something that made sense. "I got to go, man," John said, opening the door to his car. Moses pushed against the door and closed it shut.

"You need to see him 'fo you go. That's what I'm askin'."

"And what I'm askin' is why should I?"

"He yo' daddy."

"My daddy? That's bullshit, man. And you know it. I ain't got no daddy. Don't need no damn daddy. Now, why don't you get back in that truck over there and go home."

Moses surprised John and laughed. "You gon' put me in my truck, boy?"

"Old man, I ain't got time for you. I ain't in the mood."

"I understand this ain't a good time fo' you. I wouldn't be here if I didn't think this was somethin' you need to do."

"Who the hell are you to tell me what I need to do?"

"It ain't what you think."

"What I think? About Fool? I don't give a shit about Fool! He raped a fourteen-year-old girl, man! Why should I give a damn about him?"

"So you can know the truth fo' yo'self, boy!" Moses spat. "Boys don't need truth the way a grown man does."

"I don't need his kind of truth."

"Truth ain't got no kind! Or is yo' ass too dumb to know that?" John glared at him. Anger rose up in him and if Moses wasn't careful, an explosion was going to take place, and it would take place all over him.

"You need to get yo' ass away from me, old man," John growled.

"Or what, boy? Huh? You think you can whoop my ass? I might be old, son, but I can still tear even yo' big ass apart. Fuck with me," he said, staring into John's eyes. "Ain't nothin' like what you thought. All I'm askin' is come see fo' yo'self, son. You don't owe him shit, but you owe it to yo'self to know the truth. That's all I'm sayin'." Moses turned slowly, got back into his truck, and drove away.

John got into his car and drove to the liquor store.

The Little Woman

Connie had only caught a glimpse of her but recognized the woman instantly. Her heart beat wildly in her chest at the sight of the ghost of Pauline Graves heading west, strolling down the Sixteenth Street Mall, stopping occasionally to admire displays in the windows of department stores. Connie followed behind her, drawn to the woman as if she were being pulled by some invisible magnetic force. A tug of war waged inside her. Connie had never expected to see either Pauline or Earl Graves ever again. She'd never wanted to, and yet here she was, stalking the woman like some scene out of a bad movie, envisioning the moment Pauline Graves would spin on her heels and stare pathetically into Connie's eyes. Connie hurried to catch up to her, struggling to breathe through the shock of seeing this woman again. She wanted Pauline to face her, look her in the eyes, and admit that she honestly didn't know what was going on in her house, and that she had no idea that her husband had been capable of such things. And Connie would say—what? She had no idea what she'd say, or what difference it would make to say anything at all. After all, this was Pauline, not Earl. Through the years, she'd rehearsed over and over again the kinds of things she'd say to him if she ever had the chance.

"You sick mothafucka!" burned the tip of her tongue so badly sometimes, she had to fight the urge not to go back to that house in Park Hill and look for him.

Earl had paved the way for a child to become a prostitute.

He'd stolen the core of who she was. It wasn't just pussy he'd taken. It had been innocence. It had been pure, and spotless. It had been the foundation of the woman she would grow up to be. The kind of woman who put more value on herself than a cheeseburger and a cheap motel room. The kind of woman who knew she deserved more than to be touched by someone who didn't even think she deserved to know his name. Because of Earl, she'd become the kind of woman who'd learned to separate herself from the most intimate act a man and woman could share. Intimacy, for Connie, had always been the challenge. Even with Jamil, and now with John, she struggled to make sex more than that. She struggled to make love, to feel loved, and to be in love. All because Earl's nasty ass had convinced her that love had absolutely nothing to do with being intimate.

Pauline stopped in front of a shoe display, and before Connie realized what she was doing, she grabbed the woman by her arm, then stood defiantly in front of her, daring her not to look into her eyes. Connie needed Pauline to know who she was, and what Earl had done to her.

Connie's abrupt gesture startled Pauline. The woman stared back at her, unsure of what was going on. "Excuse me?" she asked timidly. "Do I know you?"

Tears quickly welled up in Connie's eyes, but she refused to let them fall. At this moment, she promised herself, she would not let this woman see her cry. Connie's mouth opened, but her words were absent.

Pauline nervously looked around, obviously uncomfortable by this woman's actions. "I think you might have confused me with someone," she said, starting to walk away.

Connie blocked her path. "Where's Earl?" she asked, her voice cracking.

Pauline stared meekly at Connie. "My husband?"

Connie locked her eyes on Pauline, holding the woman frozen where she stood.

"You know my husband?"

Connie wiped her eyes with the back of her hand. *Don't let her leave without telling her, Connie,* she said to herself. *You've got to do this. You've got to do it now, or you might not ever get the chance to do it again. Pauline's got to suffer in the truth the way you've suffered in the truth. Pauline's got to hurt the way he hurt you.*

"I know him," she practically whispered. "And I know you." Pauline wore her hair the same way she'd worn it when Connie lived with her. Pulled back in a ponytail at the nape of her neck. A light sprinkling of gray framed her small oval face.

Pauline smiled weakly. "Church? I knew you looked familiar. We go to the same church, don't we? Or we used to."

"No. We don't know each other from church." Anger welled up inside Connie, anger that this woman had no idea who she was. She'd lived with her, for God's sake! She'd lived in her house, ate at her table every night, used the same toilet. How could she not know who she was?

"Then I'm sorry. I don't recall where I know you from."

Connie made a conscious effort to uncurl her hands from fists they'd formed, then swallowed hard before answering. "I lived with you. Years ago."

Pauline didn't need to hear anymore. She quickly turned and hurried in the opposite direction, back to the monorail. She'd been looking forward to today. Pauline had planned it all week and had hoped that today would be the kind of day that opened up a brand-new life for the woman who needed one. She'd hoped to do some shopping, buy herself a new wardrobe, and maybe even get her hair done. She hadn't had her hair done in years and Lord knew she needed it. This was supposed to have been her special day, when she could indulge in herself for the first time in her life.

Connie caught up with her, then grabbed her by the arm again. "You remember me, don't you?"

Pauline anxiously looked around, embarrassed by the scene this woman was causing. "No, I don't think I do."

"Oh, you remember me!" Connie nearly screamed. "I know you do! You have to! I lived with you—and him. I know you remember me."

"I don't know you!" Pauline snapped. She yanked her arm from Connie's grasp, then started to walk away again. Connie quickly maneuvered her way around her, then pulled her into a secluded area just inside the entrance of a department store. Pauline stared into Connie's familiar light brown eyes from behind tears pooling in her own. "I thought you ran away," she sobbed. "You didn't run away far enough. I'd hoped you'd run far enough away to fall off the edge of the earth. Why? Why didn't you just keep on running?" Pauline caught the tear sliding down her cheek with the back of her hand. "Of course I remember you. But wasn't nothing special about you, girl. You think you were the only one? You think you were something special?" Pauline shook her head, then looked off in the distance past Connie's shoulder. "Well, you weren't. None of you were special." She glared at Connie, "I'm the one he married. Me. Not you. Not any of the rest of them either."

"So you know what he did to me?" Connie said through clenched teeth. It took all the restraint she had not to lash out at this woman. Pauline was actually standing there, gloating over Earl like he was the prize and she'd been the winner.

"What he did to you? How dare you stand there and whine about what he did to you! What about what all of you did to *me*! What about that?" she said, angrily pointing her finger at herself.

Connie's eyes narrowed. "What makes you think I give a damn about you?"

"You were just like the rest of them little bitches," she hissed. "Coming into my house, strutting around him like whores!"

"I was a kid!" Connie exclaimed, appalled by Pauline's accusation.

"It don't matter! You were with him, like all the rest. Like all of them."

"All of—"

"You think you were the first one?" Pauline vehemently shook her head. "You weren't the first one and you weren't the last one either. There were too, too, too many, before you and after you."

Shock washed over Connie's face. "And you let him—"

"I didn't!" Pauline growled, trying to keep from drawing too much attention to herself. "I didn't! There was nothing I could've done!"

"You could've stopped him!"

"He wasn't supposed to want you! You were older than the rest. Too old. 'She's too old,' I thought. He won't want this one, because she's too old. 'But she's so pretty, Pauline,' he said." Pauline stared at Connie, painfully remembering the expression on her husband's face every time he looked at the girl. " 'She such a pretty girl, don't you think so, Pauline?' But I told him, she's a big girl, Earl, and he agreed. He said it was time to be the kind of husband I needed him to be. He'd promised."

Pauline's memory drifted back to the kind of intimacy she shared with her husband. The only kind he'd insisted on. She'd fix her hair just the way he liked it, wearing two ponytails on either side of her head, tying a white ribbon around each of them. Pauline had always been small enough to buy clothes in the little girls' section of the store. He liked her in little girl's clothes. His favorite outfit was the plaid wool skirt, pinned at the side with the large gold safety pin, fringes hung to just above her knees. She'd wear the white cotton shirt with the ruffled collar, buttoned up to her neck, and black patent leather Mary Janes, with white socks ruffled around her ankles.

He'd make her stand across the room, then sit on the edge of the bed, while he'd be staring at her, licking his lips as if his mouth were watering. "You're so small," he'd whisper. "You're so . . . tiny."

Pauline would glance at the crotch of his pants and see his excitement rising at the sight of her. He wouldn't know it, but her excitement for him was rising in her too.

"Come here, baby," he'd coax. Slowly, she'd start to walk over to him, anticipating being wrapped up in his arms. "Not so fast," he'd say, putting up his hand to stop her. "Slow down, honey. Pretend that you're afraid of me. Pretend that you really don't want to come to me." But she did want to come to him. She craved him, even more than he'd craved her. Pauline did as she was told and hesitated before taking each step. "It's all right, baby doll. It's all right to come to me." He loved the game of coaxing her, convincing her, tricking her. Pauline would stand between his legs, trembling at the sensation of his hand gently sliding up her thigh, underneath her skirt. "That's a good little girl," he'd say soothingly. "You're such a good girl." Then he'd take her hand in his and curl her four fingers into her palm, leaving her thumb extended. Earl gently pushed her hand to her mouth. "Baby girls have to suck their thumbs to keep from crying, don't they?" He nodded. "Baby girls taste so sweet to big, bad men." Earl would pull her into his arms and press her up against his hard penis. "Baby girls don't like this. It scares them and makes them want to run away." That was her cue to struggle, and fight, and pretend she didn't want her husband, until Earl's only recourse was to force himself on her. They played this game nearly every time they made love. Pauline never liked the games, but playing along was the only way to get her husband to want her. So she played whenever he asked. But eventually he stopped asking, preferring the company of real little girls. Girls with no hair between their legs or under their arms. Girls who'd never been with a man before and who'd never miscarried babies.

Suddenly, Pauline seemed to remember she was standing inside the doorway of the department store in downtown Denver, talking to a woman her husband had chosen over her. "You weren't the only one," she whispered.

Connie had chosen not to entertain the idea that he'd molested other girls. Like most ugly things in her life, she'd concluded that if she'd just shut her eyes to it, it might be like it never happened after all. Only she'd learned lessons lately that forced her to realize that monsters don't really disappear just because you pull the covers over your head. The only way to ward them off was to turn on the light, because monsters hated to be exposed. Earl was a beast that needed to have the light shone on him so that everybody could see him for what he really was. She'd run from him her whole life and the time had come to stop running. Connie had no idea where it would come from, but she couldn't let it keep happening. She couldn't let him keep doing this to little girls, and there was only one thing left for her to do. "Earl's a child molester. A rapist. And I've gone too long without saying anything. I'm turning his sick ass in," she said coldly.

Without warning, Pauline threw her head back and laughed, then stared at Connie. "You're too late," she said defiantly. "I've already turned him in. I did, because I'm his wife, and he shouldn't have wanted anyone else but me." She glared at Connie. "Who are you to think you have that right?"

"I'm the one he raped," Connie said.

"It's over, and you ain't got no right to ever speak to me again." Pauline pulled her coat close around her and walked away. This time, Connie let her.

If she weren't so ready to be done with this mess, Pauline would've thanked that woman. Coming face to face with her had forced Pauline to say things she'd been to afraid to say before, and saying them seemed to lift the weight of the world from her shoulders. She'd turned him in because he'd needed her less and less, and because the girls were getting younger, while she grew too old for him to even want to play his games with her anymore. The last child had been six years old and her screams still echoed in Pauline's mind sometimes. *This is the last time,* she vowed while lying in bed that night. When it was over, Earl crawled in bed next to her like he always did and cried himself to sleep. Early the next morning, Pauline gathered up the little girl and took her back to social services. Shortly after that, Earl was arrested. The last time she saw her husband was in court, and Earl plead guilty. Pauline never even bothered to show up for the sentencing.

Connie chose to walk home instead of catching the monorail. She needed to let her encounter with Pauline sink in. Exorcisms. That's the only word to come to mind when it came to events in her life lately. The child in her had been convinced everything that happened in her life was because of her. Charlotte's leaving, being molested by Earl, even Jamil's betrayal, all put her on the receiving end of some twisted concepts of twisted people. *Damn! Baggage is heavy,* she thought. Especially when you don't even know you're carrying it, or can't admit to carrying it. She knew one thing, though. It was a relief to finally realize it was okay to put it down.

Lessons in Love

"That child is wiped out," Reesy said, coming down the stairs from putting Jade to bed. "Every time she comes from being with you, she passes out like an old drunk." She laughed.

"Girl, please. I'm the one who can't hang. Jade is a party animal, and you're going to have your hands full when that girl gets sixteen. Consider this a warning."

Some things were sacred, like finally coming to terms with promises made in desperation that should never be broken. Connie had whispered a promise to Jade while she carried her in her womb. She said she'd do whatever it took to make sure Jade had the best of everything. Reesy and Justin had kept their part of that promise, and Connie knew the only thing she could ever do for Jade was to keep hers.

She felt like a sprinter running around in circles, hoping to reach the finish line, where the answers to life waited for her with a gold medal. But the race she'd run was long, and the end of one lap led right into another. Maybe this race lasted a lifetime, she concluded, and the best she could hope for were lessons to help make the next lap a little easier.

"Listen . . . I uh . . . want to apologize for the other day. You were right, Reesy. You were just right." Connie swallowed, hard. "I just had no business thinking I could . . ."

Reesy breathed a sigh of relief. "It's all right, Connie. I know none of this has been easy on you."

"No, Reesy. It's never been easy. I don't think it ever will be, but then that's the bed I made, and I have to lie in it. I did get caught up in something, or at least, the idea of something. I wasn't thinking with my head, and like I said, I'm sorry for what I must've put you through."

"Connie—"

"I love her, Reesy. I know it might not always seem like it, but I love her so much it hurts sometimes."

"I know, sweetie."

"Do you?"

"I love her too, remember? If so much time hadn't passed, Connie—if Jade were younger, there's no way I'd keep her from you. But we're the only parents she knows."

"I know, Reesy. I understand that now."

"I hate this. I hate that it ever had to come to this."

"Well, if I hadn't been tripping, it never would've come to this. You and Justin have been so good to Jade. I could've never given her what the two of you have. I wouldn't know how. She needs someplace stable and safe, and she loves you so much. Whenever she's over, it's always 'Mommy this' and 'Mommy that.'" Connie's voice quivered.

"Don't do this to yourself, Connie. You made the sacrifice that only a mother who truly loved her child could make. You did what you felt was best for your baby at the time. Not many women could've done that."

"I made it look easy, didn't I? But it wasn't easy, Reesy."

"I know it wasn't. But you've got to remember, she's still such a big part of your life, and you're part of hers. You don't have to miss out on any of Jade's growing up, Connie."

"The thing is, Reesy, it's not that I don't deserve her." Reesy listened. Connie inhaled deeply, knowing that she needed to say this, and she needed to say it in a way that would make it sink in for Reesy, and for herself. "I've realized something."

"What's that?" Reesy asked quietly.

"I've realized that I am good enough to be her mother. I have been her mother this whole time, Reesy. I haven't mothered her the way most mothers do, but I've mothered her the best way I know how. I have given her the best that I have to give her. I have loved her more than my own life, and I have sacrificed for my child."

"Connie—"

"You listen to me! Until you have to give one of your children to a virtual stranger, don't ever, ever tell me I don't know how to love my daughter. Don't ever accuse me of not knowing how to take care of her, because I've taken damn good care of her, Reese, even if that meant giving her away! And I deserve her as much as you do. I always have."

Connie felt vindicated for the first time in her life. She'd made terrible mistakes, but she'd done the best she knew how to do, and in the end, she'd accomplished the only thing that mattered anyway. She'd survived.

"Who knows? Maybe before menopause sets in, I might be able to have one of those change-of-life babies." Connie attempted to laugh.

"You'll be a great mom, Connie."

"Yeah," Connie said proudly. "I will be."

John had been gone for nearly a week now, and Connie hadn't mentioned anything about him. Not that she would. Especially to Reesy, considering the way she knew Reesy felt about him. But Reesy decided to pose the question anyway. "Have you heard from John?"

"No. Not yet," Connie answered softly.

"You're expecting him to call?"

Connie shrugged. "Someday. Yeah . . . I think I'll hear from him again."

"You okay with this, Connie? I mean, I know we haven't seen eye to eye on this brotha."

"Hmmm, I think that sounds vaguely like an understatement. What do you think?"

"I'm serious, sweetie. Look, I know you cared about him, but I care about you. And I just want to know that you're okay."

"I'm fine, Reesy." Connie smiled. "I knew what I was getting into with this man. I know what kind of man he is. I've always known."

"You miss him, though. Don't you?"

"Of course I do. I loved him. Still do. And believe it or not, I know he loves me too. But he grew up hard, like I did. And sometimes, things like love don't come easy for people like us. It's something we both crave and run from, screaming, at the same time. I know it's hard for you to understand that, and I can't explain it, but I can definitely relate to it."

"I wish you could find someone . . . Look, why don't you let Justin introduce you to—"

"I have found someone, Reesy." Connie smiled.

"His name is D. J., and he's a really nice guy. Single, good looking, responsible."

Connie vehemently shook her head back and forth and mouthed the word "no" to her sister. She was absolutely in no mood to be fixed up, hooked up, or set up with anymore so-called nice guys. Her heart was full of King and there just wasn't room for anybody else. "I have found someone, Reesy."

"But he's gone, Connie."

"Maybe he is, from my life, but not from my heart. If John never comes back, then that's something I'm going to have to live with. And in case you haven't figured it out yet, girl, I'm tough. I know how to survive, with or without him, or anybody else, for that matter. I'm going to be all right."

"I think I'm learning this about you. You've got that 'tougher than she looks' thing going on." Reesy smiled. "But this guy, D. J., girl . . . Now, I've seen him, and he's fine!"

Connie sighed, then put on her coat. "I have found someone, Reesy."

"Justin will be home soon. Why don't you wait so he can give you a ride home?"

"I don't need a ride home." Connie smiled. "But thanks."

"Maybe we can do lunch this weekend," Reesy suggested, as she walked Connie to the door.

"Yeah, maybe. Your treat."

Reesy laughed. "Isn't it always?"

Connie stopped abruptly, put her hand on her hip, and glared at Reesy. "Don't trip. I got you last time and you know it."

"That's the only time too. I'm always the one breaking out the plastic to pay for those feasts you manage to choke down."

"You got amnesia, girlfriend." Reesy started to protest, but Connie put up her hand in defense. "Shush!" All of a sudden, the two sisters laughed at the memories they had of each other as children, conjured up by that one simple word.

"I'm not eight years old anymore, Constance. I don't have to shush if I don't want to," she said smartly.

"Well, I wish you would. You run your mouth too damn much."

Reesy's eyes watered, and suddenly she put her arms around Connie and hugged her. "I love you, sis. I really do," she whispered into Connie's ear.

"I love you too, Reese. Always," Connie whispered back. Despite their differences, nothing had been strong enough to keep them apart, and Connie was beginning to believe nothing ever could. "Can I see Jade next weekend? I'll take her out to the park or something. You can have her back. Promise," she joked, trying to hide the tremble in her voice.

"She'd love that."

"Me too. Bye, Reesy."

"See you next weekend, sweetie, and I love you."

"Yeah, love you too."

Connie sat alone in her apartment, watching candles flicker to the soulful vibrations of Rachelle Ferrell's voice. She believed that souls lived in the flames of candles. If she watched them long enough, she could see them struggling through life like most people. Dancing, crying, playing, and wrestling to be free. John was a lot like that. Wrestling with issues inside himself. Only he hid it better than most people did, even better than she did. But without even trying, he'd taught her something. He'd taught her the importance of living in the moment, and not taking that one moment for granted. Miracles happened in moments. Some good, some bad, but all miraculous, and if a person wasn't careful, she might miss something. Every moment with him had been magic, and no matter what happened between them she'd cherish them all. Besides, living in the present didn't leave much room for dwelling in the past. She'd wasted a lot of years doing that. Not that she expected to change overnight, but some change was better than none, and maybe, Connie concluded, she'd eventually get it right.

The phone rang, interrupting her solitude. "Hey, Little Bird."

Connie grinned from ear to ear, wondering how in the world Eddie knew she needed her. "Eddie?"

Edwina laughed. "Yeah, it's me, baby."

"How'd you—"

"Know it was time to call?" she asked, laughing. "You know me and the Lord is tight. He said you might need to talk to me."

Connie laughed. The sound of Edwina's voice had always soothed the rumblings of her soul and fell on her ears like music. Connie closed her eyes and pictured the cocoa complexion of Edwina, barking orders and bouncing her fists against her hips, then smiling when she thought Connie wasn't looking. Eddie had loved her at a time when she believed no other human being could love her. And for that, Connie would always be grateful.

"Talking to you is always exactly what I need. I wish you were still here. Don't you want to come home, Eddie?" Connie whined, like she was a kid. "Don't you? Please? For me?"

"I told you once I got here I wasn't never goin' no place else. But I'm always as close as a phone call, Little Bird. All you ever got to do is call." Eddie laughed.

"I really do miss you."

"Aw, I miss you too, Little Bird. You always been jus' like my own chil'." Eddie sniffed quietly on the other end of the phone. "You doin' all right, though? You need anything?"

"I'm fine, Eddie. Really," Connie said reassuringly. "I'm just, well, I guess I'm just finally starting to grow up. I mean, for real this time."

"You been grown, Little Bird. You was grown when we met. Remember?" Tears filled Eddie's eyes as she thought back to the scared little girl scouring around in the alley behind her restaurant. Connie was a child forced to face grown-up issues much sooner than she should've, and the pain of her experiences echoed in the things she never said. "Life been hard on you, Little Bird. But I always been proud of you, 'cause you ain't never let it beat you."

Connie sniffed. "It's come close, Eddie. Sometimes, it came real close."

"You a strong woman. Always been strong. I ain't never known all the details, but I suspected I could guess most of them. Little girls don't end up out in the street like that 'less something terrible drives them out there."

Connie cried. "I used to think it was all my fault, Eddie. Momma leaving, and . . . I used to think it was because of me."

"And what do you think now, Little Bird?" Eddie asked soothingly.

"I don't know."

"Yes, you do know. Tell me, Connie. What's the truth?"

Connie hesitated before answering. The truth had never been kind to Connie. It had never been a thing she relished, valued, or even looked forward to, because truth had always been intermingled with something ugly. But Eddie was asking her to stand toe to toe with it and look it in the eyes, and admit that she'd always been closer to it than she realized. "The truth is, I've always done what I had to do, Eddie. Right or wrong, I have always done what I felt I had to do; running away, even giving Jade to Reesy." She swallowed hard. "I did my best."

"That's all any woman can do, Little Bird. You done come through horrors I don't even want to imagine, and here you are, baby." Eddie laughed. "Strong and beautiful, with a whole life still waiting on you to live it."

Connie wiped away her tears, then smiled. "I sure hope I live the last half better than I did the first half."

"There you go again, bein' too hard on yo'self, Little Bird. I always knew there was more to you than you give yo'self credit for. I hope you know by now that you ain't even close to bein' the worst person in the world. There's so much more 'bout you that's so right and good too, honey. I knew that when I first saw yo' little evil ass— *forgive me, Lord*. You know what I mean?"

"I'm starting to, Eddie. I think I'm really starting to." Connie twirled a strand of her hair, then smiled. *Finally,* she thought. The sensation felt like butterflies in her stomach, and Connie caught herself grinning. Finally, the lesson Eddie had been trying to teach her since they'd met had started to set in, and it felt wonderful.

"Lord, I never thought I'd ever be a grandmomma!" Eddie laughed. "But I'm glad I am."

Connie smiled. "Me too, Eddie."

"How's that new man in yo' life. He treatin' you right?"

"He's very nice, Eddie. You'd like him."

"If you like him, Little Bird, then I know I will. But I know one thing."

"What's that?"

"He better be good to my Little Bird, or I sho' will get my big ass—*forgive me, Lord*—on a plane and slap him upside his head. Now, I will come back for that."

Connie laughed. "I'll be sure to let him know that, Eddie."

"Maybe y'all can come out this way one of these days, and I can meet him, and my grandbaby too."

"Definitely, Eddie. I'd love that. We all would." A tear escaped down Connie's cheek.

"Well, send me some pictures or somethin'. You got my address, Little Bird. I don't know why you don't use it."

"I will, Eddie. From now on, I sure will."

"You know I love you?"

"I love you too. More than you'll ever know."

"Oh, I know all 'bout that, Little Bird, 'cause that's how I feel 'bout you." Connie could hear Eddie smiling. "You take care, and don't forget to come see 'bout me, baby. I miss lookin' into those pretty eyes you got."

Connie smiled. "I'll be there soon. I promise."

"And bring my grandbaby," she said excitedly. "I can't wait to see my grandbaby."

"She can't wait to see you either, Eddie. Neither can I."

Connie and Eddie said their good-byes with promises to see each other soon.

Sitting alone in the dark, it was as if all the lights had been turned on all of a sudden. Mortality wasn't about loss. It had nothing to do with anything that might've been missing. She and John had been wrong about it all along. Mortality was about gain. It was about living and growing and expanding and all those wonderful things both of them had been afraid to believe in. Both of them had craved more from life than what they'd gotten, but neither of them had ever had the courage to admit it. But whether he'd ever be willing to admit it or not, Connie knew that she needed to. Maybe he'd be back someday. She hoped with all her heart that he would. But if he never did come back, she'd do what she'd always done. Connie would keep moving in the only direction that made sense. Forward. She'd been a survivor her whole life. But now it was time for her to live, and she made up her mind to start by planning a trip to Vegas to see Eddie.

"A mortality moment," she whispered, and smiled. Connie finished the last of her wine, then blew out her candles and went to bed.

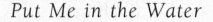

Put Me in the Water

John slowly pushed open the rickety gate leading into Roberta's yard, overcome with weeds and wildflowers. He stared at the spot on the ground where she'd fallen and watched as her ghost reappeared before him, down on her hands and knees, digging holes in the ground, for no other reason than to set a trap for her own death. She blamed him, even in her dead eyes, accusing him of being the reason she'd lost her mind that day, and her life.

John stared at the house that now looked like an old shack. The years had worn it down like they'd worn down just about everything else. He turned the knob on the door, then walked inside. He'd never seen the inside of Roberta's house, but as John looked around the small rooms, it dawned on him that he'd been born there. He had no idea why he'd stopped here. Maybe to satisfy his curiosity of seeing the place where one world started and the other ended. He and Mattie crossed paths in this house, only for a moment, and he wondered if her soul lurked here too, like Roberta's lurked outside in the yard. Wasn't much to it. A small living room, with linoleum floors peeling up in the corners. Beyond that was a bedroom, with a small kitchen behind it. There was another room in the very back of the house with a mattress on the floor stained with what looked like blood, and piss. An old wooden cane leaned against the wall in the corner.

He'd heard she'd been cool before she killed her man. Folks used to whisper about how fine she used to be when she was

a young woman. Maybe she had been, John shrugged. She killed
Charles Brooks when she found out he was cheating on her. Hell!
A divorce would've been a whole lot easier, he thought. She was
sent to a home for lunatics for some years. That's what he'd heard
growing up. John stared around the room wondering how much of
Roberta had been insane, and how much of her was just plain evil.
She'd heard voices. They spoke to her all the time. The only voices
that old woman heard were probably her own. Some people called
them conscience.

John sat outside Roberta's house, in his car. He'd gotten in it this
morning, knowing it was time for him to leave, but he had no idea
where he should go. Connie waited for him in Denver. Somebody
else waited for him someplace else. All John knew was that he
wanted to drive as far away and as fast as he could. Being in Bueller
only reminded him of why he'd left in the first place. Pieces of him
were in this town, floating around in the stratosphere like dust,
filling his lungs, threatening to choke the life out of him. Pieces
that looked like Mattie, and Agnes, Roberta, and even Fool. Trying
to put themselves back together and reunite with the core of him.
John knew that once he left this time, nothing or no one could ever
bring him back. Bueller had died with Agnes.

"Agnes ain't the only ghost you need to deal with, John King,"
Dot had told him. All of a sudden, he knew that she'd been right.
He'd exorcised two ghosts so far. Agnes, Roberta. Mattie's ghost
would probably never leave him. But there was one more he had
to deal with. One more he had to face, because John knew he'd
never get the chance again. He'd been plagued with unasked questions his whole life about Fool. Why? Why him? Why her? Fool
was probably the last person who was capable of answering the
questions he had, but John felt the need to lay eyes on the man,
to see him once and for all. He needed to hear him speak, to look
into his eyes. Maybe seeing Fool was enough to set him free from
this place altogether. Seeing Fool would finally make him tangible
to John, and if he was real, then leaving the man behind wouldn't
be hard. John was a master at leaving behind tangible things. He
started up his car, then pointed it in the direction of Solo, Texas,
a town about fifteen minutes outside Bueller. A town where he'd
find his so-called daddy.

Seed

What nuisance was this interrupting his supper? Moses wiped his mouth and started to get up from the table at the sound of the car pulling up in front of his house.

"Want me to see who it is?" Sadie asked.

"Naw. I got it." They didn't get many visitors out here, except folks trying to sell something. Whatever it was, he didn't want any and planned on telling whoever it was walking up his porch steps just that. Moses swung open the front door, surprised to see John standing there. "I didn't think you was comin'," he said, stepping aside to let John in.

"I hadn't planned on it."

"Sit down."

"I didn't come to sit down, man," John said impatiently. "I came to see Fool, then I'm heading out."

"I said sit down," Moses said sternly.

Reluctantly, John took a seat. Moses sat down in the chair across from him. "Sadie!"

"Yes?" the female voice answered from the kitchen.

"Bring us a coupla glasses of lemonade."

John laughed. "Man, I didn't come here to drink lemonade with you."

Moses glared at John. "He been waitin' on you for a long time, boy. Now . . . it's time fo' you to wait on him."

Sadie came into the room carrying two tall glasses of fresh-squeezed lemonade. She couldn't take her eyes off John. He looked so much like Adam.

"You act like you're doing me a favor by letting me see him."
"Ain't I?"

John gulped down his lemonade. It was good. "Maybe in a way you are," he said solemnly. "Maybe now I can finally lay eyes on the bastard that raped Mattie." He glared at Moses.

Moses's jaws tightened. "You ought not to talk 'bout yo' daddy like that, boy."

"I already told you. I ain't got no damn daddy."

"Then what the fuck you here for?"

"To get this over with, once and for all. To put his ass to rest." John pointed to his temple. "Here."

Moses laughed. "A man can't ever put his daddy to rest, son. Even if his daddy is dead he can't ever put him to rest. He inside you, boy. Fool been in yo' soul since the day you was born."

"Fool ain't shit to me," John growled.

"He is you."

John glared at Moses. "You going to let me see him, or what? I need to get the fuck out of this piss-ass town."

Moses pointed toward a closed door just beyond the kitchen. "He in there."

John rose slowly, then took a few steps in the direction of the room. He turned to look at Moses, who sat, grinning, with his hands resting across his bulging belly. "Go on, son."

The faint sound of music coming from Fool's room greeted John before he'd even opened the door. "Yo' daddy," Moses had called him. Fool was no man's daddy, especially not his. He was the son of a bitch who'd wreaked havoc on John's life even before his was born. *Why are you here, John?* he asked himself. *Why you really here, man? To kill? And to die?* He'd run all his life, only to end up back where he'd started. John slowly turned the knob, then quietly pushed open the door.

Now I don't mean to bother you
But I'm in distress
There's danger of me losing
All of my happiness

Faded posters and old album covers covered the walls of the small room. Pictures of Smokey Robinson and the Miracles, Sam

Cooke, Bobby Womack, Aretha Franklin, all frozen in time. Old albums and forty-fives filled every corner. There wasn't much room for more than the twin-size bed, neatly made up and taking up half the space. Near the only window was a table, and on it sat the old record player spinning a crooning Sam Cooke. Fool sat in a chair, facing the window, singing off-tune to "Cupid," oblivious to the fact that he wasn't alone.

John closed the door, then walked slowly to where Fool was sitting. He swallowed hard, then called his name. "Fool?"

Adam didn't seem to hear John and continued singing, lost in his memories and in his love of soul music. Out of all of them, he loved Sam Cooke the best. Sam Cooke was his favorite soul singer and he could listen to him all day long.

"Fool!" John called again, startling Adam.

Adam quickly sat up and reached over to turn down the volume on his record player. "That too . . . that too . . . l-loud?" he asked nervously. Sometimes Moses complained that Adam played his music too loud. He expected to see Moses standing behind him, but instead he turned and stared at the stranger standing in his room. Adam was speechless. He wasn't used to visitors. Nobody ever came to see him. Or maybe this man had come to see Moses. Or even Sadie.

John hadn't prepared himself for this. He'd spent years thinking of ways he'd break this man, only looking at him, he realized he'd been too late. Fool had already been broken. He stared up at John with one eye, black like his. White space filled the other, which was little more than a slit. A thick keloid scar stretched the length of his face from the corner of his mouth to the top of his head, covered in hair the color of snow. Adam picked up his metal walking sticks lying next to his chair on the floor, then stood to get a better look at this man standing in his room. No, he thought, peering at John. He was no stranger. Adam had seen him before. But where? Where had he . . . in his dreams. Adam's mouth fell open in astonishment. Mattie had showed him this man, but in his dreams, Adam had always thought that man had been him. Not a man who looked like him.

Years ago Adam been crippled by angry men he thought were his friends. Men who'd wanted him dead, accusing him of things he didn't understand. They beat him, nearly to death, and spat words in his face that made no sense. *Rape!* They sneered at him and growled through clenched teeth. Rape. He never even knew what that word meant. Even now, he still didn't know. Moses wouldn't let them kill him, though. He'd saved his brother's life, he'd sometimes heard that Moses had even killed for him, but he never felt right asking Moses about it. It really wasn't any of Adam's business anyway. Adam balanced on his crutches, dragging his feet to carry him closer to this man he'd dreamed of. Standing in front of John, he leaned in to get a closer look. "I know you? I know you?" He smiled, revealing open spaces where teeth should have been. "It is you," he said excitedly. "It is . . . she said . . . you was comin'. She said you . . . was comin' . . . back. Back . . . to me." Adam laughed.

John stood transfixed, frozen in awe of Fool. This retarded man, guilty of . . . what had Roberta accused him of? "Tearin' that girl apart"?

"What?" John asked, barely hearing what the man had said. "What are you talking about? Who said I was coming?"

Adam shook his head, grinning from ear to ear. That boy don't know nothin', he thought to himself. How could he not know nothin'? "You like soul music?" he asked, flipping through records. "I bet you do. I bet you . . . I bet you . . . you like soul music? You like Jerry . . . Butler? Jerry B-B-Butler?" John sat down on the bed and watched, as Fool sat back down in his chair and searched through his collection of forty-fives. "The Chi-Lites is good. The Chi-Lites . . . is good too. You like the . . . you like . . . I like the Chi-Lites." He replaced the record he was playing with another one. Adam's hands shook in the excitement of it all. How many times had she told him about this boy? Too many. Too many times she'd come to him, wearing her pretty yellow dresses and bows in her hair, smelling good and smiling. Always smiling, calling out his name. His real name . . . Adam. "Listen . . . boy. Listen . . . this here her favorite. This . . . always was . . . her favorite."

> *At first I thought it was infatuation*
> *But ooh, it lasted so long*
> *Now I find myself wanting*
> *To marry you and take you home*
> *Darlin', you . . . send me*

John started to say something, anything to get this man to be still and let John tell him whatever it was he'd come to tell him. What was that? That melody. John held his breath deep inside him, scared to death for it to be set free. "What the . . . ," he muttered to himself.

Honest you do
Honest you do

Mattie had hummed that melody on the floor of his bedroom. She'd hummed it to him, over and over, in different dreams, different nightmares, comforting herself with it, calming whatever it was that had left her spirit unsettled. The words had always managed to rest on the tip of his tongue but would never go farther than that. He listened intently to Sam Cooke, filling the room with the lyrics that matched her melody. Adam was held captive by this song. He closed his eyes and hummed quietly to himself, as the tears fell freely from his eyes.

"What the hell . . ." John snapped. "What the hell is this?" He hadn't expected this. John hadn't expected his dreams to come to life, in that small room, with that broken-down, mentally retarded man guilty of raping little girls.

His anger startled Adam, who quickly turned off the record player. "That too . . . l-loud?"

John's eyes watered as he glared at Adam. "Don't you know what you did to her, man? Don't you . . . don't you understand?" John found himself pleading, begging Adam to put it together and admit that what he'd done was wrong, instead of being caught up in something that just wasn't right.

Adam didn't understand John's anger but instinctively shied away from it, staring blankly out the window, wishing the boy would listen to the song. Mattie's song. "She said . . . you was comin'. Back to me," he murmured.

"Who? Man . . . who the hell are you talking about? You don't know me, Fool!"

He hated when folks got mad. Folks always trying to beat on somebody when they got mad, but Adam wasn't going to have any of this. This boy . . . his boy wasn't going to disrespect him.

Mattie had told him not to let any of his children disrespect him.

*And when we do have kids, Adam . . . don't you let none of 'em disrespect
you. They yo' kids. And you the daddy. You make 'em mind.*

Adam pointed a crooked finger in John's face. "Don't you . . .
You don't call me no . . . fool, boy! I know you! 'Course I . . . course
I . . . I know you!"

"Naw . . . man. You don't know me! But you knew her. Didn't
you? Mattie King? You knew her?" John prayed he could resurrect
a truthful memory from deep inside this man. And that's why he'd
come. That's why he'd needed to see Fool before leaving Texas. To
make him admit the truth about what he'd done. To make him see
the truth about what he'd done. "You remember what you did to
her, man?" He had to make this man understand the kind of pain
he'd caused Mattie. The kind of pain he'd caused Agnes. And most
of all, the kind of pain he'd caused him. "You remember how you
hurt her?"

Adam shook his head vehemently. "Naw . . . naw!"

John crouched down until he and Adam were nose to nose.
"Look at me!" he demanded. "You raped that girl. You took her,
and you raped her. Do you understand what I'm saying?"

"Naw! 'Cause she said . . . she said you was comin'."

"She didn't say shit, Fool! She's dead! And you and me . . . we
killed her! Together. We killed Mattie King! You started it, and I
finished it!"

He'd never confessed it before. Not out loud and not even to
himself, but he'd carried that responsibility with him his whole life.
That burden and guilt had been the demons he'd been running
from. Not Mattie or Roberta or even this broken man the world
called Fool.

Adam stared silently out the window. That's not what happened
at all. He knew the truth and Mattie knew the truth. The boy . . .
like everybody else . . . he didn't know the truth.

"She's dead. Do you understand that?"

"She said . . . you was . . . she said you was . . . comin' back."

"She's dead, man," John said simply.

" 'Course she . . . dead! 'Course she dead, boy! I know! I know!"
Adam pounded his fist hard against the arm of his chair. "I love
Miss Mattie, boy. How could I . . . I be the one to kill her? I love . . .
Miss Mattie, boy!"

John sighed in frustration. "You only think you loved her."

"And she love me too. She love . . . she did."

John was tired. His eyes were tired, and he rubbed them to soothe the burn. He'd been up too long. Fool was exactly what he'd been told he was. He had no concept of what he'd done to Mattie or the mess he'd made of her life. He'd never understand how many lives had been destroyed by what he'd done to that girl. It was time to go, and John started to leave. Nothing had been accomplished by coming here. Except he'd finally gotten to lay eyes on the man he'd known was his father. In Fool's mind, no crime had been committed, and none would ever be committed. As far as he was concerned, he and Mattie had been in love. John didn't know who he felt sorrier for, Fool, Mattie, or him.

Adam pulled his wallet from his back pocket, then pulled out a yellowed piece of paper, folded up and faded. He held it up to John. "Open it," he demanded. John stared at him and took it from his hand. "Right now . . . you . . . you open it . . . boy! And . . . and . . . read it. Read it too."

Slowly, John unfolded the piece of paper. Hand-drawn flowers and circles with smiling faces drawn inside them filled each corner. The years had faded the ink and the lines, but not the message of the author. John read it silently.

> Dear Adam,
> I can hardly believe you asked me that. And I'm so happy. Yes. I'll marry you and I love you too.
> Love Mattie

John folded the letter, then laid it on the table next to Adam and left.

Adam stared out the window, sobbing quietly to himself. Some-times, when he closed his eyes, he swore he could feel her warm, soft lips pressed against his. He could smell the lingering scent of her in his nostrils. Adam fought to keep his eyes closed for as long as he could, in the hopes that the angels would leave her with him this time. But they never did. These were the moments he lived for, and he'd have died for them, if only he could be sure he wouldn't lose them. Memories of Miss Mattie kept him alive. Sweet memories of the only true tenderness he'd felt in his life. The angry look in this boy's eyes told Adam he didn't understand. No one understood what Mattie King had seen in him. Sometimes, not even Adam understood. But she'd loved him, and that he knew for sure. She'd loved him and they'd made love. That's what she'd called it. Some people called it other things. Moses called it fucking. Clyde and the others had called it rape. But he liked Mattie's words for it better than anyone else's. Making love.

"How can you love a man like me, Miss Mattie? I ain't nobody like you need."

She giggled. "You so silly sometimes, Adam. You the sweetest man I know. That's how come I love you."

Things never made sense to him like they did most folks. So, they called him slow, retarded, or dumb. No matter how hard he tried, things just didn't make sense. But Mattie made sense to him. She'd let him undress her and touch places he'd only dreamed of touching on a woman. And she'd touched him too. There was nothing nasty about it, and he was never Fool to her, only Adam. Soft covered her like a blanket and he was careful not to press too hard. She made him water, his eyes, his mouth. And he prayed he'd never lose her. Losing her would be like death. She'd been gone a long time. He knew that. Looking at the boy, he figured it must've been longer than he realized. He wasn't a boy but a man. Adam's son. Mattie's son. Angry because he couldn't understand what had happened between Mattie and Adam. Nobody did.

Soul Inclination

Nobody had ever promised revelations wouldn't whoop his behind. Thinking back, John realized that most of the time that's exactly what it did. For the past twenty years, Bueller, Texas, had been the vault that locked away every truth in his life he ever needed. If he'd stayed there instead of running away, maybe he'd have found them sooner. Then again, if he hadn't left, maybe those truths would've never come out of hiding.

Whatever the case, he was a different man now than he was before he'd gone home. John had been reborn, but into what? Into whom? Deciding on a destiny had been as careless an act as flipping a two-sided coin up in the air, then choosing whatever side it landed on to find his path in life. It had been an irresponsible route, one of a boy and not a man. Real men didn't run away from life, they stood toe to toe with it, looked it square in the eye, then said, "C'mon . . . I dare you to try and whoop me!" He'd fooled himself into believing he'd done that, realizing for the first time that no, he'd never done that.

Fool and Mattie had been in love. "Damn!" he muttered to himself. A retarded man and a fourteen-year-old girl? No, it wouldn't have been hard to get that twisted at all. Misconceptions didn't mix well with love, and youth, and small-town gossip. In the end, it couldn't help but end tragically. Mattie was gone. There was no use feeling sorry for her, but Fool—Adam—had been left behind, held prisoner in 1963 and his small room, capturing memories in Sam Cooke and the Chi-Lites. Adam's truth had been handwritten by a young girl and kept securely tucked away in his wallet. That was his proof. Why he hadn't shown it to anybody else, John didn't know. Maybe he just figured that what he and Mattie had was better than the world deserved. John shrugged. "Love. Can definitely . . . fuck up a brotha's whole world."

John pulled off the highway to fill up his car. He spotted a pay phone and decided it was time to make that call.

"This had better be good," she muttered groggily, answering the phone. "Hello?"

"Hey," he said. "I know it's late . . ."

Relief warmed her from the inside out at the sound of his voice. "It's early," she corrected him.

"I was just thinking about you."

She grinned. "Oh yeah? Well, I might've been thinking about you too."

"Don't lie. Your ass was sleeping."

"You're right. And I was dreaming about you."

John laughed. "Good answer, baby girl."

"You coming home soon?"

Home. He liked the way she said that. Even more than that, he liked the way it felt inside him. Home had never been more than a word to him. But now, it stood five feet three inches tall, with pretty light brown eyes, a natural, and waited for him back in Denver, Colorado. "I'm on my way."

"I love you."

"I know."

"Aren't you ever going to say it back?"

"The next time I look into those pretty brown eyes . . . I'll say it then."

"I'm going to hold you to that, King. Now hurry up," she purred. "I'm getting cold."

"I'll be there in a minute, Baby."

Moses watched the sun set from his porch, relieved that he'd finally done the right thing. He'd atoned for his sins after all these years and maybe sleep would come easy tonight. The only person that mattered now knew the truth. At least part of it. John knew that Adam hadn't raped that girl. The other part of the truth would go to the grave with Moses.

READING GROUP GUIDE

1. John and Connie both grew up in homes where they were denied love and driven into the streets because of this. Do you feel either of them can move beyond their histories, to form lasting relationships and trust each other? Or anyone?

2. On the subject of STDs, the author feels that the African American community still seems reluctant to openly discuss or deal with these issues. Do you feel this is the case? Why or why not? And if you agree, why do you feel our community shares this attitude? What can we, as a society, do to change our way of thinking?

3. Do you feel Connie's sister, Reesy, is justified in her reaction when Connie shows interest in getting custody of Jade? Do you feel Connie's reasons for wanting custody are valid?

4. John is haunted by images of women alternating between his mother and his grandmother. What do you feel is the driving force behind John's nightmares—his conscience, or a higher, spiritual calling that he needed to answer to?

5. Regarding the events that occurred after John returned to Bueller (resolving his issues with both Agnes and meeting his father for the first time), which do you feel had the most impact on him? What kinds of changes in him/his life do you think either of these occurrences will have in the future?

6. For years, Pauline's insecurities were prevailing enough for her to allow her husband to get away with molesting foster children placed in their care. Do you think Connie's encounter with Pauline was the confrontation she needed to close the book on that portion of her life?

For more reading group suggestions visit
www.stmartins.com

Turn the page for a sneak peek at the next
not-to-be-missed prequel to
One Day I Saw a Black King

Don't Want No Sugar

Coming in a Specially Priced Hardcover
October 2004

Baby, Won't You Please Come Home

Being Mrs. Charles Brooks was more than a notion, Roberta thought, staring out the kitchen window at the memory of him driving down the road while she washed dishes left over from breakfast.

"When you gon' get tired, Roberta?" she muttered the question to herself. Roberta and Charles had been married for three years and she loved him more now than ever. She wondered if she'd ever lose the strength to love him so much but knew she wouldn't. Charles had been a bittersweet prize she'd won. She'd always known that he'd married her out of obligation. For Charles, loving Roberta had nothing to do with marrying her, but Roberta always figured it would come when it was supposed to. Charles would wake up one morning, turn to her lying in bed next to him, tell her how much he loved her, and Roberta would sigh and curl up against him, knowing it was true and that everything was fine. Years later that moment still hadn't come, but she couldn't lose hope. And when it did come, she could finally rest from the burden of carrying all the love for both of them.

Roberta sang absently to herself, "*Jaybird said to the peckerwood, I like to peck like a pecker should, But give me some, yes, give me some, I'm crazy 'bout them worms . . . you gotta give me some.*" She laughed, thinking of how she craved Charles the way that jaybird in the song craved her worm.

His friend Grady had asked Charles to drive to Clarksville in his place to repair a roof for his aunt, because something had come up and he couldn't get the time away to do it himself. It was a paying job, so Charles jumped at the opportunity, but Roberta hadn't been happy about it at all.

"Grady should be the one out there fixin' that ol' woman's roof hisself," she said out loud, scrubbing cooked egg from the cast-iron skillet. The sound of Charles Jr.'s crying trampled her thoughts. Roberta glanced, annoyed, in the direction of her son in the other room who'd been crying for well over an hour. It was times like this when she hated that boy. Roberta cringed, and then she looked over at Elizabeth, nearly four years old now, sitting quietly in the corner playing with the baby doll Granny Meryle had made for her. Elizabeth's dark wide eyes stared accusingly at Roberta.

Roberta turned her attention back to finishing the dishes and shrugged. "Sometime you jus' gotta let 'em cry," she mumbled weakly, more to herself than to the little girl. "He jus' want to be held, that's all," she said, more convincingly this time. "He always want to be held. Everybody 'round here got that boy spoiled."

Charles had him spoiled, insisting he be picked up every time he so much as opened his mouth to yawn. He had both of the children spoiled, especially Elizabeth. But the children were worrisome when he wasn't around. Elizabeth watched her constantly, waiting for her to do something wicked that would stay in her memory until she was old enough to tell her daddy about it, and CJ cried all the time. Elizabeth could be especially worrisome whenever Charles came home from work. He'd be so tired he could hardly walk in the door before the child hurled herself up into his lap and wrapped her arms tight enough around him to strangle the man.

"Get offa yo' daddy, gal!" Roberta would end up scolding her.

But Charles would protectively snuggle her close to him and kiss her cheek, almost as if he were doing it to spite Roberta. "She fine, 'Berta. She jus' givin' her daddy some of that sweet lovin', that's all."

It was moments like that when Charles seemed to want to show Roberta that he was capable of giving love to everyone but her. He'd break her heart, but she would never give up on him. Roberta ignored his indifference to her and pulled his affection from him like she pulled thread from a seam. She'd learned to do that from the beginning with Charles when he was pining over Nadine Cooper. But he'd made love to Roberta. She'd even ignored the moments when he'd called out Nadine's name instead of hers, knowing and relishing in the fact that Nadine was gone for good, and Roberta was all he had left.

How could a woman be jealous of her own child? Roberta wondered, staring woefully at Elizabeth playing quietly in the corner. But that's what she was, jealous of any woman, no matter how young or old, getting too close to him, threatening to push her off the rope she balanced on over his heart. After three years he'd never told her he loved her, but he said it to Elizabeth all the time, and to Miss Meryle, too. But the words had never escaped his mouth for Roberta's sake.

Roberta finished washing the last of the dishes and wiped her hands on her apron.

"What else? What else I got to do? What—"

There was plenty to do around that house. Things always needed cleaning, or fixing, or—Lord! Why didn't that boy just shut up? Reluctantly she walked over to the room where CJ was still crying. The seven-month-old infant sat up in his bed and looked at Roberta, staring desperately through red swollen eyes. He reached out to her, hiccupping through tears, but Roberta was devoid of the instinct to mother him. She reflexively cupped her hands over her ears as his wailing seemed to grow even louder, until his crying sounded more like screams digging into her skull like an ice pick.

She felt a slight tug at the hem of her skirt and looked down into the face of her daughter.

"Can I have a drink?" Elizabeth asked in her small voice. "Please, momma?"

"Go sit down!" Roberta snapped. The girl hesitated and then looked at her brother in his crib, as if her attempt to rescue him had failed.

"She gotta a ol' spirit. Some chillen jus' born with a ol' spirit already in 'em," Martha had told her not long after Elizabeth had been born. Roberta saw it too sometimes, wisdom of the ages behind Elizabeth's dark eyes, and it frightened her if she let it. Roberta leaned down and turned the girl in the opposite direction, then swatted her backside. "Go sit down, now! 'Fo I tan yo' hide!"

Elizabeth did as she was told and reluctantly found her place in the corner of the room.

Roberta turned her attention back to the baby. "Be quiet, CJ!" The dark shadow of contempt washed over her face. "You heard me, boy! I know you did! Now—"

CJ's screams filled the room and echoed in Roberta's ears. She was so tired of this boy crying all the damn time. She was so sick of holding him and rocking him and coddling him every second of the day. It seemed like all she did was give in to him. Just to shut him up. Just to keep him quiet.

Roberta stormed into the room, grabbed the baby, held him up in the air, and screamed into his face. "Hush! You hear me? Hush, CJ! Quiet!" His crying pierced through the air. She knew what he wanted. Roberta quickly unbuttoned her blouse, then slumped down on the bed and resentfully filled his mouth with her breast. His small hand grabbed desperately at her as he sucked hungrily on her nipple.

Roberta rocked back and forth, loathing every minute of his suckling. She'd always hated it, even more with Elizabeth, but nobody had to know. Nobody but the children, and she knew they'd never tell, because children held all the secrets about their mommas sacred. Which was as it should've been.

Makes Me Weak Way Down in My Knees

The shortest route between Bueller and Clarksville was to drive through town, and he'd have come right out of one and landed into the other in no time. He'd been asked by his best friend Grady to do some repair work for him at his great-aunt's house in Clarksville, and in the same breath he warned Charles to stay far away from his cousin Sara, who was staying with the old woman.

"She my baby cousin, man, and I know how you are. You lay one finger on her, Charles, and I'll beat yo' black ass, man—I swear!"

Charles just shook his head. He and Grady were just alike when it came to women. Both of them had always had more than their share, and neither one of them could ever get enough. They were greedy men with no bottom to them. Since he'd gotten married, though, Charles's insatiable appetite had pretty much been left hungry. Once word got out that he was marrying Roberta, cold shoulders greeted him in place of warm kisses. Besides that, Charles found himself working twelve-, sixteen-hour days with his and Grady's repair business. He felt like he'd aged a hundred years in no time at all, and Charles hardly had the time or energy he'd once had for women.

Charles drove leisurely, gazing out at the road still ahead of him, wondering who'd had the good sense to put this road back here in the first place. Charles smiled, then inhaled the cool morning air, knowing that the man who'd carved out this particular stretch of road must've been like him. He'd been in no hurry to reach his destination either, or maybe he'd just been in no real hurry to get home.

He'd always loved long drives and if he didn't have to stop, he never would've. Temptation rode in that truck with him, whispering in his ear, *Man, why don't you jus' keep on goin' and don't stop till you get to the other side of the world?* It took all the will power he had to squash it, but every now and then, like now, he listened to it and let his mind roam barefoot in all the places he'd like to go, like California. Charles didn't know a damn thing about California, except that he liked the name. It sounded like a woman's name, and he imagined her waiting for him, big and stretched out, smiling as she welcomed him with her arms open and her eyes shining. He'd heard she rested next to the ocean, and Charles had always wanted to see it. In the back of his mind he'd imagined himself wading knee-deep in it, with his pants rolled up and his hands buried in his pockets while he watched the sun sink down inside it. That's where he wanted to be.

He scratched his head, awed by how quickly life had changed directions on him. It seemed like just the other day he was a cocky sonofabitch, flitting around like a bee from one flower to another, sampling damn near any woman who'd let him. Nadine's nectar had been the sweetest, though, he thought fondly. Every now and then the essence of her still tingled the tip of his tongue and Charles found himself missing her, regretting that he never did do the one thing he should've—just loaded her into his truck and drove off with her, all the way to California. He chuckled at the thought. That old man of hers would've come running after them, but his legs would've given out long before he ever made it that far.

Charles's thoughts inevitably drifted back to Roberta and the children he'd left at home early that morning. A wife and two kids separated him from California or anywhere else other than Bueller, for that matter. He loved his children, Elizabeth and Charles Jr. Loving Roberta, however, was a different issue altogether. Lord, that woman worked his nerves. Charles had done the right thing where Roberta was concerned. He'd owned up to his responsibilities and to his mistakes and married her. Most of the time he'd even go so far as to believe he'd been a good husband, as good as he knew how to be. Four years ago Roberta had been a young girl, desperately in love with him. She hadn't changed and neither had he.

Where you been, Charles?

Whatchu need, Charles?

Where you going, Charles?

I love you, Charles.

I can't live without you, Charles.

He'd never counted on being that girl's reason for living, and he sure as hell never wanted it. But Charles had played the game of fools and got caught up in encounters too brief to change his life the way they had. At least, he'd believed they were brief at the time. Now he knew better.

"How you gon' love me when you don't even know me, Roberta?" He'd asked her that question all the time in the beginning. Roberta would stare back at him with wide eyes, as if she couldn't believe he didn't know the answer. She tugged at him all the time, trying to pull something out of him that just wasn't in him, and without even trying Charles hurt her feelings, hoping she'd finally say the one thing he wanted to hear more than anything; "I can't take this no mo', Charles, and I want you gone."

He'd be a fish blessed by the gods if she ever said that, and then Charles would swim away as fast as he could, happier than he'd been in years because she'd finally let him off that hook of her own free will.

Charles hesitated before disturbing the old woman napping in a chair on the porch of the old house. Must be Aunt Josephine, he thought to himself. He cleared his throat and removed his hat before calling out to her, "Miss Harper?"

Miss Harper bobbed her head and muttered something to herself, but she didn't wake up so Charles called out a little louder, "'Scuse me, Miss Harper."

The old woman snorted and woke up with a start. Charles was worried that he might've scared her. "Miss Harper," he said quickly, "How you doin'? My name is Charles and Grady sent me over to—"

"Grady?" she asked, staring confused at Charles. "You Grady?"

"Naw, ma'am. I ain't Grady, I'm Charles." He took a few steps closer so that she could get a better look at him. "Grady sent me over to see 'bout yo' roof that need fixin'."

Miss Harper took a deep breath and sunk back into her chair. "Boy, don't be goin' round tippin' up on folk like that. If'n I'd'a had my gun, you be leavin' up outta here with a bullet in ya."

Charles couldn't help but laugh. That old woman couldn't see him well enough to shoot him. "Yes, ma'am. I do apologize."

Miss Harper patted herself gently on the chest and then turned her attention to the young man standing at the foot of her porch. "Sho' is warm for October, ain't it?"

"Yes, ma'am. I s'pect it's gon' get cold soon 'nuff, though."

She frowned. "I don't too much care fo' the cold. The older I gets, the colder it seem to get," she said, laughing. She studied Charles intently, "Now who you say you was again?"

"My name is Charles, Miss Harper, Charles Brooks."

She thought for a moment. "Brooks. I don't reckon I know anyone named Brooks. Yo' people here in Clarksville?"

"No, my people live in Bueller by way of Oklahoma. They come out of Alabama and Tennessee, I believe."

"I see. You kin to any Trimbles? I know some Trimbles outta Oklahoma."

Impatience began to creep in, but he held it at bay, knowing how old people tended to carry on. "No, ma'am. Don't know no Trimbles."

Charles glanced at the window in time to see a young woman peep at him from behind the curtain. Just then Sara opened the screen door and stepped outside.

"Hello? Is there somethin' we can do fo' you?"

Baby cousin, he thought, staring up at this pretty dark-skinned girl on the porch. Grady was no fool. He knew that the moment Charles laid eyes on this girl, he'd trip over his own feet to get to her if he could. For a moment she reminded him of Nadine, but softer around the edges. She was the kind of girl Nadine might've been had Edward Cooper not gotten hold of her and wrapped her up in dollar bills.

"My name is Charles," he said, smiling.

"He a Brooks out of Bueller, 'cross the way, but he ain't no kin to them Trimbles outta Oklahoma," Miss Harper interjected.

"I come by to fix the roof. Yo' cousin Grady sent me."

"Oh, yes. Well—"

Miss Harper interrupted, "Sara, why don't you take him 'round back and show him where that hole is?"

"Yes, ma'am." Sara obediently led Charles to the back of the house.

Baby cousin had a fine figure on her, Charles thought, admiring her from behind. Grady had given him the blues about this girl, and for good reason.

"The hole is right over here," she explained, pointing up to the corner of the house. "Thank goodness we ain't gettin' a lot of rain and that it ain't been too cold. But if you ask me, I think the whole thing might be rotted out. Don't it look rotted out to you?"

Charles peeled his eyes off Sara long enough to examine the area she pointed to. "From here it don't look too good. Might have to replace a good part of it."

"We can't afford to fix all of it. Maybe if you could just patch it up good, that would last us awhile."

Charles shrugged. "Well, I can patch up the hole, all right, but it wouldn't be long fo' you gon' have to get somebody out here to fix it again." Charles caught a glimpse of disappointment, but this girl was too pretty for him to let that happen. "Tell you what . . . I'm gon' do my best to fix the whole thing and I won't charge you a penny mo'."

Sara hesitated at his offer. "I can't ask you to do that."

"You didn't ask me. I made the offer, and if you as smart as I think you are, then you'll take it."

Sara smiled and set Charles on fire from the inside out. "That's fine, Mr.—"

He reached out to shake her hand. "Call me Charles."

"Charles. That's fine, Charles, and thank you. Thank you so much." She walked past him back towards the front of the house, "Well, I'm gon' leave and let you get to work. I've got plenty of my own inside."

Charles watched her leave, then mumbled to himself, "Damn girl!" He shook his head, remembering quickly how pretty girls always managed to get him into trouble, or rather, his love of pretty girls. Sara disappeared around the corner and into the house, and Charles shook off the effect she'd had on him and started unloading his tools to get down to the business of fixing Miss Harper's roof.

From time to time Sara caught a glimpse of Charles from the kitchen window while he worked, careful not to let him see her. His offer not to charge them any extra money had come as such a surprise. Momma Harper didn't have much money, just what she and Seth had saved over the years in mason jars hidden under loose floorboards in the kitchen pantry. From what Sara had seen, it had been quite a bit of money, mostly pennies, dimes, nickels, silver dollars. Momma Harper had been living off that money for years, though, and she'd told Sara quite a few times that there also was money outside in back of the house that Seth had buried years ago, but she had never been able to remember where.

Sara was rolling dough for chicken and dumplings when she heard a tap on the window. She turned in time to see Charles, wiping sweat from his head with the back of his hand.

Sara opened the window. "Yes?"

"Don't mean to trouble you, Miss—"

"Sara." She smiled.

He smiled back and stared into her soft brown eyes. "Sara. I was wonderin' if I could trouble you fo' some water?"

She filled a glass with cool water and handed it to him. Charles drank it all in one gulp, then handed the glass back to her. "Thank you, kindly."

"No trouble." She blushed.

Charles put on his hat and went back to work. She hadn't noticed before, but he had dimples. Sara hadn't seen too many men with dimples, but on him they looked good. Her neighbor Mrs. Robinson had warned her about men like him, the pretty ones, slick as ice and just as cold was how she'd explained them.

"They quick to tell you all kinda sweet things, but don't you believe 'em, girl. Don't be no fool over no man, 'cause all they wanna do is crawl up yo' skirt, get what he want and leave you standin' there with a baby that look jus' like him, hangin' on yo' hip. Ain't nothin' worse than havin' a take care of a baby that look jus' like the niggah' who broke yo' heart. They make some pretty chil'ren, though."

Sara laughed. Everybody always seemed to go out of their way to make sure she knew how bad men were. Not too many people seemed to have anything good to say about men, not even Pappo. Sara watched Charles rummage through his box of tools. She'd only just met the man today, and he hadn't been anything less than kind and generous. He'd worked hard from the moment he'd come by, stopping long enough to take a drink or get a quick bite to eat. And on top of all that, he was about the most handsome man she'd ever laid eyes on. Sara shrugged and went back to her dumplings.

I've Been Saving It Up

She lay wide awake in bed that night while Momma Harper lay in the bed across the room, snoring faintly, having been asleep for hours. Sara had been living with Momma Harper for several months now, and the longer she stayed away from Timber, the harder she knew it would be for her ever to go back. She missed Pappo and the boys, though, much more than she'd ever let on. If he knew how much he'd probably make her come home, so Sara always assured him that she was fine and enjoying her new home and her new life in Clarksville more than she ever thought possible. She knew him well enough to sense loneliness in him, too. She'd always been close to him, even closer than she was to the boys, and the bond between them went beyond that of father and daughter. Sara believed it was even soul deep.

Before he'd brought her here, he'd made her promise to be a sensible girl, one who thought with her head and not with her heart.

"Young girls can be kinda silly sometimes," he'd warned her. "Fallin' fo' any kind of fool to come 'long who know how to say what he know y'all like to hear."

"But I ain't like that, Pappo. You know I—"

He put his hand up to stop her like he always did when he didn't want to be interrupted. "Me and yo' momma . . . maybe we sheltered you too much sometimes. I know we did, 'specially me." Pappo looked off into the distance across the field, but Sara could see tears glistening out of the corners of his eyes. "That's 'cause I always wanted the best fo' you, baby girl, and I never want no daughter of mine to end up with some fool who can't take care of her or treat her right."

Sara softly placed her hand on top of his. "I know, Pappo," she whispered.

"Clarksville is a big place. Things out there move faster than they do down here. Folks move fast too." He stared lovingly at her, hoping he was doing the right thing in sending her away, knowing he had no choice. "I want you to take care of yo' grandmomma and be a good girl." Ezra smiled and then corrected himself. "Be a good woman, Sara. 'Cause that's what you is now. A woman."

Sara sighed at her memories of the last time they were together. She was a woman now, and she had no idea what had changed in the moment he'd confessed that to her and the breath before, when he'd called her his "baby girl." Had the right of passage from girlhood to womanhood always been so simple? Once Pappo declared it to be so, then was it so? She was Sara Tate, the same Sara Tate she'd always been, but suddenly she'd been thrust into a new town, a new house, and womanhood, and Sara wondered if she'd ever be able to catch up with it all.

Pappo had warned her about falling in love with fools, but

he'd never told her what a fool would look like. For all she knew, she might trip and fall right on top of one and never even know it. Maybe this Charles Brooks was a fool. He'd worked hard, though.

Sara squeezed her eyes shut and rolled over on her side, facing the window. She'd cracked it just enough to let the stuffiness of the house escape into the night air. The breeze was a welcomed relief, though, and she inhaled deeply, hoping it would be enough to clear her mind so that she could finally doze off to sleep. Why did she even concern herself with Charles, anyway? He would only be around the house another day or two until he'd finished the work he'd started, and then she'd never see him again. That man probably had more women chasing after him in Bueller than he knew what to do with. She'd always imagined that the man she'd fall in love with and marry would chase after her and court her like Pappo had courted her mother. Before she died, Sara's mother used to go on about how he would bring her flowers and even how he asked her daddy for her hand in marriage. Charles didn't strike her as that kind of man. Maybe Mrs. Robinson had been right, and pretty men like him were selfish and conniving. The only thing he'd done all day was hammer on the house and drink up most of her water. Maybe tomorrow she'd charge him a penny a glass. After all, a cool glass of water wasn't always so easy to come by.